# The Brewing of Futures

Bianca Kingsley

Published by Bianca Kingsley, 2024.

THE BREWING OF FUTURES

**First edition. October 8, 2024.**

ISBN: 979-8224653676

Written by Bianca Kingsley.

# Chapter 1: The Brew of Dreams

The sun was just beginning to set, casting a golden hue over Alderwood, illuminating the amber waves of grain that surrounded the town. The quaint brick buildings, dusted with ivy, lined the streets like elderly friends reminiscing about their glory days. A few leaves danced in the autumn breeze, fluttering like confetti tossed in celebration of something yet to come. I could almost hear the faint hum of laughter and chatter from the festival preparations in the distance, a symphony of anticipation and excitement that tugged at my heartstrings.

With each passing moment, my thoughts raced faster than the whimsical gusts outside. The brewery, my family's pride and joy, stood resilient against the backdrop of the fading light, its wooden sign creaking softly as if whispering secrets of generations past. The familiar scent of malt and hops wafted through the air, wrapping around me like an old quilt—comforting, yet charged with the electricity of possibility. I leaned closer to the glass, my breath fogging it slightly, as I peered inside, half-expecting to see my father's silhouette, always bustling with purpose. But instead, there was only silence, save for the gentle fizz of fermentation bubbling in the large tanks behind me.

"Aren't you going to join the party, Lila?" A teasing voice broke through my reverie, yanking me back to reality. I turned to find Max, my childhood friend, leaning against the doorframe, his arms crossed and an amused grin dancing across his lips. His tousled hair caught the light, framing his face with a carefree charm that always seemed to draw people in like moths to a flame.

"Just soaking in the ambiance, Max," I replied, rolling my eyes playfully as I stepped away from the window. "You know, contemplating the universe and all that."

"Sure, that's what they call it these days," he smirked, his tone dripping with sarcasm. "More like wallowing in your sad attempts to connect with your father's legacy."

"Hey! I am not wallowing," I protested, though the flush in my cheeks betrayed me. Max had a knack for finding my weak spots, whether it was my overly sentimental moments or my obsessive need to make things perfect.

"Right. You're just standing there like a ghost haunting a brewery," he quipped, stepping closer. "Why don't you grab a pint and let's go have some fun? We've got a festival to get ready for."

I hesitated, my heart tugging between duty and desire. "I have a lot to do before the Brew Fest. I can't just abandon everything for a drink."

"Please, as if you haven't spent the last week pouring over family recipes and brewing notes," he said, his eyes sparkling with mischief. "Just one pint. It'll help you relax. Plus, I promise not to let you think too hard about anything while you drink."

He flashed that charming smile, the kind that had captivated every girl in Alderwood since high school, including me—though I'd never let him know how often he affected me. I sighed, knowing full well I needed a break. "Fine. One pint, but then I'm back to work."

Max grabbed my hand, pulling me toward the small tavern next door, its wooden sign swinging gently, promising warmth and laughter. Inside, the atmosphere was alive with the sounds of clinking glasses and boisterous laughter. The air was thick with the scent of grilled meats and fried dough, making my stomach grumble in eager anticipation. I felt myself begin to relax as I let the laughter of my friends wrap around me like a warm embrace.

"See? This isn't so bad," Max said, sliding a pint of amber ale in front of me. "Now, tell me about your grand plan for the festival.

Are we talking a parade of lopsided beer barrels, or something more... sophisticated?"

I chuckled, taking a sip of the frothy brew. The flavors burst on my tongue, a perfect blend of malty sweetness with a hint of bitterness that reminded me why I loved our family's craft. "Actually, I'm thinking of presenting a new recipe—one that combines our traditional methods with a twist. I want to showcase what our family stands for but also show that I can innovate."

Max raised an eyebrow, impressed. "A bold move, Lila. Are you sure you want to step out of your dad's shadow like that?"

"Honestly? No," I admitted, my voice dropping slightly as I looked down into my glass, swirling the golden liquid. "It terrifies me. But if I don't take this chance, I'll regret it forever. I want to prove that I can carry on his legacy while also making it my own."

His expression softened, and he leaned in closer, lowering his voice conspiratorially. "You've got this. And even if you don't, you know I'll be right here, cheering you on—preferably with a drink in hand."

"Only you could turn a moment of vulnerability into a toast," I teased, my heart swelling with gratitude for his unwavering support. Just then, a commotion erupted at the bar, drawing our attention. A group of locals had begun a raucous rendition of a drinking song, clapping and stomping in rhythm.

"Looks like it's showtime," Max said, standing up and pulling me into the fray. I couldn't help but laugh, feeling the weight of my worries lift as I joined in, clapping along with the laughter and camaraderie that filled the tavern.

But even amidst the revelry, a voice inside whispered doubts I couldn't shake—was I ready to stand on my own, to forge my own path while honoring my father's memory? The night slipped away in a blur of laughter and music, but as I danced, I felt the flicker of hope in my heart grow brighter. Maybe, just maybe, I could do this.

The energy in the tavern was infectious, a rhythmic pulse that drew everyone in. I laughed with old friends, my worries fading like the distant echoes of my father's expectations. The warmth of the ale coursed through me, igniting a spark that I had almost forgotten existed. As I clinked glasses with Max, the clang reverberated through my chest, a reminder that we were alive, and life was, if only for tonight, carefree.

"You know, Lila," Max began, leaning in closer, his voice a conspiratorial whisper above the din of the crowd. "If you really want to shake things up at the Brew Fest, why not introduce a new twist to your dad's classic recipes? Something that'll knock their socks off. People love surprises."

I took another sip, the beer smooth and crisp against my lips, and considered his words. "What do you mean, like... adding jalapeños to a stout?" I chuckled, picturing the faces of our regulars grimacing at the thought. "That might not go over well."

"Okay, maybe not that extreme," he replied, grinning. "But how about incorporating some local flavors? There's that new orchard on the edge of town—did you see their apple cider? It could work beautifully in a winter ale."

His suggestion danced around my mind like the autumn leaves outside. The orchard had been buzzing with activity since the harvest began, their vibrant apples promising a burst of sweetness. "You might be onto something," I admitted, excitement bubbling within me. "A spiced apple ale... I could play with that."

Max's eyes lit up as if I had just handed him the keys to a treasure chest. "There you go! See? You're a brewing genius just waiting to be unleashed. I bet your dad would be proud."

The thought sent a mix of warmth and anxiety through me. My father's approval felt like the only validation worth seeking, yet here I was, about to step out from the shadow of his legacy. "What if it's terrible? What if everyone hates it? What if it's not good enough?"

My voice wavered, the uncertainty creeping in like an unwanted guest.

"First of all, you'll never know unless you try," Max replied, his tone firm yet gentle. "And second, even if it flops, it'll be an epic story. Besides, we're in a small town. If they don't like it, you can always blame me. I'm the one who suggested it, after all."

I laughed, shaking my head at his absurdity. "You'd be the first to throw me under the bus, wouldn't you?"

"Always," he said, mockingly serious, and we clinked our glasses again, laughter spilling out like the beer frothing over the sides. The world around us blurred, and for that moment, the weight of expectation lifted.

As the night wore on, we danced and sang along to the raucous anthems of our hometown, a cacophony of voices blending into one joyful melody. Each twirl and spin felt liberating, as if I were shedding layers of doubt with every step. The festival was only days away, but instead of panic, I felt a strange thrill. Maybe I could pull this off.

By the time the tavern began to empty, the moon hung high in the sky, casting silver beams through the windows. I stepped outside, the crisp night air kissing my flushed cheeks. Max strolled beside me, our footsteps echoing softly against the cobblestones.

"I'll help you with the recipe tomorrow," he declared, his hands stuffed in his pockets. "We can experiment until we find the perfect balance. I mean, I'm practically a culinary genius myself."

"Culinary genius?" I raised an eyebrow. "The last time you cooked, you almost set your apartment on fire."

"Those were merely... experimental flames," he countered, waving his hand dismissively. "I'll have you know my microwave skills are unparalleled."

"Microwave skills? Now I'm really worried." I smirked, enjoying our banter. There was something comforting about it, a grounding force in the whirlwind of uncertainty surrounding me.

As we neared the edge of town, I spotted the sprawling orchard, its trees swaying gently in the night breeze, their branches heavy with fruit. A sudden rush of inspiration flooded me. "What if I incorporated some fresh apple slices into the brew? A little garnish, maybe? Or infused some cider directly into the mixture?"

Max nodded, his eyes gleaming with excitement. "Now you're thinking! You'll be the talk of the festival. Just imagine it—Lila Hayes, the brewing prodigy, strutting her stuff while everyone else serves boring old lagers."

A laugh escaped me, brightening the quiet night. "You really think I can do this?"

"Absolutely," he affirmed, stopping to face me. "You're Lila Hayes. You were born with a beer mug in one hand and a recipe book in the other. Don't ever doubt that."

His confidence washed over me like a warm tide, lifting the last of my lingering doubts. I was more than just my father's daughter; I had dreams of my own, bubbling beneath the surface, waiting for the right moment to burst free.

But just as I began to feel invincible, a shadow loomed in the back of my mind. What if the Brew Fest became a showcase of my inadequacies instead? What if I disappointed everyone, including myself? My breath caught in my throat as I wrestled with the thought.

"Hey, earth to Lila!" Max waved his hand in front of my face, breaking my reverie. "You're zoning out on me again. What's going on in that brilliant mind of yours?"

"Just thinking," I replied, forcing a smile. "You know, the usual existential crisis."

"Ah, yes. The 'what am I even doing with my life' spiral," he said with a mock-serious nod. "My favorite. What if I tell you that everyone else is just as clueless? Most of us are pretending we have it all figured out while actually Googling life advice at 2 a.m."

I chuckled, shaking my head. "That's oddly comforting."

"Glad to provide a sense of security in these dark times," he quipped, pulling me back into the moment. "But seriously, we'll work on this together. I won't let you face the festival alone."

We reached my front porch, and I paused, glancing back at the orchard. The trees stood strong and proud, their branches heavy with promise. Maybe I could learn a thing or two from them—root myself deep in the soil of my family's legacy while reaching out toward the sun, ready to grow.

"Thanks, Max," I said quietly, feeling the weight of gratitude settle warmly in my chest. "For believing in me."

He shrugged, a playful grin spreading across his face. "What can I say? I'm a sucker for a good underdog story. Plus, it's a lot more fun when you're not wallowing in self-doubt."

I rolled my eyes, but a smile lingered on my lips. As I stepped inside, the flickering lights of the brewery caught my eye, a lighthouse beckoning me toward uncharted waters. Tomorrow, I would face the brewing challenge head-on, not just for my father, but for myself.

The morning sun streamed through the kitchen window, illuminating the dust motes dancing in the air like tiny fairies celebrating my newfound resolve. Today was the day. I had my plan, a mixture of excitement and anxiety buzzing beneath my skin. The faint scent of coffee filled the room, grounding me as I scrolled through my notes. Each line was a testament to my determination, scribbled in a flurry of inspiration and scattered thoughts.

"Are you sure you don't want a backup plan?" my mother's voice drifted in from the living room, laced with concern. She appeared in the doorway, arms crossed, her brow furrowed. "Maybe a nice vanilla lager? Something safe?"

"Mom, I need to do this," I replied, my voice steadier than I felt. "I can't just play it safe. This is my chance to honor Dad's legacy while carving out my own path."

She sighed, glancing at my notes with a mixture of pride and apprehension. "I know you want to honor him, but the brewing business isn't easy. What if things don't go as planned?"

"What if they do?" I shot back, trying to infuse some confidence into my words. "What if I create something amazing, something that puts Alderwood on the map? I can't let fear of failure keep me from trying."

My mother studied me, her expression softening slightly. "You've always had his passion, but don't forget, it's also about the process, not just the end result."

I smiled at her, appreciating her wisdom but also feeling the weight of expectation. "I promise, I'll take my time with it. I just need to get started."

With that, I gathered my things, slipping on my favorite plaid shirt—my brewing uniform, in a way—and stepped outside, ready to meet Max for our brewing session. The cool autumn air greeted me like an old friend, filling my lungs with the scent of crisp leaves and promise.

As I approached the brewery, the morning bustle enveloped me. Townsfolk greeted each other with waves and nods, the air alive with anticipation for the Brew Fest. The brewery, a charming brick building adorned with ivy, felt like my sanctuary. I pushed open the heavy wooden door, and the familiar sounds of bubbling fermenters welcomed me.

"Lila! Ready to get your brew on?" Max's voice rang out from the back, where the brewing equipment gleamed like shiny toys waiting to be played with.

"Let's do this," I said, my heart racing as I joined him. Together, we surveyed the equipment and ingredients laid out before us. The rich aroma of malt and hops enveloped me, a reminder of everything I loved about this craft.

"Okay, what's the game plan?" Max asked, his eyes sparkling with mischief. "Are we throwing caution to the wind and winging it?"

"Actually, I thought we could start with a basic spiced apple ale," I said, detailing my ideas with increasing enthusiasm. "We'll use fresh apples from the orchard and add some cinnamon and nutmeg. It'll be the perfect fall brew."

"Now we're talking!" he exclaimed, pulling ingredients from the shelves as I scribbled down measurements and steps. The kitchen area was bustling with energy as we transformed it into our experimental brewing lab, and before long, we were immersed in the process, chatting and joking as we worked.

"You know," Max mused as he stirred the mixture, "if this goes well, we might just have to start a brewing dynasty. Lila and Max: the power couple of Alderwood Brewing."

I laughed, shaking my head. "You do realize we're just friends, right? No power couple here."

"Hey, I'm just saying," he shot back, feigning hurt. "When the world recognizes your genius, I want in on the profits. Just remember, I was your first taste-tester."

"Don't worry, I'll make sure to pay you in beer," I teased, feeling the comfort of our friendship wrap around me. But beneath the playful banter lay the undercurrent of anticipation that churned in my stomach.

As we neared the end of our brewing session, the apple mixture bubbled vigorously, and the aroma filled the room. It was intoxicating, a blend of sweetness and warmth that made me envision the smiles on everyone's faces at the festival. "This is going to be a hit," I said, my voice filled with excitement.

Max glanced at me, a serious look crossing his face. "But what if it isn't? What if we don't hit the mark? Are you ready for that?"

"Then I'll learn from it," I replied, the conviction in my voice surprising even myself. "Every great recipe has its trial and error. It's part of the process."

He nodded slowly, his eyes softening. "Just remember, I'm in this with you. We're a team."

As the day wore on, the brewing process felt almost magical. The liquid gold bubbling away felt like my hopes and dreams coming to life. With every stir, I could see a future where I didn't just exist in my father's shadow but stood confidently beside it.

After we finished brewing, we cleaned up the kitchen and decided to take a break on the patio outside, soaking in the afternoon sun. I sank into a chair, feeling the warmth seep into my skin. "Can you believe we did it?" I said, grinning at Max, who leaned back in his chair, basking in the moment.

"Absolutely. And I'm already looking forward to the taste-testing phase. Who knew brewing could be so... liberating?"

"Liberating, and delicious," I added, imagining the crisp, refreshing taste of our creation. Just then, my phone buzzed in my pocket, cutting through the moment like a jarring alarm.

"Who is it?" Max asked, eyeing me curiously.

I glanced at the screen, my heart sinking. It was a message from my father's old business partner, Thomas. The subject line read: Urgent Matter. A knot tightened in my stomach.

"What's wrong?" Max noticed my change in demeanor.

"Thomas wants to meet. He says it's about the brewery." My voice faltered, anxiety creeping in. The implications swirled in my mind—what could he possibly want? Had something gone wrong?

Max frowned. "Do you want me to come with you?"

I shook my head. "No, I think I should handle this alone. It's probably just a business matter."

"Right, because you're clearly the queen of handling business matters," he quipped, but his smile faded as he saw my concern. "Are you sure? I'm just a text away if you need me."

"I'll be fine," I reassured him, though my heart raced with uncertainty. As I stood up, the sun cast long shadows on the patio, mirroring the unease settling in my chest. "Let's just see how this goes. I'll call you afterward."

He nodded, but the worry in his eyes mirrored my own. I took a deep breath, willing my nerves to settle. I didn't want this meeting to ruin the excitement of our brewing success.

As I walked to the brewery, a sense of foreboding loomed over me, an unexpected chill that clashed with the warmth of the sun. The familiar sounds of clinking glasses and laughter faded, replaced by a heavy silence that enveloped the building. Pushing through the door, I felt an inexplicable tension in the air.

Thomas was waiting for me, his face etched with concern, as if the very fate of the brewery hung in the balance.

"Lila," he said, his voice grave. "We need to talk."

And just like that, the brewing dream I had so carefully crafted felt like it was teetering on the edge of a precipice, ready to plunge into uncertainty.

# Chapter 2: A New Recipe for Love

The festival unfolds like a vibrant tapestry, colors weaving through the air, as laughter and the tantalizing aroma of street food swirl around me. I adjust the display of artisanal bread and cheese on my booth's table, the wooden surface warm under my fingertips, and glance up at the sky, which seems to have decided to bless us with the perfect autumn day. The sun hangs low, casting a golden hue over everything, turning the ordinary into something magical, and as I survey the scene, I can't help but feel a heady mix of excitement and trepidation.

"Do you think I should add more rosemary to the focaccia?" I mumble to myself, barely registering the question as I push aside the nagging doubt that creeps in. "Or maybe I should stick with garlic? Everyone loves garlic." My thoughts tumble out as if speaking them aloud will somehow clarify the recipe in my head, as if the simple act of talking to myself could keep the chaos at bay.

It's then that I notice him. Jackson Reed, the new head brewer at Alderwood Brewing Co. He stands across the way, the very embodiment of effortless cool. His fitted shirt clings just enough to highlight strong shoulders, and there's a playful smirk dancing on his lips, like he's in on a joke that no one else knows. I try to divert my gaze, but it's like trying to look away from the sun—impossible and slightly painful. Our eyes meet, and suddenly, the world feels like it's in technicolor, every sound sharpening, every detail more vivid.

"Hey there," he calls out, his voice smooth as the finest whiskey, and I swear the air shifts, crackling with an unspoken tension. I'm momentarily caught off guard, the sight of those striking emerald eyes doing something funny to my heart. It flutters erratically as if attempting to escape the confines of my chest.

"Hi!" I manage to respond, too chipper, too eager. I focus on the table, pretending to arrange the bread as if it needs my attention.

My hands tremble slightly as I pick up a loaf, taking a moment to appreciate its crusty exterior. "You're, um, the new head brewer, right?"

"I am," he replies, stepping closer, the warmth of his presence enveloping me like a cozy blanket. "Jackson Reed. And you're the baker everyone's been talking about. I had to see the famous Bread Queen for myself."

"Bread Queen?" I chuckle, the title making me feel both flattered and ridiculous. "That sounds way too regal for someone who just spends her days kneading dough and trying not to burn her hands."

His laughter is infectious, a rich sound that makes my heart skip. "I'm not so sure about that. Everyone loves bread. It's the universal comfort food, and I have to say, I admire a good loaf."

"Is that a pick-up line, or are you just really passionate about carbs?" I fire back, raising an eyebrow, the corner of my mouth lifting in a teasing smile. I'm aware that I should probably dial back the flirtation, but something about his easy demeanor draws me in, nudging the barriers I've built around my heart.

"Maybe a bit of both," he quips, his eyes sparkling with mischief. "But I'll have you know, I have a very refined palate when it comes to beer. I can pair it with your bread, if you're up for the challenge."

"Challenge accepted," I say, my heart racing at the thought. "But just so you know, my focus is on the bread. If you can manage to keep up with my gluten game, we might just be able to make a delicious pair."

He leans on the table, clearly amused, and I find myself caught in the magnetic pull of his presence. My nerves seem to settle as we talk shop, bouncing ideas off each other about brewing techniques and flavors. It feels surprisingly easy, like we're two old friends catching up rather than two people meeting for the first time amidst the chaos of a bustling festival.

As we chat, the noise of the festival fades into a gentle hum, and the world outside our little bubble loses its urgency. I glance at the crowd, people laughing, dancing, and celebrating life, but they seem distant now, mere spectators in our intimate exchange.

"Have you ever considered brewing with bread?" he asks, and I raise an eyebrow, intrigued. "I mean, the flavor possibilities are endless. Imagine a sourdough stout. Or a wheat beer infused with your rosemary focaccia."

"Now you're just trying to make me swoon," I reply, feigning offense. "But that does sound pretty good." My heart races at the thought of crafting something together, a collision of our culinary worlds.

He leans closer, lowering his voice as if sharing a secret. "I think we could create something remarkable, you know. Pair your incredible bread with a beer brewed just for it. A little culinary romance."

"Culinary romance?" I repeat, feigning shock. "Now that's a dangerous proposition. We might just create something that could take the festival by storm."

His gaze intensifies, and I can feel the electric chemistry between us crackling like the sound of popcorn in hot oil. The moment stretches, hanging in the air, thick with possibility. Just then, the air is pierced by a sudden cheer as the festival's main event kicks off—a local band bursting into an upbeat tune, drawing people toward the stage.

"Looks like we're not the only ones trying to steal the show," Jackson says, stepping back reluctantly. "But I have a feeling this isn't the last time we'll be discussing recipes. What do you say we meet after the festival? I'd love to get your thoughts on my next brew, and maybe you could bring that focaccia I've been daydreaming about."

I blink, momentarily stunned by the invitation that feels more like a promise. "Are you asking me out for dinner, or are we just cooking up trouble in the kitchen?"

"Why not both?" he grins, and just like that, I'm swept away in a tide of excitement and uncertainty, wondering if this charming man could indeed be the unexpected twist my life so desperately craved.

As the festival unfolds, the clamor of voices and the fragrance of roasted nuts and caramelized onions wrap around me like a familiar shawl. Each laugh and shout resonates with the festive spirit, while the golden rays of the sun dance on the vibrant stalls. My booth, with its rustic charm and handmade signage, is a proud little corner of this bustling carnival, but it feels like the universe has chosen this moment to tilt a bit sideways, throwing me into the orbit of Jackson Reed.

The world rushes by in a blur, but Jackson remains a constant, a magnetic force pulling me into conversation and laughter. The way he leans against my table, his expression a mix of curiosity and amusement, sends a thrill through me. We dive deeper into the possibilities of beer and bread pairings, trading ideas like seasoned chefs sparking inspiration off each other. I can't help but notice how his eyes light up when I mention my new rosemary focaccia recipe, as if the mere thought of it is enough to awaken a dormant hunger.

"Rosemary and garlic are a match made in heaven," he insists, nodding enthusiastically. "I can already picture it. A crisp, golden crust with those herbs, perhaps paired with a light, citrusy pale ale to cut through the richness."

"Crispy crust, you say? I like the sound of that. You might just be onto something," I reply, teasing him with a raised eyebrow. "But you'd better bring your A-game if you want to impress a self-proclaimed Bread Queen."

"Is that your official title? Because I must admit, I'm a bit intimidated," he says, the corners of his mouth quirking up in a grin that makes my heart flutter. "I've dealt with tough crowds, but a Bread Queen? That's on a whole new level."

Before I can respond, an enthusiastic shout erupts nearby, drawing our attention. A crowd has gathered around a local performer, whose juggling act has captivated the audience. As the performer throws flaming torches into the air, Jackson's gaze flickers back to me, mischief dancing in his emerald eyes.

"Think you could juggle bread? Maybe we could set a new trend at the festival," he quips, and I laugh, my cheeks warming at the absurdity of the image.

"Only if you promise to catch it! I'm not prepared to serve my bread as a fire hazard," I shoot back, the banter flowing effortlessly between us. Each word feels like a thread, weaving us closer together, tightening the bond that's beginning to form.

Our conversation flows like a fine brew, rich and layered, each exchange bubbling with new ideas and playful challenges. The festival buzzes around us, but we've created our own little world, a space filled with laughter, creativity, and a simmering tension that's impossible to ignore.

After a while, the performer concludes his act to raucous applause, and the crowd disperses. Jackson glances over, then leans in closer, his voice dropping to a conspiratorial whisper. "I must confess, I didn't just come over to talk about bread and beer. I wanted to ask you something a little more... personal."

"Personal?" I echo, my heart skipping a beat. The festival seems to fade away as I lean in, curiosity piqued. "Do you mean your secret recipe for brewing, or perhaps your deep-seated desire to become a bread juggler?"

He chuckles, and the sound is like music to my ears. "No, I mean more along the lines of—would you like to join me for dinner tomorrow? Just you, me, and a shared passion for all things culinary?"

The unexpected invitation hangs in the air, vibrant and thrilling. For a moment, I'm caught off guard, the weight of the proposition swirling in my mind. It's not just dinner; it feels like an opening act to something far more profound, something that could shift the very fabric of my life.

"Are you sure you can handle that much Bread Queen?" I tease, masking my own surprise. "Dinner might not be enough to prepare you for my endless culinary rants."

He grins, leaning closer, eyes sparkling with challenge. "Bring it on. I thrive on culinary rants. You can give me the entire history of sourdough if you want. I'll even pretend to be fascinated."

"Pretend?" I reply, my voice laced with mock indignation. "You'd better not be that guy who rolls his eyes when I start talking about the magic of fermentation."

He raises his hands in mock surrender. "I promise to be a captive audience. I've got to know all the secrets behind the Bread Queen."

As we exchange a final laugh, the festival's energy swells around us, but the moment stretches like warm dough, filled with potential. Jackson's proposal lingers in my mind, the thrill of possibility tinged with a hint of nervousness. I catch a glimpse of him looking away for just a second, his expression turning serious as he scans the crowd, and suddenly I'm reminded that this connection is as delicate as the pastries I bake.

Before I can ponder too deeply, a commotion breaks out a few booths down, and I see a flash of color—my friend, Lydia, waving enthusiastically, her hair bouncing with each animated gesture. "Sophie!" she calls, her voice slicing through the festive noise. "Come help me with the chocolate fountain!"

"Duty calls," I say reluctantly, glancing back at Jackson. "But I'll definitely consider your dinner invitation, especially if you're as good at cooking as you are at charming."

"Count me in," he replies, his grin wide, and my heart does a little dance as I step away, the sweet taste of potential filling the air around us.

Lydia's frantic waving leads me to her booth, where the chocolate fountain has become a mini disaster. The once pristine setup is now a spattering of chocolate everywhere, including on her shirt, which she tries to wipe off with little success. "I could use a hand, Sophie! It's like a chocolate explosion over here!"

"Looks like someone took 'fondue' a little too seriously," I quip, stepping in to help. As we work to contain the chocolate chaos, I steal glances back at Jackson, who is chatting with a customer, his laughter ringing out, effortlessly charming everyone around him. I can't help but feel a flutter of anticipation, the kind that comes with new beginnings and the promise of something more.

Once we manage to salvage the fountain, I glance over at Jackson again, who catches my eye and winks. My stomach flips, and for a moment, I wonder if he feels this spark too, this inexplicable connection that seems to pulse between us, drawing me into his orbit.

"Okay, now tell me," Lydia says, her eyes glinting with mischief as she leans in conspiratorially. "What's going on with you and Mr. Tall, Dark, and Handsome over there? You were practically glowing when he approached you."

"Nothing's going on," I retort a bit too quickly, my cheeks flushing. "We were just discussing bread and beer. You know, normal festival stuff."

"Normal festival stuff?" Lydia scoffs, a knowing smile creeping across her face. "Honey, that looked like the start of a rom-com. Do you have any idea how long it's been since you've been on a date?"

The question hangs in the air, and I can't help but feel the weight of it. In the whirlwind of my work and baking, I had let my social life slip away, focused solely on my business and the joy of bread. But

Jackson, with his charming smile and passion for craft, feels like a breath of fresh air, a new recipe for love that I never saw coming.

As the sun begins to dip lower in the sky, casting a warm golden glow over the festival, I find myself reflecting on the unexpected possibilities that have emerged from a simple encounter. The evening promises to be filled with laughter, good food, and perhaps something even more delightful—a connection that feels as promising as the best bread rising in the oven.

As the sun begins its descent, casting a soft amber glow over the festival, I can't shake the giddiness bubbling up inside me. My booth, with its rustic charm and tantalizing aromas, feels like a small island of comfort amid the swirling chaos. The air is thick with anticipation, every moment charged with the thrill of possibility. Jackson's invitation hangs like a delicate thread between us, and the thought of our dinner lingers in my mind, sweet and enticing.

"Is it just me, or is the chocolate fountain still dripping more than it should?" Lydia's voice breaks through my reverie, her hands on her hips, chocolate smudged across her cheek. I turn to find her surveying the aftermath of our earlier mishap, a bemused smile on her lips.

"I think it's just excited about its newfound fame," I reply, stifling a laugh. "It did just put on a great show. But in all seriousness, we should probably do something about it before it becomes a chocolate slip 'n slide."

As we make our rounds, wiping down the booth and chatting with festival-goers, the warmth of the sun transforms into a gentle evening breeze. The crowd is still lively, their laughter mingling with the melodies from nearby musicians strumming their guitars, and I feel a growing anticipation for my upcoming dinner with Jackson.

"Just promise me one thing," Lydia says suddenly, her tone conspiratorial. "Don't go falling head over heels before you know if he can cook."

"Because that's the only metric of a good relationship, right?" I tease, rolling my eyes. "I'm pretty sure there are more important factors—like compatibility and whether he knows the difference between a whisk and a spatula."

"Compatibility is important, but a guy who can whip up a mean soufflé? That's a game changer," she insists, nudging me with her shoulder as we walk. "And if he doesn't like garlic, that's a red flag."

I chuckle at her exaggeration, but there's a kernel of truth in her words. "If he doesn't like garlic, then he and I aren't meant to be. It's the ultimate test of culinary compatibility."

As we continue to banter, my mind drifts back to Jackson. He's charming, witty, and undeniably attractive, with a warmth that draws me in. I can't help but wonder what it would be like to share my world with him. What if he's the kind of person who sees bread as more than just a food, but as an art form, a canvas for creativity? My heart flutters at the thought, but I'm quickly brought back to reality by a shout from the crowd.

"Look out!" A voice rises above the din, and I turn just in time to see a child dashing through the crowd, ice cream cone in hand. Time seems to slow as the cone slips from the little boy's fingers, sending a streak of chocolate and vanilla flying through the air.

"Oh no!" I gasp, instinctively raising my hands to shield my booth as the ice cream lands—splat!—smack in the middle of my rustic bread display, leaving a gooey, sticky mess.

Lydia bursts out laughing, doubling over as the crowd erupts in a chorus of gasps and laughter. "Well, that's one way to make a sweet impression!" she wheezes, and I can't help but join her, the absurdity of the moment breaking the tension like a freshly baked loaf.

With a resigned smile, I start the cleanup process, trying to salvage what I can of the bread while laughing at the situation. "I guess we'll add a new flavor to our menu—ice cream-infused focaccia," I joke, shaking my head.

As the evening wears on, the festival begins to dim, lanterns hanging from the trees flickering to life, casting a warm glow that dances across the ground. It's a picturesque scene, but my thoughts keep drifting back to Jackson, his laughter echoing in my mind. What if this dinner turns into something more? The thought sends a thrill coursing through me, but it's quickly chased away by a flutter of anxiety. What if it doesn't?

Lydia nudges me again, breaking into my thoughts. "Hey, I'm heading to catch the band. You coming?"

I glance back at my booth, still needing to clean up the remnants of the ice cream disaster, but the thought of spending the evening with Jackson pulls at me. "I think I'll stick around here for a bit. I've got some bread to salvage and thoughts to stew over."

"Fine, but don't keep staring at him like he's a loaf of sourdough or you might scare him away," she quips, winking at me before disappearing into the crowd.

With her gone, I take a deep breath, the festival's energy swirling around me, vibrant and intoxicating. I catch a glimpse of Jackson across the way, his laughter bright and carefree as he chats with a group of festival-goers. My heart races at the thought of what tomorrow could bring, yet an undercurrent of uncertainty thrums beneath my excitement.

"Okay, Sophie," I murmur to myself, shaking off the doubt. "You've got this. Just be yourself, and don't overthink it."

A few moments later, Jackson approaches, his gaze locking onto mine as he strides confidently toward my booth, the warm light illuminating his features in a way that makes my stomach flutter. "I saw the ice cream incident," he says, a teasing glint in his eyes. "Are you okay? I didn't know they had dessert wrestling at this festival."

"Surprisingly, it wasn't on the schedule," I reply with a grin, trying to keep my tone light, despite my lingering embarrassment.

"But hey, that's the risk you take when you open a booth at a food festival. It's all part of the experience, right?"

He leans against the table, crossing his arms casually. "Right. It's all fun and games until someone loses their ice cream," he quips, then adds, "So, are we still on for dinner tomorrow? I promise not to bring any dairy products that might end up airborne."

"I'm still in," I say, my pulse quickening at the thought. "As long as you don't try to serve dessert in an unconventional way."

He chuckles, the sound warm and inviting. "I can assure you that my culinary skills are more refined than that. I can handle both beer and bread without turning them into a circus act."

Just then, a loud crash resonates from the festival, and the crowd gasps. My heart races as I turn to see what's happening. A nearby stall, decorated with an elaborate display of glass jars, has tipped over, sending a cascade of colorful contents spilling across the ground.

"What now?" Jackson exclaims, his brows furrowing as he glances in the direction of the chaos.

As the crowd gathers, I feel an unsettling sense of foreboding creeping in, a tingling sensation at the base of my spine. There's something unsettling about the energy shifting, and for a moment, I'm frozen, caught between the joyous festival atmosphere and the tension brewing beneath the surface.

Jackson nudges me, breaking my reverie. "Come on, let's check it out," he urges, his tone half-excited, half-worried.

We make our way toward the scene, the air thick with a mix of anticipation and anxiety. The closer we get, the more I can see the spilled jars—glittering shards scattered across the pavement. My heart races as we push through the crowd, my mind racing with questions.

"Is anyone hurt?" I murmur, scanning the scene for signs of trouble.

Just as we reach the edge of the commotion, I hear a woman's voice rising above the clamor, filled with frustration and anger. "This was all planned! You can't just ruin everything!"

Jackson and I exchange a glance, confusion mingling with concern.

"Do you know what's going on?" I ask him, but before he can respond, a figure emerges from the crowd—one I recognize all too well.

It's someone from my past, someone I thought I'd left behind. My breath catches in my throat, my pulse quickening as their gaze locks onto mine, the tension between us palpable. The vibrant festival around me blurs, the joyful noise fading into a distant hum as uncertainty crashes over me like a wave.

"Sophie," they call, their tone laced with a mix of familiarity and something darker. "We need to talk."

The laughter, the light, and the warmth of the festival suddenly feel like they belong to another world. The ground beneath my feet seems to shift, leaving me teetering on the edge of something I can't quite grasp, and I realize that this moment may not just change my evening but the entire course of my life.

# Chapter 3: A Family Affair

The festival thrums with life, the air thick with the scents of caramelized onions and freshly baked pretzels mingling with the tangy notes of beer. Strings of fairy lights stretch like stars across the twilight sky, twinkling above laughter and music that bursts forth from every corner. I stand rooted in the crowd, a sea of faces swirling around me, and yet, my focus narrows to one: Ethan. He's there, a few yards away, leaning against a wooden post, the golden light casting shadows on his angular features. His presence pulls at me, a stubborn string tugging my heart into a place I'd thought was permanently sealed.

We used to be inseparable, two halves of a whole, sharing secrets and dreams as we climbed trees and played hide-and-seek in the sun-drenched backyard of our childhood home. But that was before grief twisted our bond into something unrecognizable. After our father's death, silence stretched between us like a taut wire, snapping with every clumsy attempt at reconnection. Now, seeing him in this vibrant scene is like watching a ghost float through a party I thought I'd been enjoying. My laughter feels distant, a mere echo of what it once was.

Jackson, my steadfast anchor in this ocean of festivity, leans closer, his voice warm and inviting. "You alright?" he asks, his eyes glancing toward Ethan, though his focus is entirely on me.

"Just... memories," I murmur, a half-hearted smile on my lips as I raise my pint, the froth spilling slightly over the edge. "It's been a while since I've seen him."

He follows my gaze, and his brow furrows. "Do you want to talk to him?"

A simple question, but layered with complexity. A thousand possibilities race through my mind—what if I say the wrong thing? What if he hates me for all the years of silence? My heart pounds, thrumming in my chest like the bass from the nearby band, and I'm momentarily distracted by the beat of the music, the pulse of the crowd.

"I don't know," I reply finally, glancing down at my drink. "It feels like I'd be diving into a pool of sharp glass. I'm not sure I'm ready for that."

Jackson nods, understanding washing over his face. "Then let's just enjoy this for now. We've got pretzels to conquer and terrible karaoke to endure. You can pretend the rest of the world doesn't exist."

I chuckle, grateful for his unwavering support. He raises his glass in a mock toast, and we clink our pints together, the sound mingling with the laughter that drifts through the air. Jackson has a way of making everything feel lighter, as if the weight of my past can be momentarily shed like a heavy cloak on a warm summer day. We meander through the festival, sampling everything from apple cider donuts to artisan cheeses, our laughter ringing out as bright as the lights above us.

But as the sun dips lower, painting the sky in strokes of orange and purple, my thoughts drift back to Ethan. I can't shake the feeling of unfinished business. It's as if a part of me remains tethered to that moment of silence, the anger we never voiced, the hurt we allowed to fester like an untreated wound.

"I'm going to grab another drink," I say suddenly, the urge to face Ethan creeping into my mind. Jackson looks at me, a mixture of concern and encouragement etched into his features.

"I'll come with you," he offers, and his presence feels like a comforting hand on my back, nudging me gently toward whatever lies ahead.

"No," I reply, surprising myself with the strength of my voice. "I need to do this on my own. Just... give me a moment?"

He studies me for a beat, then nods, a flicker of pride in his eyes. "Alright, I'll be over there if you need me." He gestures toward a cluster of people engaged in a spirited debate about which band is the best in the history of ever, then steps back, leaving me to my thoughts.

I weave through the crowd, each step a challenge against the rising tide of uncertainty swirling within me. My pulse quickens as I draw nearer to Ethan, the warm glow of the festival now feeling like a spotlight shining directly on the fractures of our relationship. The familiar ache of loss tugs at my heart, but I swallow it down and keep moving forward.

He looks different, older perhaps, the lines around his eyes more pronounced, but there's still that spark of mischief lurking in his expression—the same one that ignited our countless adventures. As I approach, he glances up, his gaze locking onto mine, and for a moment, the world around us fades into a dull hum.

"Emma?" he says, disbelief evident in his voice.

"Hey, Ethan," I reply, the words tumbling out before I can catch them, my heart hammering against my ribs like it's trying to escape.

He straightens, the space between us palpable, charged with all the things we never said. "I didn't expect to see you here."

"Neither did I," I admit, the honesty surprising us both. I take a deep breath, the air filled with the sweetness of cotton candy and the tang of fried food, grounding me in this moment that feels simultaneously surreal and achingly familiar. "How have you been?"

"Busy," he shrugs, his tone nonchalant but his eyes betraying a flicker of vulnerability. "Work, you know. Keeps me occupied."

The silence stretches, thick and heavy, the unspoken words lingering like an unfinished song. The laughter of festival-goers floats around us, a stark contrast to the tension hanging in the air. The world is alive, yet here we stand, caught in the echo of our shared past.

Ethan's eyes search mine, and for a moment, the laughter and clinking glasses fade into the background, creating an intimate bubble where it's just the two of us—siblings reunited in a world that has moved on without us. "Busy," he says again, a weak smile pulling at the corners of his mouth as if he's trying to convince himself that he's not just existing but actually living. "You know how it is. Adulting and all that."

I nod, trying to mask the tightness in my chest with a laugh. "Ah yes, the joys of adulting. Where the only constant is the laundry pile and existential dread." I can see the flicker of amusement in his eyes, but it's overshadowed by something deeper—regret, maybe? Or perhaps just the weight of years spent in silence.

"Is that what we're calling it now? Adulting?" he teases back, his voice lightening slightly. "I thought we were supposed to be thriving, you know? Crushing our dreams and whatnot."

"Oh, definitely." I take a sip of my drink, the cold beer refreshing but failing to chill the awkwardness that simmers between us. "If crushing dreams means sitting in front of a computer screen for eight hours a day, then sign me up for the next seminar."

He laughs, a genuine sound that reverberates in the warm air, and the tension between us begins to ebb just a little. "I can't believe you've ended up in a job like that. You were always the adventurous one, ready to leap off cliffs for the next thrill."

"Only metaphorical cliffs, Ethan," I reply, folding my arms, suddenly feeling the need to protect my heart. "You know I'm not one for actual risk-taking. I leave that to the adrenaline junkies and... well, you."

His expression shifts, the playfulness fading as he looks down at his drink. "Yeah, well, someone had to keep things interesting after you left for college. I remember the nights we spent plotting our escape from this town. Now it feels like I'm the only one who didn't make it."

His words hit me harder than I expected. I'd always viewed his departure from our childhood dreams as something inevitable, a sign of growing up. But to him, it felt like abandonment. A twist of guilt coils in my stomach, and I resist the urge to reach out and reassure him that he hasn't lost me. "You still have time to chase whatever dreams you want," I say, trying to keep the conversation light. "I mean, how many people can say they're still figuring it out at thirty?"

"Yeah, thirty," he says, bitterness lacing his tone. "Such a charming age. Old enough to know better but still too young to care."

I can't help but chuckle at the absurdity of it all. "You sound like an old man who's been through a midlife crisis."

Ethan's gaze lifts, a smirk creeping onto his lips. "Old man? I'll have you know I've barely aged a day since we last saw each other. I'm practically a fine wine."

I roll my eyes, leaning against the wooden railing that separates us from the bustling crowd. "If you're a fine wine, I'm afraid I'm more of a flat soda. Sweet at first, but ultimately disappointing."

"Sounds like a terrible pairing," he says, taking a step closer, the space between us shrinking. "Maybe we should trade. You'd at least add a little sparkle to my otherwise drab existence."

"Or I could just ruin yours," I retort, but the warmth in my chest betrays me. This banter feels good, like slipping on a favorite sweater that I thought I had lost. Yet, beneath the surface, I can sense the deep current of our unresolved issues pulling at us.

"Do you miss it? The adventures?" he asks, his tone growing more serious, the laughter fading like the day. "Or maybe just... us?"

The question lingers in the air, heavy with unsaid words. "Sometimes," I admit, my voice barely above a whisper. "But it's not like we can just rewind the clock, can we?"

"Maybe not," he says, his eyes narrowing thoughtfully. "But we could try. What if we just started from here? No expectations. Just... see where it goes?"

"Like a reboot?" I challenge, trying to keep the mood light even as my heart races. "What happens if the reboot crashes? Is there a backup plan?"

Ethan smiles, that old mischief flashing back into his eyes. "Well, I guess we'd just have to call in the tech support—my charming sister who always knew how to fix things."

"Tech support, huh?" I raise an eyebrow, feeling the first twinges of hope. "I can hardly fix my own Wi-Fi."

"And yet you still keep trying. That's something," he replies, and for the first time in years, I see a glimpse of the brother I used to know, the one who always believed in the power of second chances.

The weight of the conversation shifts, and I can't help but ask, "So what's stopping you from trying? From fixing whatever's wrong?"

Ethan shifts, his gaze flickering to the ground as if the answer lies hidden in the wood grain. "I guess... fear. Fear that it's too late, fear that you don't want to."

I open my mouth to respond, but before I can find the words, a raucous cheer erupts from the crowd. The band has launched into a lively tune, and I can see Jackson dancing enthusiastically, a flurry of energy that threatens to pull me back into the merriment.

"Come on," I say, gesturing toward him, the music calling to me like a siren. "Let's join the chaos. I think a little dancing might do us both good."

Ethan hesitates, glancing back at the crowd and then at me, the uncertainty etched across his face. "What if I trip and fall flat on my face?"

"Then I'll take a video and send it to Mom," I reply with a grin, my heart fluttering at the thought of us laughing together like we used to. "Trust me, the embarrassment will only make for a better family story later."

With that, Ethan chuckles, and it's a sound that pulls us both into the present, a sound of possibility. He takes a deep breath, and for a fleeting moment, I think he might actually let go of the past. "Okay, let's do this. But if I fall, you're going to have to help me up, superhero style."

I can't help but laugh, and together, we step into the crowd, the music wrapping around us like a warm embrace. The festival pulses with life, and as we dance, I can't shake the feeling that this might be the beginning of something new—something worth fighting for.

The music swells around us, an infectious rhythm that pulls Ethan and me into the crowd, where the energy crackles like electricity. I glance at him, my heart racing with a mix of anticipation and anxiety. His expression mirrors my own uncertainty, but as the first notes of an upbeat melody wash over us, it's as if an invisible thread connects our spirits, urging us to embrace the moment rather than dwell on the past.

We sway awkwardly at first, his movements stilted, as if he's unsure of the choreography that is life. I can't help but giggle, throwing my arms in exaggerated circles, attempting to loosen the tension. "Just pretend you're a leaf in the wind!" I shout over the pulsating bass, my words laced with laughter.

"More like a tree in a hurricane!" he retorts, his voice filled with mock despair as he flails his limbs in a way that only solidifies my delight. The tightness that had woven itself around my heart begins to unravel, strand by strand, and I lose myself in the moment, our laughter becoming the soundtrack of the evening.

As the song shifts, the energy in the air morphs, drawing people closer together, their faces lit with joy. Jackson dances nearby, wildly gesticulating as he attempts to incorporate some kind of interpretive dance that makes me snort with laughter. "I think he's trying to summon the spirit of a disco ball!" I shout to Ethan, who shakes his head in disbelief.

"He's definitely channeling something," Ethan replies, an amused glint in his eyes. "Maybe a particularly confused octopus?"

The banter flows effortlessly between us, a refreshing balm over the years of silence that had defined our relationship. I glance at Ethan's face, illuminated by the glow of string lights overhead, and I'm struck by the way he looks both familiar and foreign, a mosaic of memories and missed opportunities. Yet in this moment, we're just two siblings, united by shared laughter and the magic of a festival that feels almost like home.

The song transitions to a slower melody, a gentle waltz that envelops us in its embrace. The crowd begins to sway in unison, couples drawing close, lost in each other's warmth. Ethan, sensing the shift, takes a half-step back, as if suddenly shy. "I can't waltz to save my life," he admits, scratching the back of his neck, the vulnerability in his tone sending a flutter of sympathy through me.

"Neither can I!" I declare, throwing my head back in a laugh. "But I think we should give it a try. It's all about the spirit, right?"

"Or the spirit of a cocktail," he quips, glancing toward the bar where a line has formed for a round of colorful drinks.

We edge closer to the center of the crowd, and as the music envelops us, I find myself gazing into his eyes, a swirl of emotions tumbling through my mind. There's a mixture of fear and excitement, like standing at the edge of a cliff, teetering between the thrill of jumping and the instinct to hold back. "You know," I start, my voice quieter now, "we could talk about... things. If you wanted to."

"About Dad?" Ethan's tone shifts, a shadow crossing his features. "I thought we agreed to avoid the elephant in the room."

"That elephant has been tap dancing on my chest for years," I confess, trying to lighten the mood but also feeling the weight of the truth. "I think it's about time we address it."

He runs a hand through his hair, the familiar gesture reminding me of our childhood—how we'd talk late into the night, our secrets shared like treasures hidden in a garden. "I just don't want to bring up the past if it means digging up more pain. It's messy, you know?"

"Life is messy," I reply, my heart pounding in my ears. "But it's better when we're honest with each other. Otherwise, we'll just be standing here, dancing around the same ghosts."

His gaze softens, and I can see the internal struggle written across his face. "What if we're just too far gone? What if we can't fix this?"

"Maybe fixing isn't the goal," I suggest, sensing a crack in his armor. "Maybe it's about learning to live with the broken pieces."

Ethan nods slowly, absorbing my words. The music swells again, and he pulls me in closer, our bodies swaying instinctively as the melody washes over us. For the first time, I can feel the distance between us closing, a flicker of hope igniting amidst the shadows of our past.

"Okay, let's try," he murmurs, his breath warm against my ear. "Let's be real for once."

I smile, feeling a spark of something that had long been extinguished. "Real it is. But only if you promise to not trip over your own feet."

"I'll do my best, but no promises," he teases back, and the playful banter weaves a fragile thread of connection, binding us together in a way I hadn't dared to hope for.

As the night deepens, laughter and chatter swirl around us, and the festival takes on an otherworldly glow, every flickering light a reminder that life continues to flow even amid uncertainty. Jackson rejoins us, drink in hand, and the three of us weave through the crowd, sharing stories and laughter that feel more genuine with every passing moment.

But then, as if a storm brews just out of sight, the festival's energy shifts. An electric tension fills the air, and I feel it—a sudden chill that wraps around us, prickling my skin. Jackson glances toward the entrance, his expression shifting from carefree joy to something more serious. "Uh, guys... what's going on over there?"

I turn, following his gaze, and my heart plummets. A group of figures stands at the edge of the festival, their postures rigid, eyes scanning the crowd with an unsettling intensity. The laughter around us dims, uncertainty rippling through the throng of festival-goers as whispers erupt like fireworks.

"What is this?" Ethan murmurs, his brow furrowing. "Do you know them?"

"I... I think I've seen them before," I stammer, my mind racing to make sense of the sudden change in atmosphere. "It looks like trouble."

Before I can process what's happening, one of the figures breaks away from the group and strides toward us, determination etched on their face. My breath catches in my throat, recognition crashing over me like a wave. The last person I expected to see here, now storming into my life with a fierce resolve, a specter from the past that I thought I had finally escaped.

Ethan shifts beside me, his body tensing as he picks up on the shift in my demeanor. "Emma? Who is that?"

I open my mouth to respond, but no words come out. The air feels heavy with unspoken truths, and suddenly, the festival that had once felt like a celebration now pulses with the threat of something I can't quite grasp, but that promises to change everything.

# Chapter 4: Bubbles of Tension

The soft hum of the brewing kettles mingles with the sweet scent of malted barley, wrapping around me like a well-worn blanket. This place, our family's brewery, is both a sanctuary and a battleground. As I stir the mash, the grains swirl in a warm embrace, reminding me of the countless times I stood here as a child, learning the art of brewing from my father. Each grain felt like a story waiting to unfold, but now, those stories feel threatened, darkened by looming shadows of discontent.

I glance up from my workbench, where an array of hops and yeast sits waiting, like soldiers poised for battle. My brother, Ethan, leans against the wall, arms crossed, his brow furrowed in concentration as he speaks in hushed tones with our mother. Their voices are low but heated, the tension almost tangible, crackling in the air like the static before a storm. I should be focusing on perfecting our first craft beer line, but their conversation drips into my thoughts, each word a reminder of what's at stake.

"Do you really think we can just sell it and walk away?" Ethan's voice cuts through the clinking of bottles, sharp and incredulous. I freeze, heart pounding, listening intently as my mother responds, her tone a mix of frustration and desperation.

"It's not about walking away, Ethan. It's about keeping our heads above water. Business is slow, and we can't keep pouring money into this place."

Her words hit me like a splash of cold water. I set down my wooden spoon and lean closer to the doorway, peering around the corner. I need to see their faces, to gauge the weight of their words. My mother's usually warm expression is strained, shadows under her eyes deepening like the amber color of a stout. Ethan, with his wild hair and scruffy beard, looks like he's about to explode, and I can't decide if I want to storm in and defend our father's legacy or keep hiding behind this door, letting the tension roll over me like waves against the shore.

"It's Dad's legacy," Ethan insists, voice rising. "You can't just throw it away because things are tough. This place is more than just a business; it's our home."

I can't take it anymore. I push through the door, heart racing, ready to confront whatever they're planning. "You can't sell it!" The words burst out of me like the fizz of a freshly opened beer, and I immediately regret the fervor in my tone. The room turns quiet, two pairs of eyes locking onto mine, surprised and scrutinizing.

My mother sighs, rubbing her temples. "Lila, it's not that simple. We have to consider our options."

"Options?" I scoff, feeling the heat of indignation rise to my cheeks. "Options don't involve selling out everything Dad worked for! We can find a way to make this work."

Ethan watches me, his expression shifting from frustration to something softer, more vulnerable. "How, Lila? We can't just keep pouring our savings into something that's failing."

The words stab at me. They're a truth I don't want to face, but the familiar weight of responsibility settles over my shoulders. I think of the late nights spent here, the laughter echoing off the walls, the friends who walked through the doors to share stories and drink our beer. "What if we... what if we try something new? Market it differently? We could revamp the whole thing."

"What do you suggest?" my mother replies, skepticism coloring her voice.

The air is thick with tension, and I can feel the heaviness of their gazes weighing down on me. "We could host more events, craft beer tastings, maybe even a community market. We need to get people back in here."

Ethan shifts slightly, leaning against the counter, arms still crossed. "And what, pray tell, do you think we'll do in the meantime? This isn't just about ideas; it's about money."

I open my mouth to argue, but the truth lies just beneath my skin, a bubbling anxiety that threatens to spill over. "I... I'll figure it out. Just give me some time."

I can't afford to show weakness; not now. They might think I'm just an idealist, a daydreamer with grand schemes, but I know this place like I know my own heartbeat. It holds our family's history, our father's laughter, and the scent of freshly baked pretzels that lingers long after the last customer leaves.

"Look, I need to work on the new recipes," I finally say, breaking the tense silence. "If you're both so set on selling, then I'll make sure this last line is the best we've ever produced. It'll be a tribute to Dad, a final toast to everything he built."

My heart races as I retreat back into the brewing area, needing to escape the weight of their stares. Each step echoes in my ears, and I can almost hear the faint whispers of my father's voice urging me to fight for what we have. I start measuring out the hops, pouring them into a kettle, the scent of pine and citrus filling the air.

Jackson, my trusted friend, walks in just as I pour the first batch of grains into the kettle. His presence is like a balm, easing the tightness in my chest. "What's going on?" he asks, leaning against the doorway, a playful smile tugging at his lips.

"Just the usual family drama. You know, discussing our imminent demise."

He raises an eyebrow, stepping further into the room. "That sounds ominous. Care to elaborate?"

I drop my gaze to the bubbling mixture, my frustration bubbling alongside it. "Ethan and Mom are talking about selling the brewery. They think it's the only option."

Jackson frowns, leaning against the counter, arms crossed like my brother had moments ago. "That's insane. This place is your home. What are you going to do?"

"I'm going to save it," I reply, my voice stronger now, ignited by the fight that's brewing inside me. "I'll create the best craft beer this town has ever tasted, and they'll see that it's worth holding onto."

He chuckles softly, the sound a welcome reprieve from the tension. "With that kind of determination, I wouldn't bet against you. But you know it's going to take more than just a few recipes to turn things around."

"Yeah, I know. But I have ideas," I say, waving a hand as if shooing away the doubts. "I'm thinking events, tastings, collaborations with local food trucks. We need to get the community back in here. We're not just a brewery; we're part of the town's fabric."

He studies me for a moment, and I can almost see the gears turning in his head. "You know, I might have a few connections who could help with that. I've got a friend who organizes local festivals. Maybe they could feature us next time."

The prospect ignites a spark of hope. "Really? That would be amazing! If we can get our name out there, people will remember us."

His grin widens, and I feel the warmth of his support wrap around me, an anchor amidst the storm. "Let's do it then. We'll show Ethan and your mom that the brewery can thrive if we put our heads together."

And just like that, the tension that had been bubbling in my chest begins to ease. With Jackson by my side, I can almost see the path forward, illuminated by the promise of possibilities.

The hum of the brewing kettles continues to fill the air as I pour the ingredients for our newest craft beer, each one a splash of hope mixed with uncertainty. Jackson's words echo in my mind, a steady drumbeat of encouragement that somehow makes the weight of the world feel a little lighter. Yet, despite the growing excitement of our collaboration, the undercurrent of tension remains. My family's fate hangs in the balance, and the thought of Ethan and my mother selling our father's legacy feels like a betrayal that sinks deep into my chest.

As the days roll on, I find solace in the rhythm of brewing, in the way the ingredients blend and transform. Each batch becomes a new opportunity, an escape from the reality that looms outside these walls. But the tightness between my brother and me lingers like an uninvited guest. He's been quiet, his usual spark dampened by the weight of our conversations, as if he's been wrestling with some internal conflict I can't quite grasp.

"Ready for this?" Jackson asks, breaking through my brewing reverie as he steps into the backroom. The sunlight spills through the windows, casting a warm glow on the bottles stacked neatly against the wall. Today, we're bottling our first batch of craft beer, a small victory in the grand scheme of things, but it feels monumental.

"More than ready. I think this is going to be our best batch yet." I flash a grin, trying to channel my optimism into the atmosphere. Jackson, with his tousled hair and easygoing smile, brings an energy that lights up the room. But as he sets up the bottling equipment, I can't help but notice the crease in his brow.

"Let's hope the customers agree," he replies, his voice light but laced with an undertone of seriousness. "What do you think they'll say? Is it too hoppy? Too citrusy?"

"Jackson, it's beer. If it's cold and in a glass, they'll drink it," I tease, nudging him playfully. "Besides, if it doesn't fly off the shelves, I'm sure we can convince Mom to turn it into a pancake syrup. I mean, who doesn't love beer pancakes?"

His laughter dances through the room, warming my heart even as I feel the looming shadows of our family's decisions creeping back in. As we set to work, the sounds of clinking bottles and the bubbling brew create a symphony of productivity, momentarily drowning out the chaos swirling outside.

Hours later, the last bottle is capped and lined up, glistening in the afternoon sun. I wipe my hands on a towel, exhilaration mingling with exhaustion. "We did it," I say, grinning like a kid on Christmas morning. "Our first batch is ready to go."

"Now we just need to figure out how to sell it," Jackson says, leaning back against the counter, arms crossed behind his head. He looks relaxed, but I see the flicker of concern in his eyes.

"We'll have a launch party, get everyone in the community excited about it," I suggest, determination fueling my voice. "We'll call it 'The Taste of Home,' because that's what this beer represents to us. A way to celebrate our roots."

"Nice touch," he says, nodding thoughtfully. "I can help with the marketing. You know I've got a few tricks up my sleeve."

"Do you mean tricks like posting it on social media and hoping for the best?" I quip, raising an eyebrow.

He feigns offense, hand over his heart. "I'll have you know, my last post got a whole seven likes! It's practically a viral sensation."

"Seven likes? Wow, I didn't realize we were sitting on a social media goldmine."

We share a laugh, the air thick with camaraderie, but it's fleeting. As the laughter fades, the reality of our situation presses in again, an unwelcome reminder of the fragility of our plans.

That evening, while I'm washing the dishes from our bottling session, I hear Ethan's voice rise again, slicing through the quiet of the brewery. Curiosity tugs at me, and I abandon the suds to eavesdrop, my heart pounding with anticipation.

"You're being unreasonable, Mom!" he exclaims. "You can't just decide to sell everything without consulting Lila and me first. It's not just yours to give away."

His words ignite a fire in my chest, pushing me into the hallway. "You know what?" I call out, voice steady despite the adrenaline coursing through me. "If you're going to sell it, then you might as well do it without me. I refuse to let Dad's legacy be discarded just because it's inconvenient."

The moment I step into the room, the atmosphere shifts, thick with unspoken words and unprocessed emotions. Ethan's face reflects shock, while my mother's eyes dart between us, clearly caught in the middle.

"Lila, this isn't the time," she says, but I see the glimmer of conflict in her gaze.

"No, Mom. This is exactly the time. If we're going to have a conversation about our family's future, it needs to be honest. You can't make decisions without me."

"I'm trying to protect us," she snaps, her frustration bubbling over. "This place is falling apart! I can't keep pretending everything is fine when it's not!"

The weight of her words slams into me, but I refuse to back down. "I'm not saying everything is fine. But selling is not the solution. We need to fight for it, just like Dad would have."

"Dad's not here anymore!" Ethan interjects, his voice sharp enough to cut through the tension. "And it's time we face that reality. Maybe selling is the best option."

The air crackles, and I feel my heart racing, a visceral blend of anger and desperation flooding through me. "You can't mean that. You know how much this place meant to him. To us."

My words hang in the air, heavy with memories of laughter and love. I remember my father's passion for brewing, the way he'd light up when talking about each batch, each new recipe, as if he were sharing a part of himself. The thought of letting it go feels like tearing apart a piece of my soul.

Ethan takes a step back, eyes narrowing as he processes my outburst. "And what do you propose we do? Pretend everything will magically turn around because you want it to?"

I open my mouth, ready to argue, but Jackson appears at the doorway, sensing the tension. "Maybe what we need is a plan," he says, his calm demeanor grounding me. "Lila and I have been working on something. We're launching our first craft beer, and we want to do it right. If we can generate some buzz, maybe we can turn this around."

Ethan's expression softens slightly, curiosity piqued. "Really? And you think that will work?"

"I believe it can," Jackson replies, crossing his arms as he leans against the doorframe. "But we need your support, all of us. This isn't just about selling or abandoning what your father built. It's about reviving it, making it something new."

My heart swells with gratitude for Jackson. He's stepping into the fray, advocating for the brewery and our family's legacy. I can't help but feel a flicker of hope, a glimmer of possibility amidst the turmoil.

"I'm willing to try," Ethan concedes, a hint of vulnerability breaking through his previously hardened exterior. "But we all need to be on board. No more half-hearted efforts."

My mother nods, the tension in her shoulders easing slightly. "I want to believe in this. I really do. But if we're going to do it, we need to go all in."

Jackson and I exchange a glance, a silent agreement passing between us. This is our chance, our opportunity to unite and fight for what we hold dear.

"Then let's get to work," I say, a renewed sense of purpose coursing through me. "Together."

As the three of us begin to brainstorm ideas and strategies, a sense of camaraderie begins to blossom. We may have stumbled into conflict, but now we're forging a path forward, guided by the spirit of our father and the love we share for this place we call home.

As the sun dips below the horizon, casting a golden hue across the brewery, a renewed energy fills the air. The tension that once gripped my family seems to morph into something akin to determination as we gather around the old wooden table, its surface scarred and polished by years of laughter and late-night brainstorming sessions. Jackson leads the charge, sketching out ideas on a notepad while Ethan and I throw suggestions back and forth like we're in a game of catch, the stakes far higher than any friendly competition.

"I'm telling you, we need a killer tagline," Jackson says, his pen tapping rhythmically against the table. "Something that captures what this beer represents. It has to be catchy but heartfelt."

Ethan leans back in his chair, fingers rubbing his chin thoughtfully. "How about 'A Taste of Tradition'?"

"Boring!" I scoff, unable to suppress a smirk. "It sounds like something you'd read on a box of crackers. We need to connect with people. Maybe something like, 'Brewed with Heart and Hops'?"

"Or 'A Love Letter in Every Sip'?" Jackson suggests, his eyes sparkling with mischief.

Ethan rolls his eyes, but I see a smile tugging at the corners of his mouth. "That's a bit sappy, don't you think? We're not writing poetry here."

"It's not sappy; it's evocative!" I retort, crossing my arms, a playful defiance in my stance. "I want people to feel something when they drink our beer, not just gulp it down mindlessly."

Jackson chuckles, his laughter brightening the room. "I like it, actually. It's romantic, like the brewery itself—always been a place where stories are shared and memories are made."

"Okay, okay, let's not get too carried away," Ethan interjects, raising his hands in mock surrender. "We'll brainstorm later. Right now, let's focus on what we can do for the launch."

Just then, the door swings open, and my mother walks in, a bag of groceries in hand, her brow still furrowed from the earlier conversation. "What's all this?" she asks, eyeing our scattered notes with curiosity.

"Planning our grand beer launch," I reply, my voice infused with enthusiasm. "Join us! We need your wisdom."

She hesitates, glancing between us, and then sets the bag down, softening at the prospect of being included. "All right, but only if you promise not to get too wild with the ideas. I don't want to end up at some festival trying to explain why we're giving away beer-flavored pancakes."

"Only if you promise to help us with the logistics!" I counter, grinning at her. "We can't do this without you."

And just like that, the atmosphere shifts, the earlier tension fading into the background as we delve into a whirlwind of brainstorming, laughter spilling out like the foamy beer we hope to create. We brainstorm event ideas—beer tastings paired with food trucks, live music featuring local bands, and a contest for the best craft cocktail using our brew as a base. Each idea builds on the last, intertwining our hopes and dreams like vines creeping up the walls of the brewery.

After hours of planning, the initial outline takes shape, and we finally lean back, exhausted but exhilarated. "This is actually going to work," I say, glancing around the table. "We're going to make this place thrive again."

Ethan's smile is cautious, a flicker of his old self shining through the weight of responsibility. "Let's hope so. We're betting a lot on this."

"Betting?" I raise an eyebrow. "You mean investing in our future, right?"

"Semantics," he shoots back, feigning indignation.

"Either way, I think we're onto something," Jackson says, an easy smile spreading across his face. "If we market this right, we can pull in the crowds."

The excitement is palpable, and just as I begin to feel the warmth of hope settle over me, the door swings open again. The bell jingles, and in walks a figure I hadn't expected—Rebecca, the local newspaper reporter known for her sharp wit and keen insight. "Well, well, if it isn't the brewing family of the year," she quips, hands on her hips, a teasing smile on her lips.

"What brings you here?" I ask, trying to mask my surprise with casual curiosity.

"I heard whispers of a new craft beer line launching soon, and you know me, always on the lookout for the next big story."

Ethan shifts uncomfortably, and I sense the sudden tension rising again. "It's still in the planning stages," he says, his voice guarded.

"Ah, but that's the best time for a story! The anticipation, the excitement! Don't you want the community to rally behind you?" Rebecca's eyes gleam with the thrill of a scoop.

My mother looks unsure, glancing between Rebecca and the plans we've just developed. "We're not ready for publicity yet," she interjects, her tone cautious. "We want to be sure of our product before we go shouting about it."

"Nonsense! You want to create buzz, right? There's no better way than to get a little article in the local paper. Everyone loves an underdog story."

I feel the urge to jump in, but a sudden thought halts me. "What if we invite you to our launch party instead? You can see the beer, meet the people, and then decide if it's worth a write-up."

Rebecca raises an eyebrow, intrigued. "Now that's a tempting offer. Are you sure you want to risk it? If it doesn't go well, it could backfire."

Ethan exchanges a glance with me, and I can feel the weight of his uncertainty pressing against my resolve. "What if it does go well?" I counter, a spark of defiance igniting within me. "What if we blow them away with our beer and our story? We can't hide forever."

Rebecca's smile broadens. "I like your spirit. Consider me intrigued. Just make sure I get an invite—front row seat to the next big thing."

As she leaves, the room buzzes with a new energy. But as the door closes behind her, I catch a glimpse of the apprehension in Ethan's eyes. "This is a risk, Lila," he warns, his voice low. "What if we can't deliver?"

"Then we'll learn from it and keep trying," I reply, feeling a rush of conviction. "We owe it to Dad to give it everything we have."

With our plans taking shape, the night deepens, and we huddle around the table, our laughter echoing off the walls. The room feels alive, electric with possibility, yet I can't shake the unease lingering in the back of my mind.

As the last slivers of daylight fade away, a sudden crash echoes through the brewery. My heart stops, and the jovial atmosphere shatters like glass. We exchange startled glances, and without thinking, I bolt toward the sound, a surge of adrenaline propelling me forward.

As I round the corner, I find a shattered window and a figure silhouetted against the moonlight, standing just outside the broken glass. My heart races as I step closer, the tension palpable. "Who are you?" I call out, voice steadier than I feel.

The figure turns, and I catch a glimpse of a familiar face—someone I never expected to see. "I've come to talk about the brewery," they say, voice low and urgent, sending chills racing down my spine.

# Chapter 5: Brewing Secrets

The dim light of the brewery cast long shadows across the wooden beams, flickering like old ghosts lingering in the corners. The familiar scent of malt and hops enveloped me, warm and inviting, but tonight, it had an undercurrent of something else—a hint of discovery, perhaps, or maybe just the crispness of autumn seeping through the cracked windows. I had always loved this place, but lately, it felt like a mausoleum rather than a refuge. The laughter of the past, the warmth of shared moments, was replaced by an echoing silence that reverberated off the walls. The brewery felt heavy with memories that neither Ethan nor I seemed willing to unpack.

As I swept the floor, the swish of my broom was the only sound breaking the stillness. I leaned down to pick up a discarded bottle cap when a sliver of light caught my eye from the back of the room. A shadowed door, slightly ajar, beckoned to me like a siren's song. It was a door I had never noticed before, its edges hidden behind a tapestry of forgotten crates. Curiosity ignited a spark in my chest, urging me to abandon my cleaning for something much more tantalizing.

With cautious steps, I approached the door, each creak of the floorboards beneath my feet adding to the suspense. I pushed it open and was met by a small, dusty room that smelled of aged wood and nostalgia. Shelves lined with leather-bound tomes stretched toward the ceiling, their spines cracked and faded. The air was thick with the weight of history, the kind that could only be found in a space long forgotten. I could barely contain my excitement; this was a treasure trove of secrets that my father had hidden away.

My heart raced as I scanned the shelves, searching for anything that might tell me more about the recipes that had shaped our family's legacy. One volume caught my attention, its cover worn and inviting. I pulled it from the shelf, dust dancing in the golden light as it filtered through the window. The pages whispered with the softest sighs as I opened it, revealing old brewing logs filled with meticulous notes, sketches, and, strangely, some hastily written warnings.

Each entry seemed to pulse with life, recounting the trials and triumphs of brews past. My fingers trembled as I traced the lines of my father's handwriting—his thoughts, his passion captured in the ink. But there, among the eloquent descriptions of flavor profiles and fermentation times, were scrawled notes of caution. Words like "disaster," "overcarbonation," and "family reputation at stake" jumped out at me, each one striking like a thunderclap in my mind.

As I flipped through the pages, a particularly well-worn piece of parchment fell to the floor, fluttering like a moth caught in a candle's flame. I picked it up, the weight of it anchoring me in place. It was a recipe, and not just any recipe—it was for a brew my father had never mentioned, one that promised to breathe new life into our brand. My heart quickened; could this be the answer to our dwindling sales, to the silent worry lines that had etched themselves across Ethan's brow?

But then came the gnawing doubt, curling itself around my excitement. The warning notes hinted at a brewing mishap that had nearly ruined our family's name. I couldn't shake the feeling that this recipe carried with it more than just the potential for revival—it held a ghost of our past, a legacy fraught with peril. What if this was not a second chance but a noose tightening around our family's neck?

I felt the thrill of the discovery battling against the weight of caution. In my heart, I knew I had to share this with Ethan; after all, he had always been the pragmatist, the one with his feet firmly planted on the ground. Maybe he could see the potential that I was blinded by, or perhaps he'd know how to approach the ghosts lingering in the recipe's shadows.

I rushed back into the main brewing room, my heart pounding with the urgency of my discovery. But when I found Ethan, I wasn't prepared for the wave of dismissal that crashed over me. He stood by the fermentation tanks, arms crossed, a frown etched deeply across his forehead. "What is it, Anna?" he snapped, frustration dripping from his tone. "I'm busy here."

I hesitated, the excitement deflating like a punctured balloon. "Ethan, I found something—something important. A recipe, one we could use to revive the brand. But—"

He cut me off with a wave of his hand, his blue eyes stormy and distant. "We don't need another harebrained scheme, Anna. We need to stick to what we know. Dad's methods were good enough. We can't start chasing ghosts."

The sting of his words hit harder than I expected. It was as if he'd taken the hope I had nurtured and tossed it into the gears of our brewing equipment, grinding it to dust. "This could change everything," I implored, my voice tinged with desperation. "You don't understand! The logs are filled with our history, and this recipe—"

"History is what got us here. We can't afford to take risks like that. It's too late for that." His voice was cold, a stark contrast to the warmth of the room. The chasm between us widened, echoing the silence left by our father's passing.

I felt the heat of tears prick at the corners of my eyes, the sting of my brother's disbelief igniting a fire within me. How could he dismiss something so vital, so promising? The disappointment wrapped around me like a heavy cloak, suffocating the joy I had felt just moments ago.

With every heartbeat, the distance between us became an unbridgeable gulf. The past weighed heavily on my shoulders, and the secrets I had unearthed felt more like chains than keys. I stood there, torn between the urge to fight for my discovery and the realization that I might just have to face this battle alone.

The air hung thick between Ethan and me, charged with tension that crackled like a poorly wired light bulb. I could feel my heartbeat echoing in my ears, drowning out the comforting hum of the brewery's machines. It was as if we were standing on opposite shores of a vast, raging river, each of us staring into the churning waters of our own grief and stubbornness. I had never seen Ethan so resolute, a stone wall against the storm of my enthusiasm.

"Anna, we can't gamble with the family name," he said, the resolve in his voice as solid as the oak barrels lining the walls. "If that recipe was good, Dad would've used it. He knew what he was doing."

"But what if he didn't?" I shot back, frustration bubbling up like a fresh brew. "What if he was holding back? Maybe he was afraid of making the same mistakes again. We've lost so much already; it's time to reclaim what's ours."

Ethan sighed, rubbing the back of his neck as if trying to ease the tension knotting there. "Reclaiming things doesn't mean diving headfirst into uncertainty. It means building on what we have."

The words felt like icy water splashed over my hopes. I stepped back, suddenly aware of how trapped I felt in this space that had once been a sanctuary. I had been here countless times, surrounded by laughter and the sweet aroma of hops, but now it was a cage, its bars forged by grief and my brother's unwillingness to embrace change.

I turned away from him, my heart aching at the distance that had formed not just in this room but in our lives. It was like staring into a mirror that had cracked, reflecting all the ways we were falling apart. The echoes of laughter that once filled this place faded into whispers of bitterness, and the joy of brewing together felt like a distant memory.

I needed air, and I needed to think. With one last glance at Ethan—who remained unmoved, arms crossed and expression hard—I stepped out into the cool night. The crispness of the autumn air washed over me, pulling me out of the heaviness of the brewery. The moon hung low, a silvery orb casting a soft glow over the tangled vines climbing the brewery's exterior. I walked along the gravel path, the crunch beneath my boots grounding me, as if each step was a silent prayer for clarity.

The shadows danced around me as I wandered to the back of the property, where a small garden lay hidden behind a worn wooden fence. It had once been a riot of colors, but now it was a graveyard of wilted leaves and abandoned dreams. My mother had tended to it with care, each bloom a testament to her love for our family and this place. I knelt beside a withering rosebush, the scent of decay mingling with the cool breeze. It reminded me too much of what we had lost.

"What are you doing out here?" came a familiar voice, playful yet tinged with concern. I looked up to see Lila, my childhood friend, standing at the garden gate. Her wild curls framed her face, and she wore an expression of genuine curiosity, as if she could sense my turmoil from afar.

"I'm not gardening, that's for sure," I replied, attempting a laugh but failing miserably. The tightness in my chest was relentless, and the rosebush beneath my fingertips felt like a metaphor for my life—blooming and beautiful at one moment, then fading the next. "Just... thinking."

"Ah, the classic brewery crisis." She grinned, stepping into the garden, her boots crunching over the gravel. "I came to rescue you from the brewing basement. You know Ethan and his broodiness—he'll suck the fun out of anything."

"Yeah, well, I kind of brought it on myself," I admitted, brushing dirt from my hands. "I found something. A recipe, one my dad never shared. But Ethan... he thinks it's too risky."

Lila's eyebrows shot up. "A secret recipe? Now that's intriguing. What kind of risk are we talking about? Bad yeast? Stale hops? Or the more alarming risk of becoming an actual entrepreneur?"

I rolled my eyes, but a smile tugged at my lips. "You know how it is. It's not just about brewing. It's about the legacy, the family name.

And it's tied to... well, a brewing disaster from years ago. There are warnings in the margins, like our father was afraid to try again."

"Yikes. That's heavy." Lila plopped down beside me, her playful demeanor shifting to something more serious. "But think about it, Anna. You're not your dad. You're your own person, with your own ideas. Maybe this recipe could be your chance to create something new, to rewrite the narrative."

"I want to believe that, but what if I screw it up?" I confessed, a wave of vulnerability crashing over me. "What if I bring ruin to what's left of our family's name?"

"Then you learn from it. Just like brewing. You add a little more hops, adjust the yeast, and you keep going until you find the perfect balance. It's messy, but that's where the best brews come from—flaws turned into something extraordinary."

Her words hung in the air, reverberating through my doubt. I wanted to grab onto that hope, to cling to the idea that I could shape our legacy into something vibrant and alive, rather than let it wither away under the weight of old fears.

Just then, the distant sound of laughter floated from the brewery, a reminder of the life that still thrummed beneath the surface. I stood up, brushing off my knees. "You're right, Lila. I need to talk to Ethan again, not just about the recipe but about everything. We can't let this place crumble into memories."

She grinned, her eyes sparkling with mischief. "There's the Anna I know. Let's go shake some sense into that brother of yours. And if he still won't budge, we'll just have to sneak in a few late-night brews of our own."

Laughter bubbled up as I followed her back toward the brewery, a sense of determination igniting within me. The ghosts of the past might linger, but they wouldn't dictate our future. This was our family legacy, and it was time to breathe new life into it, one brew at a time.

The laughter faded as Lila and I stepped back into the brewery, the sounds of clinking glasses and jovial chatter washing over us like a wave. It felt alive in here, pulsing with energy that had been absent moments before. The warmth of the space wrapped around me, yet the tension with Ethan hung in the air, a persistent cloud I couldn't shake.

As we entered, the sight of patrons mingling, their faces glowing with excitement over the latest brew, brought a bittersweet smile to my lips. I longed for that enthusiasm, the kind that had once danced in our family's eyes before everything went quiet. I scanned the room for Ethan, finally spotting him near the bar, deep in conversation with one of our regulars, a grizzled old man named Frank. His laughter was rich and deep, but as I approached, I could see the tight lines around Ethan's mouth, the way his jaw clenched as he spoke.

I felt a flicker of resolve ignite within me, bolstered by Lila's encouragement. "Time to turn the tide," I murmured, adjusting my stance. "Do you think he'll actually listen this time?"

"Trust me, it's like trying to convince a cat to take a bath," Lila replied, rolling her eyes playfully. "But you're the only one who can even attempt it. Just remember to lead with your heart and not your fists."

With a nod, I squared my shoulders and made my way toward them. "Ethan!" I called, forcing a brightness into my tone. His eyes flickered toward me, a mix of surprise and something else—exasperation, perhaps. Frank, sensing the shift in the air, politely excused himself, leaving us standing on opposite sides of an emotional battlefield.

"Hey," Ethan said, his voice flat, as if bracing for impact.

"I found Lila, as you can see," I began, forcing myself to maintain eye contact. "But that's not what I came to talk about. I want to show you something. Something I found in that hidden room."

He crossed his arms, his posture closed off. "I don't think we need to revisit that discussion. You know where I stand."

I took a deep breath, refusing to let his dismissiveness deter me. "But you haven't heard everything yet. There's a recipe, Ethan—a real recipe! One that could revive the brewery! It's in the logs, and it's... it's not just about the beer. It's about us."

His expression didn't change, though a flicker of something caught my eye—curiosity, maybe? "I'm not interested in chasing ghosts, Anna. We have enough problems without digging up the past."

"Not chasing ghosts, Ethan. Reclaiming them." My voice rose slightly, my frustration bubbling over. "If we can't even talk about this, what's the point? We're here, now, standing on the precipice of failure. What if this recipe is our chance to turn it all around? We can't just let Dad's fears dictate our future."

The moment hung in the air, thick with unspoken words and a shared grief that had been festering like a forgotten wound. "What's so special about it?" he asked, finally softening slightly.

"Come with me," I urged, motioning for him to follow as I led him to the back room. Lila trailed behind, her eyes alight with excitement, but I felt the weight of Ethan's skepticism pressing down on me. As we stepped into the hidden space, the warm, nostalgic scent of aged wood and musty parchment enveloped us. I pointed to the open tome, the pages fluttering slightly in the draft. "Look at this—this is our history."

Ethan approached the shelf, eyes narrowing as he scanned the delicate lines of my father's handwriting. "It's just a recipe book, Anna. We've got plenty of those."

I could feel my heart quickening as I turned the pages, revealing sketches and notes that told stories I had never heard. "But this one... this is different. This recipe—my dad was careful with it. It could be what we need to breathe new life into the brewery. Just give it a chance."

As he leaned closer, I could almost see the gears turning in his mind. "What does it say?"

"Here," I pointed to a passage that described a unique combination of ingredients, one that promised a bold flavor profile that would set us apart in the market. "This could help us stand out. It's like nothing we've ever done before."

"Sure, but you also mentioned those warnings. What if we're just repeating past mistakes?" Ethan shot back, his skepticism still evident. "What if we screw this up?"

"Life is all about risks, isn't it?" Lila chimed in, attempting to lighten the mood. "I mean, you took a risk marrying that awful IPA with the peach puree last summer, and look how that turned out!"

Ethan shot her a side-eye, then focused back on the page. "That was a brilliant mistake, thank you very much. But it wasn't tied to the family legacy."

"Exactly! That's why we need to think carefully. We can adapt it, modify it to suit us," I insisted, my passion flaring like the flame of a brew kettle. "What if we take the essence of this recipe but refine it to fit what we know? It's an opportunity to honor Dad's work while carving our own path."

He fell silent, fingers brushing over the margins as if trying to glean wisdom from the warnings scrawled in his father's hurried handwriting. I could see the internal battle raging in his mind, the weight of the past wrestling with the spark of hope I had ignited.

"I need to think about it," he finally said, pulling away from the tome, the familiar tension returning as he stepped back into his protective shell. "You know how I feel about risks."

"Fine. Just don't bury your head in the sand like an ostrich," I shot back, an edge creeping into my voice. "We're already knee-deep in uncertainty. At least let's try to steer it somewhere good."

His gaze flicked to me, frustration flaring. "You think you can just waltz in here and dictate what we should do?"

"It's not dictating, Ethan! It's suggesting! This place means something to me—us! Can't you see that?"

Suddenly, a loud crash echoed from the front of the brewery, the sound jolting us from our argument. My heart raced as I exchanged a worried glance with Lila. "What was that?" I asked, dread pooling in my stomach.

"I don't know, but it sounded serious," Ethan replied, tension draining from our previous conflict as we rushed toward the source.

As we made our way back to the main room, I could see a small crowd had gathered, all eyes trained on the bar. My pulse quickened as I pushed my way through the onlookers, Lila right at my heels. The scene that unfolded before us was a jarring sight.

The bar was littered with shattered glass, and behind it stood Frank, looking bewildered and apologetic. But it wasn't just the broken bottles that caught my attention; it was the figure crouched on the ground, hastily picking up the scattered remnants. My heart sank as I recognized the unmistakable shock of dark hair—Emma, the new bartender we had recently hired.

"What happened?" I gasped, concern flooding through me.

"I tripped! I swear I didn't mean to—" she stammered, her cheeks flushed with embarrassment as she scrambled to gather the glass shards.

"Don't worry about it," Ethan said, kneeling beside her, an unexpected softness in his tone. "Just be careful. Are you hurt?"

"I'm fine, I promise! I just didn't see the floor was wet," she replied, glancing up with a sheepish smile.

But my focus shifted as something glinted in the light—a piece of glass that had a small envelope stuck to it, its edges frayed and stained. I reached out, pulling it free, my fingers brushing over the parchment as I opened it. A quick scan of the words sent a chill down my spine.

"Ethan," I said, my voice shaking. "You need to see this."

His brow furrowed as he stood, taking the letter from my hands. I could see the color draining from his face as he read, and I could only imagine the weight of what was written within those lines.

Just then, the door swung open, a gust of wind sweeping through the brewery, carrying with it the scent of rain and something darker—something that smelled like trouble.

And with it, an unsettling feeling settled in my gut, as if the storm brewing outside was merely a harbinger of the chaos that lay ahead.

# Chapter 6: A Toast to the Past

The air in the brewery was thick with the sweet scent of malt and the earthy undertones of hops, a fragrant reminder of the countless hours spent there as kids, racing through the brewing equipment like it was an elaborate playground. I stood behind the bar, wiping down the polished surface that gleamed under the warm amber lights, a faint echo of laughter and clinking glasses already beginning to swell in the background. Today marked more than just a family reunion; it was a toast to our father's legacy, a chance to celebrate the roots of our family tree, even if its branches were somewhat fractured at the moment.

"Are you sure you want to do this?" Jackson's voice cut through my thoughts, as he emerged from the backroom, a stack of bottles precariously balanced in his arms. His brow furrowed with genuine concern, and for a fleeting moment, I felt that familiar tug of gratitude for having him by my side. "You know how Ethan can be."

"Trust me," I replied, my heart racing in sync with the thrum of the brewery's lively atmosphere. "If we don't do this, we might lose the last thread connecting us to Dad." I brushed a stray hair behind my ear, my eyes scanning the room filled with old friends and loyal patrons who had stuck by us through thick and thin. "This is about honoring him, not letting the past drown us."

Jackson placed the bottles on the bar with a decisive thud, sending ripples of foam frothing from the freshly poured pints. "Fine. But if Ethan tries to flip a table, I'm not going to be responsible for what happens next." He flashed me a mischievous grin, and I couldn't help but chuckle. The tension that had been coiling inside me started to unfurl, just a bit.

As the clock inched closer to six, I busied myself with the last-minute details, arranging an array of glasses that sparkled like gems under the soft lighting. Each clink against the bar echoed memories—long afternoons spent practicing our pours, our laughter intertwining with the bubbling sounds of the brewing kettles. I could almost hear Dad's booming laughter, see him standing tall, his hands covered in flour from the pretzel dough he'd insist on making for every family gathering. He had a knack for turning ordinary moments into vibrant tapestries of joy.

"Are we ready for this?" Jackson asked, leaning against the bar, arms crossed, his demeanor both relaxed and alert.

"Ready as we'll ever be," I said, glancing at the door as it creaked open. A group of familiar faces spilled into the brewery, some smiling wide, others more subdued, yet all were warm with memories. It was a crowd of misfits and companions, each carrying a piece of our father's spirit with them.

"Ella!" a voice called out, and I turned to see Lucy, a childhood friend, her bright red hair bouncing as she approached. She enveloped me in a hug that smelled faintly of cinnamon and old leather. "I can't believe you finally got this together! Your dad would be so proud."

"Thanks, Lucy. I just wish Ethan could see that." The weight of his absence, like a phantom limb, was palpable, threatening to overshadow our efforts.

"We'll get him back," Jackson interjected, pouring a generous sample of the new brew into a glass. "If this doesn't work, I'll go full-on motivational speaker on him."

I snorted, amused by the mental image. "Yeah, I can picture it now: 'Ethan, let's talk about your feelings over a pint of hops.'"

The laughter that rippled through us felt like an anchor, grounding me as more guests trickled in. Familiar faces swirled in the haze of nostalgia, each one tugging at my heartstrings. I welcomed them with hugs and stories, the atmosphere shifting from the remnants of sadness to a symphony of cheer.

But through the joyous chaos, I couldn't shake the sight of Ethan, sulking in the corner, nursing a beer as if it were a lifeline. He wore that familiar scowl, the one I had seen too often lately, as if he were trying to protect himself from the very warmth that surrounded us. My heart ached to bridge the chasm between us, but what words could possibly traverse the bitterness that had settled like a fog between our shared memories?

"Let's raise a glass!" Jackson announced, standing on the bar with a showman's flair that drew everyone's attention. "To Ella, for pulling us all together, and to the legacy of a man who taught us how to dream over a good brew!"

The room erupted in cheers, glasses clinking like tiny thunderclaps, yet my gaze remained fixed on Ethan. I watched as he took a long pull from his glass, his eyes betraying a mix of longing and resentment. The laughter echoed around me, but inside, I felt a cold knot tighten in my stomach. This reunion was supposed to mend our bonds, but with each laugh, I felt the distance between us widen, as if I were straddling two worlds—one filled with nostalgia and the other draped in shadows.

"Ella!" Lucy pulled me back into the present, her voice laced with excitement. "Come on, you've got to try this new brew! Jackson really outdid himself."

"Yeah, Ella! Come celebrate with us!" The chorus of voices beckoned, but I couldn't tear my eyes away from Ethan. He looked so lost, like a ship adrift on a stormy sea.

"Just a minute," I murmured to Lucy, my feet moving toward the corner where he sat, framed by the golden light like a reluctant hero. I could feel the room pulsating with laughter and joy behind me, but the air felt different in this part of the brewery. It was charged, heavy with unsaid words and unresolved feelings.

"Ethan," I began, my voice steady despite the tremor of uncertainty in my heart. "Can we talk?"

"Ella," Ethan said, his voice rough as if he hadn't used it in ages. "What's there to talk about? The reunion? This...this spectacle?" He gestured vaguely toward the thrumming crowd behind me, where laughter and chatter swirled like the hops in our best brews.

I swallowed hard, the lump in my throat feeling larger than the stacks of empty kegs lining the back wall. "This isn't just a spectacle. It's a chance for us to remember. To honor Dad, to connect with everyone again." My voice felt fragile, teetering on the edge of emotion, yet I pushed on. "You can't keep hiding back here."

"Hiding?" He chuckled, but it was devoid of humor, a hollow sound that resonated in the air between us. "I'm not hiding, Ella. I'm observing. Someone has to be the rational one in this family circus."

I took a breath, trying to rein in the frustration bubbling within me. "Rational? Is that what you call pushing everyone away? Because I don't see how that's helping anyone." My heart raced, driven by the dual forces of indignation and concern. I had known Ethan long enough to understand that beneath that gruff exterior lay a brother who had once shared my dreams and fears. "You're not alone, Ethan. You never were. Just look around."

He shifted in his seat, his expression hardening, eyes narrowing as if I had just tossed a dart into the center of a target. "I don't need your pep talks, Ella. This is exactly why I didn't want to do this. I can't play happy family when everything feels broken."

"Maybe it feels broken because you refuse to let anyone in," I countered, the words spilling out before I could catch them. "You think being a wall will protect you, but all it does is isolate you more. We're all hurting, but we're here together. For Dad." I let the last words hang, hoping they would penetrate the armor he had built around himself.

Ethan's gaze dropped to the table, studying the condensation rings left by forgotten drinks, and for a moment, I thought I could see the defenses begin to crack. "You think I'm the only one hurting?

You don't know what it's like to stand there and watch everything we built crumble."

"No," I admitted, my heart aching for him. "But I do know what it's like to feel lost. We lost our father. You lost your way. But isolating yourself won't bring him back. It won't fix anything."

The silence stretched between us, thick and taut. It was the kind of silence that thrummed with unexpressed feelings, a charged atmosphere where all the unsaid words hung heavy. I could see the flicker of something—maybe regret or the desire to reconcile—swimming in his eyes. But before it could fully surface, he masked it, that familiar wall of bravado rising again. "You sound like you have it all figured out," he muttered, sarcasm dripping from each syllable. "Maybe I'm just not ready to share a beer with a ghost."

The sting of his words cut deep, and I leaned back slightly, allowing the distance between us to grow. "I'm not asking for perfection, Ethan. Just... try. For one night. Can't you do that for Dad?"

His gaze flickered past me, and for a brief moment, I thought he might just stand up and walk away, leave me in this dim corner of the brewery while the world celebrated around us. My heart pounded, a drumbeat of anxiety mingled with hope. I didn't want to lose him, not again.

"Fine." Ethan's voice was a mere whisper, barely rising above the din. "For Dad." It was a concession, a tiny crack in his façade that I would take, despite how fragile it felt.

Before I could respond, a rowdy cheer erupted from the crowd, the sound washing over us like a wave. Jackson appeared, grinning like a Cheshire cat, holding a tray laden with glasses. "What's this? A family feud? Or are you two finally ready to rejoin the living?"

"More like a family therapy session," I replied dryly, shooting Ethan a look that dared him to dispute it.

"Oh, good! I can be the therapist," Jackson announced, setting the tray down with a flourish. "Everyone knows that the best healing comes from laughter—and beer. So, what'll it be, sibling therapy or a round of toasts?"

"Let's toast," I suggested, desperate to shift the mood before it soured entirely. I picked up a glass and raised it high, channeling all the hope I could muster. "To our father! The man who taught us that a little laughter can turn any situation around."

Ethan hesitated but then reached for a glass, the motion tentative yet determined. "To Dad," he echoed, his voice steadier this time, warmth creeping into his tone as he clinked his glass against mine.

"To Dad!" Jackson chimed in, lifting his own glass, and the sound of glasses clinking filled the air, a momentary harmony that resonated with all the love and loss woven into our family's history.

As the toast lingered in the air, a wave of nostalgia washed over me. The warmth of the brewery enveloped us, the clamor of old friends sharing stories, laughter spiraling into the rafters like a song sung by the walls themselves. I took a sip of the brew, a mix of caramel notes and slight bitterness that was unmistakably Jackson's creation, and felt the tension within me begin to dissipate.

"Wow, this is actually good," Ethan remarked, an eyebrow raised in genuine surprise. "You might just have a future in this after all."

"Thanks, I think?" Jackson shot back, feigning indignation. "I was hoping for a little more enthusiasm. How about, 'This is the best thing since sliced bread?'"

Ethan laughed, and I felt a surge of relief—like the thawing of winter's grip on the world. It was a small victory, but it was a victory nonetheless. The laughter grew louder, voices blending together in a beautiful cacophony that felt more like a reunion than a funeral for our father's legacy.

Just as I began to feel hopeful, the door swung open again, ushering in a gust of cold air, and a figure I hadn't anticipated stepped inside, bringing with them a shockwave that rippled through the room. My heart dropped as I recognized the unmistakable silhouette—someone I had hoped would be absent tonight.

The air shifted as the door swung open, a gust of chilly wind cutting through the warmth of the brewery like an unwelcome specter. I squinted, my heart doing a rapid tap dance in my chest, as I recognized the figure standing in the doorway. It was Maddie, a ghost from our shared past, her silhouette framed against the fading twilight outside. Her entrance was as unexpected as a thunderclap on a clear day, sending ripples of tension through the room.

"Great, just what we need," Ethan muttered, his voice dripping with disdain as he crossed his arms, but I could see the flicker of discomfort in his eyes. He didn't want to engage, but the atmosphere around us shifted, charged with the sudden realization that the past was crashing the party in all its messy glory.

Maddie stepped inside, her presence commanding, drawing attention like a magnet. Her dark hair cascaded in waves, and her smile, while warm, carried an edge of uncertainty that mirrored my own. It had been years since we last saw each other, a chasm carved by time and choices that led us on divergent paths. But here she was, as real as the shadows of nostalgia swirling around us.

"Hey, everyone," she called, her voice carrying a blend of excitement and trepidation. "I heard there was a party, and I couldn't resist."

Her eyes locked onto mine, and I felt a rush of memories flood back—laughs shared, secrets whispered, and the bittersweet end of our friendship when life had pulled us in different directions. I was struck by the nostalgia but also the weight of unresolved feelings, like a heavy blanket pressed against my chest.

"Ella," Maddie said, her smile faltering slightly as she approached. "I didn't know you were organizing this."

"Surprise!" I managed, forcing cheerfulness into my tone, though it felt more like a mask than a genuine expression. "It's a family reunion. We thought it would be nice to celebrate Dad." I gestured toward the throng of familiar faces, hoping to diffuse the tension. "You should join us. Everyone's here."

"Yeah, it seems like a real love-fest," Ethan interjected, his sarcasm thick enough to cut through. "Just don't break anything while you're at it."

Maddie's gaze flickered to him, a hint of confusion darting across her features before she redirected her attention back to me. "I'd love to." Her tone was polite but felt weighted with the past.

As she joined the gathering crowd, I could sense the dissonance in the air, an unspoken tension settling like fog between Ethan and Maddie. I caught Jackson's eye; he looked equally perplexed by Maddie's presence, clearly aware of the potential for a drama that could rival the best soap opera plotlines.

"Is this the part where we all sit around and air our grievances?" Jackson quipped, trying to lighten the mood, but his humor fell flat. I shot him a warning glance, silently pleading for him to read the room.

"Let's focus on the celebration," I said, eager to steer the ship away from stormy waters. "We're here for Dad, after all. The last thing we need is more drama."

But as I looked over at Ethan, his expression darkening further, I felt a gnawing sense of dread settle in. Maddie and Ethan had shared more than just our father's legacy; they had shared a significant chapter of our lives, one that had ended on a note neither of them had resolved.

I wandered toward the bar, pouring myself another drink, hoping to fortify my nerves. The warm amber liquid swirled in my glass, mirroring the tumult of feelings roiling inside me. Laughter erupted from the crowd as a game of 'remember when' began, old tales of Dad's antics floating through the air like confetti. I wanted to join in, to lose myself in the joy of shared memories, but I felt anchored to the spot, a silent observer caught in a whirlwind.

"Come on, Ella!" Jackson beckoned, snapping me from my reverie. "Join us! We're about to recount the Great Pretzel Disaster of '09!"

I chuckled at the memory, the image of Dad flailing about, pretzel dough flying everywhere, sparking warmth in my heart. But as I turned back to the crowd, my gaze landed on Maddie and Ethan, both standing too close for comfort. Their eyes were locked, the air between them thick with something unspoken, something that crackled like static electricity.

"Are you two going to fight, or are we just going to pretend the past doesn't exist?" I blurted, the words escaping before I could tame them. A ripple of silence cascaded through the crowd, the laughter halting as all eyes turned to us.

Ethan opened his mouth, but Maddie beat him to it. "I'm not here to cause trouble," she said, her voice steady but edged with an underlying tension. "I came to honor your father, like everyone else."

Ethan's jaw tightened, a storm brewing in those familiar dark eyes. "Right, because that's exactly what you did when you left." The words dripped from his tongue like poison, cutting deep into the festering wound of our shared history.

A heavy silence descended, the air thickening with discomfort. I felt my heart race, anxiety clawing at me. The reunion was slipping through my fingers like sand, and I had to act fast. "Okay, how about we focus on the memories?" I suggested, my voice rising above the tension. "Does anyone want to share their favorite story about Dad?"

But before anyone could respond, the brewery door swung open again, this time with a dramatic flair, drawing even more attention. A man stepped in, tall and confident, with a grin that seemed to light up the dimly lit room. My heart sank; he was a reminder of a chapter I thought I could close.

"Did I miss the party?" he called out, his voice smooth and teasing, eyes sweeping across the room. "I heard there were free drinks, and I'll do anything for a good brew!"

"Ethan!" Maddie exclaimed, her voice laced with surprise and a hint of something else, a flicker of emotion that caught me off guard.

Ethan stiffened, the heat of the moment replaced by the chill of recognition. I stood frozen, caught between two worlds, and the air crackled with tension, every pair of eyes darting between us as we awaited the inevitable fallout. As I looked at Ethan, his expression morphed from surprise to a guarded wariness, and in that moment, I realized that nothing would ever be the same again.

The weight of the past hung heavily around us, and it was about to unleash its fury.

# Chapter 7: The Flavor of Change

The aroma of hops and malt filled the air, a heady combination that danced around me like a well-rehearsed ballet, each note of sweetness twirling around the sharp bitterness in a tantalizing embrace. As I stood in the middle of my makeshift brewing station, the sun peeked through the window, casting golden rays that shimmered on the steel brewing kettle, turning it into a small altar of my brewing dreams. Each time I stirred the mix, I could almost hear the whispers of my father guiding me, urging me to chase after the flavors that once delighted our small kitchen in summer—when he would teach me to blend different herbs and spices as if they were old friends.

Yet today, that sense of nostalgia was clouded by the looming weight of the brewing competition. The excitement that had sparked in me like a match was snuffed out by the steady drip of self-doubt that started creeping in, as insidious as a leak in the very keg I was trying to fill. I could already picture the judges, their discerning eyes inspecting every drop as if I were a culinary magician conjuring a trick rather than a novice trying to perfect her craft. "Why did I think I could do this?" I muttered under my breath, pouring the grains into the kettle with a sense of futility.

"You look like you're about to combust," Jackson's voice broke through the haze of my spiraling thoughts, a splash of cool water on my simmering anxiety. He leaned against the doorway, arms crossed, his dark hair falling into his eyes in that annoyingly charming way. "What's going on in that head of yours?"

I rolled my eyes, resisting the urge to smile at him. "Just the usual existential crisis," I replied, trying to match his teasing tone. "You know, the kind that comes with entering a brewing competition with no idea what I'm doing?"

"Ah, yes, the classic rookie mistake. You're not supposed to know what you're doing; that's what makes it fun." His grin widened, and

I couldn't help but feel a little lighter, the weight of my worries momentarily lifted by his presence.

"Fun? More like terrifying. What if I make a brew that's a disaster?" I stirred the mixture, a slow and deliberate motion that belied my internal chaos. "What if I'm just not cut out for this?"

Jackson pushed himself off the doorframe, stepping closer. "Or what if you create something extraordinary? Something that could change everything for you?" He leaned against the counter, his eyes glinting with mischief. "Besides, if disaster strikes, you can always just blame it on the hops. Nobody really knows what they're supposed to taste like anyway."

I snorted, shaking my head. "You've clearly never tasted my experimental batches. They could knock the socks off a bear and make it reconsider its life choices."

"Then let's make sure we craft something that even a bear would be proud to drink," he said, his tone earnest, a sincere challenge hidden beneath the humor. "What if you infused it with your father's spirit? You mentioned how he used to mix flavors like he was painting a masterpiece."

The thought struck me like a lightning bolt. My father had always said that brewing was an art form, not a science. His eyes would light up whenever he spoke of the flavors dancing on the palate, the unexpected combinations that could bring joy with each sip. "You think I should?" I asked, caught off guard by the surge of inspiration coursing through me.

"Why not? You have his recipes, right? His memories? Blend them together, and let it be your signature." Jackson's words wrapped around me, like a cozy blanket on a chilly night. He leaned closer, a conspiratorial glint in his eye. "Plus, if it goes wrong, we can make it into a story about how we bravely faced the brewing apocalypse together."

I couldn't help but laugh, the tension in my shoulders easing. "You make it sound so heroic. I'll just be the girl who made beer explode."

"Exactly! You'll be legendary," he teased, nudging my arm. "C'mon, let's find something that embodies your father's spirit, literally and figuratively. We can throw in some surprises, a little zing to make it memorable."

As I rifled through the boxes filled with herbs, fruits, and spices, I began to envision my father beside me, his laughter echoing in my mind. I rummaged through a jar filled with dried lavender, recalling how he once added it to a summer brew, transforming it into something ethereal, as if the sun had distilled itself into a bottle. "This... this could work," I said, holding up the jar, a flicker of excitement igniting my determination.

"Lavender, huh? Bold choice. Now we're talking." He raised an eyebrow, his interest piqued. "What else have you got hidden in here?"

"Maybe some rosemary? It's earthy, like my father. Reminds me of those long hikes we took through the woods." I rummaged deeper, each discovery an ode to his memory. "And what about orange peel? It adds a brightness, a twist."

"Bright and earthy—it's a flavor profile worth experimenting with," Jackson mused, a smile playing on his lips. "Just like us, huh?"

I shot him a skeptical glance. "You're comparing our chemistry to a brew now?"

"Absolutely. A little unexpected, a bit messy, but it could be something really good." His tone was playful, yet there was an undercurrent of sincerity that made my heart skip a beat.

With each ingredient I pulled from the shelf, a newfound confidence bubbled within me. We weren't just creating a brew; we were crafting a story, a blend of flavors that represented my journey, my father's legacy, and perhaps, the chemistry sparking between us.

I could almost hear the laughter of my father mingling with the clinking of bottles, urging me to embrace this unexpected adventure, one hop at a time.

As I measured out the lavender, the delicate buds spilling into the kettle like small purple jewels, a wave of nostalgia washed over me. Each fragrant whiff transported me back to those sun-soaked afternoons spent in my father's garden, where he would share tales of the old brewing legends while his hands coaxed life from the soil. The scent mingled with the sweetness of orange peel, igniting a spark of creativity I hadn't realized I'd lost along the way. It was as if the weight of my worries had shifted, if only temporarily, with every pinch and pour.

"Are we crafting a beer or summoning a garden party?" Jackson quipped, watching me with a bemused expression as I practically danced around the ingredients. "I half-expect you to whip out a floral arrangement next."

"Hey, don't knock it until you try it," I shot back, my mood buoyant, feeling the walls of self-doubt begin to crumble. "This could be revolutionary. Picture it: a floral brew that speaks to the heart. People will sip it, sigh dramatically, and proclaim, 'This is the taste of love!'"

"Or they'll sip it and think they've accidentally drunk potpourri," he replied, laughter bubbling in his voice. "But I like where your head's at. Let's create something that brings all the feels."

We worked side by side, a rhythm emerging between us as we measured, mixed, and stirred. The atmosphere buzzed with a shared energy, and I could feel the tension in my shoulders easing, replaced by an exhilarating buzz of creativity and camaraderie. Jackson's easy banter punctuated our efforts, his lightheartedness encouraging me to embrace this process, flaws and all.

"Okay, but seriously," he said as I pondered the next ingredient. "What's your secret weapon? Every great brew has one."

I paused, biting my lip in contemplation. "My secret weapon? I don't know. Maybe just a dash of bravery?"

He chuckled, shaking his head. "Not what I meant, but sure. We can all use a little bravery these days. I was thinking more like a flavor that surprises people."

"Right, the element of surprise," I mused, tapping my chin. "What about some ginger? It adds a zing, a little kick to wake up the senses."

"Now you're talking," Jackson said, eyes sparkling with excitement. "Let's give this brew a personality. Let's make it unforgettable!"

With newfound purpose, I grated fresh ginger into the mix, watching as the bright orange strands floated and danced in the bubbling liquid. The kitchen filled with a fragrant medley that wrapped around us like a comforting embrace. Jackson leaned against the counter, observing the transformation with a grin.

"Look at you," he said, mockingly swooning as if I were some master brewer. "Soon, you'll have a cult following, all clamoring for the 'Garden of Love' brew."

"Just wait until they taste it," I laughed, glancing at him. "They'll either love it or hate it. It's all or nothing."

"I'm banking on love," he replied, his tone shifting to something more earnest. "And if they hate it, we'll just tell them it's an acquired taste, like fine wine or abstract art."

I chuckled, shaking my head as I finished up the last touches. The brew was finally coming together, and with it, my confidence swelled. Yet just as I felt the tide of doubt receding, a shadow slipped through the doorway, darkening the vibrant atmosphere we had cultivated.

"Oh look, the local celebrity is here," Jackson muttered under his breath, and I followed his gaze to see Tara, the reigning queen of brewing competitions, stroll into the room with an air of effortless superiority. She swept her gaze around the kitchen, her perfectly coiffed hair bouncing slightly as she turned to me, a smirk already forming on her lips.

"I heard there was some amateur hour happening over here," she said, her voice dripping with condescension. "You're really going to compete? I mean, how cute."

I could feel my heart plummet, the euphoria of the moment crashing down like a poorly constructed tower of beer bottles. "I am competing, yes. Is there a problem with that?"

"Oh, sweetheart, it's adorable," she replied, stepping closer, her eyes glinting with challenge. "But this competition isn't a tea party. You'll need a lot more than herbs and flowers to impress anyone. I hope you're ready to be judged. You know what they say about comparing yourself to the best, right?"

"Yeah, they say it's a fool's errand," Jackson interjected, stepping in beside me, a protective edge to his tone. "But everyone's got to start somewhere. Even you."

Tara's eyes narrowed, but she only laughed, as if Jackson's words were nothing more than a fleeting joke. "You'll see, darling," she said, flicking her wrist dismissively. "It's a tough crowd, and they don't take kindly to amateur mistakes. Maybe you should stick to gardening."

With that, she spun on her heel and flounced out of the room, leaving a bitter taste in the air. I inhaled sharply, the momentary confidence I had felt just moments ago crumbling like old parchment.

"What a piece of work," Jackson muttered, crossing his arms, his expression one of incredulity. "Ignore her. She thrives on intimidation. Just focus on what you're creating, and don't let her get under your skin."

"Easy for you to say," I replied, trying to shake off the lingering doubt her words had sparked. "I'm just a small fish in a big pond. She's right; I don't belong here."

"Small fish, big pond, but you've got guts," he said, his voice unwavering. "You're not just here to swim; you're here to create waves."

His words resonated within me, filling the hollow space that Tara's visit had carved. "Waves, huh?" I mused, the corners of my lips curving up slightly. "I like the sound of that."

With renewed determination, I turned back to the brewing station, determined to infuse my creation with every ounce of passion I had left. As Jackson joined me, our shared laughter and banter began to weave a tapestry of resilience around us. The kitchen buzzed with possibility, the brewing competition no longer a specter but an adventure waiting to unfold.

As the afternoon sun dipped lower in the sky, the kitchen transformed into a sanctuary of warmth and light, illuminated by the gentle glow of late summer. The air buzzed with the mingling scents of rosemary, lavender, and ginger, creating a fragrant tapestry that both energized and comforted me. Each stir of the kettle sent a ripple of excitement through my veins, the clinking of utensils and the bubbling of the brew resonating like a soundtrack to my newfound determination.

"Okay, what's next on our genius plan?" Jackson asked, leaning against the counter, arms crossed, an encouraging smile plastered across his face. "We've got the floral and the zingy—now we just need a dash of magic."

"Magic, huh?" I replied, tapping my chin as I surveyed the array of ingredients spread out before us. "What about something a little unexpected? Maybe a splash of chili?"

His brows shot up, and he feigned horror. "Chili? In beer? Are we brewing for a bonfire or a beer festival? You trying to start a trend or just set my taste buds on fire?"

"Why not both?" I grinned, feeling playful. "It could give it a nice kick, make it memorable."

"Memorable like an awkward family reunion? Because that's what I'm picturing," he shot back, laughter dancing in his eyes. "But I trust your instincts. You've got the heart of a brewer and the flair of a showman. Let's do it!"

With a flourish, I grabbed a fresh chili pepper, its vibrant red color screaming for attention. I sliced it open, releasing a potent aroma that mingled with the other ingredients like an unruly guest crashing a perfectly organized party. "Okay, just a pinch," I warned myself as I dropped in a small slice, imagining how the heat would blossom against the sweetness of the orange and the earthiness of the rosemary.

As I stirred the concoction, I couldn't help but imagine Tara's dismissive sneer at my unorthodox choices. But this was my brew, and I wanted it to reflect not just my father's influence but my own spirit, one that thrived on breaking boundaries. "If I'm going to face her and the judges, I'm doing it with something they won't forget," I declared.

"You're speaking my language," Jackson said, his voice turning serious. "This is not just about the competition anymore. It's about you finding your voice. So let's make sure it's loud and clear."

With the final blend simmering, I allowed myself to bask in the moment, an almost euphoric sense of accomplishment bubbling within me. But just as I was about to pour the mixture into a glass for a taste test, a sharp ding from my phone broke the spell. I glanced down, my heart lurching at the name displayed on the screen—Eric.

"What does he want?" I muttered, hesitation creeping in as I contemplated whether to answer. The last thing I needed was another reminder of my inadequacies, especially with the competition looming.

"Who is it?" Jackson leaned closer, curiosity piqued.

"An old friend," I replied tersely, swiping my finger across the screen. "He's just... checking in."

"Checking in or checking up? There's a difference."

I shot him a look, half amused, half annoyed. "You make me sound like I'm hiding something. It's just Eric. He's harmless."

"Harmless can be a slippery slope," Jackson warned, raising an eyebrow. "Just remember that sometimes it's better to cut ties than to keep letting someone drag you down."

"Wow, you're getting very philosophical. Are you sure you're not just a poet in disguise?"

"Maybe I am. I'm certainly poetic about my beer," he replied with a wink, easing the tension.

Still, I hesitated before tapping the screen, but curiosity pulled me in. The message read: Hey, hope you're doing well! Heard you're entering that brewing competition. Let's chat soon—I have some ideas that could help.

Anxiety twisted in my stomach as I contemplated what kind of 'help' he was suggesting. The last time we had talked, he had brought up ways to capitalize on my family's legacy—like turning my father's recipes into a brand. Part of me had always resented that push, feeling like a puppet dancing to someone else's strings, but the idea of leveraging my past to create something new was undeniably tempting.

"What's it say?" Jackson asked, his curiosity getting the better of him.

I hesitated, then replied, "Just Eric being Eric. You know, trying to convince me to use my father's recipes for something commercial."

"Doesn't sound so bad," he said, leaning over to read the message on my screen. "But you should ask yourself—do you want that? Is it your vision or his?"

Before I could respond, a loud crash echoed through the house, shattering our moment. Jackson and I whipped around, eyes wide, as we searched for the source of the noise. I felt my heart race, adrenaline coursing through my veins. "What was that?"

"Maybe the brewing gods are displeased with our choices?" he joked nervously, but I could see the concern etched on his face.

"I think it came from the storage room," I replied, my voice tense as I moved toward the door. As I creaked it open, the shadows loomed larger, and I stepped inside, the scent of stale air mixing with the lingering fragrance of my brew.

Peering into the dim space, I squinted, trying to discern what had caused the commotion. Boxes were strewn across the floor, but my attention was caught by a figure shifting at the back of the room—a silhouette that felt all too familiar. "Who's there?" I called out, my heart thundering in my chest.

The figure turned slowly, and for a moment, all the air seemed to leave the room. The familiar face stared back at me, half-hidden in shadow, but unmistakable. My breath caught in my throat. "Eric?"

"Surprise," he said, a devilish grin spreading across his face. "I hope I'm not interrupting anything important."

The atmosphere shifted, tension crackling like static electricity, and suddenly, everything I thought I knew felt precariously balanced. Jackson stepped behind me, protective and tense, as the reality of Eric's unexpected appearance loomed larger than any brewing competition. This was about more than just a drink; it was about choices and paths diverging in ways I had never anticipated.

"What are you doing here?" I demanded, trying to keep my voice steady while the storm of uncertainty raged within me.

"Just wanted to see how my favorite brewer was doing," he replied smoothly, stepping into the light. "And maybe offer some of those ideas in person."

I glanced back at Jackson, whose brow furrowed with concern, and suddenly the brewing of my unique blend felt like a distant memory, overshadowed by the tension brewing between us all. As I stood there, uncertainty gripped my heart, leaving me suspended in a moment that promised to unravel everything I had worked for.

# Chapter 8: Cracked Foundations

It's hard to pinpoint the exact moment everything shifted, but I could feel the change like a tightening noose around my chest. The air crackled with tension, heavier than the mist clinging to the early morning. I watched as Ethan stood across the kitchen island, arms crossed, his brow furrowed in a way that made my heart race for all the wrong reasons. It was as if he had donned an impenetrable fortress, guarding his thoughts as fiercely as he had once protected me. The familiar scent of hops and barley wafted in from the adjoining room, a bittersweet reminder of the dreams we had crafted together, now crumbling like the floor beneath us.

"Why would you even consider selling the brewery?" I blurted out, my voice sharper than I intended. Each word felt like a small pebble ricocheting off the walls of our shared history. I had imagined a hundred scenarios in which this conversation might unfold, but the reality felt raw, jagged, and clumsy. "Do you really think that's the answer?"

His gaze hardened, and for a fleeting moment, I could see the turmoil behind his icy exterior. "What do you want me to say? That keeping it is the best idea? We're barely scraping by as it is." His words dripped with a mix of frustration and desperation, each syllable a calculated blow.

"Ethan, you're not just running a business; this is our legacy. It's our father's legacy!" My chest tightened as the memory of his laughter, the warmth of his embrace, surged through me like a tidal wave. I could almost hear my father's voice echoing in the background, reminding us that family meant everything. It was more than just recipes and hops; it was about love, resilience, and a shared dream that had been nurtured over countless late-night discussions and early-morning brew sessions.

Ethan's eyes flickered with something I couldn't quite place—was it guilt? Anger? A deep-seated pain? "Sometimes," he replied, his voice lower, as if he were confiding in a stranger rather than the woman who had shared his life, "family doesn't cut it. You know that."

The accusation hung between us like an uninvited guest, and I felt my heart plummet. "Are you saying that I'm not enough?" The words slipped out before I could catch them, and I instantly regretted the vulnerability they revealed.

"It's not about that," he sighed, rubbing the back of his neck in that way he did when he was torn between two worlds. "I just..." He paused, and the air thickened with the weight of his unspoken thoughts. "I'm just trying to do what's best for us. Maybe I'm trying to protect you."

"Protect me?" The incredulity in my voice surprised even me. "By selling the one thing that connects us to Dad? You think running away is protection?"

"Maybe it's about moving forward!" His voice rose, and the vulnerability that had flickered in his eyes was replaced by a fiery determination. "You think holding onto this place will bring him back? It won't! We have to let go!"

As the words tumbled out, the unsteady ground beneath us felt like it was beginning to crack, revealing the chaos that lurked below. The grief that had been simmering beneath the surface, fed by late-night whiskey and half-formed memories, bubbled up like the foam on a freshly poured beer. "You're wrong," I managed to say, my voice trembling. "This place is our home. I can't believe you would throw it away so easily."

His face twisted in a mix of anger and anguish, and for a moment, we were two strangers caught in a whirlwind of hurt. The laughter we once shared echoed hauntingly in the silence, each shared memory a ghost taunting us with what we had lost. It felt as if the walls of the brewery, which had stood firm for generations, were somehow crumbling around us, the memories splintering like dry wood.

"I'm done talking," he declared, turning his back on me, and my heart sank further. The sharp sound of the door slamming shut echoed through the room, reverberating against the hollow walls of our relationship.

I stormed out of the kitchen, my mind racing with a whirlwind of thoughts. The sunlight streamed through the windows, bright and blinding, as I stumbled into the backyard where the old oak tree stood sentinel, its leaves whispering secrets of the past. As I leaned against its sturdy trunk, I could feel the rough bark digging into my back, a grounding reminder of the strength that had been built over decades. But even that comfort felt frayed at the edges.

In the distance, I spotted Jackson, his lanky figure strolling towards me, a concerned frown etched across his face. I could sense his eagerness to lend an ear, to sift through the wreckage that was my life at that moment, but I was too raw, too exposed to let him in.

"Hey, everything okay?" His voice was gentle, yet I could hear the undercurrent of apprehension. Jackson had always had a knack for knowing when something was off, even if I did my best to conceal it behind a smile.

"Just peachy," I replied, my tone dripping with sarcasm, and immediately regretted it. The last thing I wanted was to snap at him. He was a good friend—someone who had always been there when the chips were down.

"Right," he said, eyebrows raised, clearly unconvinced. "You look like you've just walked out of a boxing ring."

I let out a small, humorless laugh, crossing my arms defensively. "Well, you could say I'm fighting for my life."

"Or your sanity," he shot back, a teasing grin tugging at his lips. "What happened this time? Did Ethan finally decide to take up a new hobby? Like bungee jumping or skydiving?"

His attempt at levity fell flat, and my stomach twisted with unspent anger and hurt. "He wants to sell the brewery," I blurted out, the confession spilling out before I could stop it.

Jackson's face fell, his smile evaporating like mist in the sun. "What? Seriously?"

"Yeah," I replied, struggling to find the words. "It's complicated. He thinks it's the best move for us, but I can't help but feel like he's just throwing away everything we've built. Everything Dad built."

The shadow that passed over Jackson's face was fleeting but telling. "That's a big decision. Have you talked about it?"

"Talked about it? We practically screamed at each other! He's been brewing his own beer behind my back—using our dad's recipes! It's a complete betrayal!"

The air between us thickened with unspoken truths, and Jackson's expression shifted from concern to something deeper, more intense. "Wait, what?" His eyes widened, the surprise evident in his tone. "He's been brewing without you?"

"Yeah, like it's no big deal," I snapped, my voice rising again. "He thinks he can just keep secrets and everything will be fine."

Jackson took a step closer, his eyes narrowing with a mix of disbelief and disappointment. "You deserve better than that, you know."

"I know," I whispered, the weight of his words crashing down on me. "But what do I do now? It feels like everything is crumbling, and I don't know how to hold it all together."

In that moment, the tension between us shifted, crackling with a newfound energy that set my heart racing for reasons I couldn't fully understand. The soft sunlight cast a golden hue around us, illuminating the paths we had both walked, and I realized that my fight wasn't just against Ethan's choices; it was against the ghosts of my past, the dreams that had become shackles.

The sun hung low in the sky, casting long shadows that danced across the yard like playful spirits caught between worlds. Jackson's intense gaze felt like a spotlight, illuminating the fractures in my heart that I had tried so hard to conceal. I was teetering on the edge of a precipice, and it felt as if every word he spoke was a gentle nudge, threatening to send me spiraling into the chaos below.

"You know, sometimes it's easier to keep the walls up," he said softly, his voice steady as the world around us continued its busy rhythm. "But walls can't protect you forever. They just end up trapping you inside."

The rawness of his observation settled over me, wrapping me in a cocoon of vulnerability. "What if I don't know how to bring them down?" I admitted, the confession tasting bittersweet on my tongue. "What if I'm just... stuck?"

Jackson shifted closer, his presence warm and reassuring. "Stuck isn't a permanent state, you know. Sometimes, all it takes is a little push." He offered me a half-smile, one that danced at the corners of his mouth, promising understanding, but I caught a glimpse of something else—a challenge buried beneath the surface.

"I don't need a push," I shot back, an edge creeping into my tone. "I need a magic wand to fix everything."

His laughter rolled over me like waves lapping at the shore, and I felt the tension begin to ease, if only a fraction. "Well, I left my wand in my other pants," he said, an exaggerated frown crossing his face. "But I do have a great sense of timing. How about I just distract you instead?"

The moment hung suspended, electric, and I could feel the air between us humming with something unspoken. "Distract me? How? With your amazing ability to quote bad movies?"

"Hey, my repertoire of poorly delivered lines is unparalleled!" He feigned offense, clutching his chest dramatically, and I couldn't help but chuckle. The sound startled me—was that really my laughter breaking through the heaviness?

"Okay, Mr. Hollywood, show me what you've got," I challenged, daring him to pull me further away from the chaos that loomed just behind us.

Jackson leaned against the oak tree, arms crossed, his eyes sparkling with mischief. "All right, but you asked for it. How about a classic? 'I'm not a smart man, but I know what love is.'"

"Tom Hanks in Forrest Gump?" I guessed, the familiarity of the line mingling with the sweetness of nostalgia.

"Ding, ding, ding! We have a winner!" He grinned, the tension easing even more. "But let's be honest, I could deliver that line and still get no action."

I smirked, nudging him with my shoulder. "Maybe you just need to work on your charm."

"Or maybe I should just wear a sign that says 'Single and Accepting Applications,'" he quipped, winking at me. The warmth between us was palpable, sparking something deep within me, yet the specter of Ethan loomed in the back of my mind.

"Don't sell yourself short," I said, the words slipping out before I could stop myself. "You have a lot to offer. Anyone would be lucky to have you."

His gaze softened, a flicker of sincerity cutting through the playfulness. "Thanks. But lucky doesn't seem to be my thing."

We lingered in the charged silence, the chemistry between us undeniable. But just as I began to lean into the moment, I felt a familiar pang of guilt clawing at my insides. It felt wrong to be sharing laughter and warmth when everything with Ethan was unraveling. I pulled back slightly, shaking off the moment like a chill breeze.

"I should probably get back," I said, the reluctance threading through my voice. "Ethan and I... we need to sort this out."

"Are you sure that's what you want?" Jackson asked, his brow furrowing slightly. "You don't have to dive into the storm just because it's there."

"It's not about diving in; it's about facing it," I replied, my heart hammering as I spoke. "If we don't confront this, it'll only fester. I can't just walk away from him."

"I get that. Just be careful. Sometimes storms reveal truths we're not ready to handle."

"Thanks for the warning, Captain Obvious," I shot back, my attempt at humor feeling weak. But as I turned to leave, Jackson's hand gently gripped my wrist, anchoring me in place.

"Just promise me one thing," he said, his voice low. "Promise me you won't lose yourself in the storm."

"I promise," I said, but even as the words left my lips, I could feel the weight of uncertainty pulling me back into the tumultuous tide of my feelings for Ethan.

The walk back to the brewery felt heavier, the atmosphere thick with unspoken words and unresolved emotions. The air was laced with the scent of hops, sweet and intoxicating, stirring memories of laughter and shared dreams that felt just out of reach. My heart ached at the thought of confronting Ethan, not knowing if it would mend the fractures between us or crack them wider.

As I pushed open the door, the familiar creak echoed through the empty space, a haunting reminder of the life we had built together. Ethan was at the far end of the brewery, his silhouette framed by the sunlight filtering through the large windows. He looked like a painting, caught in a moment of contemplation, but the aura of despair clung to him like a second skin.

"Ethan," I called, my voice wavering. He turned, and for a moment, our eyes locked, a thousand unsaid things swirling between us.

"I didn't think you'd come back," he admitted, his voice low, almost defeated.

"I can't just walk away from this," I replied, stepping further inside, the tension thickening with every step. "But we need to talk. Really talk."

He nodded, but the distance between us felt insurmountable, as if a chasm had opened wide, threatening to swallow us whole. "I'm sorry for earlier. I didn't mean to—"

"Neither did I," I interrupted, the hurt bubbling to the surface again. "But we can't just ignore what's happening. Not anymore."

"Right," he said, running a hand through his hair, a gesture I had come to associate with his frustration. "I didn't mean to keep secrets. It's just... I thought it was my way of coping. I didn't want to hurt you."

"By brewing beer with our father's recipes?" My tone was sharp, and I could see the flicker of guilt cross his face.

"It was supposed to be a surprise," he said, his voice small, barely a whisper. "I thought maybe if I could perfect them, we could launch a new line together. Something to keep the brewery alive."

The sincerity in his voice cut through the air like a knife, and I could see the weight of his intention hovering just above us. "But you didn't think to involve me? To share this with me?"

"I didn't want to drag you into my doubts. I thought I was doing this for us."

The irony hung heavy between us, a bitter twist of fate. "But you didn't trust me," I said, my heart aching with the realization. "You didn't trust us."

He stepped closer, desperation creeping into his expression. "I do trust you, more than anyone. I just—"

"Just what?" The question hung in the air, the answer lingering like smoke.

"Just... I thought it would save us."

"And in the process, you nearly destroyed everything." The weight of my words settled like lead in my stomach, yet there was a flicker of hope in the air, a chance to rebuild what had been lost in the storm.

"Maybe we can still fix this," he said, taking another tentative step forward, vulnerability etched into every line of his face.

"Fixing it means confronting everything. Together."

"Then let's do that," he replied, his determination sparking a flicker of warmth in my chest. "I'm ready to fight for us."

In that moment, the cracks in our foundation seemed less daunting, the storm less inevitable. It would be a journey, a winding path through the ruins of our past, but standing together felt like the first step toward a future we could both reclaim.

The warmth between us felt tenuous, like a fragile truce struck in the aftermath of a storm. I studied Ethan's face, his expression a swirling mix of determination and regret, and suddenly I was struck by the enormity of the moment. It was more than just our business or our shared history—it was about two people grappling with the ghosts of their pasts while trying to forge a future that didn't seem so daunting.

"Okay, if we're doing this, we need to lay everything out on the table," I said, my voice steadying as I took a step toward him. "No more secrets, no more half-truths. We can't fix this if we're still hiding things."

He nodded, the weight of my words sinking in. "Agreed. But you have to promise me the same. No more running away."

"I didn't run away," I protested, though I could hear the echo of my own footsteps retreating in the heat of our argument. "I needed space to think. I still do."

"Then let's take it together," he said, his eyes pleading. "We need to dig into the mess we've created. I want to know what you really think about selling the brewery. I want to know how you feel about everything."

His honesty pulled at something deep inside me, a recognition that echoed through the chaos. I drew in a breath, preparing to speak my truth. "I feel like this place is a part of who we are. Selling it feels like losing a piece of ourselves, and I don't want to let go of that legacy."

Ethan's expression shifted, his brows knitting together. "But what if holding on means drowning in debt? What if it means more pain?"

"What if holding on means finding a way to thrive?" I countered, frustration seeping into my tone. "I believe we can make this work if we put in the effort. We just need to focus on our vision and—"

"Your vision," he interrupted, his voice rising again. "What about my vision? My ideas?"

"Your ideas?" I echoed, incredulous. "The ones you've kept from me?"

A heavy silence stretched between us, thick with the weight of our unspoken fears. I could see him wrestling with his thoughts, a man caught between love and doubt.

"Let's just... let's brainstorm," I suggested, trying to defuse the tension that threatened to spill over. "Maybe we can come up with a plan together. Something that honors what Dad built while also looking to the future."

He hesitated, then nodded slowly. "I'm open to that. But I want to make it clear: if we're going to do this, we need to be honest about our limits."

"Fine," I replied, the tension beginning to ebb. "Then let's outline what we both want. You first."

"Okay," he said, his voice steadier. "I want to introduce a new line of craft beers that could appeal to a younger audience. We can use social media, collaborate with local breweries, and host tasting events. It could breathe new life into this place."

"Sounds great," I said, feeling the flicker of excitement igniting my own hopes. "But we need to also keep our core offerings. Those recipes—our father's legacy—shouldn't just fade away."

"Absolutely," he agreed, his eyes brightening with a spark of inspiration. "What if we hosted workshops where people could learn to brew using those recipes? It would be a way to keep the legacy alive while also attracting new customers."

The warmth of possibility surged between us, the old wounds beginning to heal as we shared ideas, each suggestion building on the last. It felt like we were knitting together the torn fabric of our relationship, stitching in hopes and dreams that had felt lost.

We spent the next hour tossing ideas back and forth, laughter punctuating our brainstorming like the popping of champagne corks. It was a relief, a momentary escape from the heaviness that had defined us for so long. As the sun dipped lower, casting an amber glow across the brewery, I felt a sense of clarity settling over me.

"Okay," I said, grinning. "This feels good. We're actually doing this."

Ethan leaned back against the counter, a satisfied smile spreading across his face. "See? This is what we needed. Just needed to clear the air."

But before I could bask in the moment, the front door swung open with a loud creak, cutting through our bubble of optimism. I turned, my stomach dropping at the sight of a figure framed in the doorway—Jackson, his expression stormy, eyes alight with concern.

"What's going on?" he demanded, stepping into the room. "You two looked like you were about to strangle each other, and now you're... smiling?"

"Nice to see you too, Jackson," I replied, half-joking, half-uneasy.

"Seriously," he pressed, his brow furrowing. "I just saw you two practically at each other's throats, and now it looks like you're sharing a moment of bliss. What gives?"

"Just working through some things," Ethan said, his voice casual but the tension still palpable.

"Working through things? Like brewing secrets?" Jackson shot back, his eyes darting between us. "What else aren't you telling me?"

I exchanged a glance with Ethan, the unspoken fear hanging in the air like a loaded gun. "Jackson, it's complicated. We're figuring it out."

"Complicated? You mean Ethan's little side project?"

"Jackson," I said, raising my hands in a placating gesture. "It's not what you think."

"Not what I think? So, you're telling me that brewing without her knowledge is normal?"

Ethan stepped forward, his voice firm. "We were just brainstorming, okay? Can we talk about this without making it a bigger issue?"

"Like I said, it's complicated. But it's not just about the brewery. It's about us."

Jackson's expression softened slightly, but his gaze remained intense. "I just don't want to see either of you get hurt. You're both my friends, and I can't shake the feeling that this is going to explode."

I felt the weight of his words, the truth behind them resonating deep within. "We're trying to be honest with each other. That counts for something."

"But at what cost?" Jackson shot back, the frustration creeping back into his voice. "You can't just brush things under the rug. You have to confront the real issues—before it's too late."

The tension escalated, wrapping around us like an unseen noose, tightening with each passing second. "Look," Ethan interjected, his voice steady, "we're doing the best we can. If it weren't for your interference, we might be in a better place right now."

"Ethan—"

"Don't 'Ethan' me!" he snapped, the fire in his tone igniting a spark of fear. "You think I wanted this? You think I wanted to keep secrets? I did it to protect us!"

"Protect us? Or protect yourself?" Jackson shot back, his voice ringing with disbelief.

I stepped in, desperation flooding my words. "Can we all just take a breath? This isn't helping."

But as I spoke, the air shifted again, the balance of our fragile dynamic tipping dangerously. A deafening silence fell, the room charged with unspoken truths, each of us wrestling with our emotions—betrayals, fears, and unresolved desires swirling like a tempest.

Then, as if conjured by the rising tension, the back door flew open, slamming against the wall. A figure emerged, breathless and frantic. "Guys! You need to see this!"

We all turned, confusion and dread pooling in our stomachs. The urgency in their voice sent a chill racing down my spine, a shiver of foreboding wrapping around me.

"What is it?" I asked, my heart pounding as I stepped closer, my instincts screaming that whatever was about to unfold would change everything.

"Something's happened at the brewery. Something big. You need to come see."

With a shared glance, Ethan, Jackson, and I exchanged unspoken questions—worry, confusion, and a flicker of fear passing between us. As we moved toward the door, I felt the ground shift beneath my feet, a sense of inevitability clawing at my insides.

Whatever awaited us on the other side was bound to shatter our fragile peace. The moment felt suspended in time, a breath held just before a plunge into the unknown, and as I stepped into the chaos, I knew this was just the beginning.

# Chapter 9: A Complicated Brew

The clattering of coffee cups echoed softly in the quaint little café, blending harmoniously with the faint hum of conversation that enveloped us. The smell of freshly ground coffee beans mingled with the sweet scent of cinnamon rolls, a heady mixture that often felt like a warm hug on a chilly day. I nestled deeper into the plush armchair, trying to let the aroma seep into my bones, hoping it would drown out the gnawing ache that had settled there since the fallout with Ethan. My fingers idly traced the rim of my cup, the smooth porcelain a comforting weight against my palm.

Jackson sat across from me, his gaze piercing yet gentle, like a warm fire on a cold winter night. His dark hair fell just above his brow, and every so often, he would push it back with a quick flick of his wrist, a small gesture that made my heart skip a beat. I found myself lost in the depths of his warm hazel eyes, which seemed to hold the secrets of the universe—or at least, the secrets of why my heart had begun to race in his presence. The banter between us flowed effortlessly, like an old record playing a familiar tune, yet every laugh and shared smile felt electrifyingly new.

"What's on your mind?" he asked, his voice low, like honey drizzling over toast, sweet and comforting.

I shrugged, a half-hearted attempt to mask the turmoil bubbling beneath the surface. "Just thinking about...everything." A wave of frustration washed over me, an unwelcome reminder of the chaos that had unraveled in my life.

"Everything? You know, that's a pretty big category," he teased, his lips curving into a smirk that could light up the darkest corners of my mind.

"Okay, fine, it's mostly about Ethan," I admitted, feeling the heat rise to my cheeks. "And my family. It's a bit of a mess, you know?"

"Yeah, I get that." Jackson leaned forward, his expression shifting from playful to sincere, as if he were reading the lines of an intricate script that only he could see. "But you don't have to carry it alone, you know? I'm here."

His words wrapped around me like a comforting blanket, but guilt immediately crept in, gnawing at my insides. How could I lean on him when my heart was still tangled in the remnants of a relationship that had once felt like a safe haven? The silence that hung between us felt heavy, weighted by unspoken words and emotions that hovered just out of reach.

Then, as if guided by some unseen force, our hands found each other across the table. The moment was electric, a spark igniting in the space between us. I looked down at our entwined fingers, the stark contrast of his warm skin against my coolness sending a shiver of awareness coursing through me. My heart raced, betraying the logical part of my brain that screamed at me to pull away. Instead, I found myself leaning closer, drawn to him like a moth to a flame.

"What if we just... stopped thinking for a second?" Jackson whispered, his breath brushing against my cheek, sending a cascade of shivers down my spine. His gaze was unwavering, holding mine like a tether, grounding me amidst the chaos of my thoughts.

"Stopped thinking?" I echoed, my voice barely above a whisper. The world outside faded into a blur, and all that remained was the intensity of the moment, the palpable chemistry crackling in the air between us.

"Yeah," he murmured, his thumb stroking my knuckles gently, as if trying to erase the tension that had built within me. "Just... let instinct take over."

And in that moment, it was as if time suspended itself. With a breath that felt like a lifetime in the making, I leaned in closer, surrendering to the urgency in his eyes. Our lips met, tentative at first, a brush of warmth that melted away the doubts swirling in my mind. But then, as the kiss deepened, it morphed into something wild and unrestrained, a rush of emotions that crashed over me like a tidal wave.

But just as quickly as the euphoria enveloped me, a pang of guilt sliced through the haze. I pulled back, my heart racing as the reality of my situation crashed down around me. The weight of my responsibilities loomed large, reminding me of the fractures within my family, the mess Ethan had left behind. "Jackson, I—"

"Don't," he interjected softly, his eyes clouded with understanding but edged with hurt. "I know this is complicated. I just—"

"I can't," I blurted out, a mixture of frustration and desperation coursing through me. "Not now. My family..." I trailed off, the words tangled in my throat like a stubborn vine.

"Hey," he said, his voice steady and soothing, "I'm not trying to pressure you. I just want you to know I'm here when you're ready. Whenever that is."

His respect for my boundaries was admirable, but it only made the ache in my chest grow sharper. As he withdrew, the space between us felt cavernous, a chasm of unspoken words and unresolved feelings that threatened to swallow me whole. The warmth that had ignited between us flickered like a candle in the wind, casting shadows of doubt in its wake.

With a sigh, I leaned back in my chair, the comfortable café feeling suddenly foreign, as if the walls themselves were closing in on me. "I don't know how to navigate this," I confessed, the vulnerability washing over me like a cold splash of water.

"None of us do," he replied, his gaze unwavering, as if he was searching for the right words to pull me back from the edge. "But we can figure it out together. One step at a time."

The promise lingered in the air, but I was still standing on the precipice, caught between a past I was struggling to let go of and a future that shimmered tantalizingly close yet felt dangerously out of reach.

The café, with its cozy corners and ambient glow, transformed into a refuge of sorts, yet outside the warm cocoon of our conversation, the world felt heavy. Jackson's gentle presence was a stark contrast to the chaos in my mind, a soothing balm for my frayed nerves. I sipped my coffee, its warmth barely enough to stave off the chill that clung to my heart. The barista, a young woman with brightly colored hair and an infectious laugh, whirled about, her energy infectious. She served up lattes like they were works of art, each cup adorned with elaborate foam designs, but my heart was still focused elsewhere.

"What's our plan for the night?" I asked, trying to shift the weight of my worries, needing to lighten the atmosphere, if only for a moment. Jackson, leaning back with an amused smirk, was always ready for a bit of playful banter.

"Plan? I thought we were just doing the 'sit and stare into each other's eyes' thing," he replied, eyebrows waggling in exaggerated seriousness.

"Ah, right. The classic date night," I shot back, forcing a chuckle. The joke hung in the air, a moment of levity that didn't quite mask the tension that still simmered beneath the surface.

He rolled his eyes, a playful grin spreading across his face. "I think I could get used to that. But in all seriousness, maybe we should brainstorm ideas for that charity event we were discussing?"

"Right, the charity event," I nodded, attempting to push away the weight of my emotional baggage. The community center had requested our help in organizing a fundraiser, something that felt productive amidst my swirling thoughts. "Do you think we could set up a bake sale? I can whip up my famous lemon bars, and you can... um, stand there and look charming?"

"Charming? I think I could manage that." His laughter was infectious, and for a moment, the worries of my life faded into the background. "Lemon bars, huh? You make those from scratch? I'm impressed."

I leaned in, my voice dropping conspiratorially. "Only the finest ingredients. There might even be a secret ingredient that makes them irresistible."

"Secret ingredient, huh?" He leaned closer, curiosity sparkling in his eyes. "I'm intrigued. Care to share?"

I hesitated, an impish smile creeping across my face. "It's love. And a pinch of paranoia that they'll be the worst thing anyone has ever tasted."

"Ah, yes, the recipe for success. Love and paranoia. You really are a culinary genius," he teased, and for the first time since the kiss, I felt a flicker of hope amid my swirling thoughts.

But then, as quickly as the warmth spread, a shadow slipped back in, lurking at the edges of my thoughts. My phone buzzed, shattering the moment as I glanced down to see a text from Ethan. My heart sank, the words blurring together as dread knotted in my stomach. "We need to talk." It felt like a heavy weight, a stone cast into the serene waters of my new reality.

"Everything okay?" Jackson asked, his voice laced with concern, his gaze shifting from playful to serious in an instant.

"Just... a message from Ethan," I replied, my voice small. The moment hung heavy between us, the playful atmosphere dissipating like steam from a freshly poured cup of coffee.

"Do you want to talk about it?" he asked gently, and the sincerity in his eyes made it clear he genuinely cared.

"No, not really." I shook my head, the thoughts swirling in a chaotic dance. "It's just... complicated. And frustrating."

"Relationships tend to be that way," he said, a knowing smile touching his lips. "Especially when they start off with bad communication."

"Yeah, well, communication hasn't exactly been our strong suit," I muttered, frustration threading through my voice. The truth of my situation felt suffocating.

Before Jackson could respond, my phone buzzed again. A follow-up message from Ethan read: "I'm outside." My stomach plummeted, an unexpected chill cutting through the café's warmth.

"Jackson, I think I need to—" I began, but he was already on his feet, a protective instinct flickering in his eyes.

"I'll handle this," he said, his voice low and steady, infused with a confidence I desperately needed. I opened my mouth to protest, but the determined look on his face left no room for argument.

"Fine. But don't throw any punches. I'm not ready for a dramatic exit from the café." I attempted to lighten the mood, but the words felt hollow as they left my lips.

"Only verbal punches. I promise," he replied, his eyes locking onto mine. "Just stay put." With that, he turned and strode toward the door, his posture confident, like a knight heading into battle.

I watched him walk away, a swirl of gratitude and anxiety swirling inside me. The door swung open, and Ethan stepped inside, his expression unreadable. My heart raced as I braced myself for whatever was about to unfold.

"Hey," he said, casual as if we hadn't just come off a whirlwind of emotions that left me feeling like a rubber band stretched too thin.

"Hey," I replied, my voice steady despite the storm raging within me.

"Can we talk?" His tone was cautious, the weight of unspoken words hanging between us.

"Right now? In a café full of people?" I glanced around, the patrons oblivious to the emotional tension that was about to erupt at any moment.

"Is there a better place?" His brow furrowed, and I could see the frustration creeping into his posture.

"Maybe not here," I admitted, my voice softer than I intended. "Let's step outside."

As we moved toward the door, Jackson's gaze flickered toward me, a silent question in his eyes. I shot him a quick look of reassurance, though I felt anything but reassured. The world outside was shrouded in an early evening haze, the soft glow of streetlights barely illuminating the sidewalk. The air was thick with uncertainty, and I could feel my stomach churning as Ethan led me away from the café's warmth.

Once we were outside, the chill settled over us, a stark contrast to the heated emotions simmering just beneath the surface. "So," Ethan began, his hands shoved deep in his pockets, "I know things have been rough between us."

"Rough? That's one way to put it," I replied, sarcasm lacing my words.

He sighed, glancing down the street as if searching for the right words among the passing cars. "I didn't handle things well. I should've listened, communicated better."

"Should have? You mean, you should've tried," I retorted, the frustration bubbling up. "You didn't just ignore me, you ghosted me when I needed you most."

"I know. And I'm sorry," he said, his gaze finally meeting mine. "I didn't know how to deal with everything, and I messed up."

"Messing up doesn't even begin to cover it, Ethan," I shot back, the weight of his apology feeling insufficient.

"I realize that now," he pressed, his expression earnest. "I miss you, you know? I miss what we had."

My heart twisted painfully at his words, the ache of loss mingling with a stubborn resistance. "What we had? Or what you think we had?" I challenged, unwilling to let him back in so easily.

He took a step closer, the vulnerability in his eyes making it difficult to hold my ground. "What we had was real. And I want to fix this. Can't we just talk about it?"

The tension crackled between us, a familiar dance of emotions I thought I had left behind. But now, standing in the dim light with the weight of the past pressing heavily upon me, I found myself at a crossroads. My heart was still tied to our shared memories, yet I felt the undeniable pull of something new, something I dared not name but was ready to embrace.

"I don't know, Ethan," I said, my voice trembling slightly. "Things aren't just going to go back to normal because you say you're sorry."

"Maybe they can, though," he replied, desperation edging into his tone. "Just give me a chance to prove it."

As his words hung in the air, a rush of warmth enveloped me, a reminder of all we had shared and all that had been lost. But in the shadows of my heart, another voice whispered, urging me to consider the path Jackson had opened before me. A path filled with possibility and promise, yet it felt tantalizingly close yet impossibly out of reach.

The cool night air wrapped around us like a silken shroud, amplifying the tension lingering between Ethan and me. His expression was a mix of hope and apprehension, but my heart was an unwieldy mess, tangled in emotions I could barely articulate. The lights from the café glowed behind us, a soft halo against the encroaching darkness, and for a moment, I could almost convince myself that we were still the same two people who used to laugh over late-night coffee, weaving dreams of the future like some intricate tapestry.

"Look, I get it," I said, trying to cut through the thick tension. "You want to fix things, but it's not that simple. You can't just say you miss me and expect everything to go back to normal."

"Why not?" he shot back, the spark of defiance igniting in his eyes. "Why can't we just go back to the way things were? We had something good, and I can fix it. I just need you to trust me again."

"Trust is earned, not given," I replied, the sharpness of my words surprising even me. The coolness of the night air did nothing to dampen the heat rising between us.

Ethan stepped closer, the frustration boiling over in his demeanor. "And how do you plan to earn it? By avoiding me?"

"Maybe that's what you need to figure out," I retorted, crossing my arms defensively. "You think it's just a flick of a switch? I have to process this, Ethan. I need to know what you want beyond just a fleeting moment of nostalgia."

"Can't it just be about wanting you back?" His voice softened, becoming earnest, almost pleading. "I don't want to be the one who lost you."

The vulnerability in his eyes tugged at the strings of my heart, but alongside it, doubt simmered. How many chances had I given him? How many times had I let my heart dance on the edge of hope only to have it dashed against the rocks of disappointment?

"I can't be your safety net," I said, struggling to keep my voice steady. "I can't just step back into a relationship that has been built on broken promises and misunderstandings. I need more than that."

"Then let's build something new," he said, his voice dipping low, urgency creeping in. "Let's take it slow. I'm willing to do whatever it takes."

"I don't even know what that looks like," I replied, my breath catching in my throat. It felt like we were on the precipice of something monumental, yet the ground felt shaky beneath us.

Before I could add anything else, a movement caught my eye. I turned slightly, and there was Jackson, standing just a few feet away, his expression a mix of concern and something else I couldn't quite decipher. The moment of intimacy between Ethan and me shattered like glass, and my heart sank.

"What's going on?" Jackson asked, his voice calm but firm, like a gentle wave breaking against a stubborn rock.

"Just a conversation," I said too quickly, a wave of guilt washing over me as I glanced between them. "Right, Ethan?"

"Yeah, just talking," Ethan replied, though the tension in the air suggested it was much more than that. Jackson's brows knit together, but he maintained his composure, clearly sensing the layers of unspoken words and tangled emotions hanging heavy between us.

"Look, I didn't mean to intrude," he said, his gaze flickering between us, calculating. "But I think we should wrap this up. It's getting late, and we have that charity event to plan."

I could see the storm brewing in Jackson's eyes, an amalgamation of frustration and protectiveness. It was endearing but unsettling. I found myself caught in a web of conflicting loyalties and feelings, and the weight of the moment pressed down on me.

"Yeah, that sounds good," I finally said, trying to break the tension. "We can talk more later, Ethan."

"Later," he echoed, the word heavy with meaning. "Just think about what I said. I'll be waiting."

With that, he turned and walked away, each step echoing in the silence that followed, leaving a palpable void in his wake. I felt my heart tighten as I watched him go, an instinctive urge to reach out and stop him, but the moment passed, slipping through my fingers like sand.

"Are you okay?" Jackson asked softly, stepping closer to me. The concern etched on his face pulled at something deep within me.

"I'm fine," I said, though the word felt like a flimsy shield against the reality crashing around me. "It's just... complicated."

"Complicated is an understatement," he replied, a hint of humor lacing his voice, but I could hear the seriousness beneath it. "You know you can talk to me about anything, right? I'm here for you."

"I know," I whispered, my heart swelling with appreciation. In the swirl of chaos, his steadfastness felt like a beacon, a reminder that I wasn't entirely alone.

"Why don't we get some fresh air? I could use a breath of fresh air after... whatever that was," he suggested, gesturing toward the darkened street beyond the café.

"Yeah, let's do that." I nodded, grateful for the distraction.

We stepped outside, the crisp air filling my lungs, a refreshing contrast to the tense atmosphere we'd just left behind. The streets were quiet, with only the occasional rustle of leaves and the distant hum of traffic breaking the stillness.

"Want to talk about it?" Jackson asked as we strolled down the sidewalk, hands shoved deep in his pockets, his demeanor relaxed yet attentive.

"Not really," I admitted, biting my lip. "I mean, I'm not sure what to say. It's just... complicated."

"Complicated seems to be your word of the day," he teased gently, nudging my shoulder with his own.

"Just trying to spice things up," I shot back, a smirk creeping across my face despite the heaviness weighing on my heart.

We walked in companionable silence for a moment, the cool breeze wrapping around us like a comforting embrace. Yet, beneath the surface of our lighthearted banter, a tension crackled, both exhilarating and daunting.

"Do you want to keep planning the charity event? Or maybe we could grab some food?" Jackson offered, his casual tone betraying the earnestness in his eyes.

"Food sounds good," I said, my stomach rumbling in agreement. The simple act of sharing a meal felt like a grounding choice, a way to reconnect with something uncomplicated amid the chaos swirling around me.

As we made our way to a nearby diner, the neon lights flickered, casting a warm glow that welcomed us inside. We settled into a booth, the familiar smell of burgers and fries wafting through the air, pulling at my senses.

"What's your go-to comfort food?" he asked, leaning back, his expression open and inviting.

"Definitely fries. I could live off them," I replied, grinning. "With a side of existential dread, of course."

Jackson chuckled, a deep, resonant sound that sent a ripple of warmth through me. "Ah yes, the classic pairing. What about dessert?"

"Hmm, dessert is a must. I think we can safely say ice cream is the ultimate comfort food," I declared, feeling lighter as I spoke.

He raised an eyebrow, amusement dancing in his eyes. "You're really pushing the limits of 'comfort food' here. Are you a glutton for punishment or just really passionate about your snacks?"

"Why can't it be both?" I shot back, unable to contain the laughter bubbling within me.

Just as our conversation flowed freely, my phone buzzed again, jolting me back to reality. I glanced at the screen, and my heart plummeted. Another message from Ethan flashed before my eyes: "I'm outside."

"Julia?" Jackson's voice cut through my swirling thoughts, concern lacing his tone. "What is it?"

I looked up, panic clawing at my insides. "It's Ethan. He's outside. I can't do this."

Jackson's expression shifted, and without a word, he stood up, determination radiating from him. "Stay here. I'll handle it."

"Wait!" I grasped his arm, the urgency in my voice catching him off guard. "You don't have to do anything. It's my mess."

"And I'm not letting you face it alone," he replied, his voice steady, his gaze unwavering.

The door swung open, and there was Ethan, standing in the threshold, uncertainty written all over his face. My heart raced as I looked between the two men, the storm of emotions swirling once again.

"Julia," Ethan began, but Jackson stepped forward, a fierce protectiveness igniting within him.

"Not now," Jackson interrupted, his voice low and firm. "You've already had your chance."

The air thickened with tension, a palpable current that electrified the atmosphere. My breath caught in my throat, the weight of the moment settling heavily on my shoulders. I had to choose, and the decision loomed like a shadow over us all.

With both men staring at me, the world felt like it had narrowed down to a single moment, a defining choice that would alter the course of my life forever. My heart raced, and the realization hit me hard—this was it, the culmination of everything I had been running from.

And just as I opened my mouth to speak, the ground beneath us trembled, and the air crackled with an energy that promised to

# Chapter 10: Hops and Heartbreak

The sun rose lazily over the town of Maplewood, casting a warm golden hue over the bustling streets. The familiar scent of malt and hops wafted through the open doors of our small brewery, mingling with the rich aroma of freshly brewed coffee from the café next door. I stood behind the bar, polishing the gleaming glasses, trying to keep my mind busy. The chatter of customers filled the air like a melody, but beneath it lay a different kind of music—the dissonant chords of uncertainty and longing that had become my constant companions since that fateful kiss with Jackson.

As the door swung open with a jingle, I looked up to see him walk in, that disarming smile lighting up his face. My heart raced, and I cursed myself for still being so hopelessly affected by him. "Hey, Penny," he called out, his voice smooth as the craft beer we'd been perfecting together. He moved to the bar, leaning casually against it, the sunlight catching the tousled strands of his hair, making him look almost ethereal.

"Hey," I replied, trying to sound nonchalant as I focused intently on the glass in my hand, as if it held the secrets of the universe. "How's the batch from yesterday coming along?"

"Smells divine, but you already know that." He grinned, and I felt that familiar flutter in my stomach. "I think we're onto something special here."

"Let's hope the judges agree." I attempted to match his lightness, though the weight of my feelings pressed heavily on my chest. Every moment spent with him felt like a tightrope walk between bliss and devastation.

The brewery was buzzing with life; laughter echoed off the walls, and glasses clinked in toasts, but in that moment, it felt like we were in our own world, suspended in a space filled with possibility and unspoken tension. Yet, as I poured a fresh pint, the laughter dimmed to a murmur, and I caught snippets of a conversation from a nearby table that made my heart drop.

"Did you hear about Jackson? There's a big job offer in Seattle," one patron said, his voice a low rumble.

I tried to concentrate on the foam, but it felt like I was pouring my heart out into a glass—lost and futile. Seattle? I couldn't imagine him so far away, and the thought of him leaving made my stomach twist into painful knots. I forced a smile, hoping Jackson wouldn't notice my abrupt change in demeanor.

"You okay?" he asked, his brow furrowing in concern as he leaned closer, his eyes searching mine.

"Yeah, just—" I hesitated, searching for a distraction. "Did you see the hops we're using for the next batch? They're supposed to add a floral note."

He chuckled, a sound that sent warmth through my veins, but it didn't reach my heart. "You and your hops. Always thinking ahead."

The playfulness in his tone felt like a lifeline, but the shadows of uncertainty loomed. I turned away, pretending to fiddle with the brewing equipment as if it could somehow brew away my fear.

Days passed, each filled with the same pattern—customers, brewing, and the ever-present tension between Jackson and me. We worked seamlessly together, crafting our new recipe, but beneath the surface, I felt the churning of my heart, the brewing storm of my emotions, and the looming shadow of his potential departure.

One evening, as we cleaned up after a particularly busy shift, I finally gathered the courage to bring it up. "So, Seattle," I said, trying to sound casual as I wiped the bar. "What's the deal?"

Jackson paused, his eyes narrowing slightly. "You heard about that?"

"Yeah, just a rumor I overheard." I shrugged, fighting to keep my voice steady. "Are you thinking of taking it?"

He sighed, running a hand through his hair, a gesture I had come to recognize as a sign of his frustration. "I don't know yet. It's a good opportunity, but..."

"But?" I prompted, my heart pounding.

"But I have things here that matter to me too." His gaze held mine, a flicker of something—hope, maybe? "The brewery, the competition... and you."

I felt my breath catch, his words wrapping around my heart like a warm embrace. "You know, we have something special here, Jackson. It's hard to think about losing that."

"Are you saying you want me to stay?" He stepped closer, the intensity of his gaze causing my heart to race.

"Of course I do! But you have to think about your future," I replied, trying to sound logical despite the tumult of emotions threatening to spill over. "You deserve to pursue every opportunity."

He smiled softly, a mixture of gratitude and something deeper, and in that moment, the air crackled with possibility. "And what if my opportunity is right here?"

"Then we'll win this competition together," I said, trying to keep the mood light, though the weight of unspoken feelings hung between us like a storm cloud, ready to burst. "Let's brew our way to the top."

His laugh rang out, a sound I realized I'd been longing for. "You really believe we can do this?"

"Believe? I know we can. We make a great team." I met his gaze, the warmth of his presence enveloping me, yet that flicker of doubt lingered. I was terrified of what would happen if we succeeded—or if we failed.

The following week slid by, each day blending into the next, like the layers of flavors in a well-crafted beer. The brewery buzzed with life, but inside, I felt like a tightly wound coil, ready to spring at any moment. The brewing competition loomed like a shadow, a blend of excitement and dread that tinged everything with a bittersweet edge. Jackson and I threw ourselves into our work, testing recipes and experimenting with new ingredients, but there was always that unspoken tension lingering between us, a delicate thread pulling us together yet threatening to unravel at the slightest tug.

"Okay, what do we think?" I asked, presenting our latest batch to Jackson. I could feel the adrenaline coursing through my veins as I poured a small sample into a glass, the amber liquid sparkling in the overhead lights.

Jackson lifted the glass, swirling it gently as if trying to uncover some hidden truth. "It smells incredible," he said, taking a sip, his eyes closing momentarily as he savored the flavor. "But it needs a little something... like a secret ingredient to really make it pop."

"Secret ingredient?" I teased, leaning closer, the warmth of his presence almost intoxicating. "What are you, a wizard? Do you keep magic dust in your back pocket?"

"Only for special occasions," he shot back, a playful grin dancing on his lips. "But for real, how about we add a hint of citrus? Something zesty to balance the maltiness."

I nodded, impressed by his insight. "Great idea. We'll have to test that out tomorrow. I've been wanting to try using grapefruit peel."

The playful banter helped ease some of the tension, yet I could still feel the weight of unsaid words pressing down on us. Every laugh seemed to echo against the walls, teasing the thoughts that spiraled through my mind. Jackson, with his charm and that glimmer of passion in his eyes, made it all too easy to forget about the inevitable reality that lay ahead.

As the evening wore on, the brewery began to quiet, the customers dwindling down to a few familiar faces sharing stories and laughter. The clinking of glasses became more muted, the air heavy with an intimacy I craved yet feared. It was during this peaceful lull that I decided to break the silence that had wrapped around us like a fog.

"Are you really considering that job in Seattle?" I asked, the words slipping out before I could hold them back. My heart raced as I watched his expression shift, uncertainty flickering across his features.

He leaned against the bar, his arms crossed, and sighed. "It's a great opportunity, Penny. They want me to lead a team, work on some innovative projects. It's... tempting."

"Tempting," I echoed, trying to mask the disappointment that threatened to spill over. "And what about us? What happens to our little brewing partnership?"

Jackson looked at me, the corners of his mouth twitching as if he was wrestling with something deep inside. "I don't want to lose this. You know that, right? This place, this partnership... you mean a lot to me."

His words hung in the air, rich with possibility yet tinged with a sorrow I couldn't quite place. "I just... I don't want to stand in your way, Jackson. You deserve to chase your dreams."

"And I'd chase them with you," he said, his voice steady, as if he was trying to reel me in from the ledge of my own fears. "But I also don't want to hold you back if this is your dream too."

I shook my head, frustration bubbling beneath the surface. "It's not about me. This is your career, your future. I'm just... the girl who brews beer."

He stepped closer, his eyes intense. "You're so much more than that. You're the heart of this place, Penny. You're my partner in every sense of the word."

The sincerity in his voice sent a thrill through me, but it also raised the stakes. "And what if I can't follow you? What if I'm stuck here, watching you build a life somewhere else?"

"I don't want you to feel stuck," he said, his voice softening. "Maybe we can find a way to make it work. I mean, people do long-distance all the time."

I snorted, the bitter taste of reality flooding my senses. "Long-distance? Is that really what you want? Late-night video calls and counting down the days until you visit?"

His brow furrowed, and I could see the gears turning in his head, each tick amplifying the tension between us. "I'd rather not. I want to share a life with you, not just a series of phone calls."

"You make it sound so easy," I replied, a mixture of sarcasm and vulnerability slipping into my tone. "But it's not. Life is messy and complicated. What if it doesn't work out? What if we grow apart?"

"Or what if we grow together?" he countered, a spark igniting in his eyes. "Penny, I'm willing to take the leap if you are. But it has to be both of us, not just one of us trying to hold on."

His words wrapped around me like a warm blanket, but doubt crept in, gnawing at the edges of my resolve. I wanted so desperately to believe in us, to throw caution to the wind, but the weight of uncertainty was a formidable opponent.

"I need to think about it," I finally said, my voice barely above a whisper.

"Take your time," he replied, stepping back, the space between us suddenly feeling miles apart. "But know this—I don't want to let go, Penny. Not now, not ever."

As he turned to walk away, I felt a pang of regret wash over me. The choice loomed ahead, dark and tangled like the hops in our latest brew. I wanted to grab his arm, pull him back, and let the weight of my heart decide the outcome. But as the door swung shut behind him, I was left alone with my thoughts, the echo of his words hanging in the air like the lingering scent of hops—familiar, comforting, yet tinged with the bittersweet taste of uncertainty.

The morning sun cast a golden glow over the brewery, illuminating the wooden beams and creating a warm, inviting atmosphere. I stood at the bar, watching as the first customers trickled in, their laughter and chatter melding into the comforting hum of daily life. But for me, the excitement of the brewing competition was overshadowed by the unresolved tension with Jackson. Each glance he threw my way felt loaded, a heavy freight train of unspoken words barreling down the tracks of our friendship.

"Penny! You want to take the first round?" Jackson called out, his voice breaking through my reverie. He was standing by the brewing tanks, his shirt slightly damp from the morning's work, his hair tousled in that adorable way that made my heart flutter.

"Sure! What are we pouring?" I replied, forcing a bright smile as I grabbed a glass.

"Let's start with the grapefruit batch. I think it's finally ready for the spotlight." He flashed a grin that sent a thrill racing through me.

"Perfect. I'm in," I said, pouring the beer with a practiced hand. As I filled the glass, the familiar aroma of hops and citrus filled the air, momentarily distracting me from the whirlwind of my emotions.

Customers gathered around, eager for the first taste, and I felt a rush of adrenaline. The laughter and chatter resumed, and I lost myself in the rhythm of serving, but Jackson's presence was an unyielding weight on my mind. He worked alongside me, offering comments and playful quips, yet there was an invisible barrier between us, like a thick fog that refused to lift.

"Okay, everyone!" I called out, raising my glass high. "Here's to our grapefruit brew! May it be as refreshing as a summer day and as complex as our emotions!" Laughter erupted, and I noticed Jackson's eyes spark with something—amusement, perhaps, or maybe a deeper recognition of the truth buried beneath my joke.

We served the crowd, and as the drinks flowed, so did the conversation. But as the night wore on, I caught myself glancing toward Jackson, longing to bridge the gap between us. He seemed to sense my gaze, turning his attention toward me, and in that moment, the world around us faded, leaving just the two of us standing in the warm light of the brewery.

"What's going on in that head of yours?" he asked, tilting his head, a teasing grin playing on his lips.

"Just thinking about how well this batch turned out," I replied, attempting to keep my voice steady despite the rush of emotions bubbling beneath the surface. "And how if we win the competition, we'll be the talk of the town."

"And if we lose?" He raised an eyebrow, his expression shifting to something more serious. "What happens then?"

"Then we go back to brewing, because that's what we do." I shrugged, but inside, my heart raced. "But if you go to Seattle, it'll be different."

"Penny, I—" he started, but the door swung open, interrupting our moment as a group of rowdy patrons stumbled in, laughter trailing behind them like a banner announcing chaos.

The atmosphere shifted, laughter exploding around us, and just like that, the moment slipped away. Jackson stepped back, sliding into the role of a friendly bartender, and I felt the familiar pang of disappointment knot in my stomach.

Hours passed as we served beer and mingled with the crowd, the night stretching on like the amber liquid in the glasses we poured. I laughed and chatted with customers, but in the back of my mind, I replayed our earlier conversation, wondering where I stood. Each time I caught Jackson's eye, my heart raced, only to find my bravado crumbling at the thought of what it meant for us.

Eventually, the bar began to quiet, and Jackson leaned against the counter, exhaustion etched into his features. "What do you think? Do we have a shot at this competition?"

"Absolutely," I said, feeling the spark of excitement reignite. "We've put in so much work. It's got to pay off."

"I'll hold you to that." He smiled, but there was a hesitation behind his eyes that gave me pause. "But honestly, Penny... I need to know what you want. If this job offer is pulling me away, I don't want to waste any more time pretending everything's fine."

"Why are we having this conversation when there are still customers around?" I shot back, the heat rising in my cheeks.

"Because I can't keep pretending either," he replied, his voice low and steady, a weight of sincerity in every word.

With that, I felt the tension in the air shift, thickening like syrup. "Jackson, I... I don't know if I'm ready to have this conversation."

"Then what are we doing here?" he challenged, a hint of frustration slipping through his normally easy demeanor. "I can't go to Seattle with a heart in two places."

"What if we—" I hesitated, searching for the right words. "What if we try to make this work? You know, when we win the competition, we can decide together."

His expression shifted, a glimmer of hope igniting in his eyes. "So you're saying there's a chance?"

"Why not?" I shrugged, trying to sound more confident than I felt. "Let's see where this takes us. But we need to be honest with each other."

"Honest," he echoed, nodding slowly. "I can do that. But the clock is ticking."

"I know," I whispered, a chill running down my spine as the reality of our situation crashed over me.

Just as I was about to dive deeper, the door swung open again, this time revealing the unmistakable figure of my father. He stepped inside, his face a mixture of confusion and surprise, and I felt my stomach drop.

"Penny?" he called out, his voice cutting through the haze of the moment.

"Dad?" I replied, shocked. "What are you doing here?"

He took a step forward, his eyes darting between Jackson and me, the unspoken tension suddenly palpable in the air. "I thought I'd stop by and see how things were going. I didn't expect this..." His gaze settled on Jackson, and I felt the uninvited heat of embarrassment creep into my cheeks.

"Everything's great! We're just... discussing the competition," I stammered, desperately grasping for a way to shift the mood.

But my father wasn't buying it. "Right. Well, I hope you two aren't getting too cozy. There's work to be done," he said, his tone carrying the weight of unintentional judgment.

Jackson shifted, his expression unreadable as my father continued. "I've been hearing some rumors around town, and I wanted to make sure you're both focused."

"Rumors?" I echoed, my heart racing again. "What kind of rumors?"

"Just the usual," he replied, waving a hand dismissively. "But you know how small towns are."

I exchanged a look with Jackson, uncertainty flooding the space between us. "Dad, we're fine. Really," I insisted, though I could feel the walls closing in around me.

"Fine, huh? Just make sure it stays that way," he warned, his gaze hardening. "You have a competition to win."

With that, he turned on his heel and left as abruptly as he'd come, the door swinging shut behind him, leaving a charged silence in his wake. Jackson and I stood there, tension thick enough to cut with a knife, our hopes and fears suddenly tangled in a web of uncertainty.

"What just happened?" Jackson murmured, breaking the silence.

"I have no idea," I replied, my heart pounding. The air crackled with unspoken words, the weight of my father's intrusion hanging heavily between us. I felt a storm brewing, one that could either strengthen our bond or tear it apart entirely.

"Penny," Jackson said, stepping closer, the urgency in his voice pulling me from my thoughts. "Whatever happens, we can face this together. Right?"

I opened my mouth to respond, to reassure him, but before I could utter a single word, the lights flickered overhead, and an ear-splitting crash echoed from the back of the brewery, shattering the fragile moment we'd shared. My heart raced as dread settled in my stomach.

"What was that?" I gasped, my voice barely above a whisper.

"I don't know," he said, his expression darkening with concern as we both turned toward the sound, the tension between us momentarily forgotten in the face of uncertainty.

As we rushed toward the source of the noise, I couldn't shake the feeling that whatever lay ahead was about to change everything.

# Chapter 11: Tangled Threads

The air in the brewery was thick with the smell of malt and hops, a comforting blend that clung to my skin like a second layer. I moved between the brewing stations, my fingers grazing the cool stainless steel, a grounding reminder of the task at hand. The competition loomed ahead, a beast of pressure and expectations ready to consume me whole. Each day ticked by with a maddening urgency, and I found myself running on caffeine and adrenaline, trying to distill my thoughts into something clear and cohesive.

Ethan's message had shattered my routine. His words were like glass, sharp and cutting, demanding attention I was unwilling to give. Let's talk. That simple request twisted my stomach into knots. The very notion of seeing him felt like trying to hold water in my hands—too slippery, too chaotic. Anger simmered just below the surface, and the memories of our last encounter played like a movie on repeat, the scene set in a dim corner of our childhood home, where our voices had risen until they reached a fever pitch, drowning out everything but the hurt.

I could hear the distant hum of Jackson's laughter from the adjacent room, a sound that grounded me in the chaos. He was the calm to my storm, his steady presence a comforting weight. Yet, even as I glanced toward him, there was a subtle distance in his gaze, as if he stood at the edge of my world, a mere observer rather than a participant. It was the kind of separation that made my heart ache, threading my brewing with an undercurrent of tension I couldn't shake. The way he looked at me sometimes—full of warmth and understanding—was a distraction I both craved and feared.

"Hey, are you with me?" Jackson's voice pulled me back, the melodic timbre breaking through my thoughts. He leaned against the workbench, arms crossed, a playful smile tugging at his lips. "Or have you entered the brewing zone, where no mortal man can reach you?"

I forced a grin, determined to shake off the encroaching shadows. "Sorry, just trying to figure out if I can make this hazy IPA a little more... hazy. You know, for dramatic effect." I turned back to the ingredients laid out before me, attempting to focus on the task rather than the tumult brewing in my heart.

He stepped closer, his shoulder brushing against mine, the warmth igniting a spark of something electric between us. "You always go for the dramatic effect. It's like your superpower," he teased, but there was a seriousness beneath his playful tone, a silent acknowledgment of the heaviness that lingered in the air.

"More like a curse." I let out a humorless laugh, my thoughts drifting back to Ethan. "Especially when it comes to family."

Jackson's expression shifted, the playful façade slipping away as he regarded me with a mix of empathy and understanding. "Do you want to talk about it? I mean, you don't have to, but I'm here if you need me."

The offer hung between us, a lifeline tossed into turbulent waters. My instinct was to push him away, to shove my feelings down deep where they belonged. But instead, I found myself leaning into the warmth of his concern, a small relief amidst the chaos. "It's just... Ethan wants to meet up, and I don't know if I can handle it." My voice cracked slightly, revealing the vulnerability I so desperately wanted to hide.

"Your brother?" Jackson's brow furrowed in thought. "I can see how that would be tough. You guys have been through a lot."

"A lot?" I echoed, bitterness lacing my words. "You mean a lifetime of miscommunication, betrayal, and resentment?"

Jackson nodded slowly, his gaze steady. "It's complicated. Family usually is." He reached out, brushing his fingers over mine, a small gesture that sent a jolt of awareness racing through me. "But maybe this is a chance to start untangling those threads."

"Untangling threads," I mused, imagining a complex web woven through years of history, each strand representing a moment that had pushed us apart. "It sounds like a lot of work."

"Work is good," he said, a hint of mischief in his tone. "Especially if you get to do it with someone who makes it less painful."

I laughed, the tension easing ever so slightly. "And who might that be?"

"Just a guy who knows a thing or two about brewing and isn't afraid of a little emotional labor." Jackson's grin was infectious, the corners of my mouth curving upward despite the weight in my chest.

As the banter continued, I felt a flicker of hope, ignited by the possibility of healing that hovered just out of reach. But reality crashed in, an unwelcome reminder that no amount of witty repartee could erase the truth lurking behind Ethan's request. We were tangled in a mess of shared history, and as much as I wanted to navigate this with grace, the thought of facing my brother sent my heart racing.

"Let's just get through the brewing competition," I said finally, trying to push the thought aside. "After that, maybe I'll reconsider the family reunion."

Jackson studied me, his expression softening. "I think you're stronger than you give yourself credit for. Just remember, you're not alone in this. Whatever happens with Ethan, you have me."

The sincerity in his voice wrapped around me like a warm blanket, fortifying my resolve even as I felt the shadows creeping in again. I nodded, a small gesture that held more weight than words could convey. "Thanks, Jackson. I really appreciate it."

And for a fleeting moment, the world outside the brewery faded away, leaving only the rhythmic sounds of brewing and the steady presence of someone who, despite everything, made me feel like maybe, just maybe, I could weather the storm that was brewing within my family.

The day of the brewing competition arrived like an uninvited guest, its presence looming large and unwelcome. My heart thudded against my ribcage, a relentless drummer in the chaotic symphony of my mind. I stood in front of the massive stainless steel kettle, its surface gleaming under the overhead lights, reflecting the brewing dreams I was desperate to bring to fruition. Jackson was already at my side, focused on the intricate dance of ingredients while I fought to keep my own thoughts from spiraling out of control.

"I think we should add a bit more dry hopping," he suggested, his brow furrowing in concentration. "It'll bring out the citrus notes more distinctly."

"Citrus notes, huh? Just what I need—more zest to add to the drama." I shot him a sideways glance, but the corner of my mouth betrayed me with a smile. The playful banter had become a lifeline, keeping me afloat in a sea of uncertainty.

Jackson chuckled, the sound warm and inviting. "You're telling me you'd rather brew a dull lager than embrace a little drama? I must be hearing things."

"Only if you plan on being my dramatic sidekick," I quipped back, feeling the tension in my chest ease slightly as the rhythm of our conversation settled in like a familiar tune.

We worked side by side, our movements synchronizing like a well-rehearsed dance. I watched as he poured in the hops, the green pellets cascading down like confetti, a little celebration in the midst of chaos. Each gesture felt natural, yet each laugh we shared ignited a spark of something deeper, something that danced just beneath the surface of our brewing camaraderie.

In the background, the clattering of equipment and murmurs of competitors filled the air, a buzzing hive of anticipation. I tried to focus on the task at hand, but the shadow of Ethan loomed larger with each passing moment. The urge to confront my brother, to finally clear the air, was a relentless itch I couldn't scratch.

As I poured the malt into the kettle, my mind drifted to our childhood—Ethan's laughter echoing through the hallways of our old house, our arguments over who got to choose the first movie on family nights, the way we had once been inseparable. The memories tugged at my heart, each recollection a reminder of the bond we had once shared before the cracks began to show.

"Hey, penny for your thoughts," Jackson said, interrupting the bittersweet reverie.

"I was just thinking about how brewing is a lot like family," I said, mixing the contents vigorously. "Sometimes it takes a little heat to bring out the best flavors, but too much can ruin the whole batch."

"Wise words from a brewing guru," he said, his eyes twinkling with mischief. "Just remember, you control the heat. Don't let it control you."

His reassurance hung in the air, a soothing balm against the backdrop of brewing chaos and familial strife. I nodded, trying to internalize the wisdom as I glanced toward the competition area. Each table was a microcosm of tension and excitement, rivals ready to showcase their creations. But instead of fear, I felt a flicker of determination, a spark ignited by Jackson's belief in me.

Before I could sink into that sense of empowerment, the clamor of voices drew my attention. My heart sank when I spotted Ethan across the room, flanked by competitors, his laughter ringing out like a bell. The sight struck me like a punch to the gut, a reminder of everything I wished to forget. He seemed at ease, the very picture of confidence, and I couldn't help but wonder if he felt any of the turmoil that churned within me.

"Hey, everything okay?" Jackson's voice broke through my spiraling thoughts, and I turned to find him studying me with concern.

"Just... family drama," I sighed, trying to shrug it off, but the weight of it felt almost tangible.

"You want me to distract you?" Jackson asked, an eyebrow raised. "I could do a dramatic reading of the brewing manual. Very riveting stuff."

I laughed, grateful for his ability to lighten the mood. "Only if you can throw in some interpretive dance moves."

"Now we're talking. I've always felt my true calling was in the fine art of hops interpretation," he replied, striking a mock pose.

The laughter that erupted between us was like a breath of fresh air, clearing the storm clouds that had been threatening to engulf me. Yet, even as the joy enveloped me, I knew the competition would soon force me to confront the tumultuous relationship with my brother. The thought was both terrifying and exhilarating.

As the clock ticked down, I caught sight of the judges—a trio of stern-faced experts peering over the brewing tables with critical eyes. My heart raced again as I finished the final touches on my creation. I meticulously adjusted the ingredients, hoping to infuse my unique spin into the brew.

"Let's taste it before the judges do," Jackson suggested, his enthusiasm infectious. "You know, just in case it tastes like regret and bad decisions."

"Good plan." I poured a sample into a small cup and handed it to him. His expression shifted to one of seriousness as he took a cautious sip, his eyes narrowing in concentration.

"What do you think?" I held my breath, my heart pounding.

Jackson's brow furrowed. "It's... interesting. There's a boldness here, but it's like you're holding back. Don't be afraid to let it shine, you know?"

I felt a flicker of frustration at his observation. "Easy for you to say. You're not the one with family expectations riding on your shoulders."

He set the cup down, his expression softening. "I get that, but what if this is your moment to show who you are? To break free from what's expected and just... be you?"

The weight of his words pressed against me like a warm embrace. In that moment, I realized he was right. I was holding back, afraid to let my true self out of the cage I'd built around my emotions. It was time to let go, to embrace the heat and the chaos—not just in brewing, but in my life as well.

With renewed determination, I adjusted the final ingredient, adding a touch of citrus that danced on the edge of audacity. "Here's to bold choices," I murmured, pouring the mixture into the judging cup.

"Now that's the spirit," Jackson replied, his eyes gleaming with pride as he stepped back to let me take center stage. I took a deep breath, feeling the thrill of the competition wash over me, mingling with the bittersweet taste of my family's legacy. The stage was set, and I was ready to face whatever awaited me—brotherly confrontation and all.

As the judges began to make their rounds, my heart thrummed in my chest like a restless bird, eager to take flight but tethered to the ground by anxiety. I stood at my table, a flurry of nerves and anticipation swirling within me, while the spotlight of the competition bore down, illuminating my creation with its unforgiving gaze. Each judge was an embodiment of scrutiny, their expressions a careful blend of skepticism and mild curiosity.

I glanced over at Jackson, who was set up at the adjacent table, a picture of calm efficiency. He was chatting with one of the judges, his charisma effortless, a stark contrast to the tension coiling in my own stomach. I felt a flash of gratitude for his steady presence amidst the chaos, a reminder that I wasn't entirely alone in this maelstrom of expectations.

"Next up, we have..." The lead judge's voice rang out, but my focus was drifting, lingering on the way Jackson animatedly gestured, bringing his words to life as he poured a sample for his own creation. I shook my head, scolding myself for allowing distraction to creep in. This was my moment to shine, to demonstrate what I could do when the heat was on. I needed to stay sharp and present.

As the judges reached my table, I squared my shoulders, plastering on a confident smile that felt more like a mask than a genuine expression. "Welcome! I'm excited for you to try my latest brew," I said, my voice surprisingly steady despite the whirlwind of emotions swirling within.

"Let's see what you've crafted here," the lead judge replied, his tone professional yet tinged with intrigue. He lifted the glass, the golden liquid catching the light, casting tiny rainbows against the polished wood of the table.

With each sip the judges took, the silence around us thickened. I held my breath, caught between hope and dread as they murmured their assessments to one another. The tension grew heavier, each pause feeling like a lifetime. My eyes darted to Jackson, who caught my gaze and offered a subtle thumbs-up, a flicker of encouragement that eased my nerves.

"Bold flavor profile," one of the judges finally said, breaking the silence. "But I sense there's more to it than just a hoppy bite. What's the story behind this brew?"

I took a deep breath, ready to unveil the heart of my creation. "This brew reflects my journey through a chaotic family history. Each flavor represents a different chapter—sour notes for the struggles, sweet undertones for the triumphs. I wanted to create something that resonates with the complexity of life itself."

The judges nodded, their expressions softening. I could see that they appreciated the backstory, the emotion interwoven into the very fabric of my brew. But just as I allowed myself to relax, Ethan's voice sliced through the atmosphere like a blade.

"Interesting interpretation," he said, stepping forward from the shadows, his presence crashing into the moment like an unexpected storm. "But isn't brewing supposed to be more about technique than therapy?"

A chill spread through me, and I felt my confidence falter, the laughter of the judges turning into a murmur of discomfort. "Ethan, this isn't the time," I snapped, a flicker of anger igniting in my chest.

"Of course it is. Everyone loves a good drama," he retorted, his smirk a mask of insincerity. "Besides, I'd hate for you to distract them from the actual brewing skills required to win this competition."

I took a step forward, a wave of indignation swelling within me. "And I'd hate for you to act like you own this competition just because you're my brother. This is about my work, my craft."

"Craft is one thing; theatrics are another," Ethan shot back, his eyes narrowing. The judges shifted uncomfortably, caught in the crossfire of our sibling rivalry. I could feel the air thickening, each breath becoming heavier as my emotions spiraled out of control.

"Can we not do this here?" Jackson interjected, his voice calm yet firm, stepping into the breach. "This is a place for creativity, not conflict."

Ethan rolled his eyes, dismissing Jackson with a wave of his hand. "And who are you, exactly? Just some guy who thinks he can brew?"

The insult struck harder than I expected, igniting a protective instinct within me. "He's more than that," I said, standing shoulder to shoulder with Jackson. "He's helped me through this competition when I felt like giving up. Maybe you could learn something from him."

Ethan's gaze flickered between us, surprise mingling with contempt. "Really? You think he's the answer to your problems?"

Before I could respond, the lead judge cleared his throat, attempting to regain control of the situation. "Let's focus on the brews, shall we? This is a competition, and we're here to evaluate your creations."

"Fine. Let's get back to it," I replied, trying to keep my tone steady as I turned my back to Ethan, the frustration boiling just beneath the surface. The atmosphere was taut, each judge's gaze shifting back and forth like spectators at a tennis match.

The tension in the air crackled as the judging resumed. I forced myself to focus on the task at hand, but my heart raced with the underlying current of conflict. When Ethan stepped back, the relief was almost palpable. I forced a smile, even as I felt the weight of our encounter hang over me like a dark cloud.

When it was finally Jackson's turn to present, I watched him with a mix of admiration and anxiety. He poured his brew with precision, the rich amber liquid flowing gracefully into the glasses. "What I've created here is a blend of tradition and innovation," he explained, his voice steady. "It's about honoring the past while embracing the future. Just like life."

The judges nodded, clearly engaged. I could see the respect in their eyes as they sampled his creation, their expressions turning thoughtful.

As the judges conferred, I glanced at Ethan, who was talking animatedly with another competitor. A feeling of unease settled in my stomach, the remnants of our argument simmering beneath the surface. It was like standing on the edge of a precipice, knowing a leap was inevitable but unprepared for the fall.

"Alright, time's up!" the lead judge declared, his voice cutting through my swirling thoughts. "We'll announce the winners shortly."

The room buzzed with excitement, the competitors exchanging hopeful glances. I took a moment to breathe, steeling myself for the impending results. Just as I thought the tension might dissolve, a loud crash echoed through the space. All heads turned toward the sound—a table had collapsed, ingredients and glassware spilling onto the floor like broken dreams.

Ethan rushed to assist, his competitive nature compelling him to help rather than gloat. My heart raced. In the chaos, my gaze locked onto Jackson, who appeared equally stunned.

Then, in the midst of the confusion, my phone buzzed violently in my pocket. I fished it out, glancing at the screen—and my blood ran cold. A message from Ethan, his words glaringly clear: I know about Jackson. I know everything.

The words sent a chill up my spine, turning my world upside down. In that moment, the competition faded, the judges' voices became a distant hum, and all I could focus on was the overwhelming dread that gripped me. My heart raced with questions and the weight of impending confrontation, as uncertainty loomed over me like a shadow, darkening everything I had just begun to build.

# Chapter 12: Unexpected Ingredients

The day of the competition dawned with a brightness that belied the brewing storm, both meteorologically and emotionally. I stood at the edge of the park, the air filled with the sharp, yeasty scent of hops and barley that beckoned from the rows of tents, each representing a different brewery eager to showcase their finest creations. The park was an emerald jewel, vibrant and alive, as if the universe had conspired to amplify our enthusiasm with a dazzling backdrop of blooming flowers and cheerful chatter.

As I took a deep breath, the kind that tasted of ambition and nerves, I caught a glimpse of Jackson across the way. He was adjusting his own booth, muscles flexing under the bright sun as he expertly tied down tarps, but his focus seemed fragmented. I knew that look well—the mingling of hope and anxiety. Jackson had been my anchor through this process, a steady hand guiding me while I waded through the sometimes murky waters of brewing and competition. Today, however, the shadows of doubt danced across his face like the impending storm clouds lurking on the horizon.

"Hey!" I called, waving my hands as I approached, a smile plastered on my face, even though my insides were roiling. "Need a hand?"

His lips quirked into a half-smile, the kind that ignited a flutter in my chest, but his brow furrowed deeper as he scanned the skies. "I'm not sure we'll need a hand if this storm actually hits," he replied, his voice low and serious.

"Let it come," I said with a bravado that surprised even me. "I've dealt with worse. Remember the Great Sourdough Disaster of last summer? If I survived that, I can handle anything."

"Yeah, but that was just bread," he chuckled, his laughter warm and rich, almost a comfort against the foreboding atmosphere. "This is... beer. And people will actually be judging us based on it."

I rolled my eyes playfully, crossing my arms. "And you think they won't judge me for spilling flour everywhere? At least if we mess up here, it'll be liquid and not a sticky mess."

With a flick of my hair, I turned back to my booth, the soft fabric of my apron fluttering like a flag in the light breeze. I had spent the last few weeks meticulously crafting a brew that was a nod to my father's classic recipe, the one he had brewed in our backyard as I watched with wide-eyed wonder. But today, I intended to put my spin on it, mixing in a hint of lavender and a dash of something unexpected—an aromatic citrus twist that I had discovered while experimenting late one night in my kitchen.

I arranged my ingredients with the precision of an artist, each bottle and spice jar a palette of flavors waiting to be transformed into something extraordinary. Jackson leaned against the booth, his arms crossed, watching me with an intensity that made my heart race. "You really believe in this brew, don't you?"

"Of course," I replied, glancing up at him. "It's not just about the beer, Jackson. It's about telling a story. My story. It's about my father and me, the long afternoons we spent brewing, and now I want to honor that while adding my own twist. If that doesn't deserve a ribbon, then I don't know what does."

He nodded, a glimmer of pride in his eyes, but the clouds overhead rolled ominously, darkening our playful banter. Just as I began to measure out my lavender, a sudden gust of wind swept through the park, ruffling banners and sending a chill down my spine. A murmur swept through the crowd as everyone instinctively began securing their tents and displays.

"Here we go," Jackson muttered, his hands flying into action.

"Don't panic!" I shouted, a grin creeping back onto my face, despite the rising chaos. "This is just nature's way of adding some drama!"

With a determination fueled by adrenaline, we worked together, securing our booth against the wind. Tension crackled in the air, but amidst the frantic energy, we found ourselves locked in a moment that felt suspended in time. The raindrops began to fall, soft at first, then in a sudden torrential downpour.

"Uh-oh!" I laughed, my voice barely audible above the roaring storm. "I think the universe wants to wash away my carefully laid plans."

"Maybe it wants to create something new," Jackson said, his eyes twinkling despite the downpour. "Like a water feature! Or a disaster."

As I chuckled, I felt a rush of warmth between us, something electric that made me forget about the wet ground beneath my feet. He moved closer, reaching out to tuck a strand of wet hair behind my ear, his fingers grazing my skin in a way that sent delightful shivers down my spine.

"See?" he said softly, our laughter mingling with the sound of the rain. "Even in a storm, we're making memories."

Just then, the storm reached its crescendo, and a peal of thunder split the air, causing me to jump. "Okay, fine! You win. Let's go inside and wait this out!"

Jackson laughed, taking my hand and pulling me toward the nearest tent, our laughter mingling with the chaos around us. The world outside blurred, the vibrant colors of the park now a smudged canvas, but in that moment, all I could see was him.

We stumbled into the tent, breathless and soaked, and I couldn't help but grin as I looked around at the other competitors, equally drenched and bewildered. "Well, at least we're not the only ones," I said, scanning the room. "And we might as well make the best of it."

"I have a feeling this is going to be a competition no one will forget," Jackson replied, his tone light yet tinged with something deeper.

"Just wait until they taste my brew!" I shot back, my spirit ignited by the thrill of the unexpected. "It's going to knock their socks off. And if it doesn't, at least we'll have a hilarious story to tell."

In that little bubble of camaraderie, the brewing storm felt less like a disaster and more like an unexpected ingredient in our story, enhancing the flavor of the day rather than washing it away. And as we shared laughter and soaked camaraderie, I realized that no matter the outcome of the competition, this moment—this connection with Jackson—was a victory in itself.

Raindrops drummed on the canvas above us, a chaotic symphony that drowned out the rest of the world, leaving only the vivid colors of our makeshift refuge. The tent buzzed with nervous energy, a melting pot of rival breweries and enthusiastic amateurs, each hoping to capture the hearts of the judges with their concoctions. I leaned against one of the sturdy poles, shivering slightly from the cool air that rushed in with the storm, and caught Jackson's eye. He flashed a reassuring grin, one that sent a jolt of warmth through me, banishing the chill that lingered.

"Have you thought about what you'll do if the power goes out?" he asked, the corners of his mouth quirking up. "You know, besides turning into a dramatic, soggy mess?"

"Let's not get ahead of ourselves," I replied, rolling my eyes but unable to suppress a smile. "I'll just throw my brew into the river and let nature take its course. It's bound to be better than half the stuff I've tasted this morning."

Jackson laughed, the sound brightening the dim tent as thunder rumbled outside, a gentle reminder of nature's authority. "You'd better hope that storm doesn't turn into a flood. That might actually drown your dreams."

"Or just my recipe," I shot back, feigning despair. "At least it would be a dramatic exit from my brewing career."

The tension in the tent began to ease, buoyed by our banter. I watched as other competitors huddled around their tables, some nervously adjusting labels on their bottles, others sharing last-minute adjustments to their recipes, every face a mix of determination and trepidation. I felt a rush of gratitude for the comfort Jackson provided, an anchor amidst the brewing storm—pun intended.

"Want to help me mix my secret ingredient?" I asked, raising an eyebrow mischievously. "It's essential for the competition."

"Secret ingredient?" he echoed, leaning in closer, his curiosity piqued. "Now I'm intrigued. What is it?"

"Patience and a sprinkle of despair!" I grinned, holding up a small vial containing the vibrant, citrusy essence I'd concocted. "I decided to go with something that captures the chaos of today's weather. If I can blend in some sunshine, maybe my beer can fight off the storm."

"Or it could turn out tasting like a desperate cocktail at a failed barbecue," he teased, reaching for the vial. "But I'm willing to risk it for the sake of art."

He carefully poured the contents into the mixing bowl I had set up earlier, a medley of hops and grains that had already begun to transform under his attentive eye. Watching him work was mesmerizing; he moved with a confidence that filled me with a sense of awe. I couldn't help but admire how he embodied the spirit of creativity, transforming chaos into something beautiful.

"Do you ever think about how this whole brewing thing started?" he asked, his brow furrowed in thought. "I mean, did you envision it becoming this—whatever this is?"

"Honestly?" I paused, the storm outside roaring as if to emphasize my words. "I thought I'd be spending my weekends perfecting a recipe and maybe impressing some friends. But here I am, neck-deep in rain and competition. It's wild."

"Wild is one way to put it," he said, shaking his head with a smile. "You're like a brewing superhero, conquering storms and creating liquid magic."

"And here you are, my trusty sidekick," I teased, nudging him playfully. "I couldn't do it without your charming support. You keep me grounded, you know."

"I try my best," he replied, his expression softening as he caught my gaze. For a brief moment, the laughter faded, leaving behind an intensity that made my heart race. It felt as if the storm outside paled in comparison to the tempest brewing between us.

The chaos of the tent melted away as we lingered in that moment, each heartbeat resonating with unspoken words. Then, just as quickly, the moment was shattered by a loud crash outside, the sound of a tent collapsing under the weight of the rain. The din erupted into panic as competitors rushed to save their equipment and ingredients, and the air thickened with urgency.

"Looks like we're back to reality!" I exclaimed, pushing my nervousness aside. "We need to secure our stuff."

Jackson nodded, the spell between us broken as we sprang into action. Together, we scrambled to gather our supplies, fastening loose ends and preparing to protect our precious ingredients. The tent trembled as the storm intensified, but somehow, I felt invincible alongside him.

As the rain poured down, a sense of determination surged within me. I wasn't just participating in this competition; I was claiming my place among the breweries, cementing my identity as a brewer. Every drop of rain that pelted the canvas overhead felt like a challenge, an opportunity to rise above.

"Alright!" I shouted, rallying the nearby competitors. "Let's show this storm we mean business!"

Jackson caught my eye, his expression filled with admiration as he joined in, helping to steady the booth. "That's the spirit! Storms don't stand a chance against us."

Our camaraderie shifted the atmosphere, transforming the frenetic energy into a collaborative frenzy. We secured the tables and adjusted the tents, laughter punctuating the serious undertones of our task. The spirit of competition had morphed into something deeper—an unexpected community forged in adversity.

As we fought against the elements, I realized how much I had come to appreciate Jackson's presence. He wasn't just a supporter; he was a catalyst, encouraging me to embrace my passion and challenge the norms of brewing. His playful jabs and easy laughter soothed my worries, giving me the courage to face the storm with renewed vigor.

Finally, after what felt like an eternity of scurrying, we managed to stabilize our booth. Drenched and laughing, we collapsed against the table, panting from the effort. "Did we just survive an apocalypse?" I asked, wiping my brow as I surveyed the bustling tent.

"More like a torrential downpour with a side of brewing madness," Jackson replied, chuckling. "But we're still standing, so I'd call it a win."

As the rain continued to pour, I turned my attention back to the brewing process, my heart pounding with excitement. "Okay, time to finish what we started," I said, my voice steady with newfound determination. "Let's make this the best batch ever."

The chaos around us faded into the background as we worked side by side, hands moving in perfect sync. Each ingredient that went into the mix felt like a piece of our shared experience—a journey woven together in the rain and laughter, punctuated by the unexpected ingredients of life. And in that moment, with Jackson by my side, I felt ready to embrace whatever came next, storm or not.

The chaos of the storm had transformed our little brewing haven into a frantic symphony of clattering bottles and fluttering tarps. I could hardly tell where the laughter ended and the panic began as we set to work. Jackson and I moved in a rhythm that felt oddly choreographed, our hands flying between securing the booth and checking on our precious ingredients. The rain pelted the tent like an orchestra gone rogue, but somehow, in the heart of the tempest, I felt invigorated.

"Alright, Mr. Sidekick," I said, tossing a playful glance his way. "What's our game plan for taking on the judges? Should we unleash our secret weapon now, or wait for the dramatic reveal?"

He raised an eyebrow, feigning deep contemplation. "I don't know. Maybe we should save it for a grand finale. Something like, 'And now, behold!' while we dramatically sweep aside the curtain to reveal... a very wet booth."

I snorted, nearly spilling the carefully measured hops in my hands. "If we keep this up, our grand reveal will be more like 'And now, behold our soggy mess!'"

He laughed, the sound mixing with the rhythm of the rain. "I'd still be proud. Besides, who knew brewing could be such an exhilarating cardio workout? You're really working up a sweat here."

"Oh, you think this is cardio?" I grinned, taking a deep breath as I began pouring the last of my ingredients into the mixing bowl. "Just wait until we have to haul these heavy kegs across the field for judging. That's when the real workout starts."

The atmosphere in the tent shifted as the competitors around us began to take notice of our infectious energy. More than a few heads turned, and I could see a spark of camaraderie igniting between the rival breweries, our shared struggle transforming competition into connection. It was amazing how quickly a storm could dissolve the barriers between us, drawing out laughter and encouragement instead of tension.

"Okay, let's get this brew finalized before the storm turns into a full-on monsoon," I said, stepping closer to Jackson as I prepared to mix the ingredients. "I think we need a little more of that secret twist, don't you?"

He leaned in, and I caught the warmth of his breath brushing against my ear as he whispered, "Only if you promise me one thing."

"What's that?" I asked, half-ignoring the way my heart raced at his proximity.

"No matter what happens, we'll keep this fun. We might end up soaking wet and completely mad, but we'll do it together."

"Deal," I said, unable to suppress a smile. "Besides, if I crash and burn, I can always blame you for my terrible choice in sidekicks."

"Fair enough," he said, his voice low and earnest. "But I'm going to need you to at least pretend to take some of the blame if we actually win."

"Now you're just getting greedy."

With a laugh, I poured the last of the citrus-infused concoction into our mixing bowl, the vibrant colors swirling together in a delightful dance. I could almost taste the freshness in the air, an invigorating mix of hops and sunshine battling against the looming clouds. My heart raced as I anticipated the magic of what we were about to create.

"Okay, let's do this," I said, raising my mixing spoon like a sword. "Together!"

With a flourish, I plunged the spoon into the mix, stirring with determination. Jackson joined in, his movements strong and steady beside me. Our eyes locked, and the moment felt charged with unspoken possibilities. The world around us faded into a blur as we became lost in the process, our laughter mingling with the sound of the storm, a joyful symphony that played only for us.

Just as we were about to pour the mixture into our brewing vessel, a sudden silence fell over the tent. The rain had lessened, but something else had entered the atmosphere—a tension that prickled at my skin. The other competitors had turned toward the entrance, their faces drawn with a mixture of disbelief and fear.

"What's happening?" I whispered, my heart skipping a beat.

Jackson followed my gaze, and his expression turned serious. "I don't know, but it doesn't look good."

The tent flap whipped open, revealing a figure silhouetted against the dim light outside. The wind howled, carrying the scent of rain and something else—a hint of smoke that curled ominously in the air. I squinted, trying to see past the figure, but the shadows obscured everything behind them.

"Ladies and gentlemen!" the figure boomed, their voice echoing through the space like a clarion call. "We have a situation!"

Jackson and I exchanged worried glances, and the energy in the tent shifted dramatically, a wave of tension sweeping through the competitors. I could feel my heart racing as the figure stepped into the light, revealing themselves to be a frazzled event coordinator, drenched but determined. "The river is rising dangerously fast. We need to evacuate!"

"Evacuate?" I echoed, my heart sinking. "But the competition—"

"Is at risk of being washed away!" they shouted, urgency dripping from their words. "We don't have much time. Grab your things and follow me!"

The tent erupted into chaos. Bottles clinked and clattered as competitors scrambled to pack up their brews, the thrill of the competition suddenly overshadowed by fear. My heart raced as I looked to Jackson, uncertainty clouding my thoughts. This was not how I envisioned this day unfolding, not when I was so close to making my mark.

"We can't leave yet," I insisted, my voice rising over the din. "I need to finish my brew!"

"Listen," Jackson said, grabbing my arm gently. "I know how much this means to you, but safety comes first. We'll have other chances. Let's get out of here."

I hesitated, the weight of my dreams heavy in my chest. But the rising tide of panic around us was infectious. I took one last look at my half-finished brew, a symbol of everything I had poured into this competition. It felt like a piece of me, just waiting to be unleashed.

"Fine," I relented, my voice shaky. "Let's grab what we can."

As we hastily stuffed supplies into our bags, the energy around us surged, each competitor driven by adrenaline. Jackson and I moved in sync, our hands flying as we raced against the clock. Just as we were about to make our escape, a loud crack echoed through the tent—an ominous sound that sent chills racing down my spine.

The lights flickered, and the tent shuddered as if in response. My heart dropped as I turned to see a nearby support pole splintering, the tent threatening to collapse in on itself. "We need to go—now!" I shouted, my voice barely cutting through the cacophony.

As we dashed for the exit, I caught one last glimpse of my brewing station, the ingredients swirling together in chaos, a bittersweet reminder of what was slipping away. Just then, another loud crack split the air, and the tent began to buckle.

"Run!" Jackson yelled, pulling me along as the fabric overhead began to cave in.

We stumbled out into the storm, the rain now pouring in earnest, but I felt a rush of determination surge through me. We were not just leaving; we were fighting against the rising tide of uncertainty.

But as we burst into the open, something caught my eye—something dark and swirling just beyond the riverbank. My breath caught in my throat as I realized that the river wasn't just rising; it was transforming, churning violently as if stirred by an unseen force.

And then, out of the mist, a shadow emerged—a boat, battered and tumbling in the angry waves, barreling toward us like a force of nature itself.

"Look out!" I screamed, yanking Jackson to the side as the world around us descended into chaos, and the storm surged ever higher.

# Chapter 13: Bitter and Sweet

The air was crisp, filled with the fragrant aftermath of the storm that had rolled through just hours before, leaving everything washed and vibrant under the now brilliant sun. A brilliant blue canvas stretched overhead, punctuated by a few defiant clouds that seemed reluctant to leave the stage. My heart raced, not just from the lingering energy of the tempest, but from the impending competition that had me teetering on the edge of excitement and anxiety. I could feel the pulse of the festival in my veins, a heady mix of anticipation and the overwhelming aroma of hops and malt that wafted from the nearby brewing tents.

I stood in front of my booth, which had transformed from a simple table into a tapestry of my labor—handcrafted signage, gleaming bottles of my special brew, and a smattering of colorful hops that lent a whimsical touch. Yet, beneath the surface of my carefully arranged display, I felt a thrum of insecurity. The stakes felt higher than ever, especially now that Ethan had decided to step up his game. He was here, by my side, a silent support with his hands tucked casually into his pockets, his demeanor more serious than I remembered. His presence was both reassuring and disconcerting, like a familiar song playing at the wrong tempo.

As I adjusted the labels on my bottles, I couldn't help but steal glances at him. Ethan had a way of commanding attention without even trying—his tousled hair glinted under the sun, and those deep-set eyes held a world of secrets that both intrigued and annoyed me. After everything, after the storm of our emotions, here he was, helping to make this day as perfect as it could be. I wanted to be mad at him for the confusion he had left in his wake, but part of me was thankful. Each shared glance seemed to weave us back together, thread by fragile thread, but with every soft smile, I felt the fragility of our situation.

"Are you ready?" he asked, breaking my reverie, his voice a low rumble that sent a shiver up my spine.

I shot him a wry smile. "Ready to either crush it or make a complete fool of myself?"

"Isn't that the spirit of competition?" he replied, his lips curving into that infuriating grin that seemed to promise mischief. "Either way, I'm here for it."

The warmth of his support wrapped around me like a comforting blanket, momentarily easing the simmering anxiety beneath the surface. Just then, the announcer's voice boomed through the crowd, vibrant and alive, sending a ripple of excitement through the assembled competitors and onlookers alike. The judges were making their rounds, and the weight of their scrutiny hung in the air like an electric charge.

As I prepared to showcase my brew, I caught sight of Jackson. He was across the way, his booth bursting with activity as his fans clamored for a taste of his latest creation. A swell of pride filled me as I watched him; he had worked hard for this moment. But pride quickly twisted into a pang of jealousy when I saw him sharing a laugh with another competitor, a woman with hair as bright as sunshine and a smile that could light up the gloomiest of days. I wanted to be happy for him, truly I did, but my heart betrayed me, twisting and tightening at the sight. It felt like a reminder of everything I was afraid of—his success, his charm, and the way he seemed to shine in every light.

"Hey, you're up!" Ethan nudged me gently, pulling me from my spiraling thoughts. "Don't let him distract you."

"Easier said than done," I muttered, taking a deep breath. With a flick of my wrist, I adjusted my hair, pushing aside the tangled emotions and stepping forward, ready to embrace whatever came next.

The moment my name echoed over the crowd, a strange mix of exhilaration and dread washed over me. I stepped up to my booth, the world fading to a dull roar around me. My hands trembled slightly as I poured a sample for the judges, their eyes scrutinizing every detail with an intensity that made my skin prickle. Each swirl of liquid seemed to mock my uncertainty, the subtle aromas wafting up like a siren's call. I focused on the moment, on the craft, on the passion that had brought me here.

"This is delightful," one of the judges said, taking a sip. Her eyebrows shot up in surprise, a smile breaking across her face. "You've really captured the essence of the season with this brew."

I grinned, my heart lifting, buoyed by her enthusiasm.

As the judges continued to sample my creation, I caught sight of Jackson again, and this time he was watching me. Our eyes met, and for a brief moment, the world around us faded. In that charged silence, something passed between us—a recognition, a connection. But before I could decipher it, the moment shattered as he turned his attention back to his own booth, laughter erupting from his friends.

My heart sank again, a reminder of the distance that remained, but there was no time to dwell. I had to stay focused. The judges were moving on, and my moment in the spotlight was slipping away like grains of sand.

The air buzzed with anticipation as they called for the next competitor, and I found myself retreating into my mind, piecing together the tattered threads of my emotions. With every passing moment, I realized that this brewing world was far more intricate than I had anticipated. With every turn, my feelings for Jackson became a tangled mess of hope and jealousy, each layer adding depth to my already complicated heart. The competition, the judges, and even the whispers of the crowd faded into the background. What mattered now was what came next.

As the competition wore on, the sun arched higher, illuminating the festival grounds in a warm glow that almost felt like a promise. I moved through the crowd, each step a cautious exploration of my emotions, careful not to trip over the remnants of my jealousy or the weight of my aspirations. Laughter and chatter floated around me, mingling with the clinking of glasses and the occasional shout of delight as someone sampled a particularly outstanding brew. It was a scene of joy, yet I couldn't shake the feeling of being slightly out of sync with the rhythm of the day.

Ethan, who had taken to mingling among the guests, cast a few sidelong glances my way. "You know, you could smile once in a while," he teased, sidling up to me after chatting with a group of enthusiasts. "You look like you're about to face a firing squad, not a beer festival."

"Thanks for the vote of confidence," I shot back, arching an eyebrow. "I'll add 'smile' to my list of brewing tips."

He chuckled, that infectious sound pulling me out of my internal spiral. "Seriously, you're doing great. Just remember to breathe. We don't want you passing out in front of the judges."

I rolled my eyes, playfully nudging him. "You're so supportive, you know that?"

"Always here for moral support," he grinned, brushing off the mockery as if it were a light dusting of flour.

And just like that, the tension in my shoulders eased a fraction. As I scanned the crowd, I caught a glimpse of Jackson again, surrounded by admirers, his charisma radiating like the sun that bathed the festival in warmth. He was in his element, a genuine smile lighting up his face, and I couldn't help but feel a bittersweet tug at my heart.

With the judges still roaming, I decided it was time to stretch my legs and gather my thoughts. I wandered towards a quieter area of the festival, where the noise faded into a low hum. A small wooden gazebo stood nearby, draped with fairy lights that twinkled like stars. I leaned against the railing, letting the gentle breeze cool my flushed cheeks.

"Lost in thought, or just lost?" a voice pulled me from my reverie.

I looked up to see Jackson approaching, his hands tucked into his pockets, the very picture of casual confidence. "I didn't realize I was on the menu for today's special," I replied, my tone teasing despite the fluttering in my chest.

He chuckled, his eyes crinkling at the corners. "It's a buffet of emotions today, isn't it? I mean, everyone's here showcasing their best, and yet..."

"Yet we're all hiding something," I finished for him, feeling a weight in my own heart.

Jackson stepped closer, his expression shifting from playful to sincere. "You've got something special brewing, you know. I tasted it. Your passion shines through."

"Passion doesn't always translate to success," I replied, a shadow of doubt creeping into my voice. "This world is brutal, and every good brew comes with a story that's not always sweet."

He leaned against the railing, mirroring my stance. "Aren't stories what make the best brews? It's all about the journey, not just the outcome. Besides, I think you're more formidable than you give yourself credit for."

My heart fluttered at his words, and yet, a nagging thought pulled me back. "Formidable, huh? Well, maybe it takes a little more than being formidable to break into this industry."

"Is that a challenge?" he asked, a playful glint in his eye.

"Maybe," I smirked, feeling emboldened. "Or maybe I just need a little motivation."

"Consider it given," he replied, laughter dancing in his voice. "But you have to promise me something. If you win today, you'll let me take you out to celebrate—my treat."

"And if I don't?" I asked, feigning nonchalance, though I felt the weight of his challenge.

"Then you'll let me buy you a drink, and we can commiserate over our losses. Deal?"

"Deal," I said, and a strange thrill surged through me, one that felt less about the competition and more about the connection we were forging—layer by layer, with every conversation and shared glance.

Just as the tension between us began to crackle, a commotion pulled my attention back to the festival. A cluster of competitors erupted into laughter, pointing toward the judges who had gathered at the edge of the lawn. Apparently, one of them had tripped over a rogue cooler, sending a cascade of bottles clattering to the ground. I couldn't help but laugh at the sight; even the judges weren't immune to the chaos of the day.

"See? Everyone's human," Jackson said, chuckling at the scene. "Even the ones with the power to make or break us."

"Right?" I replied, amusement dancing in my voice. "We're all just a few misplaced bottles away from disaster."

He met my gaze, and I sensed the moment stretch between us, charged with possibilities. Yet, before I could delve deeper into the tangled threads of my feelings, a loud cheer erupted from the crowd, drawing our attention back to the main stage.

"Looks like they're announcing some awards," Jackson said, his tone shifting back to the gravity of the moment. "You should head back."

"Right, the show must go on," I murmured, though the flicker of nerves stirred in my stomach.

As we made our way back through the crowd, the announcer's voice echoed, drawing every ear toward the stage. "And now, for a special recognition award..."

My heart raced in tandem with the crowd's mounting excitement. I stood tall, forcing my breath to slow as I leaned into the atmosphere, feeling every heartbeat resonating around me. Jackson stood beside me, a steady presence that somehow anchored my swirling thoughts.

"And the award goes to... Jackson Harper!"

The crowd erupted in applause, and I found myself clapping as well, a surge of pride filling me despite the small twinge of jealousy that followed. He stepped forward, grinning widely as he accepted the award, his enthusiasm palpable.

In that moment, watching him shine, I felt an unexpected warmth wash over me. I knew I had to celebrate his victory, even as the emotions tangled within me like vines. But deep down, beneath the celebration, I recognized that this brewing world was only becoming more intricate, more compelling, and even more bittersweet.

As the applause for Jackson faded, I couldn't shake the buoyancy in the air, a mix of celebration and the heavy charge of unspoken words swirling around us like the aromas of the competing brews. Jackson was all smiles, basking in the limelight, and it made my heart flutter with a blend of admiration and an unexpected pinch of longing. I was still standing near the stage, trying to capture the moment in my mind while the world around me began to buzz with renewed energy.

"Congratulations, Jackson!" I called, waving my hand through the crowd to get his attention. As he turned, the genuine joy on his face was contagious, and for a moment, the pang of jealousy faded, replaced by the warmth of shared happiness.

"Thanks! You should've seen my face when they called my name!" he exclaimed, his eyes sparkling like the trophies they handed out. "I thought I was going to trip over my own feet."

"Your face was priceless. Like a kid on Christmas morning." I chuckled, trying to keep the mood light while my heart tugged me in another direction. "Did you thank your fan club?"

He gestured to the small crowd still clamoring around him, a group of competitors and admirers hanging on his every word. "I tried! But it's hard to be gracious when everyone's asking for selfies. I think I'll need an agent soon."

"Oh, definitely. You're going to need one to navigate your stardom in the brewing world." I smirked, but beneath the playful banter, I could feel a longing building in my chest. "What's next for you, rock star?"

Before he could respond, Ethan appeared at my side, his expression unreadable. "We should probably get back to the booth. The judges will be wrapping up soon, and I'd hate to miss their verdict on your brew."

I shot Ethan a quick glance, half-expecting to see a hint of possessiveness in his demeanor, but all I saw was concern. "Right," I said, forcing myself to pivot back to the task at hand, even though I could feel the weight of Jackson's gaze still lingering on me.

As we walked back, Ethan fell into step beside me, his presence both grounding and oddly unsettling. "You did great out there," he said, his tone genuine. "I mean it. You handled the pressure like a pro."

"Thanks. But I think I still need a few more practice rounds before I can confidently call myself a pro."

Ethan smirked. "You're way ahead of the curve. Just wait until you see the judges' reactions to your brew. They're going to be blown away."

The crowd around us swelled, a tide of excitement carrying us forward as the announcer prepared to reveal the competition's winners. My heart raced; this moment felt monumental, as if the culmination of all my hard work hung in the balance. I glanced over my shoulder, catching Jackson still mingling, his laughter ringing like a bell through the festival's cacophony.

"Should we start a betting pool for who wins?" Ethan mused, trying to lighten the mood as we reached our booth, though I sensed a tension creeping back into his words. "I'll put ten bucks on you, just to keep the stakes interesting."

"You're going to regret that if I flop," I joked, but my smile didn't quite reach my eyes.

"We both know you're not going to flop. Just look at you." He paused, studying me with an intensity that made my breath hitch. "You've got this. I believe in you."

His confidence was almost tangible, and I found myself needing that affirmation. "Thanks, Ethan. I really appreciate it."

Just then, the announcer's voice broke through the chatter, crisp and authoritative. "And now, for the moment you've all been waiting for—the winners of this year's brewing competition!"

I felt my heart leap into my throat, a rush of adrenaline coursing through my veins as I tried to focus on the announcer's words. "First up, the award for Best in Show..."

The crowd quieted, and I could hear the sound of my heart pounding in my ears. Every fiber of my being was on high alert as I clung to Ethan's reassuring presence.

"...the award goes to... Bree Hartley!"

A wave of shock washed over me, quickly morphing into exhilaration as the crowd erupted into applause. I felt a jolt of disbelief, followed by the realization that my name had been called. As I stepped forward, the applause faded into a mix of cheers and gasps, and I could hardly hear the announcer over the pounding in my chest.

"Bree, come on up!" Ethan urged, giving me a gentle push toward the stage.

I felt like a deer in headlights, my mind racing, but I managed to smile, lifting my chin as I made my way to the front. The spotlight washed over me, warm and inviting, but it also felt like a spotlight on all my insecurities. My hands trembled as I accepted the award, the cold metal grounding me in this surreal moment.

"Congratulations, Bree!" the announcer beamed, his enthusiasm contagious. "Tell us about your winning brew!"

I opened my mouth, the words a jumble in my brain, but the cheers from the crowd spurred me on. "Thank you! I created this brew to embody the spirit of the season—a blend of autumn flavors, rich and complex, just like the journey that led me here."

As I spoke, I saw Jackson in the crowd, his expression a mix of pride and admiration. The warmth from the applause washed over me like a wave, but in that moment, I noticed something out of the corner of my eye.

A shadow moved behind the crowd, a figure I couldn't quite make out, but something about it made my heart race for entirely different reasons. I scanned the faces in the audience, searching for clarity, but the crowd shifted, blocking my view.

"I couldn't have done this without the support of my friends and my partner, Ethan," I continued, hoping to pull my focus back to the moment, but my thoughts were fraying at the edges. The weight of the award felt heavier in my hands, a stark reminder of the complexities that lay beneath the surface of this victory.

Just as I wrapped up my speech, the shadow materialized again, clearer this time, and my breath caught in my throat. A figure slipped out from behind the crowd, and with it came a familiar face, one I thought I had left behind.

"Surprise!" came a voice, lilting and playful, cutting through the noise of the festival.

I froze, my heart dropping as I stared in disbelief. It was her, the ghost of my past—a specter I thought I'd never have to face again. My mind raced, emotions crashing over me like the tide, and the applause faded into a distant roar.

This brewing world was far more complicated than I could have ever imagined, and just when I thought I had carved out my space, the past had a way of rising to the surface, ready to throw everything into chaos once more.

# Chapter 14: The Rising Tide

The scent of malt and hops swirled around me, intoxicating and familiar, like a warm embrace from a long-lost friend. My hands moved instinctively, pouring and stirring, the rhythmic clinking of glass and metal providing a sort of soundtrack to my brewing ritual. Each batch I crafted felt like an extension of myself, a reflection of my hopes and dreams—something tangible I could cling to while everything around me threatened to unravel. It was an anchor in the storm brewing within my heart.

Ethan was my partner in this venture, his laughter cutting through the tension like a sudden gust of wind through the stillness. He had this way of lighting up the dim corners of my mind, the shadows where doubt liked to lurk. "Are you trying to brew your worries away?" he teased one afternoon as he handed me a fresh bag of hops, his dark curls falling just slightly over his brow. His smirk was a mixture of mischief and understanding, and it tugged at something deep within me.

"Maybe," I replied, a smile breaking through my earlier somber mood. "Or I might just be channeling my inner mad scientist." I scooped the hops into the brew kettle, relishing the way the earthy aroma enveloped us. "If you're lucky, I might just create a potion to keep you around a little longer." The words slipped out before I could second-guess their weight, but Ethan's eyes sparkled with amusement, even as a flicker of something deeper lingered in the air between us.

He leaned against the counter, arms crossed, watching me as if I were a captivating puzzle he was desperate to solve. "You know, you could just ask me to stay. No potions necessary." His voice was light, but there was an undercurrent of seriousness, a suggestion that made my heart race.

The moment hung there, charged with unspoken implications. My mind drifted to Jackson—the impending job offer, the bittersweet way he'd spoken about his dreams. I had always admired his ambition, his relentless pursuit of a future that beckoned him. But now, with the threat of his departure looming over me, I felt like I was on the edge of a cliff, my heart dangling dangerously close to the abyss.

"Speaking of staying," I began, forcing myself to break the tension. "Have you thought any more about that recipe for the seasonal brew? I was thinking something with a hint of citrus..." I trailed off, but the conversation had shifted in a way I wasn't ready to confront. Ethan nodded, a thoughtful expression crossing his face as he focused on the brewing process rather than the charged atmosphere.

Yet, even as we resumed our work, my thoughts spun like the grains swirling in the mash. Each measured step in the brewing process felt heavier, weighed down by the thought of Jackson packing his bags and walking away from everything we'd built. Every laughter-filled moment we'd shared echoed in my mind, memories colliding with the harsh reality that our shared dreams could soon fade into mere memories.

As the week unfolded, Jackson's news became an unwelcome specter in my mind. He hadn't said much beyond the job offer—just enough to leave me in a whirlwind of emotions, spinning between pride and fear. I admired his ambition, his desire to chase his dreams, yet the thought of him leaving felt like losing a piece of myself. I tried to drown out my worries in brewing, pouring my frustration and desperation into each batch, my fingers deftly weaving through the ingredients, creating something new, something hopeful.

"Hey," Ethan said one evening, catching me mid-pour as I tried to balance an overwhelming tide of emotions. "You've been a bit quiet. Is everything okay?" His gaze was steady, and I knew he could see through my carefully crafted facade.

I took a breath, the sweet and bitter aroma of the brew mixing in the air, filling my lungs with courage. "I just... I don't know how to handle this Jackson situation," I admitted, my voice barely above a whisper. "He's considering taking this job, and I can't help but feel like everything we've built is crumbling." I ran a hand through my hair, the frustration and sadness spilling over. "It feels selfish to want him to stay, but how can I not fight for something that means so much to me?"

Ethan's expression shifted, the playfulness giving way to a serious contemplation. "You have to tell him how you feel. If he's important to you, you can't just stand back and hope he'll make the right choice." His words hung in the air, resonating with the truth that my heart already knew. But it was so much easier to hide behind the brew kettle than to confront the raw reality of my feelings.

"I don't want to be that person," I murmured. "What if it makes him feel trapped? I wouldn't want him to choose me out of obligation." The irony wasn't lost on me; I was living in a world built on choices and flavors, yet the thought of laying my heart on the line felt like standing naked in front of a crowd.

"Sometimes the hardest choices lead to the best outcomes," Ethan replied gently, his eyes meeting mine with a sincerity that sent shivers down my spine. "You'll never know if you don't try."

As the evening wore on, I found myself standing in the dim light of the brewery, the weight of my uncertainty pressing down like the last grains of sugar before fermentation. The rising tide of my emotions surged, a tempest brewing just beneath the surface, threatening to spill over. I knew I had to take a leap—into the unknown, into the vulnerability that came with laying my heart bare.

The following days passed in a haze of hops and malt, each brewing session becoming a sanctuary for my swirling thoughts. I found myself retreating to the brewery, inhaling deeply the comforting aromas as I lost myself in the rhythm of the process. Each boil, each stir of the mash, felt like an exercise in alchemy, transforming the weight of my worries into something vibrant and effervescent. Ethan and I had begun to sync in our creativity, bouncing ideas back and forth like the bubbles rising in a freshly poured pint, and for that brief time, I felt lighter.

"Okay, hear me out," Ethan said one evening, his eyes gleaming with mischief as he tossed a slice of orange into the air like a juggler. "What if we named our new brew 'Ethan's Elixir' and marketed it as a cure for heartbreak?"

I raised an eyebrow, pretending to consider his suggestion seriously. "Are you sure that wouldn't just exacerbate the heartbreak? People might end up drowning their sorrows instead of healing them." I couldn't help but laugh, the sound bursting out of me, lightening the tension that had coiled in my chest for far too long.

"Maybe that's the point," he shot back, mock seriousness etched on his face. "You know, there's a fine line between healing and forgetting." He leaned closer, the space between us shrinking, and my heart raced as I realized just how charged our banter had become. "Besides, what better way to deal with heartbreak than over a good drink?"

A warmth spread through me at his teasing. It was easy to lose myself in the laughter, to forget the storm brewing outside the brewery door. But that storm loomed ever closer, the reality of Jackson's impending departure darkening the edges of my happiness. The laughter faded, replaced by the weight of my thoughts pressing down like an unrelenting tide.

As we prepared for the local brew festival—a showcase of our hard work and creativity—my mind kept circling back to Jackson. He had not brought up the job offer again, leaving a gaping hole in our conversations. Each time I tried to navigate the topic, the words caught in my throat, tangled in a mess of conflicting emotions. I felt like a ship lost at sea, desperately searching for a lighthouse to guide me home.

"Hey, you've got that look again," Ethan remarked one afternoon, his tone shifting from playful to concerned as he studied me over the rim of a glass filled with our latest batch. "What's going on in that brilliant mind of yours?"

"Just thinking about Jackson," I confessed, my voice softer than I intended. "He hasn't really talked about the job since that day. It's like... it's hanging over us like a cloud, and I don't know how to clear it."

Ethan nodded slowly, his expression shifting into something more serious. "You can't let fear keep you from saying what you feel. You deserve to know where you stand, and so does he."

His words echoed in my mind as the festival approached, the buzz of excitement mingling with my dread. I needed to talk to Jackson, to lay bare my heart and face whatever came next, but a part of me hesitated. What if he decided to leave? What if I lost him and the bridge we'd built together crumbled under the weight of my own vulnerability?

The night before the festival, I stood in the brewery, the soft glow of the overhead lights casting a warm halo around me as I checked our final preparations. Ethan had gone home, leaving me alone with my thoughts and the clattering of bottles lining the shelves. I poured myself a small sample of our latest brew, the golden liquid sparkling like liquid sunshine in my glass. I raised it to my lips, letting the crisp flavors wash over me—floral notes dancing on my tongue, a hint of bitterness grounding it.

"Here's to new beginnings," I murmured to the empty room, my reflection glimmering back at me from the glass. The silence enveloped me, but I couldn't escape the sense of urgency building within.

I glanced at my phone, its screen illuminating with a message from Jackson. My heart raced as I opened it, my pulse quickening with every word I read: Hey! Can we meet tomorrow before the festival? I have something to talk about.

My stomach dropped, a mix of anxiety and hope swirling together in a chaotic dance. This could be it—the moment I'd been dreading and yearning for. I tapped back a quick response, my fingers shaking slightly: Absolutely. Can't wait to see you.

I spent the night tossing and turning, the excitement and trepidation battling for dominance. Morning came too soon, the sun shining brightly as I threw on my favorite flannel, the one that made me feel both cozy and brave. I brewed a pot of coffee, letting the rich aroma seep into my bones as I mentally prepared myself for what lay ahead.

The festival grounds buzzed with activity, a cacophony of laughter, music, and the tantalizing scents of various brews wafting through the air. Colorful banners fluttered in the breeze, each stall brimming with life. I set up our booth, my hands moving on autopilot as I arranged the bottles and promotional materials, but my mind was elsewhere—on Jackson, on the conversation we were about to have.

Finally, he arrived, a wave of energy following him as he approached, his smile as bright as the sun overhead. "Hey!" he called out, his voice cutting through the noise. "You look great!"

"Thanks! You're not so bad yourself." I flashed him a grin, my heart racing as I gestured toward the booth. "Ready to show off our masterpiece?"

"Absolutely." He stepped behind the counter, his presence bringing an ease to the chaos. As we poured samples for eager festival-goers, I stole glances at him, the way his hands moved effortlessly, the laughter that came easily. But beneath the surface, a current of tension simmered, a reminder of the conversation waiting just beneath our playful banter.

After a flurry of customers, we found a moment of reprieve, leaning against the table as the sun began to dip low in the sky, casting a warm glow over everything. "So," I began, my voice steady despite the storm in my chest, "you wanted to talk?"

Jackson's expression shifted, the lightheartedness replaced by something heavier. "Yeah, I've been doing a lot of thinking since I got that job offer." He paused, taking a deep breath, and my heart thudded in my chest, an anxious rhythm echoing my unease.

"I can't help but feel like this might change everything between us," he continued, his gaze steady, unwavering. "I want to be honest with you about what I'm feeling."

The air crackled with anticipation as he spoke, the festival fading into the background, our surroundings blurring into a distant hum. I held my breath, knowing this moment could either tether us closer or set us adrift in opposing currents.

The warmth of Jackson's gaze sent a flutter through my chest as he leaned against the booth, the sounds of the festival fading into a distant hum. "I don't want to leave," he said, his voice steady but tinged with an unmistakable gravity. "But this job... it's everything I've been working toward. It feels like the right next step, you know?"

"Of course, I get that." My mind raced, scrambling to grasp the reality of his words. The bittersweet truth settled in the pit of my stomach like a heavy stone. "But what about everything we've built here? What about us?" The words tumbled out before I could catch them, raw and unfiltered.

Jackson ran a hand through his hair, a nervous habit of his that I had come to recognize all too well. "That's the thing. I care about you, I really do. But if I take this job, it could change everything for me. I'd be in a different city, a different world." His eyes searched mine, a mixture of hope and fear swimming within them. "I just need to know if we can make this work, even if I'm not here physically."

The tension in the air crackled like static electricity, and I fought to keep my composure. "Jackson, this isn't just about distance. This is about the life we're building together, isn't it? Can we really say we're in this if we're miles apart?"

He opened his mouth to respond, but the moment stretched long and taut, each heartbeat echoing in the silence. My mind flickered back to the late nights we had spent in the brewery, the laughter, the warmth of our friendship blossoming into something deeper. But now, standing on the precipice of a decision, everything felt precarious, as if the slightest misstep could send us tumbling into an abyss.

"I don't want to lose you," Jackson finally said, his voice barely above a whisper. The sincerity in his tone pierced through the walls I had built around my heart. "You've become such an important part of my life, and I can't imagine leaving without trying to figure this out."

I took a deep breath, forcing my mind to sift through the jumbled emotions swirling inside me. "Then let's talk about it. Let's figure out how we can make it work, because I'm not ready to just let this go." My voice gained strength with each word, buoyed by a fierce determination that surprised me. "If this is meant to be, we'll find a way."

As if summoned by the universe, Ethan appeared at the edge of our booth, his expression shifting from playful to concerned as he sensed the weight of the conversation. "Hey, everything good over here?" He offered a quick smile, but the warmth didn't quite reach his eyes.

"Yeah," I said too quickly, still locking eyes with Jackson. "Just figuring some stuff out." I could sense the unspoken questions hanging between us, a tension threading through the air that Ethan wasn't quite ready to dissect.

"Alright, but let me know if you need anything," he replied, his gaze lingering on Jackson for just a moment longer before he turned to help a customer.

Jackson's eyes flickered back to me, his brow furrowing slightly. "Is it weird that I want to talk about this in front of him?"

I shook my head, the chaos of my thoughts swirling like the last few drops of beer left in a pint. "Not at all. If anything, it feels more real this way. We're all in this together, right?"

"Together," he echoed, his gaze intense. "That's what I'm afraid of losing. I don't want to be the guy who chases his dreams at the expense of the people he cares about."

"Then don't be that guy," I said, my voice resolute. "You have the chance to build something incredible for yourself, and I want to support you. But we need to figure out how to keep this connection alive."

The festival buzzed around us, the excitement palpable, yet all I could focus on was the magnetic pull between us. Jackson took a deep breath, as if steeling himself for what came next. "What if I told you I was thinking of taking a leave of absence instead? Just to give us time to figure things out?"

I blinked, the proposition settling over me like a warm blanket. "Are you serious? You'd really do that?" The prospect was both exhilarating and terrifying. The thought of him delaying a dream felt like a safety net being stretched taut, and I could only hope it would hold.

"I mean, it's a risk, but so is everything else, right? You could start exploring new ideas, and I'd be here, trying to make it work between us." The earnestness in his eyes spoke volumes, igniting a flicker of hope within me.

"And what about the job? They might not be willing to wait," I replied, a frown creasing my forehead. The reality of the situation loomed large, dark clouds gathering around the edges of our hopeful conversation.

Jackson shrugged, a hint of mischief flashing in his smile. "Let them come to me. It's not every day you get an offer like this, but it's also not every day you realize what really matters."

A rush of warmth flooded through me, a bittersweet blend of admiration and fear. "You're going to make this decision with your heart, aren't you?" I said, half-teasing, half-incredulous.

"Isn't that what we're all trying to do?" He leaned closer, the space between us shrinking as the festival lights twinkled like stars above. "Just figuring it out as we go."

I swallowed hard, battling a sudden wave of emotions. "It's a big risk, Jackson."

"It is," he replied softly, a hint of uncertainty clouding his expression. "But maybe it's a risk worth taking."

The moment lingered, charged and potent. Just as I felt my pulse quicken in response to the weight of his words, a loud crash erupted from nearby—a toppled stall, glass shattering against the ground, punctuating the air with chaos.

Startled, we both turned our heads, the sudden noise yanking us from our intimate cocoon. As the crowd gasped and rushed to help, I caught sight of Ethan sprinting toward the commotion. My heart sank as I followed him, the brief connection between Jackson and me feeling fragile and fleeting.

"Stay here!" I shouted to Jackson over the noise, my instincts kicking in as I dashed after Ethan. The scene unfolded like a slow-motion disaster—people scrambling, a vendor shouting for help. It was as if the world had shifted on its axis, throwing everything into disarray.

As I reached the stall, I caught a glimpse of Ethan, kneeling to help a woman who had fallen, her ankle twisted at an unnatural angle. "I need some ice!" he yelled, and I rushed forward, panic surging through me.

"Right here!" I grabbed a nearby cooler, ready to help, but as I turned back, Jackson stood a few paces away, his expression unreadable. The uncertainty of our conversation faded momentarily, replaced by the chaos of the festival.

And just when I thought I could catch my breath, I saw Jackson's face transform from concern to something darker as he spoke to someone just beyond my line of sight. The words were muffled, but the intensity in his eyes sent a shiver down my spine.

"Wait, what are you saying?" My heart raced as I edged closer, the world around me fading into a blur.

Jackson's jaw tightened, and I strained to hear, but the festival sounds roared back to life, drowning out the critical moment unfolding before me. The rush of bodies and noise created a disorienting whirlwind, but as I leaned in closer, the truth began to crystallize.

He looked over at me, his expression shifting from concern to something more profound, and in that instant, the very foundation of our conversation cracked beneath my feet. I had just realized that what I thought was an offer for a new beginning might instead be a stark ultimatum.

# Chapter 15: Brewing Connections

The evening air wrapped around us like a warm, comforting blanket, the soft hum of laughter and clinking glasses drifting up from the brewery below. The rooftop was a hidden gem, a place where the city felt like a living, breathing entity—each flickering light a heartbeat pulsing in the night. I could see the glow of the sunset lingering on the horizon, its hues of orange and pink surrendering to the deep navy of twilight, and for a moment, I let myself forget the weight of the world. I focused instead on the man beside me, Jackson, his presence a steady anchor amidst the swirling tide of my thoughts.

"Why do you look like you're contemplating the meaning of life?" he quipped, a playful grin spreading across his face, illuminated by the string lights strung overhead. The warm glow danced across his features, revealing the lines of worry etched into his brow. I knew that grin well—it was the one that told me he was trying to lighten the mood, to keep me from spiraling into the vortex of my own fears.

I chuckled, a soft sound that felt foreign amid the tension bubbling beneath the surface. "I guess I'm just thinking about how it feels to have everything you want within reach but still feel like you might lose it all at any moment." The honesty of my words hung in the air between us, heavy yet freeing.

His laughter faded, replaced by a more serious expression. "You're not going to lose me, you know. Unless you push me away." There was a gentleness in his tone that made my heart clench, a truth I couldn't ignore. I turned my gaze to the skyline, trying to steady my racing heart, yet all I could see was the very real possibility of our lives taking drastically different paths.

"Do you think I want to push you away?" I asked, my voice a mere whisper as I sought the courage to unravel the tangled emotions swirling within me. "I got this job offer, Jackson. It's everything I've worked for, and yet... here we are." The words tasted bitter on my tongue, a sharp contrast to the sweet beer we'd been sipping, each sip a reminder of the carefree moments we shared before this weight settled between us.

"You're terrified, and you have every right to be," he said, his eyes locking onto mine, intense and unwavering. "But it's not just you who's scared. I feel it too."

I wanted to reach out, to close the distance between us, but I felt stuck—caught in a web of expectations and dreams that felt both tantalizing and suffocating. "I don't want to lose you, Jackson. This job could take me away from here, from us. What if it changes everything?"

He leaned back, the wood of the rooftop creaking under him, the cool metal railing framing his silhouette against the starry sky. "What if it doesn't? What if it opens new doors for both of us? You deserve to chase your dreams, and I want to be there to cheer you on. But I also want you to know that I'm here for you, no matter where you go."

The sincerity of his words struck a chord deep within me, resonating in a way that felt both terrifying and exhilarating. I could see the weight of family expectations etched in his eyes, the pressure he felt to uphold a legacy that felt more like a shackle than a blessing. It was a burden I understood all too well. "You're carrying a lot on your shoulders, aren't you?"

He sighed, a sound filled with resignation. "My family has this vision for me, for what I should be doing with my life. But the truth is, I don't always want that. I want to carve my own path, just like you."

The vulnerability in his admission made my heart ache, and I could feel the walls between us crumbling. We were two lost souls, standing at a crossroads, clinging to the hope that together we could forge a new direction. "Maybe we can help each other," I suggested, my voice soft yet resolute. "Support each other as we figure this out."

"Yeah?" His smile returned, lighting up his face like the stars above us. "You'd want to be my partner in crime? The two of us against the world?"

"Always," I replied, a spark of joy igniting within me. But then the reminder of the looming decision settled heavily in my stomach again, a ghost that wouldn't let go. "I just... I don't want to be the reason you feel like you have to choose between me and your family. That's not fair."

He reached over, taking my hand in his, the warmth of his touch sending ripples of comfort through me. "And I don't want you to feel like you have to choose between your dreams and me. We're not just one thing, you know? We can be many things—friends, lovers, dreamers. Whatever we make of it."

There was a sweetness in his gaze, a tenderness that made my heart race. In that moment, I felt the barriers fall away, revealing the raw honesty we both craved. "What if we make a pact?" I proposed, my eyes searching his for any hint of hesitation. "A promise to always communicate, no matter what happens? If one of us feels like we're drifting, we talk it out."

"I love that idea," he said, squeezing my hand gently, sealing the promise with a shared warmth that sent a rush of hope surging through me. The stars twinkled above, a silent witness to our fragile yet fierce connection, and for the first time in a long while, I felt like we were ready to face whatever came next together.

The night air shimmered with possibilities, the gentle murmur of the city below a reminder of the life that pulsed just outside our little bubble. Jackson's hand still held mine, our fingers intertwined, a lifeline anchoring me to the moment. We were standing on the precipice of something beautiful, yet the shadows of uncertainty loomed just out of reach, their whispers curling around us like smoke. I stole a glance at him, his profile stark against the star-speckled sky, and felt a pang of determination. I had to be brave.

"Okay," I said, breaking the weighty silence that wrapped around us like a fog. "Let's pretend I take this job. What does that mean for us?" My heart thudded, the question hanging heavy in the air, laced with both hope and dread.

Jackson tilted his head, considering. "Well, if you take it, we get to visit each other in new cities. You could show me the best local coffee spots, and I'd drag you to every brewery I could find. Think of it as a never-ending adventure." He flashed that mischievous grin that made my stomach flutter, and for a heartbeat, the weight lifted, the future momentarily brightening.

I laughed, the sound a mixture of disbelief and affection. "You think I'll just hop on a plane every weekend? Have you seen my bank account? I can barely afford lunch, let alone a round-trip flight to visit my favorite guy in another state."

"Touché," he conceded, leaning closer, the playful glint in his eyes returning. "But that's what credit cards are for, right? We could get matching ones and call it our 'couples' travel fund.'"

The absurdity of the idea made me chuckle, yet I couldn't help but notice how quickly he'd pivoted to make light of my fears. His charm was both a blessing and a curse, a way of sidestepping the deeper conversation that still loomed over us like an uninvited guest. "Jackson, seriously," I said, my tone shifting slightly, the laughter fading into something more somber. "What happens if we grow apart? I can't just pretend that won't happen."

He paused, the easy banter evaporating, replaced by an earnestness that made my heart race. "You think I'm going to let some distance come between us? I'm not that easy to shake off."

"Have you ever tried?" I asked, raising an eyebrow. "You could just as easily put your family's expectations ahead of everything else."

His expression turned contemplative. "You know, you're right. But I don't want to be that person. I want to fight for what we have." The sincerity in his voice sent a thrill through me, but doubt still clung to the edges of my thoughts. "Besides," he added, a grin creeping back onto his face, "I have a feeling you're not the type to give up without a good fight either."

"Damn straight," I replied, matching his grin with one of my own, but the unease still tugged at my insides. Our laughter faded into a comfortable silence, the city lights winking at us like old friends, as if encouraging our burgeoning connection.

The conversation shifted, weaving in and out of the more mundane aspects of life, like the ridiculous new trend of pineapple on pizza or whether cereal was a soup. As Jackson argued passionately for the pizza toppings, I found myself stealing glances at him, my heart swelling with affection. There was something intoxicating about his passion, the way he brought life to even the most trivial topics, igniting my own enthusiasm.

But beneath the banter, the shadows of reality lingered, reminding me of the uncertainty that lay ahead. "You know," I started, hesitant but compelled to share more of myself. "My dad always wanted me to take over his business. He had this vision of a family legacy, and for years, I tried to fit into that mold. But it never felt right. I've always wanted something different, something I could call my own."

Jackson nodded, his eyes softening as he listened. "That's tough. I get it. My family has always had plans for me too—expectations that sometimes feel like a weight I can't escape. But you're breaking free, and that's something to be proud of."

"Yet, here I am, terrified to make that leap," I confessed, my voice barely above a whisper. "What if I choose my dreams and it means sacrificing what we have?"

"Let's not think of it as a sacrifice," he replied, his tone firm yet gentle. "Think of it as investing in yourself. And if I'm being honest, I want you to take that leap. You're too talented not to."

The warmth of his encouragement enveloped me like a well-worn blanket, soothing the jagged edges of my anxiety. "You really believe that?" I asked, surprised by the wave of gratitude that washed over me.

"Absolutely. But only if you believe it too," he replied, his gaze piercing yet tender. The intensity of our connection wrapped around us like a shroud, the world beyond the rooftop fading into a hazy blur.

"Okay, I'll try," I said, my voice firming with conviction, though the uncertainties still danced in my mind. "But you have to promise me something in return."

"Anything," he said, leaning in, the atmosphere crackling with anticipation.

"If things get complicated, we have to talk about it. No ignoring it, no pretending it doesn't exist. Just... honest conversations, no matter how hard they might be."

He nodded solemnly, the gravity of my words sinking in. "Agreed. No matter what. I promise."

Our eyes locked, an unspoken understanding passing between us, the weight of our promises creating a bond that felt almost palpable. The breeze whispered through the rooftop, rustling the leaves of the small potted plants scattered around, as if applauding our shared resolve.

Just as I felt the sense of clarity settle in, a loud crash shattered the moment. We turned to see a group of rowdy patrons spilling onto the rooftop, laughter echoing like a mischievous storm. The sudden intrusion broke our spell, and I couldn't help but chuckle at the irony of it all.

"See?" Jackson said, his eyes sparkling with mischief. "Even the universe can't resist crashing our moment. Maybe it's a sign that we should take this leap together, no matter how chaotic it gets."

I laughed, the tension easing as I absorbed his infectious energy. "Well, if that's the case, then bring on the chaos. I'm ready."

With a shared grin, we turned back to the bustling crowd, the night alive with possibilities, and for the first time in a long while, the future felt less like a weight and more like an open road stretching before us.

The rooftop pulsed with energy as the group of rowdy patrons commandeered the space, their laughter brightening the air. Suddenly, the night felt less like an intimate haven and more like a lively carnival, the infectious buzz sweeping away the weight of our earlier conversation. I caught Jackson's eye, his grin widening in response to my raised eyebrow, and we exchanged knowing glances that seemed to say, "Well, this should be interesting."

As they settled in around us, claiming tables and spilling drinks, I leaned closer to Jackson, our earlier promises lingering in the air like a delicate web. "So much for our heartfelt moment, huh?" I teased, trying to reclaim the lightness of the night.

He chuckled, his eyes dancing with mischief. "What's a little chaos among friends? I'd say it adds a nice touch of unpredictability."

"Unpredictable is one way to put it," I replied, feigning a serious tone as I surveyed the boisterous group. "More like a tornado of joy and questionable life choices."

Jackson laughed, and I loved that sound—rich and genuine. We both knew we had stepped into a new dynamic, where laughter served as a balm to the insecurities lingering in our hearts. The chaos of the crowd blurred the lines of our previous conversation, and I found myself drawn into the whirlpool of energy around us.

As I turned my attention back to the group, I was greeted by the sight of an exuberant woman in a bright floral dress, balancing a tray of drinks like a circus performer. "Get ready for a toast!" she announced, her voice bubbling with enthusiasm. "Tonight, we celebrate life, love, and the thrill of not knowing what tomorrow brings!"

The crowd erupted in cheers, glasses clinking together in a joyful cacophony. I smiled, swept up in the moment, though a part of me remained tethered to the thoughts that had danced in my mind only moments before. Jackson nudged my shoulder, and I turned to him, my heart racing as his playful expression beckoned for my attention.

"Think we should join in?" he asked, gesturing to the makeshift celebration. "It could be a good distraction."

"Distraction?" I echoed, raising an eyebrow. "Or a calculated risk? This feels like the perfect setup for a disastrous karaoke moment."

"Disastrous is just another word for unforgettable," he shot back, his eyes gleaming with challenge. "Come on, let's make some memories."

With a deep breath, I nodded, my pulse quickening at the thought of stepping into the unknown. Together, we wove through the crowd, the warmth of the evening wrapping around us like an embrace. Jackson grabbed a couple of drinks—one for each of us—and handed me mine with a flourish.

"Your magic potion," he declared, raising his glass. "To the unpredictable journey ahead."

I clinked my glass against his, the sound ringing clear amidst the joyful noise. "To the adventure!" I replied, and as I took a sip, I felt the vibrant energy of the night seep into my bones. It was exhilarating and terrifying all at once.

As the night wore on, we found ourselves immersed in conversation with new friends, sharing stories, laughter, and even the occasional toast. Jackson's presence remained a constant source of strength beside me, and I marveled at how easy it was to let go, even just for a moment. Yet, beneath the laughter, a flicker of unease lingered—a reminder of the unresolved tension tethered between us.

The crowd began to drift into spontaneous games, one of which involved a rather enthusiastic game of "Truth or Dare." As the group huddled together, I caught Jackson's eye and smirked. "Ready to face your demons?"

He grinned back, mischief dancing in his gaze. "Only if you are."

I felt the thrill of challenge ignite between us. The group called for a dare, and Jackson, with his trademark bravado, volunteered first. "I dare you to serenade the person you find the most attractive here," he declared, casting a cheeky glance my way.

Gasps and laughter erupted from the crowd, and I couldn't help but roll my eyes, fully aware that the mischievous glint in his eye was aimed directly at me. "Oh, come on! That's just cruel!" I protested, though my heart raced at the thought.

"Only if you're too chicken to take it," he teased, leaning closer as the group rallied behind him, chanting for me to take the plunge.

With a determined nod, I leaned in and whispered, "Fine, but only if you join me." The laughter that followed was infectious, and I felt a rush of adrenaline surge through me.

Jackson's expression shifted from playful to sincere as he caught my gaze. "Okay, but I'll only join if you promise to go first. I need to see how it's done."

With a deep breath, I stepped into the center of the circle, my heart pounding. The crowd quieted, anticipation crackling in the air. I felt the weight of their gazes and the thump of my heartbeat in my ears. I cleared my throat, channeling all my bravado, and started humming the first few notes of a silly, romantic ballad I could never have imagined singing in public.

Laughter erupted, but I embraced it, spinning the ridiculousness into something enjoyable. Jackson joined in with his deep voice, and we found ourselves harmonizing in a way that felt utterly absurd yet exhilarating. The crowd cheered, clapping along as we belted out the

THE BREWING OF FUTURES

lyrics, our voices blending in a chaotic symphony of laughter and camaraderie.

In the midst of it all, I caught a glimpse of something more in Jackson's eyes—an appreciation, a connection that transcended the silliness of the moment. When the song ended, the crowd erupted into applause, and I stumbled back into Jackson's side, breathless and giddy.

"You were amazing!" he exclaimed, laughter dancing in his voice. "Who knew you had such hidden talents?"

"Ha! Hidden talents or a desperate need to impress a crowd?" I quipped, my heart still racing.

As the next round of dares began, I felt the undeniable pull between us deepen, like an invisible thread weaving our fates together. The night continued to swirl around us, each moment a thread in a tapestry I wasn't quite sure how to navigate. Then, as I leaned against the railing, the cool metal grounding me in the chaotic energy of the night, my phone buzzed in my pocket.

I pulled it out, glancing at the screen, my breath catching in my throat. An email notification flashed before my eyes, the subject line emblazoned with the name of the company that had made the job offer. The words swirled before me, a harbinger of the decision that lay ahead, a decision that could change everything.

"Everything okay?" Jackson asked, noticing my sudden stillness.

I swallowed hard, my heart pounding louder than the music around us. "I... I think I need to step away for a second."

He nodded, concern flickering across his features. "Do you want me to come with you?"

"No," I replied, my voice steadier than I felt. "I'll be right back. Just give me a moment."

As I made my way to the quieter edge of the rooftop, I could feel Jackson's gaze on me, an anchor tethering me to reality. I opened the email, my pulse racing as I read the words that could seal my fate.

The world around me faded into a blur as I stared at the screen, my heart pounding in a rhythm of uncertainty and dread, unaware that just beyond my line of sight, a familiar figure was approaching, their intentions shadowed in darkness.

# Chapter 16: A Recipe for Reconciliation

The air hung heavy with the scent of freshly baked bread, the warm embrace of yeast and flour mingling with the crisp autumn breeze that filtered through the half-open windows of the bakery. I found myself losing track of time as I kneaded the dough, each push and fold releasing the tension built up over the past few weeks. Ethan had taken to visiting the bakery more frequently, his presence like a sunbeam cutting through the morning fog, illuminating the darker corners of my doubts. We'd been brainstorming for our upcoming launch party, each idea igniting a spark of enthusiasm that I hadn't felt in ages. The chatter of our laughter echoed off the walls, blending with the comforting sounds of clinking pans and the occasional hiss of the espresso machine.

"Have you considered adding a signature drink?" Ethan suggested, wiping a smear of flour from his cheek with the back of his hand. His eyes sparkled with a mix of mischief and determination that I found infectious. "Something that pairs perfectly with your pastries but also tells our story. Something that brings people together."

"Like what? A 'Sibling Reconciliation' cocktail?" I shot back with a grin, my hands momentarily pausing in their rhythm. "Maybe a splash of bitters to capture all the years of resentment?"

Ethan laughed, a deep, throaty sound that sent a warmth racing through me. "Only if we include a hint of cinnamon to represent the sweet memories we're trying to create. A recipe for reconciliation, if you will."

"Okay, that's actually not a terrible idea," I conceded, nodding as I envisioned the vibrant cocktail swirling with hues of amber and garnished with a twist of citrus. Perhaps we could even infuse it with herbs from the garden, something fresh and unexpected.

Our conversation flowed easily, an effortless dance between laughter and earnest discussion. With every shared memory, I felt the walls I'd built around my heart begin to crumble. Perhaps I had been too hard on Ethan, holding onto resentment like a shield, convinced he was the sole architect of our family's disarray. But here he was, throwing himself into the revival of our father's legacy with a passion I hadn't anticipated. It made me wonder if I was looking at him through the wrong lens all along.

The bakery filled with the rich aroma of baked goods, and I lost myself in the rhythm of work, rolling out pastries, measuring out ingredients with precise care. Each movement was meditative, allowing my thoughts to wander freely. The challenges we faced were daunting—Jackson's job offer looming like a dark cloud overhead, uncertainty pressing down on my shoulders—but there was an undeniable thrill in pursuing this venture with Ethan. It felt right.

As the sun dipped below the horizon, painting the sky in shades of orange and pink, I glanced outside to see Jackson standing by the curb, his silhouette framed against the glowing backdrop. He was on the phone, his face serious, but I could see the slight tilt of his lips that suggested he was talking to a friend. My heart sank, a heavy stone in my chest. The idea of him leaving to chase his dreams was both exhilarating and terrifying. The thought of him walking away sent waves of panic crashing through me, and I turned back to my work, trying to drown out the tumultuous emotions swirling within.

But as I continued kneading the dough, each punch a silent protest against the uncertainty of it all, I couldn't shake the feeling that this was a pivotal moment. It felt wrong to want him to stay simply because of my own fears. Jackson was meant for bigger things, but the thought of watching him pursue those dreams, knowing I might lose him in the process, twisted my insides like a cruel game.

When he finally walked into the bakery, the warmth radiating from the ovens paled in comparison to the light he brought with him. His eyes searched the room, landing on me, and the usual spark of joy that ignited between us was tempered with something heavier. I could feel the weight of his decision hanging in the air, palpable and thick.

"Hey," he said softly, running a hand through his hair, displacing the strands that always fell charmingly into his eyes. "What are you up to?"

"Just experimenting with a new pastry for the launch party," I replied, forcing a smile that didn't quite reach my eyes. I didn't want to burden him with my fears, not now. "Want to help?"

"Only if I get to taste test," he teased, stepping closer, his warm breath brushing against my skin as he leaned in to peek at the ingredients scattered across the counter. "What's the secret ingredient? Heartache? Regret?"

"Definitely some heartache," I quipped, folding the dough with a flourish. "But if you're lucky, maybe I'll throw in a dash of hope."

Jackson chuckled, the sound like music to my ears, but the laughter faded as the moment hung between us, heavy and charged. He looked at me with those piercing blue eyes, and I felt like he could see right through the facade I was trying to maintain. "Are you okay?"

"Just thinking," I replied, my voice catching slightly. "About the party, about the future. You know how it is."

"Yeah," he said, his expression shifting to something more serious. "About the job, too?"

I nodded, unable to find the words. It was a tangled web of emotions, and each thread pulled tighter as I felt the ground beneath us shifting. The laughter and banter that usually flowed so easily between us felt more like a fragile truce, holding back a tide of uncertainty that threatened to crash over us both.

"Whatever you decide, I'll support you," I managed, trying to mask the tightness in my chest. But even as I said it, I felt a wave of panic rise within me. The thought of losing him was almost unbearable, like watching a piece of myself drift away into the distance, leaving behind only echoes of what once was.

Jackson reached out, brushing his fingers against mine, the warmth of his touch grounding me in that moment. "You know, sometimes it feels like we're just two kids playing house, trying to figure out how to adult. And I wish I could tell you that I've got it all figured out."

I laughed lightly, the sound echoing in the warm, fragrant air. "Believe me, I'm right there with you. I've been winging it since the day we opened this place."

"But you're not alone," he said, his voice steady and reassuring. "We're in this together, right? Whatever comes next, we'll figure it out."

And in that moment, I believed him. I wanted to believe him. Because amidst the uncertainty and chaos, there was a thread of something beautiful and vibrant, weaving through the tapestry of our lives, drawing us closer even as the world outside spun in unpredictable directions.

The first rays of sunlight crept through the bakery window, casting a warm glow over the wooden countertops where flour dust danced in the air like tiny fairies celebrating the morning. I had arrived early, my heart brimming with anticipation as I prepared for what I hoped would be a day filled with creativity and purpose. The lingering scent of cinnamon and vanilla still hung in the air from yesterday's batch of pastries, remnants of sweetness that provided a comforting backdrop to the uncertain emotions swirling inside me.

Ethan was already there, his hands expertly shaping dough into perfect little crescents, a concentration etched on his brow that somehow made him even more endearing. Watching him work was like observing a painter lost in their masterpiece, every gesture deliberate and precise. I felt a pang of admiration mixed with guilt, as if I was intruding on a moment that was not entirely mine. Was it really fair for me to question the depth of his commitment when he was so visibly dedicated?

"Need a sous-chef?" I asked, leaning against the counter, my arms crossed.

He looked up, a flour-dusted smile spreading across his face. "Only if you're okay with getting your hands messy. I can't promise a neat kitchen."

"I thrive in chaos," I replied, stepping closer to him. "Plus, I could use the distraction from the weight of the world."

With a nod of understanding, he tossed a handful of flour into the air, a playful gesture that had me giggling and swatting at the cloud that settled around us. It was moments like these that reminded me of our childhood, when we would have flour fights instead of disagreements, laughing until our stomachs hurt. It was a reminder that perhaps reconciliation didn't have to be a heavy, burdensome task; sometimes, it could be woven into the fabric of laughter and light-heartedness.

As we worked side by side, our conversation flowed like a well-crafted recipe. We discussed flavors, colors, and inspirations, drawing from the depths of our shared memories. The bakery was slowly transforming from a mere business into a canvas for our creativity, each new idea feeling like a stroke of paint on an unfinished masterpiece.

"Okay, picture this," Ethan said, his eyes lighting up with enthusiasm. "What if we did a seasonal pastry inspired by the first snowfall? Something flaky with layers, filled with spiced pear and topped with a dusting of powdered sugar that looks like snowflakes?"

"Now you're talking," I replied, my heart racing at the thought of such a creation. "But we need a name that captures the magic. How about 'Winter's Whisper'?"

"Or 'Frosted Dreams'?" he countered, his tone playful. "Though it sounds like a cheesy holiday card."

We both burst into laughter, and I felt the knot of tension in my stomach loosen a little. It was these moments of connection that made the upcoming launch party feel more like a celebration than a stressful event. But beneath the surface, the reality of Jackson's impending decision lingered, like an uninvited guest hovering at the edge of our joyful conversation.

As if summoned by my thoughts, Jackson strolled in, the morning light catching the tousled waves of his hair. His presence was magnetic, an easy blend of charm and comfort that filled the bakery with a unique energy. "Good morning, doughnuts," he greeted, leaning casually against the doorframe, an amused smile playing on his lips.

"Doughnuts?" I echoed, crossing my arms dramatically. "I'll have you know we're crafting a winter masterpiece here."

"Ah, the pastry equivalent of a snowman," he quipped, stepping inside and inspecting our work. "I'd say you two have it handled. I'm more of a cookie kind of guy, but I'll gladly sample anything that comes out of this delightful chaos."

Ethan shot me a conspiratorial glance, and I couldn't help but return his grin. Jackson had a way of making light of heavy moments, as if he could sense the underlying tension and wanted to smooth it over with laughter. But even as he joked, I could see a flicker of uncertainty in his eyes. The job offer was hanging like a dark cloud above our heads, and I wished I could shake it off like a pesky fly.

As we continued to bake, our trio of conversations swirled around pastries, memories, and dreams. Yet with every laugh, I felt the nagging worry in the back of my mind—a constant reminder that Jackson might soon leave to chase a dream that didn't include me.

In a brief lull, I glanced at him, his eyes sparkling with a playful challenge as he dared me to bring up the topic we both avoided. "So, what's the scoop with your big decision?" I asked, trying to keep my tone light, but the weight of the question hung heavily in the air.

Jackson leaned against the counter, his expression shifting to one of contemplation. "Honestly, I've been going back and forth. This opportunity could open doors I didn't even know existed, but... I don't know if I'm ready to leave everything behind."

Ethan glanced between us, sensing the shift in energy. "That's a tough spot to be in," he offered, his voice earnest. "But it sounds like it's also a huge opportunity."

"It is," Jackson replied, rubbing the back of his neck. "But I also feel this connection here, with you both. It's hard to imagine walking away from it."

My heart clenched painfully in my chest. "You have to do what's right for you, Jackson. We'll support you, no matter what. But..." I hesitated, searching for the right words. "I just hope you know how much you'll be missed if you go."

His gaze softened, and I could see the flicker of conflict in his eyes. "It's like choosing between a dream and something real, isn't it?"

Ethan interjected, his voice steady. "It's not an easy choice, but what if it's both? Maybe you can pursue your dreams while still holding onto the people and things that matter most."

Jackson nodded slowly, the tension easing slightly. "Yeah, I guess I can try to make it work. I just wish I didn't have to choose."

As we dove back into our work, the atmosphere lightened, and the bakery began to feel like a sanctuary. Yet, as the hours passed, I couldn't shake the feeling that something had changed, as if the very foundation of our trio had been subtly reshaped. There was a delicate balance in the air, and I was acutely aware that every laugh, every pastry we crafted, was imbued with the knowledge that change was inevitable.

Amidst the laughter and the delightful chaos of flour and frosting, I realized that perhaps this was what reconciliation truly felt like—a mix of sweetness and uncertainty, the beginnings of something new. And as the first batch of our winter pastries emerged from the oven, golden and fragrant, I felt a small glimmer of hope that maybe, just maybe, we could find a way to make it all work.

The smell of fresh pastries wafted through the bakery as the sun dipped lower in the sky, casting a golden hue that danced across the wooden counters. I stood in front of the oven, peering through the glass as the latest batch of "Winter's Whisper" pastries puffed up beautifully. Each one was a small testament to our hard work, and the sight brought a sense of pride that warmed me from the inside out. The anticipation of our launch party had transformed the bakery into a creative haven, but with each rising pastry, I could feel the shadows of uncertainty creeping back in.

Jackson leaned against the counter, arms crossed, watching me with an intensity that made my heart race. "You know, if I keep watching you, I might start believing you're a pastry wizard or something," he teased, a smile breaking through his otherwise contemplative demeanor.

"I'd like to think my magic comes from countless hours of failed attempts," I shot back, rolling my eyes playfully. "For every pastry that rises, there's probably five that ended up as glorified frisbees."

He chuckled, shaking his head. "You really have a knack for self-deprecation, don't you? But seriously, these look incredible. I'm excited for the party. I mean, how could anyone resist a pastry that promises to whisper sweet nothings?"

I smirked, letting his words hang in the air like the warmth of the oven. "As long as it doesn't whisper to you about how I've been avoiding our conversation regarding your job offer."

The moment hung heavily between us, filled with the unsaid words that danced around our conversations like the flour in the air. He shifted, his expression shifting from playful to serious, the corners of his mouth turning down ever so slightly. "You know I'm trying to figure it out. It's just—"

"Complicated," I finished for him, feeling the familiar twinge of anxiety tightening in my chest. "And you don't have to figure it out alone, Jackson. Just... talk to me."

He sighed, his shoulders dropping as if the weight of his dilemma bore down on him. "I don't want to let you down. Or Ethan. Or anyone, really. This opportunity is huge, but leaving everything behind... it feels wrong."

"It's not wrong to pursue your dreams," I encouraged, my voice softening. "It's brave. But I also don't want you to feel like you're abandoning us. There's room for both—you can chase your dream and still have us in your life."

He regarded me for a moment, a flicker of vulnerability in his eyes. "I just wish it didn't feel like I had to choose between what's best for me and what's best for us."

Ethan entered the kitchen, a new batch of dough under his arm, and the tension cracked like an egg. "Hey, what's the brooding about? We're supposed to be dreaming up pastry greatness, not existential crises."

Jackson shrugged, casting a sideways glance at me. "Just trying to navigate life's decisions. You know, the usual."

Ethan placed the dough on the counter and flashed a conspiratorial grin. "Ah, the classic struggle of adulthood. I say we make a pact: if you choose to leave, you'll come back every other weekend for a 'Jackson-tasting session.' Just to keep our spirits high. Deal?"

A smile broke across Jackson's face, and I felt a lightness return to the room. "I could live with that. But only if you promise to keep making these 'Winter's Whisper' pastries. They might just be the only reason I'd come back."

The mood lifted, but the reality of Jackson's choice still lingered beneath the surface, like an undercurrent threatening to pull us all under. As we threw ourselves into creating new pastries, our laughter echoed off the walls, the warmth of camaraderie wrapping around us.

The afternoon melted into evening, and we found ourselves in a whirlwind of flour, butter, and vibrant conversation. Jackson playfully challenged Ethan to a "whisk-off," both of them putting on exaggerated poses as they whipped cream, while I stood back, trying to stifle my laughter.

But as night fell and the bakery emptied, the weight of the day settled heavily on my shoulders. With the glow of the overhead lights casting long shadows, I busied myself cleaning, stealing glances at Jackson who was lost in thought, a frown tugging at his lips.

"Hey, can I ask you something?" I finally said, breaking the silence that had enveloped us.

"Sure," he replied, his tone casual, but I could see the tension in his shoulders.

"Are you really leaning towards taking the job?" My heart raced as I asked, the fear of the answer tightening around me like a vise.

He paused, his gaze searching mine. "Honestly? I don't know. I'm torn. But I think I might take it. I want to make something of myself, you know? And as much as I love this place, it feels like my time is running out."

The finality of his words hung heavy in the air, wrapping around us like the warmth from the oven. It felt like a countdown to an inevitable goodbye, and I fought against the flood of emotions surging within me. "What about us? What about... this?" I gestured to the bakery, the warmth of our shared moments, the laughter that had become a lifeline.

His expression softened, yet a shadow crossed his face. "You're important to me, you know that. But I need to see what else is out there. I can't keep living in the bakery, even if it is filled with pastries and your charming face."

I couldn't help but laugh, despite the sting of his words. "So you're saying my charm is a consolation prize?"

"No, not like that," he rushed to explain, stepping closer. "What I'm saying is that there's a whole world waiting for me. I need to find my place in it, and it might not include this bakery or, well, us."

His words pierced through the warmth of the moment, and I felt the ground beneath me shift. The laughter we'd shared felt distant, as if we were standing on different shores of an emotional ocean, each wave threatening to carry us away from each other.

Just as I opened my mouth to respond, the bakery door swung open, a gust of cold air sweeping in. A figure stepped inside, silhouetted against the dim light, and my heart raced at the unexpected interruption.

"Hey, I hope I'm not interrupting anything important," said a familiar voice, and I turned to see someone I hadn't expected. My heart sank, a heavy weight settling in my stomach.

The person standing in the doorway was a ghost from my past, someone who had the power to upend everything I had tried to rebuild. "I just wanted to talk."

And just like that, the carefully crafted world we had been shaping began to unravel, leaving me standing on the edge of a precipice, the uncertainty looming ever closer.

# Chapter 17: Pour Decisions

The air was thick with the mingling scents of hops and malt, the warm glow of the brewery lights reflecting off the polished wooden bar. I leaned over the counter, busily adjusting the floral arrangements for the launch party. A cluster of sunflowers, their golden faces shining brightly, added a cheerful contrast to the earthy tones of the brewery. This place, with its brick walls and rustic charm, had always felt like home. Yet tonight, it thrummed with a nervous energy I couldn't shake.

Ethan had left early, the remnants of our recent tension lingering like the faintest trace of a bad memory. We had patched things up, or at least agreed to a ceasefire. It was the kind of compromise that made me feel both relieved and anxious. With the launch party looming closer, I could sense that our father's legacy weighed heavier than ever. Each recipe, each bottle we were about to unveil, was steeped in stories and moments that could easily slip through my fingers if I didn't handle them with care.

Jackson walked in, his silhouette a blend of confidence and warmth that had become a familiar comfort. As he approached, I found myself momentarily lost in the deep brown of his eyes, those expressive orbs that seemed to draw me in like a well-crafted brew—rich, complex, and undeniably intoxicating.

"Need a hand?" he asked, leaning against the bar with a casual grace, his fingers brushing lightly against a row of empty pint glasses.

"More like a miracle," I replied, trying to keep the playful banter alive despite the storm of thoughts swirling in my head. "I'm convinced the sunflowers are plotting against me."

He chuckled, the sound reverberating through the brewery, mingling with the laughter of a couple seated at a table nearby. "If they start whispering secrets, we might need a whole new plan for the party."

"Yeah, because that's exactly what I need. Sunflower espionage," I shot back, feeling the tension from earlier dissipate a little. His smile was infectious, and I found myself leaning into our easy camaraderie.

As we arranged the flowers and set up tables, I stole glances at him, reveling in the way he moved—fluid, confident, entirely at ease in this world we had both grown to love. Jackson was the kind of person who made everything feel less daunting, a balm for the chaotic mix of emotions that clung to me. But then, amidst our shared laughter and the soft clinking of glasses, I spotted her.

The woman stood by the entrance, her dark hair cascading over one shoulder, laughter spilling from her lips like music. Jackson's laughter joined hers, and my stomach twisted into an uncomfortable knot. I tried to focus on the flower arrangements, but my heart raced as I watched them, the ease of their interaction igniting an unexpected flame of jealousy.

"What do you think?" I asked, attempting to draw my gaze away from the scene that seemed to loom larger with every heartbeat.

"About the flowers?" he responded, looking genuinely curious.

"No, about..." My voice trailed off, my thoughts disjointed as I gestured vaguely in the direction of the entrance. The woman was now leaning in closer to him, their shared laughter echoing through the brewery like a chorus I didn't want to be a part of.

Jackson caught the shift in my mood, his brows knitting together in concern. "You okay?"

"Yeah, just peachy," I replied, the sarcasm slipping through my lips before I could swallow it back. "Do you know her?"

"Who? Oh, that's just—"

"Just?" I cut him off, a sharpness in my voice that surprised even me. "You're being awfully casual about this."

He raised his hands in surrender, his expression shifting from surprise to understanding. "Okay, look, she's just someone I met through work. We were discussing some collaboration ideas for the brewery. It's nothing."

"Right," I said, my heart racing as I crossed my arms, the coolness of my skin barely masking the heat rising within me. "Nothing at all."

The more he tried to explain, the more I felt the green-eyed monster creeping in, wrapping its tendrils around my chest and squeezing tighter. "Is it wrong that I don't like the idea of you getting cozy with anyone else?" I blurted out, the truth spilling from my lips like the last dregs of a well-shaken cocktail.

His surprise was palpable. "Is that really what you think? I thought we were just friends, working toward the same goal here."

I felt a mix of frustration and embarrassment wash over me. "Yeah, well, friends don't lean in and laugh like that," I snapped, gesturing again toward the entrance, my voice sharper than I intended.

"Are you serious? We're just getting the party off the ground, and you're jealous? Over nothing?"

The air between us crackled with tension, every word an electric shock. I couldn't believe I'd let my insecurities seep into our working relationship.

"Jackson, it's not nothing!" I countered, my heart pounding in my chest as I stepped closer, wanting to close the distance but also terrified of the consequences. "This isn't just business for me. It's my family, our history, our dad's recipes."

He sighed, running a hand through his hair in that way that made my heart flutter. "And what about us? What are we?"

The question hung in the air like a question mark at the end of a punchline, and suddenly, I felt exposed, my walls crumbling. I couldn't hide behind the pretense of professionalism anymore. "I... I don't know," I admitted, the truth flowing out before I could grasp it back.

The silence that followed was heavy, charged with unspoken words and raw emotions. I could see the wheels turning in his mind, the uncertainty mirrored in his eyes. He opened his mouth to speak, but no sound came out. Instead, he stepped closer, and in that moment, everything shifted.

The air around us crackled with tension, a live wire connecting our unspoken feelings. I could see the surprise morphing into something deeper in Jackson's eyes—something that hinted at a shared understanding, a recognition of the emotions swirling between us like the steam rising from the freshly brewed coffee behind the bar. His presence, once so comforting, now felt charged with uncertainty, and my heart raced as I awaited his response.

"What are we?" he repeated, a faint incredulity in his voice that was equal parts curiosity and concern. "You've got me wondering what you want this to be."

I wanted to say something profound, something that would untangle the mess of emotions roiling inside me. But all that came out was a breathless, "I want to know if we're more than just... this." I gestured to the bottles and the chaotic scene of preparations around us, the laughter from the other patrons fading into a dull hum.

His expression shifted from surprise to contemplation, those deep brown eyes searching mine, as if he could decipher the intricate puzzle that was me. "I think we are," he said slowly, his voice low, almost reverent. "But we've been dancing around it, haven't we?"

The truth hung between us, a thin thread that tethered our unspoken desires to the reality we were navigating. It felt reckless to dive into this conversation, but I had already committed to the plunge, my heart racing like a rollercoaster about to crest its highest peak.

"Why do you think I'm here, Jackson?" I replied, my voice barely above a whisper, filled with a mix of fear and exhilaration. "Why do you think I've been working late nights, decorating for a party that should be just another business venture?"

"Because you care," he said simply, his gaze steady and intense. "About the brewery, about honoring your dad's legacy. And maybe a little bit about me?"

A grin tugged at the corner of my mouth, the kind of smile that felt foreign and wonderful all at once. "Maybe a lot about you," I confessed, feeling the heat rise to my cheeks, my usual composure teetering on the edge of vulnerability.

Before he could respond, I felt the ground shift beneath my feet as the woman from earlier sauntered over, her laughter ringing out like an alarm bell, pulling me back from the precipice of something profound. "Jackson!" she exclaimed, her voice bright and bubbly. "I was just telling the guys about this amazing brew I had at another brewery last week."

My stomach twisted, and I could feel my irritation bubbling back up like an overactive fermenter. "Great," I mumbled under my breath, crossing my arms in a defensive posture. The ease with which she spoke to him made my insides churn, as if she were mocking the delicate moment we'd just been sharing.

Jackson turned to her, a polite smile plastered on his face, and my heart sank. "Yeah, sounds interesting," he replied, clearly distracted. He didn't glance back at me, and I suddenly felt like a ghost in my own life, fading into the background as someone else took the stage.

"Can you believe how close we are to the launch?" she continued, her eyes sparkling as she leaned closer to him, her laughter mingling with the clink of glasses. "I can't wait to try your dad's new recipes."

I bristled at the possessiveness creeping in again, the sharp edge of jealousy cutting deeper. "Oh, I'm sure he's been waiting for your approval," I interjected, my voice sharper than I intended.

Jackson's expression shifted, his amusement faltering as he turned back to me. "Avery, don't—"

"No, let's just be real here," I interrupted, my voice rising slightly. "You can't be this friendly with every woman who strolls in."

The woman blinked, her surprise palpable as Jackson's face hardened, the easygoing air between us now thick with tension. "This isn't what I meant—"

"Clearly," I shot back, feeling the fight ignite within me. "You're inviting her into our moment."

"Avery!" he said, his voice a mix of frustration and disbelief. "You think I'm inviting her? I'm just trying to be polite!"

Politeness had a funny way of morphing into something else entirely, and I could feel the weight of the moment shifting. "I guess I'm just not sure what that means anymore," I retorted, throwing my hands up in exasperation. "Do we have a label? A boundary? Because right now, I feel like I'm just one of your brewery projects."

The woman stood there, clearly baffled, and I could almost hear her thoughts racing. "I'll just... um, head back to my friends," she finally muttered, retreating as if the tension in the air was contagious.

Once she was gone, the silence was deafening. Jackson pinched the bridge of his nose, clearly grappling with the fallout of our argument. "You're overreacting," he said finally, his voice taut. "I'm not interested in her like that."

"Then what do you want?" I shot back, my heart pounding as the weight of my own insecurities pressed down on me. "Because I don't want to keep playing this game."

He stepped closer, closing the distance that had felt insurmountable only moments ago. "I want you, Avery. It's always been you," he said, his voice low and earnest. "But I can't keep walking on eggshells around you, either."

My heart raced, torn between the relief of his admission and the frustration that had driven me to this brink in the first place. "So what do we do now?"

"We talk," he replied, his gaze unwavering. "We figure this out together."

The sincerity in his eyes melted the edges of my defensiveness, and as I studied him, I felt a flicker of hope stir within me. "You mean like adults?" I asked, a playful tone slipping back into my voice despite the heaviness in the air.

"Exactly," he said, a smile breaking through the tension, and I couldn't help but mirror it. "No more games, no more confusion. Just us."

"Okay," I agreed, allowing myself to relax into the moment. "But if we're doing this, you need to promise me something."

"Anything."

"No more flirting with random women who sidle up to you at the bar. It's not cool."

He chuckled, a rich sound that sent warmth through my chest. "I can promise you that. But I might need a little help defining 'flirting.'"

"Trust me, you'll know it when you see it," I replied, smirking. "Consider it a part of your ongoing education."

Jackson shook his head, laughter still lacing his voice. "I can handle that."

As we stood there, the world around us faded, the weight of my worries lifting as we forged a new path forward together. The tension of the moment transformed into something more—a promise, a partnership, an unwritten future filled with the warmth of possibility.

The moment hung in the air like the last note of a favorite song, lingering just long enough for its resonance to become intoxicating. Jackson's gaze held mine with a gravity that felt both terrifying and exhilarating. In the warmth of his presence, I began to sense the invisible barriers we had built around ourselves start to crumble, revealing the raw truths we had both been avoiding.

"Okay, so where do we start?" I asked, forcing my voice to remain steady, even as my heart raced at the thought of this newfound openness.

"Let's not start with 'Why are you jealous?'" he suggested, a mischievous glint in his eyes that reminded me of the boyish charm I had first found so endearing. "That seems like a trap."

I laughed, a genuine sound that dispelled some of the tension. "Fair point. How about we talk about our actual feelings, then? I can't be the only one with a confession lurking in the shadows."

"Confessions, huh? This sounds like a game," he replied, leaning back against the bar with a casual ease that belied the weight of our conversation. "I confess that I think you're incredibly talented. Your passion for this place? It's magnetic."

"Flattery will get you everywhere," I teased, though I could feel the blush creeping up my cheeks. "What else? I'll go first. I'm terrified of failing this launch. It feels like our father's legacy rests on my shoulders."

He nodded, his expression shifting to something serious. "I get that. I feel the same pressure. We both want this to succeed for him."

"That's why I want us to work together, to truly be a team," I insisted, my heart racing again at the implications. "But if we're going to do this, we need to be honest with each other. No more second-guessing. We can't keep holding back."

"I agree," he said, his voice steady, filled with determination. "But I also don't want to scare you off by diving too deep too fast."

"Too late for that," I shot back, a wry smile spreading across my face. "We've already gone for a dip."

He grinned, and for a moment, the weight of our previous tensions dissipated, replaced by something lighter. But as the moment unfolded, I felt a flicker of anxiety creeping back. "So what happens if one of us pulls back?"

"We don't," he said firmly. "We don't let that happen. That's the deal."

Before I could respond, Ethan strolled back into the brewery, his expression unreadable as he surveyed the scene. I could feel the tension in the air shift again, the lightheartedness between Jackson and me retreating like the tide before a storm.

"Hey, what's up?" Ethan asked, a hint of wariness in his voice as he caught my eye. "I thought you were both working on the tasting menu."

"We were just discussing some last-minute details," I replied, forcing a smile that felt like it might crack under pressure. "You know how it is before a big event."

Ethan's gaze flicked between us, a spark of suspicion igniting in his eyes. "Right. Just remember, we need to stay focused on the launch."

"Of course," Jackson said smoothly, though I could sense the underlying tension. "We're on it."

I could feel my stomach knotting as the weight of expectations settled back into the atmosphere, the playful banter I had shared with Jackson now feeling like a fragile bubble waiting to burst. Ethan's presence, though well-intentioned, felt stifling, and I could see the way he was trying to assess the situation.

"Let's just go over the final arrangements," he suggested, pulling a clipboard from under his arm, his demeanor shifting to that of a commander preparing for battle. "I want to make sure everything is ready. We can't afford any slip-ups."

"Got it," I said, trying to keep my tone upbeat. I shot a glance at Jackson, who met my gaze with a shared understanding, a silent acknowledgment of the complicated web we were weaving.

As we went through the checklist, discussing logistics and details, I couldn't shake the feeling that something was off. Ethan's focus on perfection felt like a mask, concealing his own insecurities beneath layers of bravado. But every time I glanced at Jackson, the warmth in his eyes reminded me that this was more than just a business venture—it was personal.

Hours slipped by in a blur of preparations and late-night brainstorming sessions, and by the time we were wrapping up, the air was thick with anticipation. We had survived the initial wave of tension, but I could still feel the currents shifting beneath the surface, pulling me toward something I wasn't ready to confront.

"Can we take a break?" I suggested, my voice edged with fatigue. "I need to clear my head for a minute."

"Sure," Jackson said, his expression turning soft, his concern evident. "Want to step outside?"

"Yeah, let's do that," I agreed, grateful for a moment away from the brewing storm inside the brewery.

We stepped into the cool night air, the stars twinkling like little promises above us. I inhaled deeply, letting the crispness wash over me as I leaned against the cool brick wall, the reality of our conversation settling in.

"Better?" he asked, his tone gentle as he stood beside me, close enough for me to feel the warmth radiating from him.

"A little," I admitted, my heart racing as I fought against the whirlwind of emotions stirring within me. "I just... I don't want this to end up being too complicated."

"It doesn't have to be," he reassured, his voice steady. "But we have to be honest with ourselves."

I took a deep breath, steeling myself for what I was about to say. "Jackson, I really like you. I think I've liked you for a while now, but—"

Just then, a loud crash erupted from inside the brewery, echoing into the night like thunder. Our conversation came to an abrupt halt as our heads snapped toward the source of the noise. Panic gripped my chest as I rushed inside, Jackson hot on my heels.

What met us in the brewery sent my heart racing: bottles were shattered across the floor, a cascade of glass glinting ominously in the dim light. But it wasn't just the wreckage that struck fear into my heart; it was the figure standing in the midst of the chaos.

"Ethan!" I called, rushing forward as the pieces clicked into place. He was bent over a table, his expression dark and stormy. "What happened?"

He turned, and in that instant, I realized he wasn't alone. Another figure stood behind him, cloaked in shadows, a familiar face that sent shockwaves through me.

"Surprise!" the figure shouted, stepping into the light with a wicked grin that sent chills down my spine.

And just like that, everything I thought I knew began to unravel, leaving me teetering on the edge of a precipice, uncertain of what awaited me on the other side.

# Chapter 18: Crumbling Foundations

The brewery buzzes around me like a swarm of bees, the air thick with the sweet, yeasty scent of fermentation and the vibrant chatter of my team. I maneuver through the crowd, my heart a lead weight in my chest, each familiar face reflecting the joy I should be feeling. But every laugh, every clink of glasses, echoes with the absence of Jackson. It's maddening how a single argument can unravel everything—our chemistry, our plans, and my peace of mind.

Ethan, ever the stalwart friend, hovers nearby, his brow creased in concern. "Hey, you okay?" he asks, his voice a low rumble amidst the clamor. His hand rests on my shoulder, a comforting gesture, yet it feels like an anchor dragging me deeper into the depths of my own turmoil.

I plaster a smile on my face, the kind that doesn't quite reach my eyes. "Of course! Just busy. You know how it is before a big launch." My voice wavers slightly, a betraying quiver that I hope he doesn't notice.

Ethan narrows his eyes, scrutinizing me like I'm a complicated recipe he can't quite get right. "Sure. Busy, right." He leans closer, lowering his voice as if the barrels of beer can eavesdrop. "You need to talk to him, you know. This silent treatment won't solve anything."

His words hang heavy between us, a reminder of the unspoken truths I'd rather ignore. I turn to scan the brewery, the wooden beams overhead reminding me of the foundations we built together, both in business and in our relationship. They seem solid enough, yet I can feel them quaking under the weight of my doubts.

"Maybe," I concede, feigning nonchalance. "But it's complicated. We both said things we didn't mean."

Ethan's sigh is laced with frustration. "Or maybe things you did mean. There's a difference, you know." He retreats slightly, leaving me

with my thoughts, which swirl chaotically like the hops we use for
our latest brew.

The team's laughter drifts toward me again, and I can't help but
feel a twinge of longing. We've come so far, transforming this
once-derelict space into a lively hub of creativity and craft. I should
be savoring every moment, but all I can think about is Jackson. His
absence feels like a ghost, haunting the corners of my mind and
clouding my every thought.

Just as I attempt to immerse myself in the preparations, a loud
crash breaks through the noise, sending a ripple of panic through
the brewery. My heart races as I rush toward the sound, praying it's
not something catastrophic. I round the corner to find a group of
employees staring in horror at a fallen stack of kegs, their shiny metal
sides glistening under the overhead lights. A slow horror dawns on
me; it looks like a scene straight out of a slapstick comedy, but there's
no room for laughter now.

"Everyone, step back!" I shout, slipping into my leadership role
like a well-worn jacket. My mind races through possible solutions,
but the tightness in my chest doesn't ease. My gaze lands on Jackson,
who has just emerged from the storage room, his face a mix of
concern and annoyance. "What happened?" he demands, quickly
assessing the situation.

"The kegs fell!" I reply, urgency dripping from my voice. "We
need to secure the area and make sure no one got hurt."

Jackson moves closer, his presence igniting the air between us
with an electric tension. "I'll help with the clean-up," he says, rolling
up his sleeves. "Just show me what to do."

I nod, relief washing over me. Working alongside him is a balm
to my wounded heart, the rhythm of our movements almost
instinctual. As we begin the tedious task of lifting and stacking the
fallen kegs, the silence hangs between us, charged with all the things

left unsaid. Each time our arms brush against one another, a spark ignites, rekindling the warmth I had thought extinguished.

"Isn't this a fun way to spend a Monday?" I say, trying to inject some levity into the heavy atmosphere. My attempt at humor lands like a thud, but Jackson smirks, a flicker of the old banter shining through the cracks in our strained dynamic.

"Oh, absolutely. Nothing screams 'team bonding' like lifting heavy metal and dodging minor disasters," he replies, his voice teasing yet laced with sincerity.

The playful exchange draws me in, reminding me of the connection we used to share. For a moment, we're just two friends working together, and the world outside the brewery fades into the background noise of laughter and clinking glasses.

But then, as we straighten up, our eyes lock, and the air thickens with unspoken feelings. The weight of everything hangs heavy in that moment—regret, longing, the fear of losing something beautiful. I open my mouth, ready to bridge the gap, but the words catch in my throat. What if it's too late? What if the foundation we built is already crumbling?

Jackson breaks the silence first, his expression shifting from playful to serious. "Listen, I know things got out of hand. I didn't mean to—"

"Neither did I," I interject, the truth spilling out before I can stop it. "I just felt... overwhelmed. I thought we were on the same page, but then it felt like everything shifted."

He runs a hand through his hair, the gesture both familiar and foreign. "I thought we were too. I just didn't expect you to... to pull away."

The honesty in his tone pulls at something deep within me. "It's not about you. I just didn't know how to process everything we were juggling—the launch, our relationship, the future."

Jackson steps closer, the air crackling between us, thick with tension and possibility. "We can figure it out. Together."

In that moment, the weight of uncertainty lifts, if only slightly. Maybe the foundations can be rebuilt, stronger than before. As we stand surrounded by fallen kegs and the hum of life continuing around us, I realize that sometimes, it takes a disaster to shake things up, to clear away the rubble and give us a chance to rebuild.

The rhythm of our collaboration slowly morphs into a dance, the kind that makes the mundane seem electric. We lift the last of the kegs into place, our hands brushing against each other, sending jolts of energy crackling through the air. I can feel my pulse quicken with each fleeting touch, a reminder of how effortlessly we used to fit together, like puzzle pieces that had only recently discovered the perfect picture they formed. The atmosphere hums with anticipation and something more—an undeniable tension that hangs between us like the sweet scent of hops.

"Well, look at us, saving the day," Jackson quips, dusting his hands off on his jeans, a half-smile teasing the corners of his mouth. "Who knew we were such a dynamic duo? Next thing you know, we'll be wearing matching capes and saving the brewery from rogue kegs."

I chuckle, grateful for the moment of levity. "Right! Maybe we can even add 'keg rescue' to our resumes. A solid life skill if I ever saw one." I shoot him a playful grin, feeling the cracks in our relationship begin to mend, if only just.

The tension begins to thaw, replaced by the warmth of shared laughter, but I can't shake the nagging thought of the unresolved issues lurking in the corners of my mind. I take a breath, steeling myself for the next conversation we need to have. The launch party looms on the horizon, a massive event that has consumed my every thought, and I need him by my side—both for the work and for what it represents. But how do I say that without reopening wounds?

Before I can spiral too far into my thoughts, Ethan ambles over, his grin stretching wide. "So, are we still on for that launch party practice run this weekend?" He glances between us, eyebrow raised, the perceptiveness of his gaze not lost on me.

"Absolutely," I reply, feeling a flicker of resolve ignite in my chest. "We need to finalize the menu, and Jackson can help with the pairing suggestions." I meet Jackson's eyes, a silent plea lurking beneath the surface. He nods, and for a brief moment, we are in sync again.

"Pairing beer with food? Now that's a subject I can get behind," Jackson says, his enthusiasm returning. "I can whip up some amazing suggestions that'll blow everyone away. Just give me a few hours with the kitchen and a couple of my favorite brews."

Ethan laughs, shaking his head. "I'm not sure the kitchen can handle both of your creativity and those brews at once. It might explode. I'm still picking up the pieces from the last time you two got together in the kitchen."

"Hey, that was one time!" I protest, though I can't help but laugh at the memory of our last culinary adventure gone wrong. "And the fire was minimal. Barely a scorched pan. We really should be praised for our willingness to experiment, if anything."

"Right, because who doesn't want a side of chaos with their dinner?" Jackson counters, a teasing glint in his eyes. "Let's just hope the launch party doesn't end up being a 'greatest hits of brewery mishaps.'"

The conversation flows easily, the banter rekindling the spark that once defined our relationship. But beneath the lightheartedness, I can still feel the weight of the unaddressed conflict, simmering just beneath the surface. I glance at Jackson, his expression warm but guarded, and wonder if I'll ever find the right moment to breach the topic that looms like an unwelcome shadow.

As we wrap up for the day, I take a moment to gather my thoughts, the tension rising like the yeast in our barrels. The noise of the brewery fades, and I'm left in the stillness of my own mind. Ethan lingers nearby, the weight of his concern palpable as he waits for me to voice my thoughts. I can feel him watching, assessing, ready to swoop in with advice if necessary.

"Can we talk?" I finally ask, my voice barely a whisper against the backdrop of clinking glasses and laughter.

"Of course," he replies, his tone earnest. We step away from the bustle, finding a quiet corner where the distant hum of conversation fades into a dull murmur. I take a deep breath, the words caught in my throat, like a cork stuck in a bottle, ready to pop with the right nudge.

"About the launch party..." I start, and he leans in, his expression attentive. "I think we need to be on the same page. We can't let our personal stuff get in the way of what we've built here."

His eyes narrow slightly, understanding flickering there. "I agree. We both know how important this launch is. It's our chance to show everyone what we can do together."

I nod, but the unsteady beat of my heart quickens as I gather my thoughts. "But... it's hard. I miss the way we used to be—how easily we worked together. I'm worried that if we don't sort this out, it will all fall apart. The party, our partnership, everything."

"Do you think we can fix it?" Jackson's voice is steady, but I see the uncertainty there, too, a vulnerability I haven't seen in a while. It hits me that he's just as invested in this as I am, and that gives me hope.

"I want to," I say, searching his eyes for a glimmer of understanding. "But we need to stop pretending everything is fine. We need to address what happened between us."

The silence stretches between us, heavy with unsaid words and feelings. Then, as if a dam has burst, Jackson sighs deeply. "You're right. I felt like we were drifting, and I didn't know how to pull us back together without making it worse. I didn't want to push you away further."

"That's what I feared too," I admit, the honesty slipping out like a breath held too long. "But we can't keep doing this. We need to talk about our expectations, about what we want—together and separately."

He nods, his expression softening as he meets my gaze. "I can do that. I want us to work this out. Not just for the brewery, but for us. I don't want to lose what we have."

With that simple admission, the weight of uncertainty begins to lift, replaced by a glimmer of possibility. The foundation of our relationship, though cracked, still has the potential to be rebuilt, stronger and more resilient. As we stand there, a renewed sense of purpose ignites between us, sparking the hope that maybe we can navigate the brewing storm together.

The conversation hangs in the air like a fine mist, both fragile and electric, crackling with potential. Jackson's expression is earnest, the lines around his eyes softening as he absorbs my words. A flicker of hope ignites within me, the kind that feels like the first ray of sunlight breaking through a storm. We stand there, suspended in this moment of vulnerability, and I realize that honesty might be the anchor we need to navigate these turbulent waters.

"Let's make a pact," I say, my voice steadying with newfound determination. "No more running. No more avoidance. We tackle everything head-on—from the brewery to us."

"Deal," he replies, a grin breaking through the tension, though there's still an edge of seriousness in his eyes. "But I reserve the right to suggest beer pairings for all serious conversations. You know, to keep things light."

"Perfect. I'll bring the snacks," I reply, my heart swelling with a warmth that had felt distant just moments ago. "But only if you promise not to throw any kegs at me in frustration."

His laughter fills the space, and for a heartbeat, it feels like we've stepped back into our familiar rhythm, the kind where even silence is comfortable. We can be a team again, not just in business but in everything.

The atmosphere in the brewery is charged as we make our way back to the others, the weight of our conversation transforming into an undercurrent of anticipation. I can feel the energy around us shifting, the camaraderie that had faltered slowly reigniting. Jackson starts to throw out ideas for the launch party, weaving in the playful banter we had once shared effortlessly.

"What about a signature beer for the event?" he proposes, his eyes lighting up. "Something bold, a little unexpected. Like a black cherry stout or a hibiscus lager?"

"Only if we can pair it with some fancy cheese," I counter, grinning. "You know, to keep up the air of sophistication."

"Oh, right. Because nothing screams 'elegance' like a cheese platter with funky names. What's next, artisanal crackers with names longer than the ingredients list?"

I chuckle, picturing the scene. "Absolutely. And we can even have a cheese sommelier on standby to explain the 'subtle notes of aged gouda.'"

"Now that's a good idea," he muses, "but only if we can pass it off as a tasting flight. It sounds more official that way."

As we brainstorm together, I can feel the tension dissolving into a shared purpose. It's exhilarating, like the first warm breeze of spring after a long winter. I catch Ethan's eye from across the room, and he gives me a thumbs-up, a silent affirmation that everything is heading in the right direction.

But then, as if the universe is determined to throw a wrench into our newfound harmony, the door swings open with a loud bang. A gust of wind carries in a flurry of fallen leaves and the unmistakable scent of rain. The familiar face that steps in, however, is the last person I expected to see: my estranged sister, Clara.

Her presence is like a thunderclap, jolting everyone into silence. Clara and I had always had a complicated relationship—more of a series of earthquakes that left emotional scars rather than sibling camaraderie. The years have been filled with misunderstandings and unsaid apologies, leaving our bond hanging by a thread. She scans the brewery, her expression unreadable until her gaze lands on me, and a mix of recognition and something akin to regret flickers in her eyes.

"Wow, look at you. All grown up and running a business," she remarks, her tone laced with both admiration and sarcasm. "I barely recognized you in all this... success."

"Clara," I breathe, caught between joy and dread. "What are you doing here?"

"I came to see how you're doing," she replies, folding her arms, a defensive posture that tells me she's bracing for impact. "I thought maybe... it was time we talked."

Jackson glances at me, his brow furrowing in concern, the banter of moments ago fading like mist in the morning sun. I can feel the gravity of the situation settling in. "I'm not sure now's the best time," I manage, a knot forming in my stomach.

"Is there ever a 'best time' for anything real?" she challenges, stepping closer. "We can't keep pretending this isn't important. You can't ignore me forever, especially not now."

Her words resonate deeply, unearthing a swirl of emotions I'd rather keep buried. "I've got a lot on my plate right now, Clara. The launch party is just around the corner, and—"

"Right, the party," she interrupts, waving her hand dismissively. "Is that all you care about now? The brewery and your perfect little life?"

"Clara, that's not fair," I counter, frustration boiling just beneath the surface. "You know it's not just about that. This is my dream—something I've worked hard for."

"And what about the family?" she presses, her voice rising slightly. "What about us? You think ignoring everything will make it disappear?"

Jackson steps forward, his expression a mix of protectiveness and curiosity. "Maybe we should take a moment," he suggests, his tone calm. "This seems like a conversation that deserves some space."

"No, it deserves to be said right now," Clara insists, her eyes blazing. "Because you know what? I'm tired of being the sister you pretend doesn't exist. I'm here to fix this."

Her declaration hangs heavily in the air, thick with tension and unspoken grievances. My heart races, emotions warring within me. The walls I've built around myself feel like they're crumbling, the foundations of my carefully curated world threatening to give way under the pressure.

"Clara, I..." I start, but my words falter as I struggle to form a coherent thought. Everything I thought I knew about my sister shifts beneath my feet, and I feel the ground shaking once again.

Just then, the door swings open again, this time revealing a figure cloaked in shadows. The newcomer steps forward, and as the dim light catches their face, recognition washes over me—a familiar but unwelcome sight.

"Looks like I arrived just in time," my mother says, her voice smooth and unsettling. "What's all this commotion about?"

Panic grips my chest as I take in the sight of her. The past rushes back, a flood of unresolved emotions threatening to pull me under. "What are you doing here?" I ask, my voice barely above a whisper, the words coated in a mixture of dread and disbelief.

"I heard there was a family reunion," she replies, her smile far too sweet, masking a tension I can sense in the air. "And I thought it might be nice to catch up with everyone."

The room seems to constrict around me, the atmosphere charged with the weight of years of unresolved conflict. I glance between Clara and my mother, feeling like a puppet caught in the strings of a long-forgotten drama. The brewery, once a sanctuary filled with laughter and creativity, now feels like a stage for an impending disaster.

And just when I thought the ground beneath me couldn't shake any harder, I realize that the foundations I thought I could rebuild might be crumbling faster than I ever anticipated.

# Chapter 19: The Tipping Point

The launch party pulsates with a vibrancy that crackles in the air like the static before a summer storm. Strings of fairy lights twinkle overhead, casting a warm glow over the jubilant crowd. Laughter and chatter meld into a symphony of celebration, a testament to the countless hours we poured into crafting our newest line. I stand beside Ethan, his warm presence grounding me amidst the whirlwind of excitement. His smile is infectious, and I can feel the pulse of pride in the way he stands tall, but a weight sits heavily in my chest, a reminder of Jackson's absence.

Everywhere I look, I see familiar faces—friends and family gathered to support us, their cheers a soft backdrop to the chaos in my heart. I take a sip from the cup in my hand, the crisp taste of our latest brew sending a jolt of energy through me. It's delicious, a complex blend of flavors that dances on the tongue, but all I can think about is Jackson. I had hoped he'd be here, standing beside me, sharing in this moment. The idea of him laughing at one of Ethan's goofy jokes or debating the flavor notes with a customer is almost too perfect to imagine. I force a smile, but it doesn't reach my eyes.

The moment is fleeting, and just as I begin to lose myself in the joyous atmosphere, a loud bang interrupts the celebration. My heart drops, and I turn to see a plume of foam erupting from one of the brewing stations. The sight is almost comical at first, a scene straight from a slapstick comedy where the protagonist accidentally triggers a ridiculous chain reaction. But the panic that quickly sweeps through the crowd is palpable, and I'm yanked from my reverie.

Ethan's brow furrows as he turns to me, concern etched across his features. "We need to help!" he shouts over the rising din of surprised gasps and frantic voices. Without thinking, I nod, my feet already moving toward the source of the chaos, adrenaline sharpening my senses. I weave through the crowd, the joyous celebration now transformed into a frantic mission.

As I approach the brewing station, I'm met with a sight that could only be described as glorious mayhem. Foam spills over like a frothy waterfall, creating a slippery barrier that threatens to engulf the entire table. A couple of guests stand back, hands covering their mouths in shock, while others rush forward with paper towels and cups, attempting to salvage what they can. The once-festive atmosphere is now tinged with urgency and a hint of absurdity.

"Grab that hose!" I call to Ethan, who has followed closely behind. He lunges forward, a determined look on his face, and together we work to contain the chaotic spill. Our hands move in a practiced rhythm, even amidst the chaos. I can feel the tension in the air shift as we rally together with our friends, each of us diving into the mess, laughing despite the absurdity of it all. I can't help but smile as Ethan playfully squirts foam at our mutual friend Mia, who squeals in mock horror. Laughter mixes with shouts, a cacophony that somehow brings comfort amidst the turmoil.

And then, amidst the laughter and chaos, I catch sight of a familiar figure entering through the crowd. Jackson. His presence pulls at the very fabric of my being, igniting a familiar warmth that spreads through me, though mixed with an undeniable pang of longing. He scans the room, his eyes searching, and for a moment, time stands still. The chaos fades, and all I can see is him—the way his hair falls just slightly out of place, the determined set of his jaw, the way his presence seems to command the space around him. I almost forget the foam disaster unfolding at my feet.

As if sensing my gaze, Jackson's eyes finally land on me. A flicker of recognition passes between us, igniting something deep within me. My heart races, and I fight the urge to run to him, to close the distance that has stretched between us for too long. Instead, I focus on the task at hand, forcing myself to maintain control as we work together. But my mind is a swirling mix of memories, of laughter shared and arguments had, of moments that felt so right until they didn't.

"Need some help?" Jackson's voice cuts through the noise, smooth and steady, pulling me from my reverie. He strides forward, stepping into the fray like a knight ready to battle the absurdity of the moment. My heart swells at the sight of him, the way he dives into the chaos, helping us contain the eruption, his confidence shining even in this ridiculous situation.

"Just a minor explosion!" I quip, attempting to keep the mood light, though I feel a flutter of nerves. "We're just testing how much foam one brew can produce!" I can't help the grin that breaks through, the shared laughter of the moment drawing me closer to him, even as I fight the tumult of emotions swirling within me.

"Next time, let's stick to something a bit less explosive, shall we?" Jackson replies, his lips curving into that half-smile I've missed so much. It's a small victory, this moment of connection, but it feels monumental amidst the brewing storm of uncertainty between us.

As we continue to work side by side, the connection between us reignites. It's electric, charged with unspoken words and unresolved feelings. Every glance shared, every brush of our arms sends a jolt through me, a reminder of what we once had, and what we might still have if I find the courage to fight for it. In this moment, surrounded by chaos, laughter, and the familiar warmth of Jackson's presence, I realize something profound. Our love has the power to weather any storm, and I'm not ready to let it slip through my fingers again.

With the foam finally tamed, the remnants of our chaotic escapade linger like a playful ghost. Guests have returned to their chatter, the moment of crisis transforming into a legendary tale to be shared over future pints. I wipe my hands on a towel, but the satisfaction of rescuing our launch feels overshadowed by the palpable tension swirling around Jackson and me. He stands close, his presence both a balm and a burn, igniting the dormant embers of our unresolved past.

"Can you believe we almost drowned in brew?" I say, my voice light, but the weight of unspoken words lingers between us.

"Only you could turn a launch party into a foam party," Jackson replies, laughter glinting in his eyes. It's a playful jab, one that echoes the warmth of our shared history, yet I sense a deeper layer beneath his words. He's here, yet the gap remains, filled with everything left unsaid.

Just as I gather the courage to delve deeper, Mia bounds over, her excitement infectious. "You guys saved the day! I can't believe it! This is definitely going in the highlight reel for our social media!" Her enthusiasm is like a gust of fresh air, momentarily lifting the heaviness that lingers in my heart.

"Highlight reel, huh? Maybe we should add an explosion warning next time," I tease, nudging Ethan as he joins us, a twinkle of mischief in his eyes. "We might need a liability waiver."

"Right after you sign the 'I promise never to brew anything with Jackson again' waiver," Ethan shoots back, and I can't help but laugh.

Amid the banter, I steal a glance at Jackson, who seems momentarily lost in thought. There's something about the way he stares into the distance, a furrow in his brow that hints at the unspoken conversation simmering beneath the surface. My heart races at the thought of addressing it, but as the party continues to unfold around us, it feels almost impossible to breach the chasm that has developed between us.

"Hey, you two!" Mia breaks through my thoughts, her eyes alight with mischief. "I just had the best idea! How about we do a tasting right now? The crowd is buzzing, and we need to showcase our new flavors!"

"Great idea! Let's get them involved," Ethan agrees, clearly eager to shift the energy back into celebration mode. I watch as Mia rounds up a few friends, gathering them to create an impromptu tasting table.

Jackson leans closer, his voice low enough that only I can hear. "You know, you really did a great job with the brewing this time. The flavors are phenomenal. I'm proud of you."

His compliment sends a warm rush through me, a bittersweet reminder of the camaraderie we once shared. "Thanks. I just—" I hesitate, grappling with the urge to reach for the truth, to unravel the tension between us. "I just wish you could have been part of the process."

The words hang in the air, a palpable truth lingering between us like a charged current. Jackson's expression softens, and I can see the flicker of vulnerability in his eyes. "I wish I could have too." He looks away, a storm of thoughts crossing his face. "But life got in the way, didn't it?"

"Yeah, life," I echo, frustration bubbling beneath my skin. "It's funny how it can make a mess of everything, isn't it?"

"I think it's a bit more than funny," he retorts, a hint of bitterness lacing his words. "It's downright unfair sometimes."

Before I can respond, Mia returns, dragging a few friends behind her. "All right, everyone, gather 'round! We're about to start the tasting, and trust me, you don't want to miss out on these flavors!"

With a flourish, she gestures toward the table laden with our creations. The crowd responds eagerly, laughter and chatter rising once more, drowning out the unsaid tension between Jackson and me. As the tasting commences, I bury myself in the task at hand, relishing the distraction while stealing glances at Jackson, who stands a few feet away, engaging with our guests.

"Okay, what do you think?" Mia asks as we pour samples for our eager patrons.

"It's really good, Mia. The hints of citrus in this one are fantastic," I reply, forcing my focus back to the task at hand.

Ethan jumps in, his enthusiasm contagious. "And the chocolate notes in this brew? Pure magic! I think we might have to expand our lineup."

As I pour, I notice Jackson's laughter drawing my attention once more. He seems to slip back into his element, engaging with our friends and chatting animatedly about the brewing process. It's a sight I adore, the way he can light up a room, and yet it gnaws at me—the distance between us is stark and palpable.

With each sample poured, I feel a mix of pride and longing. The new flavors we created together resonate with the crowd, but it feels bittersweet without Jackson by my side. The night unfolds with energy, and the tension between us simmers just beneath the surface, threatening to boil over.

As the tasting winds down, I decide to approach Jackson. "So, what do you think?" I ask, my heart pounding as I navigate the crowd, hoping to bridge the gap.

"It's amazing," he replies, his eyes lighting up, but there's an undercurrent of something more. "You really knocked it out of the park. I'm impressed."

"Thanks, but it's more than just the flavors, Jackson. It's the heart behind them—the passion we poured into this."

He nods, a shadow crossing his face. "Passion can be complicated, though."

"Complicated like us?" I challenge, crossing my arms, unable to keep the words at bay. The crowd blurs around us as I zero in on him.

"I didn't mean it like that," he says, though the way he avoids my gaze tells me otherwise.

"Then how did you mean it?" The words tumble out, each one tinged with frustration and vulnerability. I've been tiptoeing around this moment for too long, and I'm ready to confront whatever is lurking beneath the surface.

"Maybe I'm just scared," he admits, his voice barely above a whisper.

"Scared? Of what?"

"Of us. Of what we could be or could have been." His honesty hangs in the air, raw and unsettling.

"Maybe we should stop being scared, then," I suggest, my heart pounding as I search his eyes for a sign of understanding.

"I don't know how," he says, his expression a mix of longing and uncertainty.

"Then let's figure it out together," I say, my resolve strengthening with each word. "We've always been better when we're together."

And in that moment, surrounded by the remnants of our launch party, with laughter echoing in the distance, I realize that perhaps the messiness of life—and love—is what makes it all worthwhile.

The air crackles with a mix of excitement and tension as I stand beside Jackson, our shoulders nearly touching as we navigate this uncharted territory. Guests mill around us, oblivious to the emotional storm brewing just beyond the frothy chaos. I take a deep breath, the scent of hops and warm malt wrapping around me like a cozy blanket, both comforting and intoxicating. It's a reminder of what we've built, yet also a stark contrast to the uncertainty lingering in Jackson's gaze.

"You know, this isn't just about the brews," I say, my voice steadying as I attempt to pierce through the wall between us. "It's about everything we've gone through together."

Jackson leans against the table, arms crossed, the playful light in his eyes dimming as he processes my words. "Is it really, though? Because I feel like I'm standing on the edge of a cliff, ready to fall into a canyon of uncertainty."

"Then let's take that leap together," I respond, the words tumbling out before I can catch them. "You and me, we've always been better together."

He scoffs softly, but there's a flicker of hope beneath the surface. "Better together? That's easy to say, but what about when the ground crumbles beneath us?"

"Then we build something new." I step closer, closing the distance that feels like a chasm. "You can't keep running, Jackson. Not from me, not from us."

His eyes search mine, a vulnerability lurking just beneath the surface. "It's not just me running, you know. It's the whole world pulling us in different directions."

"Then let's make our own direction," I say, frustration edging into my tone. "Why let the world dictate our choices? We're not just brewers; we're a team."

Before he can respond, Mia bounds back over, her enthusiasm a sudden jolt that cuts through our moment. "You two are seriously the best. I think the crowd is loving the brews, but I'm pretty sure they're loving the drama even more!" She winks, clearly not aware of the undercurrents swirling between us.

"Drama? What drama?" I laugh, grateful for the reprieve but also annoyed that our moment is slipping through my fingers like the foam we just battled.

"The one that happens when two people who clearly have chemistry spend too much time together," Mia quips, her eyes glinting with mischief. "And then they just have to kiss."

The suggestion hangs in the air, heavy with unfulfilled possibilities. My heart races, and I glance at Jackson, whose cheeks have flushed slightly. The tension is electric, a moment suspended in time that teeters on the brink of something extraordinary.

"Maybe we should stop keeping the crowd waiting," Jackson says, forcing a smile as he pushes off the table, clearly retreating behind his walls once more. "Let's get back to the brews."

I watch him step away, a wave of frustration washing over me. "You can't just brush this aside!" I call after him, but the noise of the party swallows my words.

As we move back into the fray, I can feel the distance between us widen. The laughter and chatter envelop us, a warm blanket of camaraderie and celebration, yet I feel cold inside, the ache of unspoken words lingering like a shadow. I dive back into the tasting, trying to lose myself in the activity, but my heart remains tethered to the conversation left hanging in the air.

Moments pass, each filled with the delightful buzz of tasting our creations and hearing guests rave about the flavors. I pour a sample for a smiling couple, their faces lighting up with delight as they savor the blend. Each clink of glasses, each cheer, reminds me of why we do this, why I love this business, but the nagging thought of Jackson's retreat stings.

"Hey! Let's get a picture with the brew crew!" Mia calls, her voice slicing through my thoughts like a refreshing breeze. She gathers our friends around, and I manage a smile as we pose, holding up pints like trophies. The camera flashes, capturing this moment of joy, yet my heart feels heavy. I search the crowd for Jackson, but he's nowhere to be seen.

The laughter fades as the crowd moves on, and a quiet settles over the brewing station. I glance around, my eyes landing on Ethan, who seems to sense my turmoil. He walks over, his brow creased in concern. "Hey, are you okay? You seem a bit... distracted."

"I'm fine," I say, though the tremor in my voice betrays me.

"Look, I know you've got a lot on your plate, but Jackson..." Ethan trails off, his gaze searching mine. "He's not the only one struggling. You're carrying a lot of weight too, and it's okay to admit it."

"I just..." I hesitate, caught between wanting to vent my frustrations and fearing the vulnerability it requires. "I thought we were on the same page, you know? But now I feel like we're worlds apart."

Ethan nods, his expression sympathetic. "It's tough when you want something so badly but feel like you're fighting against the tides. But you need to talk to him."

"I know," I admit, the lump in my throat tightening. "But every time I try, it's like he pulls away."

"Then maybe it's time for a bold move," Ethan suggests, his eyes twinkling with mischief. "You're the brewmaster here. Take charge."

"Bold move? Like what? Throwing him into a vat of hops?" I scoff, but a spark of mischief ignites in my chest.

"No, but something that shows him you're serious. You're not just about brews; you're about him too. Show him what he's missing."

With a newfound determination, I scan the room, searching for Jackson. The idea of doing something daring sends my heart racing. And then, just as I spot him standing by the bar, a thought strikes me.

"Ethan, hold my beer." I hand him my cup, striding toward Jackson with purpose. The crowd fades into a blur as I weave through, adrenaline surging.

"Hey!" I call, my voice cutting through the laughter, and Jackson turns, surprise flickering across his features.

Before he can speak, I close the distance between us, my heart pounding louder than the party around us. "We need to talk," I say, urgency coloring my tone.

"I—" he begins, but I don't let him finish.

"Now," I insist, taking his hand and leading him away from the noise, toward a quieter corner of the venue where the music fades into a low hum.

"What's going on?" he asks, concern etched in his brow as he pulls me to a stop, eyes locking onto mine.

"Jackson, this isn't just about brewing anymore. It's about us. You and me. We can't keep pretending we don't have something real here."

He opens his mouth to respond, but before he can speak, I lean closer, my heart racing as I realize I'm about to take that leap I've been avoiding. "You have to know that I want you in my life, in whatever way that looks like. I'm ready to fight for us."

The air hangs heavy, charged with unspoken words and possibilities. Jackson's gaze softens, and for a moment, it feels like everything could shift.

But just as he opens his mouth, a loud crash echoes from the main area, pulling our attention. The party comes to an abrupt halt as the sound reverberates through the space, and my stomach drops.

"What was that?" I ask, dread creeping in.

Jackson's expression shifts from contemplation to alarm, and without another word, we both rush back into the fray, hearts pounding in unison.

As we break through the crowd, we come to a halt at the bar, where chaos has erupted. A display of bottles has toppled over, shattering onto the floor like a cascade of broken promises. Amidst the shattered glass, one bottle lies eerily intact, the label boldly declaring the flavor we had all been raving about. But it's not the spilled drinks that capture my attention.

In the center of it all, I spot a figure crumpled on the ground, a familiar silhouette shrouded in panic.

"Is that Mia?" I gasp, and Jackson's eyes widen in horror as we push through the throngs of guests now frozen in shock.

My heart races as I kneel beside her, the crowd fading into the background. "Mia! Are you okay?"

Her eyes flutter open, confusion washing over her face, and then... fear. "There was someone... someone with a mask..."

The world tilts on its axis as I lock eyes with Jackson, realization dawning like a chilling wave. The night has taken a turn I never expected, and as I grasp Mia's hand, I know this is just the beginning of something far more complex.

# Chapter 20: A Brewed Awakening

The vibrant atmosphere of the brewery buzzes like an electric current, alive with chatter and laughter, a heady mix of hops and ambition wafting through the air. I watch the crowd, their faces illuminated by the warm glow of string lights overhead, each one lost in their own world of hops and camaraderie. My heart races, not just from the thrill of the launch party but from the flicker of unspoken tension crackling between Jackson and me. It's as if the space between us is a taut wire, vibrating with every stolen glance and half-smile. The last remnants of my nerves are swept away in the joy of seeing our hard work pay off, but something deep within me churns with apprehension.

I set my glass down, the sound echoing slightly in the bustling environment, and take a moment to soak it all in. The sight of our brews being savored—golden ales glinting like treasure in the light, rich stouts swirling in deep, dark pools—fills me with an indescribable pride. Yet, amid the celebration, a disquiet lingers. It gnaws at me, urging me to address the storm brewing in the spaces between us.

Jackson is a force of nature, his presence commanding yet effortlessly comforting. I can't help but admire the way he engages with our guests, his laughter mingling with theirs, as he shares stories about the brewing process. There's a charisma in him that draws people closer, a magnetic pull that has me teetering on the edge of something both exhilarating and terrifying. But as I watch him from a distance, I can't shake the feeling that he's retreating into his own world, one where I'm no longer a part.

With the last toast still echoing in the air, I summon the courage to approach him. My heart pounds like the pulse of the music in the background, each beat urging me to confront the weight that has settled between us. "Hey, can we talk?" I manage to say, my voice barely rising above the clinking of glasses and the ebb of laughter.

He glances at me, his brow furrowing slightly, as if considering the weight of my words. There's a moment, a brief pause where the world seems to fall away, leaving just the two of us standing in this small, sacred bubble. "Sure," he replies, a tentative smile playing on his lips. The moment feels charged, electric, as we step outside, the cool night air wrapping around us like a blanket.

The stars shimmer above us, scattered jewels in the vast expanse of the sky, and I breathe in deeply, trying to steady my racing heart. "It's been an incredible night, hasn't it?" I start, my voice wavering slightly.

"Yeah, it has," he replies, his gaze lingering on the horizon, as if searching for something beyond our immediate reality. "I didn't think we'd pull it off like this."

A silence settles, thick and heavy, and I know this is my moment. I can't let the opportunity slip away like grains of sand through my fingers. "I'm really proud of us, you know? But..." I trail off, the unsaid words swirling in my mind. "I feel like something's changed between us."

Jackson turns to me, his expression shifting from the contemplative to the concerned. "What do you mean?"

"It's like there's this wall between us," I confess, my voice trembling slightly. "I can't shake the feeling that something's off. And I'm scared—scared of losing you." The admission spills from my lips, raw and unfiltered, my vulnerability hanging in the air like a fragile thread.

His expression softens, and for a heartbeat, I see the flicker of understanding dance across his face. "You think I'm going anywhere?" he asks, his voice low, almost tender. "I mean, I thought we were on the same page."

I shake my head, frustration bubbling up within me. "But it feels like we're not! You're always so... distant lately. I don't want to assume, but it's like you're slipping away."

Jackson runs a hand through his hair, the gesture filled with uncertainty. "You're right. I've been caught up in my own head, worrying about the future. With the brewery taking off, I'm terrified of what's next. What if I'm not enough?" The admission is a weighty one, and I can see the fear etched into his features, lines of worry tracing paths around his mouth.

"Jackson, you are enough," I say, stepping closer, desperate to bridge the divide. "You've built something incredible here, and I believe in you. But you have to let me in. We're a team."

For a moment, we stand there, locked in a shared gaze that feels both electric and terrifying. The night hums around us, an unseen orchestra playing the melody of our unspoken fears and desires. "I just thought that maybe you'd be better off without me," he admits, his voice cracking slightly, a note of vulnerability spilling into the cool air.

"Better off? How could you think that? I need you—your passion, your creativity. We can face the uncertainty together." I can feel the warmth of my words wrapping around us, a promise woven into the fabric of the night.

Jackson's eyes search mine, as if looking for a lifeline in the turbulent sea of our emotions. "What if it doesn't work out?" he whispers, the fear lingering in the air like a ghost.

"Then we'll figure it out together," I reply fiercely, the conviction in my voice surprising even me. "But we owe it to ourselves to try. To fight for this. For us."

The tension shifts, morphing from uncertainty to a glimmer of hope. His expression softens, the shadows of doubt lifting ever so slightly. "Okay," he says, his voice steadying. "Let's try."

And in that moment, the air crackles with promise, a renewed spark igniting between us, a vow to face whatever comes next hand in hand.

The night air hums with anticipation, a gentle breeze ruffling the strands of hair that have escaped my ponytail. Jackson and I stand together, the weight of our earlier conversation hanging like a promise between us. I can't help but steal glances at him, tracing the strong line of his jaw and the way his eyes reflect the starlit sky. There's a flicker of something in his expression—hope, maybe? It's enough to make my heart flutter with a mix of excitement and dread.

We slip back inside, where the remnants of our celebration lie scattered like confetti, remnants of laughter still echoing against the walls. Empty glasses line the bar, and the sticky floors bear witness to our joyous chaos. I grab a towel, ready to tackle the cleanup. Jackson joins me, his presence a comforting weight beside me. The silence is no longer strained but filled with an undercurrent of something unspoken, a shared understanding that feels like a fragile truce.

"Do you think they liked it?" I ask, tossing a dirty rag into a nearby bucket.

"Did you see the way they were drinking? I'd say we have a hit on our hands," he replies, a lopsided grin breaking across his face. It lights up his features, and I can't help but smile back, my heart warming at the sight.

"I can't believe we actually did it. All those late nights and questionable brewing decisions." I lean against the bar, my eyes sparkling with mischief. "Remember the batch that tasted like burnt rubber?"

Jackson chuckles, shaking his head. "I still have nightmares about that one. I thought you were going to throw me out of the brewery for good."

"Oh, please. If I'd thrown you out, who would I have had to blame for the terrible idea of adding jalapeños to a stout?" I tease, crossing my arms and raising an eyebrow.

He laughs again, the sound rich and warm, and I feel that familiar flutter in my stomach. "I thought it would be a culinary breakthrough."

"More like a culinary catastrophe," I say, rolling my eyes dramatically. "But hey, at least we learned what not to do."

The laughter dies down, leaving a comfortable silence in its wake. We work side by side, the rhythm of our movements syncing as we clean up the aftermath of our triumph. But my thoughts drift back to that weight, that moment of vulnerability. I need to keep the momentum going; we've opened a door, and I'm not about to let it close.

"Jackson," I begin, glancing up to meet his gaze. "About earlier... I meant what I said. We really do need to face things together, don't you think?"

He pauses, his hands resting against the bar as he considers my words. "Yeah, I think we do," he says slowly, his tone measured. "I don't want to pretend everything is fine when it's not. It's just... I've never really had anyone to rely on like this before."

I feel a rush of warmth, a strange combination of affection and empathy washing over me. "Neither have I, honestly. I've always had to figure things out alone. But you're not alone anymore. I promise."

He nods, a smile tugging at the corners of his mouth. "Okay, let's figure this out. Together."

Before I can respond, the door swings open with a loud creak, and in walks Emma, our resident beer connoisseur and self-appointed hype woman. She's a whirlwind of energy, her hair a wild halo of curls, and she sweeps into the room like a summer storm.

"You two! I just had to come back and tell you—everyone is still buzzing about tonight! I overheard a group saying they'd never tasted anything like your pale ale. They want to know when the next batch is ready!"

"Did you get their names? We should send them a thank you," Jackson says, his enthusiasm infectious.

"Already on it!" she replies, pulling out her phone and tapping away furiously. "But seriously, you guys are going to blow up. This is just the beginning!"

As she bounces around the room, cleaning up some of the empty glasses and stacking them in the sink, I feel a swell of gratitude. Emma has always been our biggest supporter, the one who can light up a room with her laughter. She's the kind of friend who would dive into a shark tank just to prove a point—fierce and unyielding.

"Thanks, Emma. You always know how to make us feel like rock stars," I say, tossing her a towel as she spills a few glasses while moving.

"Damn right! If you two don't start planning for a bigger space, I'll be forced to take matters into my own hands. I know a guy who runs a food truck, and he owes me a favor. We could do a pop-up event together. Just imagine! Your beer, his food..." She trails off, eyes sparkling with excitement.

"Food trucks and beer? Now that's a combination I can get behind," I say, laughing.

"I'd say it's a recipe for success," Jackson adds, his eyes lighting up with the idea.

Emma glances at us, her smile widening. "See? This is the magic I'm talking about! You two are meant for this. Just wait until you start brewing seasonal beers; people are going to flock to you like moths to a flame."

Jackson leans closer, lowering his voice conspiratorially. "You think we could do a pumpkin spice ale?"

Emma gasps dramatically, clutching her chest as if struck by lightning. "You genius! I can already taste it! We can market it as the

'Ultimate Fall Experience'! Picture it—autumn leaves, cozy sweaters, and a pint of pumpkin spice ale in hand. It'll be a hit!"

The warmth in the room grows, a blend of enthusiasm and laughter that feels almost electric. But then, like a sudden chill in the air, a wave of doubt washes over me. What if this success comes at a cost? What if the weight of expectation suffocates us?

"Okay, okay, one thing at a time," I interject, trying to steady the whirlwind of ideas. "Let's focus on what we've just launched before we dive into pumpkin spice dreams."

Emma rolls her eyes but nods, her exuberance undiminished. "Fine, fine. But just so you know, I'm keeping a running list of ideas. You two are not getting away that easily!"

As she continues her spirited chatter about potential collaborations and marketing strategies, Jackson's gaze meets mine across the room. In that fleeting moment, an unspoken agreement forms—no matter what lies ahead, we'll face it together. The laughter surrounds us like a warm embrace, knitting our hearts together in a tapestry of shared dreams, ambitions, and the gentle tug of something more profound that both excites and terrifies me.

The echoes of laughter linger as the last few guests filter out of the brewery, leaving behind an intoxicating mix of warmth and lingering chatter. I watch Emma bustle around, her energy undiminished by the long night, as she stacks chairs and wipes down tables with the enthusiasm of someone who just discovered her favorite song on repeat. It's a relief to see that despite the weight of the conversation Jackson and I had earlier, the spirit of our success fills the room like a sweet scent that refuses to dissipate.

"Okay, team," Emma announces, her hands on her hips, a faux-serious look crossing her face. "We've officially conquered the launch party. Now, who's ready for a celebratory dance-off?"

Jackson smirks, leaning back against the bar, arms crossed, looking far too relaxed for someone who's just shared their deepest fears. "I'll sit this one out, thanks. My coordination skills have been rated 'unsatisfactory' by various parties."

"Oh come on!" Emma pouts, the corners of her mouth twitching with suppressed laughter. "Are you telling me you can brew the best beer in town but can't dance? What kind of tragedy is that?"

I chuckle at their banter, the lightness of their teasing making it easier to ignore the unease that still stirs within me. "Honestly, I'm with Jackson. I prefer to keep my dancing confined to the safety of my living room," I confess, my laughter ringing genuine.

Emma throws her head back, feigning shock. "You two are a couple of squares! Next thing I know, you'll be suggesting we sit around and discuss... taxes or something equally dull."

"Whoa there, let's not go that far. Taxes are a hard pass," Jackson responds, raising his hands in mock surrender, and I can't help but grin at the ease of his demeanor. Maybe tonight wasn't so bad after all.

After a few more minutes of cleaning, the atmosphere shifts, and the excitement begins to settle into a calm satisfaction. Emma finally flops down onto one of the barstools, letting out an exaggerated sigh. "I think I've earned a beer for all my hard work tonight. Who's with me?"

"I can manage that," Jackson replies, already pouring himself a glass, and I can't help but admire the way he moves with practiced ease, a master in his element.

"Make that two, please," I call out, plopping down beside Emma. "After tonight, I need something to celebrate. Or to wash away the anxiety."

"Both, I think," Jackson says, his smile warm as he fills a second glass and slides it over to me.

As the rich, frothy liquid swirls in my glass, I take a moment to appreciate the moment—the way laughter and lingering conversations weave through the brewery, the soft clink of glasses, the smell of hops still lingering in the air. It's a tapestry of connection, a testament to our hard work. But the thought of what's looming over Jackson and me lurks at the edges of my mind, a shadow threatening to eclipse the happiness of tonight.

"Seriously, though, what's next for you two?" Emma asks, her curiosity evident. "You've got to have a plan. All this momentum can't just fizzle out like yesterday's stale beer."

I exchange a glance with Jackson, both of us momentarily lost in the depths of our thoughts. "Well, we've talked about doing some seasonal brews," I start, feeling a renewed sense of purpose washing over me. "A fall-inspired lineup sounds promising, and maybe we could do a collaboration with local food vendors."

"Absolutely! The pumpkin spice ale is still on the table!" Emma chimes in, her eyes alight with excitement.

Jackson chuckles, shaking his head. "Pumpkin spice is a slippery slope. Next thing you know, we'll be brewing eggnog beer for Christmas."

"Challenge accepted," I say with a wink, and we all burst into laughter, the tension in the room easing just a fraction.

But as the night drifts on, the laughter becomes a muted backdrop to my swirling thoughts. Jackson is still processing everything from earlier, and while I'm buoyed by the camaraderie, I can't help but feel the weight of our unsaid fears creeping back in. What does the future really hold for us?

"Hey, what's going on in that head of yours?" Emma nudges me gently, her tone shifting from playful to concerned.

I take a sip of my beer, its familiar bitterness a grounding force. "Just thinking about how much we've accomplished but also how quickly things can change," I admit, my voice quieter, the words spilling out before I can rein them in.

"Hey," Jackson says softly, leaning closer, his presence a comforting balm. "No one is going to take this away from us. We're in this together, remember?"

I nod, but deep down, a niggling doubt lingers. "But what if we can't keep it up? What if the next batch doesn't hit like this one? Or what if we can't handle the pressure?" The words tumble out, and I feel exposed, my insecurities laid bare in the dim light of the brewery.

Jackson's brow furrows, a mix of concern and determination crossing his features. "Then we adapt. We always adapt. That's what we do, right? Look how far we've come."

Emma leans in, her voice earnest. "You two are a team. And teams lean on each other. Don't forget that. I've seen you both fight for this. Don't let fear dim your shine."

Before I can respond, the bell above the door jingles, slicing through the warmth of our conversation like a cold draft. A figure steps in, silhouetted against the light outside, and my stomach drops.

It's Leah, the head of the local brewery association, her expression unreadable as she strides in, a folder clutched tightly in her hand. The moment she catches sight of us, her eyes narrow, a flicker of something inscrutable crossing her face.

"Sorry to barge in unannounced," she says, her voice crisp, cutting through the jovial atmosphere. "But we need to talk."

Jackson's expression shifts, a shadow of concern flashing in his eyes. "About what?"

Leah steps closer, and the air around us feels charged, the laughter dissipating like smoke. "About the future of your brewery. We have some concerns."

The words hang in the air like a storm cloud, the sudden shift in energy making my heart race. I exchange a worried glance with Jackson, the uncertainty bubbling to the surface once more. What could she possibly want?

Before I can voice my concerns, Leah opens the folder, revealing papers that seem to pulse with gravity. My breath catches as I realize that whatever she's about to say could change everything we've worked for.

"We've received reports...."

# Chapter 21: Rising Tides

The sun hung low over the horizon, casting a warm, golden glow across the brewery's rustic interior, where the intoxicating aroma of hops and malt danced in the air. As I stirred the bubbling cauldron of our newest brew, I could feel the energy thrumming through the space, mingling with the sounds of laughter and clinking glasses from the taproom. It was a symphony of joy, the heartbeat of a dream finally coming to life. This wasn't just any brew; it was the one we'd named after our father, a tribute brewed with both love and an unsparing sense of duty.

Ethan, my older brother and ever the perfectionist, stood beside me, his brow furrowed in concentration as he jotted down notes. "This batch needs a little more of the Cascade hops," he said, adjusting his glasses with a serious look that could only be described as adorable on him. I could feel the weight of his expectations settling heavily on my shoulders, but I embraced it. We were about to enter a regional brewing competition—a rite of passage in the brewing world, and a chance to shine outside the shadow of our father's legacy.

"More hops, less hops," I teased, grinning at him, "what's next, a secret ingredient? Should we throw in a dash of cinnamon and call it a 'brew-tiful surprise'?" The corners of his mouth twitched upward, betraying the tension that had wound itself tightly around him for days.

"Very funny, but this is serious business, Remi. We can't let any distractions pull us away from perfecting this recipe," he replied, but I could hear the lightness creeping back into his voice. I loved moments like these, where I could see the boy he used to be before the weight of our family legacy pulled him down. The laughter was an anchor, and I clung to it like a lifebuoy in a storm.

The brewing process became our shared language, a conversation spoken through the rhythms of measurements and the careful art of balancing flavors. But with every hour we spent perfecting our craft, I couldn't shake the feeling that Ethan was drifting, like a ship untethered from its mooring. He was becoming more ambitious, hungry for recognition, and with it came a distance that crept into our once inseparable bond. I missed the easy camaraderie we had built over the years, and I felt a pang of sadness each time he turned his back to me, consumed by thoughts of accolades and competition.

As I mixed in the final ingredients, my phone buzzed on the counter. It was a message from Jackson, the quiet yet charming guy who had slipped into my life like a perfectly timed plot twist. "Late-night brainstorming session? I've got a few wild ideas to toss around." A smile spread across my face as I imagined his disheveled hair and easy grin, the way he always leaned in just a little too close, as if sharing a secret.

"Can I bring my A-game?" I texted back, my heart racing at the thought of our late-night sessions, where we tossed back ideas like we were tasting our newest brews, some bitter, some sweet, all of them with a kick. Jackson had this way of pulling me into his world, his passion for brewing intoxicating me more than the finest ales.

With a quick glance at Ethan, I stepped outside, letting the crisp evening air wash over me. The brewing competition was looming, and with every step, my mind whirled with thoughts of flavors, aromas, and the potential for glory. But the whispers of doubt began to slither in, creeping through the cracks in my confidence. Would I be able to stand on that stage, shoulder to shoulder with Ethan, and not falter under the weight of expectation?

Jackson was waiting by the porch, his back turned as he gazed out at the sprawling fields. The setting sun cast a halo around him, illuminating the sharp angles of his jaw and the soft curl of his hair.

"You're late," he teased without turning around, his voice light and playful, instantly easing the tension coiled tightly within me.

"I was busy trying to save the world of brewing," I shot back, stepping beside him, my shoulder brushing against his. There was something electric in that touch, a warmth that ignited a spark of something deeper than friendship.

"Or just perfecting your dad's legacy," he replied, and the laughter faded from his voice. The weight of our family's expectations hung between us like an invisible thread, fragile yet unbreakable. I could see the flicker of understanding in his eyes, the way he recognized the burden I carried, and it made my heart flutter.

"Ethan is determined to win," I confessed, casting my gaze out at the horizon where the sky melted into a wash of vibrant colors. "Sometimes I think he's forgotten why we're doing this. It's not just about the competition; it's about honoring our father."

Jackson turned to me, his expression serious, and for a moment, I felt a wave of vulnerability crash over me. "You know it's okay to want more for yourself, right? You don't have to carry that weight alone." His voice was low and steady, like a calming tide, and it resonated with the chaos swirling inside me.

"But what if wanting more means leaving Ethan behind?" The words tumbled out, and I was surprised at their clarity. The thought of losing my brother, of watching him become a stranger in pursuit of some unattainable goal, terrified me.

"It doesn't have to be an either-or situation. You can support him while still finding your own way," Jackson replied, leaning closer, the warmth radiating off him comforting me like a well-worn blanket.

In that moment, I felt something shift between us, a recognition of shared ambitions and fears, layered beneath the surface of playful banter. It was an unspoken agreement, a promise that maybe, just maybe, we could navigate the tides of our lives together, even as the currents threatened to pull us apart.

The sun dipped lower, bathing the brewery in twilight, the light shifting to a soft lavender hue that made everything seem dreamlike. I could hear the hum of conversation from the taproom as patrons toasted our latest creation, and for a moment, I reveled in the satisfaction of having brought a little joy to their lives. But as I moved about, checking our supplies and mentally organizing the chaos of the competition ahead, a nagging sense of imbalance settled deep in my stomach, threatening to eclipse my enthusiasm.

Ethan had thrown himself into his work, obsessively poring over recipes and brewing techniques. I could almost see the gears turning in his head, each tick of ambition pulling him further away from the brother I had known. His laughter, once frequent, now escaped him like a shy bird, hidden away under layers of pressure and expectation. I found myself torn, wanting to cheer him on while also yearning for the easy banter we once shared.

"Hey, beer wizard," I called out as I leaned against the workbench, trying to inject some levity into the room. "You've been so serious lately; I half-expect you to start wearing a lab coat. What's next, goggles?"

He looked up from his notes, his brow furrowed, and the corners of his mouth twitched ever so slightly. "If I could concoct a potion that would make us win, I'd wear a full hazmat suit."

"Well, then, let's get brewing, Doctor Brewmaster. We have a competition to crush!" I flashed a playful smile, hoping to see a flicker of the Ethan who used to joke about brewing spells that would attract customers like moths to a flame.

"Right," he said, straightening up. "Let's focus on the recipe." The dismissal stung more than I wanted to admit, but I could hardly blame him. With our father's legacy looming over us, every moment felt heavy with potential failure, and I could see Ethan spiraling into a cyclone of ambition.

The following day, we hosted a small tasting session to gather feedback from some of our most loyal customers. The brewery buzzed with energy as people milled about, sampling our creations and sharing laughs. Jackson arrived, late as usual, but the casual confidence he exuded always made me smile. He slipped through the crowd like he belonged there, a cool breeze that stirred the warm air around him.

"Sorry, I got caught up in a discussion about the finer points of hop selection," he said with a grin, leaning close enough for me to catch a hint of his cologne—something earthy and invigorating. "You'd think brewers were chemists with how seriously they take their ingredients."

I laughed, enjoying the easy back-and-forth we'd developed. "Maybe they are chemists in disguise. We're just too busy perfecting our art to notice."

As we moved from table to table, discussing flavors and preferences with patrons, I felt the tension of the last few days ebbing away. Jackson had a way of making the ordinary feel extraordinary, as if every conversation held the potential for a revelation. When we reached a couple who were sampling our latest brew, I leaned in and asked, "What do you think? Too much citrus, or just enough to keep you coming back for more?"

"Oh, definitely just enough!" the woman exclaimed, her eyes sparkling. "It's like summer in a bottle!"

"Summer in a bottle?" Jackson chimed in, raising an eyebrow. "I'll have to remember that for my next marketing pitch. 'Get your summer fix, no sunscreen required.'"

"Perfect! And we'll call it our 'beach in a bottle' collection," I added, my mind racing with the possibilities. The laughter and chatter wrapped around us like a cozy blanket, and I could feel Jackson's presence steadying me, like the firm foundation beneath a house.

But as the afternoon unfolded, I noticed Ethan standing off to the side, his arms crossed, watching us with a tight-lipped smile that didn't quite reach his eyes. The weight of his gaze pressed down on me, a reminder that while I found solace in this camaraderie, he felt increasingly isolated. I was caught between two worlds, wanting to chase after my dreams while feeling tethered to my brother's expectations.

"Hey," Jackson said softly, drawing my attention back. "You good? You seem a little... off."

I sighed, glancing toward Ethan before turning back to him. "I just worry about Ethan. He's been so intense lately, and I feel like I'm losing him."

"Maybe he needs a reminder of what you two are really brewing for," Jackson suggested, his voice warm and reassuring. "Why not have a chat with him? He might just be too caught up to see what really matters."

As evening settled in, casting a deep indigo shadow over the brewery, I finally mustered the courage to approach Ethan. I found him staring at the last barrel of our brew, deep in thought. "Ethan," I began, my voice steady despite the uncertainty swirling in my chest, "can we talk?"

He turned, and for a brief moment, I thought I saw the vulnerability flicker in his eyes before he masked it with determination. "Sure. What's on your mind?"

"I know you're focused on the competition, but I miss the brother I used to joke with, the one who would sneak me sips of his favorite brews just to see my face scrunch up. I want us to be in this together, not just as business partners but as siblings."

His expression softened, and for a heartbeat, the tension broke. "I get it, Remi. I've just been trying to do everything right, and it feels like the pressure is on. I don't want to let you down."

"You won't. But you need to let me in. This isn't just your legacy; it's ours. We can't forget what we're building together."

Ethan's shoulders relaxed slightly, and I could see the weight of his ambition start to lift. "I guess I've been so focused on winning that I forgot to enjoy the ride."

Before I could respond, Jackson stepped up behind me, his presence grounding. "You know, the best brews are made when the brewmasters remember to enjoy the process. It's all about balance, right?"

Ethan turned to Jackson, and for the first time, I saw a spark of camaraderie between them. "You're right. Maybe I've been so caught up in the competition that I forgot what really matters."

"Exactly. And besides, it's not like you'll be going against anyone too tough." Jackson shot me a knowing glance, and I couldn't help but laugh.

Ethan joined in, the sound bubbling up like the foam on our freshly brewed beer. "Alright, let's make this fun again. Who knows? Maybe we'll surprise ourselves."

As the laughter echoed around us, the atmosphere shifted, and I felt the familiar warmth of our brother-sister bond wrapping around me like a comforting embrace. With Jackson by my side and Ethan finally emerging from the shadow of his ambition, I sensed that we were on the brink of something extraordinary—a blend of dreams, challenges, and laughter, all brewing together, waiting to unfold.

The atmosphere in the brewery had shifted, the weight of expectations replaced by a sense of camaraderie that made everything feel a bit lighter. With Ethan cracking jokes again, I found myself swept up in the energy, every laugh echoing like a soft drumbeat. The three of us—Ethan, Jackson, and I—had turned our brewing sessions into a blend of strategy meetings and playful banter, a recipe for camaraderie that sparked inspiration as much as it did joy.

As we stood at the brew kettle, Jackson peered into the bubbling mixture with a seriousness that made me stifle a laugh. "So, what's the plan for our next batch? We could go bold with a smoked porter, or maybe something fruity that makes you feel like you're sipping on a summer day." His grin was infectious, and I found myself leaning closer, captivated by the way his eyes sparkled with enthusiasm.

"I'm thinking something that embodies our family's spirit," I mused, trying to strike a balance between playful experimentation and honoring our father's legacy. "Maybe a honey wheat? It's light and approachable, but with a little complexity. Kind of like us, right?"

"Us?" Ethan quipped, raising an eyebrow. "I'm not sure you could ever be described as 'light and approachable.' More like 'fierce and unapologetic.'"

"Touché," I shot back, playfully nudging him with my elbow. "But I like to think there's a little sweetness to balance out the boldness. Just like our brews, there's always a hidden flavor."

As we discussed flavor profiles and ingredient pairings, I felt a wave of relief wash over me. I didn't want to lose this connection with Ethan, and Jackson's presence seemed to pull him back into the fold. It was refreshing, like a cool breeze after a sweltering summer day. Yet, beneath the lightheartedness, I sensed an undercurrent of tension. Despite the laughter, Ethan's ambition loomed larger than ever, and I could feel the clock ticking down to the competition, inching closer with every passing day.

Over the next week, our late nights became filled with tastings and tweaks, each iteration bringing us closer to a brew we could proudly enter. Jackson and I often stole glances, an unspoken bond forming with each shared joke and secret smile. We had fallen into a rhythm, one that was as intoxicating as the brews we crafted, and I couldn't shake the feeling that the chemistry between us was more than just business.

One evening, after a particularly grueling round of taste-testing, I decided to take a break. "I need some fresh air," I announced, slipping out to the back porch where the stars twinkled like scattered diamonds across the dark sky. The brewery was a sanctuary, and standing there, I could almost hear the ghosts of my father's laughter mingling with the memories of countless summers spent in the sun, all of it feeding into the heart of what we were building.

As I inhaled the crisp night air, I felt Jackson's presence beside me. "You okay?" he asked, his voice soft, as though he were afraid to disrupt the serenity of the moment.

"Just thinking," I replied, leaning against the railing. "About how much we've changed. About everything we're risking for this competition."

Jackson glanced up at the stars, his expression contemplative. "Sometimes, the biggest risks lead to the best rewards. You know that better than anyone."

"Yeah, but what if we fail?" I confessed, the words slipping out before I could stop them. "What if I fail? I don't want to let my dad down."

"Hey," he said, turning to face me, his intensity drawing me in. "You're not going to fail. You've got a talent for this, Remi. Just remember that the competition is a chance to celebrate what you've created. It's not the end-all, be-all."

His reassurance wrapped around me like a warm blanket, and I felt the flutter of something deeper growing between us. Just as I opened my mouth to respond, the door swung open behind us, and Ethan stepped outside, his brow furrowed.

"Guys, I need to talk to you," he said, his voice strained.

The lighthearted moment evaporated like mist in the morning sun. Jackson and I exchanged worried glances, the shift in Ethan's tone setting off alarm bells in my mind.

"Sure, what's up?" I asked, trying to keep my voice steady as dread coiled in my stomach.

"I overheard some things," Ethan began, running a hand through his hair in a gesture of frustration. "Some of the other brewers are already strategizing on how to undermine us. They think our success with the last brew was a fluke, and they're not just going to let us walk away with the win."

"Undermine us?" I echoed, incredulous. "What do you mean?"

"There are rumors about sabotaging our booth," he said, the words coming out in a rush. "We need to be careful. I can't let anyone tarnish our family's name."

"Wait," Jackson interjected, his expression shifting from concern to determination. "What are you suggesting? Should we change our recipe? Go for something totally different?"

"No, we need to stick to our guns," Ethan replied, his voice sharper than I'd ever heard it. "But we also need a plan. We can't just let them have free rein. We have to prepare for anything."

The tension escalated around us, thick and electric. I could feel the weight of the world pressing down on my shoulders, the enormity of our endeavor becoming glaringly real. "We'll be ready for whatever they throw at us," I said, trying to inject some confidence into the room. "We've put too much into this to let anyone take it away."

"Exactly," Jackson chimed in, his fierce gaze meeting mine. "We'll work together, come up with a strategy that leaves them speechless. They'll wish they hadn't crossed us."

Ethan's eyes flickered between us, and for a brief moment, the tension softened. "Alright, let's do this. We've worked too hard to let a few jealous brewers knock us down."

The determination pulsed in the air, a shared commitment to rise above the fray. But as we plotted our next moves, a shadow of doubt crept into my mind. The stakes were higher than I had anticipated, and with each plan we laid out, the fear of failure coiled tighter.

Just then, my phone buzzed in my pocket, pulling my attention away from the brewing storm around us. I fished it out, glancing at the screen. A message from an unknown number flashed ominously: "You don't know what you're up against. Stop now, before it's too late."

I felt a chill race down my spine, the weight of the words hanging in the air like a bad omen. I looked up, my heart pounding. "Guys, we may have a bigger problem than we thought."

The room fell silent, the atmosphere thick with tension, and in that moment, I realized we were standing on the precipice of something far more dangerous than a brewing competition. We had awakened a force we hadn't seen coming, and I feared it was already too late to turn back.

# Chapter 22: Stirrings of Doubt

The kitchen buzzes with an energy that's almost electric, the faint scent of caramelized sugar swirling in the air, mingling with the nutty aroma of freshly ground coffee beans. I stand at the counter, my hands buried in a mound of dough, flour dusting my arms like fairy dust, remnants of my relentless pursuit of the perfect pastry. My mind, however, is far from the buttery crescents rising in the oven. Instead, it spirals like a whisk through the swirling doubts that have settled into my gut since Ethan broached the subject of Jackson.

"Are you even listening to me?" Ethan's voice cuts through the warmth of the kitchen, sharp as the knife I've just set aside. He leans against the doorframe, arms crossed, brow furrowed in that all-too-familiar way that makes my heart flutter uneasily. "I'm serious, Nora. You need to focus. This competition isn't just about you. It's about us. Our family business."

I force a smile, but it feels strained, the corners of my lips twitching awkwardly. The way Ethan's tone sharpens each word sends a little prick of guilt through me. How did we end up here, tangled in this web of expectations? I glance at the mixing bowl, where the dough quietly waits, a reminder of the dreams we've been building together, dreams that now seem perilously close to unraveling.

"I know, I know," I murmur, kneading the dough with a bit more force, as if my frustration can be worked into the mixture. "It's just... Jackson is good at this. I thought it might help us. You know how hard we've worked." My words hang in the air like a bad omen, heavy with implications.

Ethan's eyes narrow, the familiar protective gleam turning into something sharper, almost resentful. "Help? You mean the guy who's always hovering around? You really think he has our best interests at heart? What does he want, Nora?" His voice is a low rumble, full of frustration that makes my heart race—not from fear, but from a deep-rooted loyalty that feels like it's being stretched to its limits.

"It's not like that," I protest, but the truth is, there's an inexplicable connection I have with Jackson. It feels effortless, like mixing batter on a quiet Sunday morning. He makes me laugh, and when he's around, the air seems lighter, as if the world outside our bakery fades into a soft blur. But I can't say that. Not to Ethan, who has always been my anchor, my partner in this chaotic dance of flour and frosting. "He just... he knows things. And he wants to help. I thought it could be good for us."

Ethan's expression hardens, the distance between us swelling like a rising soufflé. "Or he wants to take what's ours. I don't trust him. And I don't understand why you're so keen on letting him into our lives." The weight of his words presses against me, wrapping around my chest like a vise.

"Ethan, please," I say, my voice dropping to a whisper as I wipe my hands on my apron, the fabric still warm from the oven's embrace. "I care about our business, our dream, but I'm not sure if we can do this alone anymore. I'm... I'm starting to think that maybe collaboration might lead to something better."

The moment my words settle, a silence envelops us, thick and tangible. I can almost hear the clock ticking away the seconds, each one echoing with the unspoken tension that now fills the room. I take a step closer to Ethan, searching for the bridge that once connected us, the warmth of our shared dreams dimming in the shadow of doubt. "Can't we just think about this? I don't want to fight."

"I just want us to win, Nora," he replies, his voice softer but laced with an urgency that tugs at my heart. "I want you to win."

And there it is again—the chasm that yawns wider every time we try to navigate this new territory. The competition looms closer, a specter haunting our every move, and I can feel the weight of our ambition pressing down on my shoulders, heavier than the trays of pastries we carry. Every sweet treat, every perfectly glazed doughnut seems to carry the burden of our fractured trust, the sweetness of our dreams tinged with a bitter aftertaste.

As I watch Ethan wrestle with his emotions, I can't help but wonder if I'm betraying him in my search for clarity. Jackson's offer of help stirs something deep within me, a desire to break free from the constraints that have held me back for so long. Yet, I'm not sure if that freedom comes at the cost of my relationship with my brother. The stakes have never felt higher, the weight of family ties binding me to a decision I'm not ready to make.

"I just need to think," I finally say, breaking the silence that has become our unwelcome companion. The words taste like ash on my tongue, but they slip out anyway, a plea for understanding, a request for space. "Can we... can we take a step back? Just for a moment?"

Ethan's eyes flicker with a mix of frustration and hurt, and in that instant, I see the vulnerability beneath his protective facade. "Fine," he says, the single word heavy with resignation. "But you need to figure out where your loyalty lies. Because I can't do this alone."

He turns and walks away, the sound of his footsteps fading into the distance, leaving me alone in the kitchen, surrounded by the ghosts of our aspirations. I take a deep breath, the scent of yeast and sugar filling my lungs, as I stare at the dough that reflects my inner turmoil. It's as if every fold and knead is a whisper of my conflict, a reminder that my heart is caught in a tug-of-war between two worlds.

The sun dipped low in the sky, casting a golden hue through the bakery windows as I rolled out my latest batch of dough. The warmth of the day faded into a cool evening, wrapping around me like a comforting blanket. I tried to channel the stillness into my work, but the unease gnawed at my thoughts. Each swirl of the rolling pin became a desperate plea for clarity, for reassurance that I was still grounded in my path. Flour dust floated through the air, illuminated like tiny stars caught in a sunbeam, reminding me that even the smallest particles could create something beautiful.

Jackson appeared in the doorway, his silhouette framed by the fading light. He looked almost heroic, a knight in flour-dusted armor, ready to rescue me from my swirling doubts. I couldn't help but smile at the sight of him, his tousled hair catching the last rays of sunlight. "Hey, wonder woman," he said, the teasing glint in his eye softening the weight on my heart. "Are you trying to bake a new universe, or just the best croissants in town?"

"Maybe a bit of both," I replied, my voice light, though a hint of tension lingered beneath. "The universe needs a solid breakfast, don't you think?" I raised an eyebrow, trying to lighten the mood, but the smile on Jackson's face faltered for just a moment, the reality of my internal struggle flickering behind my laughter.

He stepped inside, the familiar scent of his cologne blending with the sweet and yeasty air. "I could help you with that. You know, if you need an extra pair of hands—or someone to taste test." He grinned, his playful nature a welcome balm to the chaotic thoughts in my mind.

"I might just take you up on that," I said, kneading the dough with renewed vigor. As I worked, I felt his presence anchoring me, but also stirring something deeper within—something both exciting and terrifying. "What are you doing here, anyway? I thought you had a big event tonight."

"Postponed," he replied, sliding onto a stool by the counter, an uninvited guest in my internal dialogue. "My plans for the evening were less important than helping you out. Plus, I had to check on you after your brother practically chewed my head off at the café."

I rolled my eyes, the corners of my mouth tugging upward despite the circumstances. "That sounds about right. He's been a little overprotective lately."

"Overprotective or overbearing?" he quipped, raising an eyebrow in mock accusation. "There's a fine line, you know."

"Fine, maybe a little of both," I admitted, stirring the thoughts in my mind as I stirred the bowl of dough. "But he's right to worry. We've put so much into this competition, and if I'm being honest, my head's been a mess."

Jackson leaned forward, a serious look crossing his face. "What's really going on, Nora? You don't seem like yourself lately. It's like you're wrestling with two separate lives."

The honesty in his words struck a chord, and I found myself trapped between the urge to confide in him and the desire to maintain some semblance of control. "I don't know. I guess I'm just trying to figure out how to balance everything," I said, my voice softer now, tinged with vulnerability. "Ethan wants to hold onto our dreams tightly, but it feels like the tighter he grips, the more I want to break free."

"Break free?" Jackson echoed, his brow furrowing slightly. "Break free how?"

I paused, my hands resting on the counter as I searched for the right words, the weight of our conversation shifting the air around us. "I love what we've built together, but sometimes I wonder if there's more out there for me. I want to grow, to explore new ideas. But I don't want to hurt Ethan. He's... he's my brother."

"Brothers can be protective, but they can also hold you back if you let them," he said, his voice low but firm. "You have to do what's right for you, Nora. At the end of the day, it's your life. You're not just an extension of your family."

His words lingered in the air, a revelation I had skirted around for weeks. I wanted to embrace them, to dance in the freedom they offered, yet fear twisted within me. "What if my choice tears us apart?" I asked, my heart racing as I thought about Ethan's hurt, his frustration.

"Isn't it already tearing you apart?" Jackson countered gently. "You're standing at a crossroads. You can't keep pretending that everything's fine. You owe it to yourself—and to him—to be honest."

I wanted to argue, to pull back from the precipice he was nudging me toward, but something deep inside me stirred. "You're right," I whispered, the admission feeling like a weight lifting from my shoulders. "I've been holding back, trying to protect everyone but myself."

"Then let's figure this out together," he said, his tone softening as he reached for the dough, his fingers brushing mine in a casual yet electrifying gesture. "You don't have to do it alone."

As we worked side by side, laughter erupted between us like the bubbling of a well-crafted sourdough. He offered ridiculous suggestions about flavor pairings—bacon-infused chocolate croissants, anyone?—and each suggestion made my heart soar and crack all at once. His presence felt like a warm embrace, urging me to embrace the unexpected twists of life rather than shy away from them.

Just as we reached the perfect point of fluffiness in the dough, the doorbell jingled, slicing through our lighthearted banter. I glanced up to see Ethan standing there, arms crossed, his expression an intricate tapestry of annoyance and concern.

"Jackson," he said, his tone clipped, "what are you doing here?"

"Helping out," Jackson replied coolly, a hint of challenge glimmering in his eyes. "Nora needed an extra hand."

"I see that," Ethan said, his voice icy enough to chill the warm air around us. "And I guess my sister doesn't need me anymore."

The tension that had briefly melted in our laughter snapped back into place, thickening the atmosphere as if the walls themselves were closing in. I felt the world tilt, caught between the two people I cared for most, each representing different paths—one tethered to loyalty and familiarity, the other a wildflower growing in unexpected soil.

"Ethan, it's not like that," I said, rushing to bridge the chasm forming between them. But deep inside, I realized I couldn't promise anything. Not anymore.

The tension in the bakery was palpable, like the crisp air before a thunderstorm. Jackson stood with his arms crossed, casting a side-eye at Ethan that could curdle milk. I could practically hear the unspoken words ricocheting off the walls as I fought to navigate the precarious tightrope of loyalty strung between them. The aroma of freshly baked bread wafted around us, a comforting backdrop to this culinary battlefield where emotions simmered hotter than the ovens.

"Seriously, Jackson?" Ethan's voice sliced through the silence, sharp enough to cut through dough. "You think it's a good idea to swoop in here like some pastry knight? You know we have a plan."

"Yeah, I do know the plan, but maybe it needs a little tweaking," Jackson shot back, his tone teasing yet firm. "I mean, have you tasted her croissants? They could practically fly off the shelves on their own."

"Don't humor him," Ethan retorted, turning his gaze toward me, the urgency in his eyes mirroring the rising heat from the ovens. "Nora, this isn't a game. It's our business. You're not just playing with flour; you're playing with our future."

I opened my mouth to defend Jackson, to explain that his presence felt like an infusion of creativity and energy, but the words stalled in my throat. Instead, I found myself caught in a storm of loyalty and ambition, each emotion vying for dominance. My heart raced, but not from the stress of the competition—rather from the weight of the choices looming over me.

"Look, Ethan," I finally said, my voice steadier than I felt. "Jackson's not here to take anything from us. He wants to help. Can't you see that?"

"Help or sabotage? There's a difference," Ethan shot back, his jaw tightening as he stepped closer to Jackson, the two of them locked in a standoff that felt all too familiar. "You think I'm just going to let him interfere?"

"Maybe you should let her make that decision," Jackson said, lifting his chin defiantly, his expression a mixture of annoyance and concern. "This is Nora's dream, too. It's time she gets to choose what that looks like."

The moment hung between us, heavy and fraught with unsaid truths. I could feel the ground shifting beneath my feet as both of their gazes turned to me, the proverbial ball now firmly in my court. I opened my mouth to speak, my heart pounding like a drum in my chest. But before I could formulate my thoughts, the doorbell jingled again, breaking the tension like a fragile eggshell.

A woman stepped inside, her energy electric and out of place amid our brewing storm. With fiery red hair and an infectious grin, she scanned the room until her eyes landed on me. "Nora! I'm so glad to find you here," she exclaimed, bounding over with an exuberance that felt like a breath of fresh air in our stifling atmosphere. "I've heard incredible things about your bakery!"

"Um, thank you?" I replied, slightly bewildered by her enthusiasm. "I'm glad you think so."

"Are you kidding? I'm Carla, by the way. I'm a food blogger and culinary school grad," she announced, thrusting her hand toward me, palm open and inviting. "I'm here for a project, and I just had to see if the croissants lived up to the hype. I can already tell they do!"

Ethan and Jackson's attention momentarily shifted to her, their expressions softening as they took in her energy. I seized the opportunity, a small spark of hope igniting within me. "Well, we're just about to bake some fresh batches. Would you like to help? It's a bit chaotic, but you might just enjoy it."

"Chaos is my middle name!" Carla laughed, and her laughter echoed in the kitchen, warming the air around us. "I'm in!"

As we moved together, mixing and shaping the dough, I felt a sense of camaraderie building, a welcome distraction from the simmering conflict just moments before. With Jackson tossing flour at Carla, who retaliated with a spritz of water, the bakery morphed into a scene of playful chaos. My heart swelled as I watched them laugh, but an undercurrent of tension still twisted in my gut, whispering reminders of my unresolved dilemmas.

Ethan's arms remained crossed, but even he couldn't suppress a smile as he observed the friendly chaos. "Okay, I'll admit, this is entertaining," he said, a hint of warmth creeping into his tone. "But we're still on a tight timeline. We can't afford to mess this up."

"Don't worry, Captain Serious," Carla shot back with a wink. "This is all part of the creative process! You've got to let it flow, like the dough." She paused, her gaze flicking between the three of us. "And it's clear you guys have some... interesting dynamics going on."

"Interesting is one word for it," Jackson quipped, casting a sly glance at Ethan. "More like a soap opera without the dramatic music."

"Just what we need," Ethan muttered, rolling his eyes. "An audience for our sibling drama."

The lighthearted banter helped chip away at the walls I had erected around my fears, yet they still loomed ominously in the background. Just as I began to feel buoyed by our new team spirit, Carla's phone buzzed on the countertop, vibrating like a warning bell. She glanced down at the screen, her expression shifting from playful to serious in a heartbeat.

"Uh-oh, looks like my editor wants a word," she said, biting her lip. "I might need to step out for a moment."

"Don't worry about it. We can handle the rest," I said, my voice steady despite the sudden swell of anxiety. "We'll be right here when you're done."

Carla nodded, slipping outside with a hurried wave, leaving an odd silence in her wake. The warmth of our laughter faded, and the kitchen felt suddenly colder, the playful chaos replaced by the charged atmosphere that had settled in before.

"Nice distraction," Ethan said, turning to Jackson with a mix of sarcasm and relief. "But we still need to talk about this."

"Talk about what, exactly?" Jackson shot back, his tone defensive. "That she's not just a pastry chef? That she's capable of being more than just someone who bakes for you?"

"Guys, let's not do this now," I interjected, my heart racing again as I felt the familiar tension return. "I need to focus on the competition, not on another argument."

"Is it really about the competition, or is it about making sure everyone else is happy while you're stuck in the middle?" Ethan asked, his voice strained with frustration. "Because I can tell you, it's tearing you apart."

Before I could respond, the door swung open again, this time with a force that sent a rush of cold air swirling into the kitchen. A tall figure stepped inside, and I recognized him instantly: Marcus, the head judge for the upcoming competition. His presence was a sudden and unwelcome storm cloud, casting a shadow over our already precarious moment.

"Good evening, everyone," he announced, his gaze piercing through the tension. "I hope I'm not interrupting anything important."

His words hung in the air, filled with implications I couldn't quite grasp. My pulse quickened, anxiety mixing with the brewing storm of emotions as I struggled to read the room. I could feel the weight of my decisions pressing down on me, each heartbeat a reminder that I was standing at a crossroads where everything could change in an instant.

"Actually, you might be," Ethan replied, his tone uncharacteristically tense as he met Marcus's gaze. "We were just about to have a serious discussion about our strategy."

"Strategy?" Marcus echoed, a hint of curiosity in his eyes. "Now that sounds interesting."

And just like that, the ground beneath me felt unsteady, the swirling winds of uncertainty spiraling faster as the looming competition threatened to shatter the fragile alliances I had built.

# Chapter 23: Colliding Worlds

The air was electric, charged with the vibrant pulse of a crowd drawn together by a shared passion for craft brewing. The venue transformed into a kaleidoscope of activity: booths adorned with twinkling fairy lights, banners fluttering like excited flags, and the intoxicating aromas of malt and hops swirling together, tempting even the most discerning of palates. As I stood behind our booth, surrounded by the artful arrangements of our carefully curated beers, my heart fluttered with an excitement that bordered on mania. Today was more than just a competition; it was a chance to showcase everything we had poured into our brews and, in some ways, into each other.

Ethan was at my side, his presence a mixture of steady confidence and a subtle apprehension that mirrored my own. He adjusted the display, ensuring our bottles were aligned with obsessive precision. The way he focused on the task, tongue peeking out ever so slightly from the corner of his mouth, made my heart skip a beat. I wanted to reach out, to brush my fingers against his arm and reassure him that we were ready, that we were a team. But instead, I busied myself with a half-empty glass of our signature brew, the fizzy liquid a comforting companion.

"Do you think we'll make a splash?" I asked, trying to keep my tone light, though an undercurrent of anxiety threaded through my words. My eyes flicked to Jackson, who was deep in conversation with a rival competitor. He looked effortless, his charm radiating like sunlight, drawing people in like moths to a flame.

Ethan glanced in the same direction, his expression unreadable. "He seems to have that effect on people," he said, a hint of something unnameable in his voice. I caught the slight tension in his jaw, the way his eyes narrowed ever so slightly. It was a look that stung more than I expected.

I rolled my shoulders back, willing away the jealousy clawing at my insides. "I just... I need to talk to him. I can't let this day go by without making things clear."

Before Ethan could respond, I slipped away, the sea of faces blurring together as I approached Jackson. He was animated, laughing, his entire being illuminated by the thrill of competition. I could feel the magnetic pull between us, the undeniable chemistry that thrummed in the air.

"Hey," I said, my voice steady despite the tumult in my chest. His gaze met mine, and for a heartbeat, the world around us faded. The other competitors and the chaos of the venue became mere background noise as I took in the way his smile lit up his face.

"Fancy seeing you here," he replied, his voice playful, teasing. "What's a girl like you doing at a competition like this? Shouldn't you be off sipping something fruity and Instagramming your lunch?"

I laughed, but it felt more like a nervous giggle. "Very funny. I'm here to win, thank you very much. I thought you'd be busy charming the judges, not chatting up the competition."

"Oh, but you know I save my best lines for you," he shot back, and the intensity in his eyes sent a thrill racing through me.

"Jackson, we need to talk. About us." The words hung between us, heavy and electric, a challenge I dared to throw into the air.

His smile faltered, and the lightness evaporated. "Is this about what happened last week? Because I thought we were—"

"Complicated? Yeah, I get it. But today feels different. The stakes are high, and I can't keep pretending that what we have is just a casual fling." My heart pounded, every beat echoing in my ears as I held his gaze.

"Who says it's just a fling?" he replied, voice low and serious.

The moment was fragile, suspended in time, until Ethan's voice sliced through the atmosphere like a cold knife. "Hey! Are you two ready to get this show on the road? We've got a competition to win!"

I turned to see him striding toward us, his brow furrowed in a mix of annoyance and urgency. The tension between Jackson and me snapped like a brittle thread, and I felt the heat rising in my cheeks as I stepped back, breaking the spell.

"Right, of course. Just... give me a second." I couldn't hide the frustration in my voice, the ungracious interruption boiling under the surface. I felt Jackson's eyes on me, and for a moment, I was acutely aware of the weight of what had been unsaid, the moment suspended like a note waiting to resolve.

As Ethan pulled me back toward our booth, I shot a glance over my shoulder, desperate to catch Jackson's expression, to find some hint of how he felt amidst the whirlwind of competition. But he stood there, arms crossed, a shadow of contemplation crossing his face, leaving me with more questions than answers.

"Focus, okay?" Ethan said, his tone clipped as he arranged our bottles, the meticulousness bordering on frantic. "We can't let anything distract us from the goal."

I nodded, but my thoughts were still tangled in the electric moment I'd shared with Jackson. Ethan continued to fidget, his movements sharp and decisive, but my mind wandered to the way Jackson's eyes had sparkled with mischief and promise, the warmth of his presence lingering like a fragrant aftertaste.

As the judges made their rounds, the energy surged around us, competitors chatting and laughing, their enthusiasm infectious. I took a deep breath, pushing aside my conflicting emotions. The stakes were higher than ever, and I couldn't let the tremors of my heart derail our hard work. We were a team, after all, and I needed to remember that above everything else. Yet the specter of Jackson loomed large, a whirlwind of possibility that threatened to sweep me off my feet just when I thought I'd finally found solid ground.

"Let's make some magic happen," Ethan said, his voice steady, pulling me back into the moment. I looked at him and saw not just my partner in brewing but also a friend who believed in our vision. Together, we could brew something extraordinary. But as I poured our first samples, the image of Jackson lingered at the edge of my mind, a reminder that in this vibrant world of competition and craft, everything was about to change.

The competition unfolded around us like a fever dream, a swirling tapestry of laughter, clinking glasses, and the heady aroma of hops that danced through the air. As I poured the first samples of our brew, a tantalizing blend of citrus and caramel, I felt a rush of adrenaline, a reminder that I was here to showcase my craft. The booth became a small sanctuary amid the chaos, filled with the soft glow of our lighting and the promise of success.

"Not bad, right?" Ethan said, nudging me with his elbow, his eyes sparkling with excitement as he watched the first wave of tasters approach. I couldn't help but smile back, the warmth of his enthusiasm contagious. Together, we had poured our hearts into every step of this process—from recipe creation to branding, and now, standing before the crowd, it felt like all our efforts might finally bear fruit.

The first tasters leaned in, their expressions eager and expectant. I carefully filled their glasses, the golden liquid catching the light just so, creating tiny rainbows that shimmered in their eyes. "Here you go, folks! A taste of sunshine in a bottle," I proclaimed, channeling my inner pitchwoman. They took a sip, and the silence that followed was thick with anticipation.

"Wow! This is incredible!" One woman exclaimed, her eyes widening in delight. The rush of approval sent a thrill through me, but my gaze darted back toward Jackson's booth, where he was engaging with the crowd, laughter ringing out like a melody. He had this effortless charm, the kind that drew people in and held them rapt. My heart sank just a little. Could I compete with that?

"Hey, you're killing it!" Ethan's voice broke my reverie as he flashed me a grin, and I realized I had been lost in my thoughts while he was serving customers with an infectious energy. "You need to keep the conversation flowing. Remember, it's not just about the beer. It's about the experience!"

I nodded, shaking off the remnants of envy clinging to my mind. "Right! The experience. Let's create a moment." I turned to the next group of tasters, leaning in slightly, my voice playful. "So, what brings you to our little corner of craft paradise?"

They responded eagerly, sharing stories about their brewing adventures and what they hoped to find at the competition. As I listened, I felt the tension from earlier begin to fade, replaced by a sense of camaraderie that seemed to envelop us all. I was in my element, weaving connections over shared interests, and it felt good—so good that I almost forgot about Jackson.

Almost.

Throughout the day, I caught glimpses of him, his laughter ringing out over the chatter, each sound like a siren song that pulled at my heart. It was ridiculous how much he affected me; just the sight of him could send my stomach into a delightful knot. But every time I tried to approach, my feet felt like lead, caught in a tug-of-war between my desire to speak to him and the nagging doubts swirling in my mind.

"Is everything okay?" Ethan asked during a lull, his brow furrowing slightly as he glanced in Jackson's direction. "You seem a bit... distracted."

"Just thinking about how to stand out," I replied, forcing a lightness into my voice. "It's a competitive atmosphere, and I need to keep my game face on."

He nodded, clearly not buying my attempt at nonchalance. "You're doing great, but don't forget why we're here. You know, beyond winning."

The gentle reminder hit home. This was about more than just the competition; it was about sharing our passion, about the joy of brewing itself. But the nagging thought of Jackson lingered in the back of my mind like a ghost, refusing to let me fully embrace the moment.

As the afternoon sun began to dip, casting a warm golden hue over the venue, I saw Jackson walk over, a bottle of his own brew in hand. My heart raced, and I forced myself to smile, determined to project confidence.

"Looks like you're keeping busy," he said, his tone teasing yet warm as he nodded toward our booth. "Is this where I tell you how incredible your beer is, or do you want me to be more original?"

"Originality is overrated," I shot back, leaning against the table, unable to hide the grin tugging at my lips. "Besides, who needs originality when you've got charm?"

He laughed, the sound a delightful mixture of amusement and admiration. "Touché. But really, it's impressive. You've got a great thing going here."

"Thanks! We've worked hard to make it happen. You know how it is." I leaned in, a rush of courage pushing me forward. "But I've been meaning to talk to you, about what we started last week."

His expression shifted, a flicker of something indecipherable crossing his face. "Yeah? I figured we'd left that behind. It was all a bit... intense."

"Intense, sure. But that doesn't mean it wasn't real." The words tumbled out before I could catch them, the urgency of my feelings pressing to the surface. "What we shared—what I felt—that was real."

"Are you sure you want to revisit this right now? We're in the middle of a competition, and I—"

"I do want to revisit it. Because I don't want to pretend anymore. Not with you, not with myself." The honesty surged within me, warming my chest like a freshly brewed cup of coffee on a chilly morning.

Jackson's gaze softened, and for a moment, I felt as if the world around us faded into a blur, leaving just the two of us suspended in a fragile bubble of possibility. "You really mean that, don't you?" he asked, his voice lower now, threading through the noise like a soft melody.

"I do. But if this conversation is too much right now, I get it. We can talk later," I said, my heart pounding with uncertainty. I watched as the emotions flickered across his face, a reflection of the struggle that mirrored my own.

The moment lingered, charged with unspoken words and emotions swirling like the hops in a brewing kettle. Just as I felt hope blooming in my chest, Ethan interrupted once more, his tone urgent as he pulled me aside. "We've got a line forming, and the judges are coming! Are you ready?"

With a deep breath, I tore my gaze away from Jackson, the anticipation and anxiety mixing together like a complex brew. "Yeah, I'm ready," I replied, though my heart still ached for the words I hadn't finished.

As I turned back to the booth, the world resumed its frenetic pace, the cheers and laughter washing over me like waves. I had come here to make a mark, to share our creations, but in the whirlwind of competition, my heart remained tethered to Jackson. I couldn't shake the feeling that our story was only just beginning, and the brewing tension between us was destined to erupt, transforming everything I thought I knew about love, competition, and the craft we both cherished.

The competition roared to life, a cacophony of laughter and clinking glasses weaving through the air like a vibrant tapestry. As the crowd swelled around us, I threw myself into the task of pouring samples, reveling in the sheer energy that pulsed through the venue.

The judges made their rounds, tasting and critiquing with discerning eyes, but I found my focus drifting toward Jackson more than I'd like to admit.

"Hey! Save some charm for our customers!" Ethan teased, snapping me back to the moment. He was at my side, organizing our display with an intensity that made me feel both grateful and a little guilty. I could see his determination shining through, a stark reminder that this competition meant a great deal to both of us.

"Right. My bad!" I laughed, forcing my attention back to the eager faces in front of us. "What can I get you all? Sunshine in a glass or a little bit of moonlit magic?"

The crowd laughed, the atmosphere lightening under the weight of our banter. I poured another sample, listening to the compliments roll in, each one a small victory that chipped away at the doubt I had carried with me all day.

Yet, every time I caught Jackson's eye across the room, the buoyancy I felt would falter, replaced by a tidal wave of uncertainty. There was a magnetism between us that felt too potent to ignore, yet every interaction seemed to dance around the real conversation we needed to have. It was as if we were both playing a game of chicken, waiting for one of us to blink and declare the rules.

As I poured another round, a familiar figure stepped up beside me, his brow knitted with a mix of excitement and concern. "You're really working it today," Jackson said, his voice laced with sincerity. The warmth in his eyes melted some of the tension still coiling in my chest.

"Thanks! It's easier when the crowd is this lively," I replied, holding his gaze for a moment longer than intended. "But I still owe you a proper chat."

"Can't we just have a drink instead?" he replied, a mischievous grin creeping across his face. "I'm pretty sure you're brewing something fantastic. Why not celebrate?"

"Because I need to tell you—"

"Or you could just try my brew first." He interrupted, lifting a bottle he had in hand, its label gleaming with ambition. "A little friendly competition?"

I sighed, half-amused and half-exasperated. "Jackson, you're dodging the conversation!"

"Maybe I'm just trying to lighten the mood before we plunge into the depths of emotional discourse." His smile was disarming, the kind that made it difficult to remain serious. "How about this—if I win, you owe me a date. If you win, I'll sit down and listen. Deal?"

"Are you serious?" I narrowed my eyes playfully. "You think you can distract me with a wager? I'll take that bet."

The challenge hung in the air, each of us grinning like we were in on a secret joke. I poured a generous glass of our brew and handed it to him. "Alright, then. May the best brewer win!"

As the competition unfolded, it was impossible not to get caught up in the thrill of the moment. We went back and forth, teasing and challenging each other with each sip. The stakes felt impossibly high, not just for the competition but for what loomed unsaid between us.

At last, we both poured our brews for the judges. They took sips, the tension thickening like a well-cooked stew, and I felt my heart racing. I could barely catch Jackson's eye; we both knew that this was more than just beer—it was a metaphor for everything left unresolved between us.

"May I have your attention, please!" A voice boomed from the stage, and the crowd hushed, eyes turning toward the judges. I squeezed Jackson's arm for a moment, my heart pounding. This was it. "After much deliberation, we are ready to announce the winners of this year's craft brewing competition..."

Jackson leaned in closer, his breath warm against my ear, igniting my senses. "Whatever happens, just know that I'm glad you're here."

The judges continued, each word a drumroll of anticipation. "In third place, we have a standout brew that captured our attention with its unique flavor profile: the Lavender Wheat from Greenfield Brewing!"

The crowd erupted in applause, and I clapped along, the excitement buzzing in my veins. My fingers brushed against Jackson's, a momentary spark igniting between us. He grinned, clearly caught up in the atmosphere, and I couldn't help but smile back.

"And now, for second place..." Another pause, the room holding its breath. "The Dark Chocolate Stout from Moonlit Brewing!"

More applause. My heart sank a little, but I forced myself to remain upbeat, leaning into the adrenaline. I caught Jackson's gaze, both of us sharing a silent acknowledgment of how far we had come.

"And finally, in first place, the winner of this year's competition..." The moment stretched into eternity, the air thick with possibility. "Is the Citrus Cream Ale from Briarstone Brewing!"

The applause erupted, and for a fleeting moment, I felt the breath leave my lungs. I stood frozen, staring at the judges, disappointment washing over me. A hand landed on my shoulder, and I turned to find Ethan, his expression a mixture of pride and concern.

"We'll get them next time," he said gently. "You were amazing."

But I could barely hear him over the noise in my head, the realization settling heavy in my heart. I had poured my passion into every sip, and yet, it hadn't been enough. My gaze flitted back to Jackson, who was applauding with genuine enthusiasm, his smile infectious, but it only twisted the knife deeper.

Just then, the crowd surged toward the stage, eager to congratulate the winners. I felt lost in the sea of faces, disappointment and frustration battling inside me. And then, out of nowhere, a voice called out from the crowd.

"Wait! Before everyone scatters, I have something to say!" It was one of the judges, his voice cutting through the chatter. All eyes turned to him, the room descending into a hush once more.

"I want to take a moment to highlight a particular brew that didn't win but deserves special recognition for its bold flavor and unique approach." My stomach dropped, curiosity mingling with dread. "I'd like to commend the Tropical Sunrise from Briarstone Brewing, whose creativity and execution captivated our judges. This brew, though not awarded today, has a potential that simply cannot be overlooked."

A wave of whispers rippled through the crowd, my heart racing as I felt Jackson step closer to me, curiosity lighting his eyes.

"Did you hear that?" he murmured, a grin spreading across his face. "They're talking about you!"

"I can't believe it," I said, my heart fluttering with unexpected excitement. It was a glimmer of recognition amidst the disappointment, and I felt a flicker of hope.

"And for that reason," the judge continued, "we invite the brewer to join us for an exclusive mentorship program with some of the industry's best. Congratulations!"

My mouth fell open in disbelief as the crowd erupted into applause, and I caught sight of Jackson's astonished expression. Just when I thought I had lost everything, the universe threw me a lifeline.

But before I could react, before I could fully grasp what this meant, I noticed a figure slip through the crowd—one that I hadn't expected to see. A face from my past, someone who had sworn to stay away. My breath caught in my throat as my stomach twisted with a combination of dread and recognition.

"Seriously?" I whispered, feeling the color drain from my face. "What are you doing here?"

The world around me blurred as the familiar figure moved closer, a mischievous smile spreading across their face. "I came to shake things up," they said, the glint in their eyes promising chaos. "And it looks like I've found the perfect moment to do just that."

The air crackled with tension as my heart raced, and I stood frozen, torn between the triumph of my brewing success and the looming uncertainty that now threatened to overshadow it all.

# Chapter 24: Chasing Shadows

The air was electric, charged with anticipation and the scent of freshly ground coffee wafting from the bustling stalls around me. I maneuvered through the crowd, feeling the thrum of excitement ripple through my veins like the espresso I'd so expertly brewed. Each face was a blur of enthusiasm and nerves, yet amid the chaos, I found my anchor in Ethan, who stood beside me, his eyes darting like sparrows in search of shelter. I could practically see the wheels turning in his mind, each anxious thought tumbling over the next, creating a cacophony that threatened to drown out the excitement around us.

"Look at them," he said, nodding toward a group of competitors across the tent, their faces painted with determination. "Do you think we stand a chance?"

His voice was laced with trepidation, and it twisted my stomach into knots. The weight of our family legacy felt heavier today, like a leaden cloak that had been draped over my shoulders since I could remember. With every competition, every brewing session, we weren't just representing ourselves; we were carrying the hopes and dreams of everyone who had come before us—our parents, our grandparents, each one a shadow whispering in our ears, urging us forward while simultaneously weighing us down.

"Of course, we do!" I replied, forcing enthusiasm into my voice, though my heart wasn't quite convinced. "Our coffee is the best in the county. Trust me." I shot him a smile, hoping to dispel the clouds gathering in his blue-gray eyes.

He sighed, raking a hand through his tousled hair, the action both endearing and exasperating. "I just don't want to let anyone down."

Before I could respond, a familiar face broke through the crowd, its presence sending a surge of warmth through my chest. Jackson was striding toward us, his confident smile disarming. His dark hair caught the sunlight, creating a halo around his head, and for a moment, everything else faded into the background. Jackson was a reminder of what could be—a distraction from the weight of expectations.

"Hey, you two!" he called out, his voice smooth like the dark roast we'd perfected. "Are you ready to blow the judges away?"

I could feel Ethan stiffen beside me, and I quickly glanced at him, noting the tension that had returned to his shoulders. Jackson's enthusiasm was infectious, but it felt like a spotlight shining on my own uncertainty, magnifying the chasm between my brother's hopes and my own tangled feelings for the competition.

"Absolutely," I said, a little too quickly. I plastered a grin on my face, determined to keep the spirits high. "We've got our secret weapon brewing back at our stall."

"Oh?" Jackson raised an eyebrow, his expression teasing yet intrigued. "What's the secret? You know I can't resist a good mystery."

Ethan shifted uncomfortably, glancing between us. "It's just a new blend," he said, his tone betraying the anxiety that lingered beneath the surface. "Nothing too fancy."

Jackson's eyes sparkled with mischief. "Nothing too fancy? I doubt that. You two have a knack for surprises. I'm just hoping to see you both in the finals."

I felt a pang of warmth at his words, but it quickly twisted into something more complex—a mixture of loyalty to Ethan and the fluttering excitement of Jackson's presence. "We'll do our best," I said, though I could sense a storm brewing within me.

As the competition commenced, I watched competitors take their turns, each more skilled than the last. The judges, with their discerning palates and steely gazes, examined every pour and every aroma with meticulous scrutiny. The energy was palpable, and I thrived on it, even as a gnawing anxiety settled in my chest.

When it was finally our turn, I felt my heart hammering like a war drum. We approached our station, and I exchanged a glance with Ethan, who seemed more nervous than ever. I placed my hand on his arm, giving it a reassuring squeeze. "We've got this."

We poured our first brew, the rich, dark liquid swirling in the judges' cups, and I couldn't help but feel a rush of pride. This was our creation, a product of countless late nights and frantic experiments, and I wanted nothing more than for it to be recognized.

But as we served our brew, I caught sight of Jackson at the judges' table, chatting with one of the judges, his laughter ringing out like music. The sight of him sent a jolt through me, a reminder of the world outside of this coffee bubble. My mind wandered, chasing shadows of doubt and desire that flickered at the edges of my consciousness.

After our turn, Ethan pulled me aside, his expression clouded with worry. "What if we don't make it?" he asked, his voice barely above a whisper. "What if all this work was for nothing?"

I could see the uncertainty gnawing at him, and I fought to find the right words. "Ethan, we've worked too hard to let fear win. This is just one competition. It doesn't define us."

But as I spoke, doubt began to fester within me too, a gnawing reminder that this moment was a crossroads. It was at this moment, with the tension between us, that Jackson returned, his demeanor suddenly serious.

"Can I talk to you for a second?" he asked, glancing at Ethan, whose anxiety only seemed to deepen.

"Sure," I replied, my stomach twisting in knots. What could he possibly want to discuss now?

He led me a few steps away from the crowd, and I could feel the weight of Ethan's gaze boring into my back. "I just got some news," he said, his expression shifting to something more solemn. "I've been offered a position in Seattle."

The words hung in the air like an unresolved note, a sharp edge slicing through the atmosphere. My heart raced, caught between shock and confusion. Seattle? "That's... incredible, right?" I managed, though my voice trembled slightly, betraying the swirling emotions beneath the surface.

"It is, but I have to decide soon," he said, his eyes searching mine for a response. "And I wanted you to hear it from me before you heard it from anyone else."

As the reality of his words sank in, I felt the world around me shift, the vibrant colors dulling to gray. My head spun with the implications—could he really leave? Did I want him to stay? "What about... us?" I asked, my voice barely above a whisper, the words escaping like fragile butterflies.

Jackson's expression softened, but there was a flicker of uncertainty there too. "I don't know, to be honest. It feels like the right opportunity, but I can't help but think about what it means for us."

The shadows of uncertainty loomed larger, heavy and suffocating. I felt torn, suspended in a moment that seemed to stretch on forever. Behind us, Ethan stood with his arms crossed, his worry evident, yet the bond I felt with Jackson was undeniable. The line between loyalty to my brother and my growing feelings for Jackson blurred, and the stakes of this competition suddenly felt far less significant compared to the emotional storm brewing in my chest.

"I need some time to think," I finally said, a whisper of resolve beneath the weight of my confusion. "We all do."

As I turned back toward the competition, I felt the lingering tension wrap around me like a shroud, a bittersweet reminder that while the competition was just beginning, my heart was already racing toward an uncertain finish line.

The buzz of the competition hung in the air like the rich aroma of the coffee brewing in our stall, but now it felt more like a cacophony of tension rather than the sweet symphony of camaraderie I had hoped for. I glanced back at Jackson, who stood a few feet away, lost in conversation with another competitor, his animated gestures a stark contrast to the knot in my stomach. His presence was intoxicating, yet right now, it felt like a storm brewing on the horizon. I turned my attention back to Ethan, whose anxiety was palpable, and I knew I had to keep our spirits high.

"Remember the first competition we did?" I asked, a nostalgic smile creeping onto my face. "We nearly set the kitchen on fire trying to impress the judges with that caramel drizzle."

He chuckled softly, his posture relaxing a fraction. "I thought you were going to burn the house down," he replied, his lips twitching at the memory. "I still can't believe we pulled it off without a trip to the ER."

"Clearly, we've come a long way since then," I said, nodding toward the judges who were deep in conversation, their notes scribbled on clipboards like ancient runes waiting to be deciphered. "Today's just another step in our journey."

But even as I spoke, doubt curled around my heart like ivy creeping up a crumbling wall. Ethan was counting on me, and I couldn't shake the feeling that my head—and my heart—were drifting in opposite directions. Just as I began to lose myself in the moment, trying to summon the optimism I was so desperate to cling to, Jackson reappeared, his expression more serious than before.

"I need to talk to you both," he said, drawing us away from the thrumming energy of the crowd. Ethan's brow furrowed in concern, and my pulse quickened in response to the sudden shift in mood. "It's about the job offer."

The air between us thickened, the weight of his words hanging heavily. "I thought we were done discussing that," I said, my voice barely above a whisper, as if speaking too loudly might shatter the fragile bubble we were encased in.

"I know, but things have changed." Jackson ran a hand through his hair, his eyes darting between us. "I wasn't going to say anything until after the competition, but I got an opportunity to work with a coffee company in Seattle that's practically a dream come true. They want me to head their marketing strategy."

"That's amazing!" I exclaimed, but my excitement felt hollow. "You should go for it. It's a fantastic opportunity."

Ethan's silence was palpable, a void where his usual banter would have filled the space. I turned to him, desperately searching for a glimmer of support, but found only a storm brewing in his eyes. "You can't just leave," he said, his voice strained. "Not now, not after everything we've worked for."

"I'm not trying to leave," Jackson said, frustration creeping into his tone. "But this isn't just some casual offer. It's a chance to build something significant. I've worked my ass off to get to this point."

"And what about us?" I asked, my voice cracking as I stepped into the emotional chasm that was widening between us. "What does this mean for our relationship?"

Jackson opened his mouth, then closed it, his expression a mix of regret and confusion. "I don't want to lose you, but I can't ignore what's right in front of me. I need to think about my future."

Ethan turned away, his hands clenched at his sides, a silent protest against the unraveling of the plan we had forged together. "You both need to do what's best for yourselves," he finally said, his voice low, the weight of his words resonating deeply. "I just can't believe you would choose a job over... us."

"Don't you see?" Jackson replied, his frustration palpable. "This could help us, too! If I succeed in Seattle, it could mean more for our brand. More for all of us."

"Is that what you think?" Ethan scoffed, the hurt lacing his words sharper than any knife. "You're talking about leaving when we've just poured our hearts into this competition. It feels like you're abandoning us."

A chill settled between us, freezing the enthusiasm I had fought so hard to kindle. I opened my mouth to intervene, but the words were caught in my throat, tangled with the chaos of my emotions. "Let's just focus on the competition for now," I said, desperate to steer us away from this impasse. "We can figure everything out afterward."

"Right," Jackson said, his voice flat, disappointment shadowing his features. "I'll go back to the booth."

Ethan's shoulders sagged, the tension between us palpable as Jackson walked away, the space he left behind suddenly feeling cavernous. I reached for Ethan's arm, squeezing it gently, but he pulled away, eyes darting back to the judges who had returned to their stations. "This isn't just about the competition," he said, his voice barely a whisper. "You know that, right?"

"I know," I replied, desperation creeping into my tone. "But can we just focus on this? Please?"

We turned back to the booth, the clamor of the crowd washing over us, and I could see Jackson already preparing our next brew, a dark cloud hovering over him. My heart ached at the sight, a pang of longing and confusion intertwining with the bitter taste of coffee on my tongue.

As the competition continued, each team took their turn, the atmosphere electric with the buzz of creativity and passion. Our stall was a whirlwind of activity, the scents of brewing coffee mingling with the chatter of enthusiastic patrons. But beneath the surface, I felt the tension simmering, a slow burn that threatened to ignite at any moment.

With every pour and every smile, I could sense Ethan's frustration rising, his energy dipping like the brew in our carafe. I couldn't blame him. Our hopes, our dreams—everything we had poured into this competition felt overshadowed by the storm brewing between Jackson and us.

"Hey, Ethan," I said, trying to coax a smile from him. "Remember the way we used to blend our flavors back at home? The cinnamon and chocolate fiasco? We thought we'd invented something revolutionary."

He cracked a small smile at the memory, the corners of his mouth lifting just a touch. "Yeah, and you nearly set your hair on fire trying to toast the cinnamon. Classic."

"Just think of today as one big experiment," I suggested, injecting a note of levity into the air. "And hey, if we don't win, we'll still have all the stories to tell, right? Stories we can laugh about when we're old and gray."

"Sure, but I'd prefer to win," he said, the spark of his competitive spirit returning. "Let's just nail this brew."

We resumed our preparations, but as we worked side by side, I could feel Jackson's presence lingering in the background, the unresolved tension gnawing at the edges of my focus. The more I tried to ignore it, the more it pulsed like a drumbeat beneath the surface.

Just as we finished our next batch, I caught sight of Jackson again, and something shifted in the way he spoke to the judges. He was charming and animated, an aura of confidence radiating from him that pulled me in. And suddenly, the weight of our earlier conversation crashed back into my consciousness. I had to confront this uncertainty before it spiraled any further.

As I watched Jackson from across the stall, his laughter ringing out like music, I couldn't help but feel an undeniable pull. Maybe it was the coffee swirling in my veins or the ache of my heart, but I knew I had to make a decision. Was I ready to chase after the shadows of uncertainty, or was it time to step into the light, even if it meant risking everything I had built with Ethan?

The competition pulsed around me, a vibrant mix of clinking cups, enthusiastic chatter, and the heady aroma of coffee mingling with sweat and anticipation. Each round brought its own unique wave of tension, and I felt as though I were caught in a riptide, fighting against the current while desperately trying to keep my footing. Jackson was a dazzling comet in the chaotic night sky, his laughter echoing across the crowd, but the gravitational pull of his news loomed larger than ever.

"Let's focus," Ethan said, breaking me from my reverie. He was back at our stall, arranging the cups with a practiced precision that spoke of our countless hours spent preparing for this moment. The meticulousness of his movements grounded me, reminding me of the brother I had always leaned on. "We need to present a solid front. You're not still hung up on that conversation, are you?"

"Of course not!" I exclaimed too loudly, feeling the heat rise in my cheeks. "I mean, yes. Maybe a little?"

He shot me a knowing look, eyebrows raised in that familiar brotherly way that said, You're not fooling anyone. I sighed, rubbing the back of my neck. "It's just... Jackson is so passionate. I want to support him, but I also can't ignore how much this competition means to us."

"Let's not turn this into a family therapy session," he replied, his tone light, but I could sense the edge beneath it. "We're here to win. So let's win, okay? One cup at a time."

I nodded, taking a deep breath to steady myself. "Right. One cup at a time."

With renewed determination, I dove into the rhythm of our preparation, pouring, grinding, and brewing with precision. Every cup we served brought a small victory, each positive nod from the judges a moment of fleeting elation. But no matter how much I immersed myself in the task, the thought of Jackson's potential departure nagged at the back of my mind like an unsung melody that refused to leave me in peace.

The crowd swelled, and with it came an influx of caffeine-fueled energy. Competitors rallied together, exchanging playful jabs and tips while families and friends cheered loudly, igniting a communal spirit that reverberated through the air. It was in this chaos that I spotted Jackson again, standing near the judges, his charm evident in the way he gestured animatedly. Each laugh that escaped his lips felt like an unintentional reminder of what I stood to lose.

"Hey! Are you two ready to dazzle the judges?" Jackson's voice cut through the noise, his grin infectious.

"Ready as we'll ever be," Ethan replied, tension loosening just a bit as he took in Jackson's energy. "Just trying not to trip over our own feet."

"Or your own dreams," I added with a teasing smile. "That would be a real tragedy."

Jackson's gaze lingered on me for a moment longer than necessary, and I felt a strange flutter in my chest, a pull I couldn't quite decipher. "Just don't forget about me when you're basking in glory," he shot back playfully, and for a moment, I allowed myself to enjoy the lightness of the exchange, the way we could dance around our feelings without acknowledging them head-on.

"Glory, huh?" Ethan said, chuckling. "We're aiming for a participation trophy at best."

"Yeah, well, at least we'll have stories to tell," I countered, hoping to dissolve the tension that crackled in the air. "When we're old and gray, reminiscing about this wild ride."

Jackson tilted his head, the mischief in his eyes softening. "I'd like to be part of that story, you know."

The moment hung between us, suspended in time. I felt the weight of his words, an unspoken promise that both thrilled and terrified me. But before I could respond, the head judge approached our stall, clipboard in hand, ready to assess our offering.

"Let's give them a show," Ethan murmured, snapping me back to reality.

We dove into our performance, working seamlessly as a team, the rhythm of our actions synchronized like a well-rehearsed dance. I poured, Ethan added the finishing touches, and together we presented our coffee with pride. The judges sipped, their faces inscrutable as they took notes, and I felt a rush of adrenaline.

But in the midst of our brewing ballet, a sudden crash erupted from the far side of the tent, jolting everyone into a startled hush. A competitor's table had toppled over, sending cups flying and coffee splattering everywhere. Gasps filled the air, and the chaotic scene unfolded like a slow-motion film, capturing the panic and disarray.

I caught sight of Jackson dashing toward the commotion, a determined look on his face as he sought to help the fallen competitor. My heart raced, caught in a tug-of-war between admiration and worry. Why was I feeling this mix of fear and attraction?

Ethan followed my gaze, concern etched on his features. "Should we help?"

"Yes, we should," I replied, my heart in my throat as I watched Jackson lift cups off the ground, his hands deft and quick. "Let's make sure everyone's okay."

As we rushed over, I felt a surge of purpose. We might have our own competition to focus on, but this was a community built on passion and shared love for coffee, and I couldn't abandon that ethos in our moment of desperation.

"Are you alright?" I asked the competitor, who was frantically trying to gather her spilled supplies. Jackson stood beside me, the tension in his posture easing as he helped her collect her things.

"I think so," she gasped, shaking her head in disbelief. "I just wanted to make a good impression, and now I've ruined everything."

I knelt beside her, our eyes meeting. "You've still got time. Don't give up. Here, let us help."

Jackson glanced at me, a flicker of gratitude in his gaze, and I could feel the world around us fading away. Suddenly, it felt less like a competition and more like a shared journey, a collective fight against the odds.

As we helped her reset her station, I caught Jackson's eye again, and for the briefest moment, the chaos faded into the background. The two of us stood shoulder to shoulder, a silent understanding passing between us. Whatever was happening, whatever storms brewed on the horizon, we were navigating this journey together, even if we were unsure of where it would lead.

Then, out of nowhere, the head judge approached our makeshift rescue team, his brow furrowed with concern. "I need to speak with you, Jackson."

My heart plummeted as I watched Jackson's expression shift to something serious. He turned toward me, and in that moment, I could see the questions swirling in his eyes. "I'll be right back," he said, and as he walked away, the air between us felt charged, electric with unsaid words and unfulfilled promises.

Ethan and I stood there, the competitor finally thanking us, her spirit lifted slightly as she resumed her preparations. I felt the weight of uncertainty pressing down on me, a familiar ache that threatened to unravel everything I had built.

"What was that about?" Ethan asked, crossing his arms.

"I don't know," I said, biting my lip. "But it didn't look good."

Before we could speculate further, the judges' voice boomed across the tent, announcing a break in the competition. A ripple of murmurs spread through the crowd, and I felt my stomach tighten. The world around me suddenly felt fragile, each passing moment heavy with anticipation.

And then, like a flash of lightning splitting the sky, I saw Jackson standing at the judge's table, his face a mask of disbelief as he leaned in closer, his eyes wide with shock. The crowd shifted, and I could barely make out the words exchanged, but I sensed the tension crackling in the air.

In that instant, everything shifted. My heart raced as I strained to hear, desperate for answers. I could feel the weight of the moment building, and the uncertainty that had shadowed me all day now blossomed into something more significant, more terrifying.

And just as the tension reached its peak, Jackson turned back toward me, his expression unreadable. The world fell silent, and I knew that whatever news he had received would change everything.

"Julia," he called, urgency in his voice. "You need to come here. Now."

I exchanged a glance with Ethan, dread pooling in my stomach. I felt the ground shift beneath my feet, the foundations of my world trembling as I rushed toward Jackson, the horizon before me dark and uncertain.

# Chapter 25: Cracks in the Foundation

The air outside is crisp, a refreshing contrast to the charged atmosphere we just left behind. Jackson leads the way into the dimly lit courtyard, his hands stuffed deep in his pockets, shoulders hunched against the chill. The stars twinkle like scattered diamonds, indifferent to the whirlwind of emotions swirling within me. I take a moment to breathe, inhaling the mingled scents of damp earth and blooming jasmine, letting them anchor me as I grapple with the bittersweet victory we've just experienced.

"Hey," Jackson says, breaking the silence, his voice light yet laden with unspoken truths. "I know it wasn't what you wanted, but you guys did great out there. Honorable mention is no small feat."

I nod, a smile creeping onto my face despite the disappointment lodged like a stone in my throat. "Thanks. I guess I just thought we had a shot at winning." My words hang in the air, heavy with the weight of unmet expectations.

"You did have a shot," he reassures, leaning against the rough stone wall. "It's just... the judges are a fickle bunch. Who knows what they were really looking for?" He shrugs, an effortless movement that seems to encapsulate his laid-back nature.

A soft laugh escapes me, the tension in my chest easing slightly. "Fickle? That's a kind way to put it. I'm starting to think they were just looking for reasons to tear us apart."

"Don't be dramatic," Jackson replies with a playful roll of his eyes. "But, hey, at least we're not going home empty-handed, right?"

Just then, a gust of wind sweeps through, rustling the leaves overhead, and I shiver. "Right," I reply, though it feels like an empty sentiment. My gaze drifts back toward the brightly lit hall, where laughter and chatter spill through the doors, masking my lingering uncertainty. Inside, Ethan is probably surrounded by his friends, celebrating our small victory, and I can't help but feel a pang of longing to be with him—though the space between us feels larger than it did moments ago.

"Do you think he's okay?" I ask, my voice barely rising above the rustling leaves. Jackson glances back toward the hall, brow furrowed, and I wonder if he can sense my worry, how it hangs in the air between us.

"Honestly? I think he's putting on a brave face," Jackson replies, his gaze thoughtful. "He cares a lot about this, you know? And he probably feels the pressure more than you realize."

"Yeah," I murmur, feeling the reality of our situation settle uncomfortably in my chest. "But it shouldn't just be about him. We're a team."

"Sometimes, teams don't mean the same thing to everyone," Jackson observes, his tone thoughtful. "Maybe he needs to hear that from you. Open up a little. You're both holding back, and it's not just about the competition anymore."

As he speaks, the weight of his words settles over me, making it hard to breathe. "You're right. I should talk to him," I say, almost as a mantra, trying to convince myself that it will be that simple. But as I prepare to turn back, the moonlight casts a shadow of doubt over my resolve.

"Go on," Jackson urges, his smile encouraging. "You've got this."

Taking a deep breath, I turn away from him and head back towards the hall. Each step feels heavier than the last, my heart drumming a nervous beat against my ribs. Inside, the atmosphere is electric, filled with the sound of clinking glasses and boisterous laughter. I search the crowd for Ethan, and when I spot him at the edge of the dance floor, my breath hitches. He's standing with his friends, his smile bright but his eyes distant. It's as if he's physically present but emotionally miles away, a feeling that mirrors my own inner turmoil.

I approach cautiously, feeling the chatter around me fade into a dull roar. When he catches sight of me, his expression shifts, a flicker of relief mingling with something I can't quite identify. It's all there, an emotional cocktail bubbling just beneath the surface.

"Hey, there you are!" he exclaims, a little too loudly, as if he's trying to mask the tension that crackles between us.

"Hey," I reply, struggling to keep my voice steady. "I wanted to talk. Can we step outside for a moment?"

His brow arches, surprise evident. "Now? In the middle of the celebration?"

"Yes, now," I insist, my heart racing as I take his hand and lead him away from the crowd. We slip through the door and into the night air, the world outside a stark contrast to the lively scene within.

Ethan watches me with an unreadable expression, and I feel the weight of my words hovering on the tip of my tongue, trapped in the cage of my anxiety. "I know tonight didn't go as we hoped," I begin, the words tumbling out in a rush. "But I need you to know that I'm here. I'm not going anywhere, no matter what."

He opens his mouth, then closes it again, a flicker of something—fear, maybe?—passing through his eyes. "It's not just about the competition, is it?"

"No, it's not," I admit, the air thickening with unspoken truths. "I've been feeling... distant from you, and I'm scared that this might be more than just a bump in the road."

His gaze sharpens, the realization dawning upon him. "You feel it too?"

"Like the ground beneath us is cracking," I say, my voice barely a whisper. "I don't want to lose us over a trophy or an honorable mention."

Ethan steps closer, the warmth of his body a stark contrast to the cool night. "You're not going to lose me. But we need to talk about what's really going on between us."

Just as his words hang in the air, we lean in, the tension crackling around us like static electricity, but the moment is shattered as Jackson's voice calls out from behind us, pulling me back to reality.

The moment hangs in the air like the taste of stale champagne, fizzled and forgotten. Jackson's voice cuts through my thoughts, pulling me back from the edge of that electric moment with Ethan. "Hey, you two, come on! We're celebrating here!" His carefree tone is like a buoy tossed into turbulent waters, reminding me of the world we've stepped away from.

I turn, watching as Jackson waves enthusiastically, his smile bright and unguarded, a stark contrast to the tightness in my chest. It's difficult not to feel like a pretender in this vibrant celebration. Behind him, the crowd pulses with laughter, and I catch glimpses of familiar faces, each one smiling with an enthusiasm I can't quite muster. It feels like I've stepped into someone else's story, one that's bursting with joy while I'm stuck on a precipice, peering into the uncertainty below.

Ethan shifts beside me, his presence a comforting weight. "Maybe we should go back inside," he suggests, his tone betraying none of the vulnerability that lingers just beneath the surface.

"Yeah, I guess," I reply, though I'm hesitant. The flicker of connection we almost ignited feels fragile, like a candle flickering in a draft. I'm not ready to extinguish it just yet.

"Or," Jackson interjects, his eyes gleaming with mischief, "we could go for an impromptu adventure. Who says we have to stick around here?"

I glance at Ethan, who raises an eyebrow, a playful spark igniting in his gaze. "Adventure sounds tempting," he replies, the tension in his shoulders easing just a bit. "What did you have in mind?"

Jackson's grin widens. "Let's grab a few drinks and head down to the river. It's only a ten-minute walk, and I have a stash of those fancy sparkling waters you love."

The idea of leaving the stifling atmosphere behind is appealing, and the thought of sitting by the river, surrounded by the sounds of nature and the distant hum of the city, sparks a flicker of excitement in my chest. "Okay," I say, glancing at Ethan, who nods.

Before we know it, we're navigating through the lively throng, weaving between laughter and clinking glasses. The night air is rich with the scent of roasted nuts and sweet pastries from a nearby vendor, a sensory explosion that grounds me amid the whirlwind of emotions. As we step outside, the cool air hits my face like a splash of cold water, awakening me from my daze.

The path to the river is lined with twinkling lights strung between trees, creating a fairy-tale ambiance that contrasts sharply with the tumultuous feelings swirling within me. I fall into step beside Ethan, the tension between us stretching like a tightrope, both exhilarating and terrifying.

"You're quieter than usual," he says, his voice teasing, as if he's testing the waters.

"Just saving my energy for the epic after-party," I quip back, hoping to deflect the gravity of our earlier conversation.

"Right, because an after-party with sparkling water is exactly what everyone dreams of," he retorts, chuckling.

"Don't knock it. Sparkling water is the drink of champions," I declare, my tone playful. "Besides, I'll bring the real party with my amazing storytelling skills."

"Now that's a claim I'll have to see to believe," he counters, smirking at me with a challenge in his eyes.

As we near the riverbank, the sound of water rushing against the stones fills my ears, a calming rhythm that lulls my racing thoughts. Jackson leads the way, already bubbling over with enthusiasm. He crouches near the water, tossing in a pebble and watching it skip across the surface, each ripple spreading outward like our unspoken worries.

"Okay, who's in for a toast?" Jackson calls, producing a couple of cans of sparkling water from his backpack, the sunlight glinting off them like little beacons of hope.

"I guess that's our champagne," I laugh, the sound of it bright and unguarded, cutting through the lingering tension.

Ethan takes a can, holding it up like a trophy. "To honorable mentions and spontaneous adventures!"

"Cheers!" we chime in unison, our voices echoing off the water as we clink our cans together.

The first sip is crisp and refreshing, a burst of citrus and bubbles that dances on my tongue, somehow managing to dissolve some of the anxiety coiling in my stomach. I glance at Ethan, and for a moment, our eyes lock, the air between us thick with everything left unsaid.

"Okay, storyteller," Jackson nudges, clearly oblivious to the current simmering between us. "Regale us with tales of your most embarrassing moments!"

"Oh, now that's a low blow," I protest, laughing despite myself. "You're going to regret asking me that."

"Never! Give us the good stuff!"

I launch into a tale of a disastrous bake sale where I mistook baking powder for baking soda, resulting in a kitchen explosion that left my mother convinced I was trying to create a new form of modern art. Laughter erupts, Jackson doubling over, while Ethan leans against a tree, a genuine smile lighting his face.

"Okay, that one takes the cake—literally," he says, shaking his head. "But you've got to do better than that. You can't just skim the surface."

"Fine, fine! You want real dirt?" I grin mischievously. "I once went on a date where I accidentally called my date by my ex's name. Talk about a conversation killer!"

Ethan bursts into laughter, the sound rich and melodic, sending warmth spiraling through me. "And he didn't run for the hills? You must have some serious charm."

"Clearly, it wasn't my charm that kept him around," I reply, winking.

We continue to swap stories, each laugh pulling us closer, weaving a tapestry of camaraderie against the backdrop of the river. Yet, beneath the surface of the lighthearted banter, an undercurrent of unspoken feelings surges, threatening to breach the fragile walls we've built around ourselves.

As the night deepens, and the stars reflect on the water, I feel that old ache return, the weight of what's unsaid becoming heavier. I steal glances at Ethan, his face illuminated by the soft glow of the moon, and I can't shake the feeling that the path we're on is diverging, each moment pulling us toward a crossroads.

"Alright, enough about me," I finally say, shifting the focus back to him. "What's the most embarrassing thing you've ever done?"

He pauses, a playful glint in his eye. "Oh, I have a good one. But it's going to cost you..."

Before he can finish, a loud splash breaks the moment, and we all turn to see Jackson, arms outstretched, having lost his balance and toppled into the river. His surprised expression is comical, and we burst into uncontrollable laughter, the sound reverberating into the night, washing away some of the tension that had lingered like a cloud above us.

"Rescue me!" Jackson sputters, his laughter mingling with the water as he flounders, splashing us in the process.

"Okay, okay! Hero to the rescue!" Ethan shouts, darting towards the riverbank, his earlier uncertainty forgotten in the rush of the moment. I can't help but smile, the warmth of camaraderie mingling with the chill of the air, and for a fleeting moment, everything feels just right, even as the cracks in the foundation of our relationships threaten to deepen once more.

Jackson, still sputtering and dripping wet, has completely upended the moment. His laughter pierces the night like a firework, bright and surprising, drawing both Ethan and me back from the precipice of our unresolved tension. As Ethan rushes to help him, I can't help but laugh at the ridiculousness of it all. The sight of Jackson, soaked from head to toe, splashing around like a bewildered puppy in the moonlight is enough to lighten my heart, even if just for a fleeting moment.

"Okay, maybe I went a little overboard," Jackson says, wiping water from his face. "But can you blame me? This is the most fun I've had in weeks!" He turns to me, eyes sparkling. "You should have seen your face when I fell! Pure horror and amusement all at once."

"Hey, at least you're making a splash in the competition, even if it's not the way we planned," I quip, still chuckling.

Ethan stands next to Jackson, his expression a mix of amusement and disbelief. "You really are something else, you know that?" he says, shaking his head in mock exasperation.

"Guilty as charged!" Jackson replies, arms raised in mock surrender. "But you both love me for it." He takes a step back, the water still glistening on his clothes, and strikes a dramatic pose. "Behold! The Great River Explorer!"

I can't help but laugh again, the sound bubbling up from somewhere deep within me. The laughter feels like a release, washing away some of the earlier weight pressing on my chest. But beneath it all, I can still feel the threads of tension weaving their way back into the fabric of our evening, a quiet reminder of the conversation I had been so eager to start.

After a few more moments of laughter, I glance at Ethan, who is still watching Jackson with that same smile that makes my heart flutter. It's not just the laughter that's shared; it's the comfort of friendship, the unspoken bond that's tethered us together through thick and thin. Yet, even as I feel that warmth, I can sense the distance creeping back in, shadows settling between us like a fog.

"Alright, Great River Explorer," Ethan says, stepping closer, "let's get you dried off. We can't have you catching a cold before the next big adventure." He places a hand on Jackson's shoulder, guiding him away from the water's edge.

"Aw, but I was just getting to the good part," Jackson protests, though he follows Ethan, a playful pout on his face.

"I think we've had enough excitement for one night. You can save the river tales for the morning."

As we start to walk back towards the main path, I fall into step beside Ethan. The sound of Jackson's chatter fades into the background, and a comfortable silence settles between us. My heart races as I struggle with the urge to break that silence, to say what's been on my mind ever since we stepped outside.

"You were really great back there," I finally say, breaking the quiet. "I mean, you handled everything with Jackson like a pro. He's lucky to have you as a friend."

Ethan glances at me, his expression shifting, a flicker of something deeper passing between us. "He's lucky to have you too. You always know how to bring the energy back, even when it feels like everything is falling apart."

I catch his gaze, and the moment feels charged, a silent acknowledgment of the turmoil that lingers beneath our surface. "It's just... I don't want to feel distant from you, Ethan. I want us to talk about what's been happening."

He opens his mouth, but before he can respond, Jackson, ever the disruptor, interjects, "Did someone say my name? Because I think I heard 'distant' and 'tension' in the same breath!"

"Are you eavesdropping again?" I retort, laughter escaping despite my best efforts to stay serious.

"Eavesdropping is such a strong word. I prefer 'situationally aware.'" Jackson smirks, his eyes dancing with mischief. "What's the scoop? Are we spilling tea or just avoiding it like a true professional?"

"Professional avoidance, mostly," I say, casting a sidelong glance at Ethan, who is trying hard not to smile.

"Classic," Jackson replies, leaning back against a lamppost, still dripping with water but completely unfazed. "You two should just stop pretending and admit how great you are together. It's like watching a rom-com in real life."

Ethan looks at me, a soft smile playing on his lips. "Is it really that obvious?"

"Obvious? It's practically glowing in the dark!" Jackson exclaims, throwing his hands up for emphasis. "You guys are like peanut butter and jelly. Just meant to be."

The warmth that spreads through me at his words is a curious mixture of embarrassment and elation. I can feel my cheeks flush, and I glance away, pretending to be deeply fascinated by the way the streetlights reflect off the water.

"Okay, maybe we are a little like peanut butter and jelly," I admit, teasingly. "But that doesn't mean we're ready for the sandwich assembly line yet."

"Let's just say we're more of an 'open-faced' sandwich at this point," Ethan adds, his tone light but his eyes serious. "No pressure."

"An open-faced sandwich sounds messy," I shoot back, my heart pounding in my chest. The playful banter provides a welcome distraction, but deep down, I know the conversation still hangs in the air, waiting to be addressed.

Jackson snickers. "I love that we're mixing metaphors now. But seriously, you two need to figure this out. You're either going to end up as a great sandwich or a great disaster."

"What kind of disaster?" I ask, intrigued.

"Oh, you know—like one of those three-alarm fires that make for great stories but leave everyone scrambling," he replies with a grin.

Ethan chuckles, and I can't help but smile at the ridiculousness of it all. Yet, beneath the laughter, there's a growing sense of urgency. Jackson's words linger like a ghost, echoing the very fears I've been harboring.

As we make our way back to the main event, Jackson suddenly stops, his expression shifting from playful to serious. "Wait, did you hear that?"

"What?" I ask, straining to listen over the distant sounds of laughter and music from the hall.

"Sounds like someone's in trouble," he replies, his brow furrowing. "I think it's coming from over there." He gestures towards a darker stretch of the path that veers away from the light, the shadows deepening ominously.

"Are you sure?" Ethan asks, his voice dropping as he scans the area.

"Yeah, I'm positive. It sounded like—"

Before he can finish, a piercing scream shatters the night air, sending chills down my spine. The sound echoes through the stillness, sharp and desperate.

"Let's go!" Ethan shouts, and without waiting for a response, he sprints towards the sound. Jackson and I exchange frantic glances before following closely behind, adrenaline surging as the shadows close in around us.

As we dash down the path, the night transforms into a blur of uncertainty and fear, the laughter fading into the distance, replaced by an urgency that feels all too real. My heart races as we approach the source of the commotion, each step heavy with dread.

Just as we round the corner, the sight that greets us stops me in my tracks. A figure looms in the shadows, their posture threatening and unfamiliar. Fear grips my chest, a hard knot that makes it difficult to breathe, as everything I thought I knew about this night unravels in an instant.

"Get back!" I hear Jackson shout, and in that moment, everything shifts.

# Chapter 26: Brewing Storms

The aroma of hops and barley hung thick in the air, weaving through the coppery warmth of the brewery like an old friend. I leaned against the polished wooden bar, my fingers tracing the grain as I took a deep breath, hoping the familiar scent would anchor me against the tempest swirling in my mind. The gentle hum of machinery buzzed in the background, harmonizing with the soft chatter of patrons, a contrast to the tumultuous thoughts crowding my brain. Just a few days after the competition, everything had changed, yet nothing felt truly different. Jackson's laughter echoed in my ears, a soothing melody that played on repeat, but the joy it brought was clouded by an oppressive weight.

I poured a pint of our seasonal ale, amber and effervescent, its bubbles racing to the surface, each pop a reminder of the life I had chosen to lead. A few days ago, that choice felt simple, a clear path marked by ambition and camaraderie. But standing here now, uncertainty churned like a brewing storm on the horizon, dark clouds creeping closer, threatening to drown out the sunlight. The clink of glasses and the low murmur of conversation faded into white noise as my thoughts spiraled back to Ethan.

He had always been the dependable one, the rock upon which our family business rested. Yet, in his drive to revolutionize our father's legacy, I felt his vision eclipsing my own desires, pressing me into a role I wasn't ready to accept. The late-night discussions had grown tense, each of his suggestions—take on more responsibilities, take the lead on new projects—sounding less like advice and more like orders. I was a cog in his grand machine, and the more I resisted, the harder he pushed.

"Dani," he had said, his voice clipped, eyes dark with frustration, "you need to step up. This isn't just my business. It's ours."

And therein lay the rub. It felt like he was claiming a path for both of us, but I was standing still, anchored by doubt. Every time I thought I could take a step forward, the ground beneath me felt more unstable. I knew how it felt to carry our family's legacy; I had grown up with it whispering in my ear, telling me where to go and what to do. But now it screamed, drowning out my own voice.

The door swung open with a soft jingle, and the chilly breeze carried in a fresh wave of excitement. Jackson stepped through, his cheeks flushed from the cold, a bright grin lighting up his face like a beacon in the dark. He was a storm of his own kind, unpredictable yet thrilling, and I couldn't help but smile in return, the tension in my chest easing just a fraction.

"Hey, what are you doing in here?" he asked, moving closer, the warmth of his presence wrapping around me like a cozy blanket. "I thought you were going to help with the tasting tonight."

"Needed a moment," I replied, my voice softer than I intended, like I was revealing a secret. "Ethan and I had... a disagreement."

Jackson raised an eyebrow, his curiosity piqued. "About the business?"

I sighed, the weight of my emotions crashing over me again. "It's more complicated than that. He wants me to take on more, and I just... I don't know if I'm ready for all of it. And then there's us."

A shadow flickered across his face, the brightness dimming slightly as he processed my words. "What do you mean, 'us'?" His tone was playful, but the underlying concern was palpable.

"Exactly that. I love what we have, but I can't shake the feeling that I'm being pulled in too many directions. I'm afraid of losing it all—losing you, losing my place in the family, losing myself."

Jackson stepped closer, his fingers brushing against mine, sending a spark through my body. "You're not going to lose me," he said firmly, his voice steady as if he were grounding me in reality. "We can figure this out together. I mean, what's love if it doesn't help us face our storms?"

His words ignited something within me, a flicker of hope amidst the turmoil. Maybe it wasn't all so dire. Maybe, with Jackson by my side, I could weather this storm, navigate through the confusion, and find my footing again.

"But what if it doesn't work out?" I whispered, my heart racing at the thought. "What if I can't balance everything?"

"Then we'll adapt. That's what we do, right? Look at this place," he gestured broadly, the brewery around us humming with life, a testament to resilience and hard work. "It didn't just pop up overnight. It took time, failures, and a lot of beer."

I couldn't help but chuckle at his comparison, the tension in my chest lightening as laughter bubbled to the surface. "Beer solves everything, huh?"

"Absolutely," he grinned, a teasing glint in his eye. "But in all seriousness, you're not alone in this. You've got me."

The sincerity in his gaze steadied me, dispelling the doubts swirling like dark clouds above. I took a sip of my ale, the crispness tingling on my tongue, a reminder of the simple pleasures still available in the midst of chaos. The brew was a reflection of us—crafted with care, with unexpected notes that danced together in harmony.

Just then, the lights flickered overhead, a sudden crackle of energy that seemed to mirror the tension building in the air. I looked up, surprised by the abrupt shift. Outside, a storm rolled in, dark clouds swirling ominously above, echoing the storm brewing inside me. The electricity buzzed, matching the rush of adrenaline coursing through my veins, setting my heart racing as the first raindrops began to tap against the windows.

Jackson's hand tightened around mine, grounding me in the moment as we both watched the tempest approach. It felt like the world was on the brink of change, and the winds of uncertainty were howling louder than ever. Yet, as I stood beside him, I realized that love was not merely a balm; it was a force of nature, fierce and unpredictable, capable of withstanding even the most tumultuous storms.

The rain intensified, tapping against the brewery windows like a drumroll for the moment ahead, as if the universe were conspiring to drown out my doubts. Jackson's presence felt electric, grounding yet exhilarating. I watched as he leaned against the bar, his expression a perfect blend of concern and playful mischief. "You know," he began, a teasing lilt in his voice, "if the world outside is anything like what's happening in here, we might be better off hunkering down with a few pints and pretending we're on a deserted island."

I rolled my eyes but couldn't suppress the smile creeping across my lips. "Oh, yes, because nothing says 'paradise' quite like the scent of hops and damp wood." I waved my hand dramatically, as if I were presenting a fine art piece. "Truly, the aroma of fermented barley is the epitome of relaxation."

He chuckled, the sound warm and inviting. "I'll take what I can get, especially if it comes with your sarcastic commentary. But in all seriousness, Dani, it's okay to feel overwhelmed. You're trying to juggle a lot, and I admire how you handle everything."

"Thanks, but flattery won't get you a discount on beer," I shot back, though the compliment did warm my heart. "Still, I feel like I'm on the brink of a meltdown. Ethan keeps pushing me, and I just... I don't know how to keep everyone happy."

His expression shifted, a flicker of understanding in his eyes. "You don't have to be the glue holding everything together. You're not a fixer-upper project; you're a whole house. If you need to take a step back and breathe, then do it. No one is going to blame you for wanting to breathe."

"Not even Ethan?" I asked, my voice softening. I leaned against the bar, my fingers idly toying with the condensation on my glass, feeling the coolness seep into my skin.

Jackson's gaze darkened slightly, a hint of frustration surfacing. "Ethan will adjust. He's passionate, maybe a bit too much at times, but he'll understand. He has to. This is about you, not just the business."

I nodded, the weight of his words settling in. Maybe he was right. But the fear of disappointing Ethan loomed large. The thought felt like a rock in my stomach, a weight that shifted uncomfortably with every movement. Just then, the door swung open, the storm outside roaring to life as a couple of friends from the competition stumbled in, laughter spilling over the threshold like a burst dam.

"Dani! Jackson! You've got to see this!" shouted one of them, waving an arm like he'd just discovered the cure for boredom. "We've got a surprise brewing outside!"

A collective cheer erupted, pulling me from my thoughts, and Jackson shared a conspiratorial glance with me. "What do you think? Should we go see what all the fuss is about?"

"Why not? I could use a distraction." The thought of venturing into the rain felt invigorating, a way to shake off the clouds that had settled in my mind.

As we stepped outside, the chill of the rain mixed with the heat of the competition buzz. Our friends had gathered near a makeshift outdoor stage, where a local band had set up amidst the downpour, determined to play regardless of the weather. The music floated through the air, an upbeat melody that begged us to dance.

"Who's crazy enough to play in this weather?" I shouted over the rain, laughing as I stepped closer, feeling the droplets pelt my face like nature's confetti.

Jackson grinned, his eyes sparkling with mischief. "Apparently, we are!" He grabbed my hand, pulling me into the throng of laughing, dancing bodies, abandoning any pretense of self-consciousness. The music thumped in time with my heartbeat, and for a moment, everything else faded into the background.

As I twirled in the rain, my worries sloshing away like the puddles forming at my feet, I felt the tension ebb. I caught Jackson's eye, and the world around us melted into a blur. He moved closer, lifting my chin gently, the warmth of his gaze cutting through the storm. "This is what life is about, right? Just letting go."

"Right," I replied breathlessly, caught between the rain, the music, and the electric current that sparked between us. "But I can't shake the feeling that everything will come crashing down once this moment ends."

"Maybe it won't," he challenged, his eyes earnest. "Maybe it's just a different beginning."

Before I could respond, he leaned in, his lips brushing against mine. It was a soft kiss, tentative at first, but the world around us ignited with energy. The rain, the laughter, the music—it all melded into a perfect symphony of chaos and calm. When we pulled apart, I was breathless, the storm no longer a weight but a companion.

"See?" he teased, laughter bubbling in his throat. "Nothing to worry about when you're with me. Just storms and music."

The moment felt fleeting, like a summer rain that could evaporate at any second. I wished desperately to hold onto it, to let it envelop me and shield me from the reality that awaited. But reality had its claws in me.

"I just wish I could keep this feeling," I admitted, gazing out into the crowd, feeling the energy pulse like a living thing. "But once the rain stops, once the music fades, everything will come rushing back."

"Only if you let it," Jackson countered, his tone earnest. "You have a choice. You can either drown in your worries or dance in the rain. I vote for dancing."

"Easy for you to say," I shot back, though the laughter in my voice was genuine. "You're not the one balancing a family business and a burgeoning relationship."

He stepped closer, his hand resting on my shoulder, his expression serious for a heartbeat. "You're more than capable, Dani. Just don't forget that it's okay to choose yourself sometimes."

Just then, Ethan emerged from the crowd, his expression stormy, a contrast to the festive chaos around us. The sight of him sent a jolt through my system, a mix of unease and determination swirling inside me.

"Dani!" he called, his voice cutting through the jubilant noise, making me flinch slightly. "We need to talk."

I exchanged a quick glance with Jackson, the weight of uncertainty crashing back down. Suddenly, the rain felt heavier, as if it was soaking in all the unresolved tension between us.

"Can it wait?" I asked, a desperate plea hidden beneath my bravado.

"No," he replied, his voice firm. "It can't."

My heart sank as I took a step back from Jackson, the warmth of his presence suddenly feeling far away. The vibrant energy surrounding us seemed to fade as I faced Ethan, my resolve wavering in the face of impending confrontation. The storm within me raged as I braced for the inevitable fallout, knowing that the world I had tried to escape was closing in once again.

Ethan's approach felt like a thunderclap against the backdrop of my momentary bliss. I took a steadying breath, trying to shake off the lingering warmth of Jackson's kiss, but the chill of uncertainty wrapped around me like a wet blanket. Ethan stood before me, rain-soaked and tense, a stark reminder that reality had a way of intruding just when I thought I had found an escape.

"Dani, can we talk?" he insisted, a note of urgency threading through his words.

"Can it wait until after the song?" I replied, gesturing to the band who had launched into an upbeat tune that had the crowd swaying and laughing. "It's kind of hard to have a serious discussion about life decisions when everyone else is celebrating."

"Now isn't a good time, Dani!" His voice rose slightly, cutting through the lively atmosphere, and a hush fell over us. The weight of his tone settled heavily around us like an unwelcome fog, and I couldn't help but feel the warmth of the moment slipping away.

Jackson stepped forward, his posture protective, but I could see a flicker of concern in his eyes. "Maybe we can find a quieter spot to talk," he suggested, a hint of tension in his voice. "There's no reason to ruin everyone's fun."

Ethan shot him a look that could have frozen fire. "This is family business, Jackson. I don't think you understand how this works."

I felt an unpleasant twist in my stomach at Ethan's tone. It was a warning shot fired across our bow, and I didn't appreciate it. "I do understand, Ethan," I interjected, my voice steadier than I felt. "But I'm not a child, and I don't need you to dictate who I can talk to."

His eyes narrowed, and I could see the argument brewing behind them. "This isn't just about you and Jackson. This is about the future of the business."

"You mean your future," I snapped back, surprised by the sharpness of my own voice. "You're acting like I'm just a piece on your chessboard. You want me to make moves without even asking what I want."

The air between us crackled with tension, the storm outside reflecting the one unfolding in our little corner of the world. Jackson moved back slightly, his hand brushing against mine, as if reminding me that I didn't have to face this alone.

"I'm trying to protect what Dad built," Ethan pressed, his voice rising. "You think I want to push you? I'm doing this because I care about you, about us."

"By pushing me away?" I shot back, my heart racing. "It doesn't feel like you care. It feels like you're just trying to mold me into someone I'm not."

"I'm trying to help you grow!" he exclaimed, exasperation evident in his voice. "You want to be part of this, right? Or are you just going to keep running off to your little fantasy land with Jackson?"

"Maybe I want to be happy!" I countered, the words spilling out before I could stop them. I was tired of the pressure, tired of feeling like I had to choose between my family and my heart. "Maybe I want to explore what that looks like without your shadow looming over me!"

The words hung in the air, a bitter truth that settled between us like an uninvited guest. The laughter and music faded into the background, the world narrowing down to just the three of us—my brother, my potential lover, and me, stuck in a storm of emotions that felt all too familiar.

Ethan's expression shifted, a vulnerability flickering through the facade of anger. "I just don't want to lose you," he said, his voice quieter now, laced with desperation. "I need to know you're in this with me. That you care about the family and what we've built."

"I do care," I whispered, feeling my resolve waver under the weight of his gaze. "But I also need to figure out what I want, not what you expect of me."

Jackson's grip tightened around my hand, his presence a steadying force against the emotional tempest. "Dani," he said softly, "you don't owe anyone anything. You're not just a cog in the family machine. You deserve to find your own path."

As I searched Jackson's eyes, a sense of clarity washed over me, an understanding that sometimes the hardest choices were the ones worth making. Ethan needed to realize that his version of our family's future wasn't the only one that mattered.

"Ethan," I began, taking a deep breath. "You need to understand that I want to be part of this family, but I can't do it your way. I need the freedom to find my own voice, my own direction. I can't keep living in your shadow."

Ethan opened his mouth, but before he could respond, a loud crack of thunder rolled overhead, reverberating through the night, causing everyone around us to jump. A sudden gust of wind blew through, sending raindrops flying like tiny daggers, and the band paused mid-song, eyes wide with surprise.

"Looks like the storm is here for real!" someone shouted, laughter bubbling through the crowd as they cheered, oblivious to the tension still simmering between us.

Ethan shook his head, frustration etched on his features. "This isn't over," he said, his voice low, and a warning glare shot between us.

"Ethan—" I started, but he turned on his heel and stormed back toward the gathering crowd, leaving a wake of silence in his path.

"Great," I muttered, the taste of defeat lingering on my tongue. I turned to Jackson, my heart still pounding from our confrontation. "I can't believe he just left like that."

"It's okay," Jackson said, his voice steady. "You stood your ground. That's what matters. You have to carve out your own space."

As I looked at him, the storm inside me raged on, battling with the warmth of his reassurance. But then something shifted in the air—a change so sudden it sent a shiver down my spine.

A shriek cut through the atmosphere, piercing the revelry as a figure stumbled into the light of the brewery's entrance, drenched and gasping for breath. My heart stopped as I recognized the wild eyes of a familiar face, panic etched deep in the lines of her expression.

"Dani!" she shouted, her voice cracking like thunder. "You need to come quick! It's Ethan! He's...he's in trouble!"

The world tilted, and my heart plummeted into the depths of my stomach. The carefree laughter of the crowd faded, the music became a distant memory, and I was left standing in the pouring rain, clutching Jackson's hand, feeling as though everything I'd fought for was about to come crashing down.

# Chapter 27: Fork in the Road

The aftermath of our fight clings to me like the sticky residue of spilled honey, sweet yet suffocating, the kind that seeps into every crevice of my mind. Ethan and I had always been a storm, a wild dance of laughter and sharp words, but this time, the tempest felt different. It raged within me, a hurricane of unspoken fears and frayed emotions that twisted and turned with the chaos of my ambitions. Just beyond the quaint facade of Alderwood, the summer festival loomed like a mirage—an oasis of excitement, but also a mirror reflecting the fissures in my heart.

Jackson had tried to be the voice of reason. "Take a step back, Ava," he said, his brow furrowed in that way that made him look more like a concerned brother than a friend. "Reassess your priorities. What do you really want?" He punctuated his point with a shrug, the weight of his own ambitions pressing down on him like an anchor. I could see it in his eyes; he had dreams too, ones that shimmered just out of reach. But right now, all I could think about was the gaping hole left by Ethan's absence.

So, I did what any rational person would do—I went wandering through the vibrant streets of Alderwood, where the sun dipped low, casting a golden glow that made the world feel alive. The air was fragrant with a bouquet of street food, where vendors served up spicy tacos and sweet funnel cakes, the clamor of laughter and chatter filling the spaces between. It was a tapestry of sound and color, each thread woven tightly together, yet I felt like an outsider, watching it all unfold from behind a glass wall.

Families ambled by, their laughter spilling over like the sparkling lemonade in their cups. Children chased after one another, their shrieks of joy punctuating the warm evening air, while couples walked hand in hand, lost in the comfort of each other's presence. A pang of longing twisted in my chest as I caught sight of a young couple stealing kisses beneath the twinkling lights strung overhead. I ached for that connection—the kind that felt electric, grounding, and so heartbreakingly real.

With every step, I could almost hear Ethan's laughter, rich and deep, resonating in the back of my mind like a melody I couldn't quite place. I craved the sound of his voice, the way he could effortlessly shift from playful banter to a serious conversation about our future, discussing our dreams for the brewery like they were sacred secrets meant only for us. But now, that future felt as distant as the stars overhead. What had we become?

A flicker of movement caught my eye—a splash of red and gold as a street performer juggled flaming torches, captivating an audience that had gathered like moths to a flame. Their applause broke through my reverie, snapping me back to the present, and I couldn't help but smile at the sheer joy of it all. But joy felt like a foreign concept, tangled up in my thoughts of Ethan, my heart swelling with memories of how we used to share moments like these, both enthralled by the magic of the world.

I made my way toward the heart of the festival, where the sound of live music pulsed through the crowd, drawing me in. The band played an upbeat tune, the kind that made you want to sway your hips and forget the burdens of life, yet my feet felt rooted to the ground. I lingered at the edge of the crowd, allowing the energy to wash over me, but the vibrant notes only served as a reminder of the quiet emptiness inside me.

"Ava!" A voice broke through my melancholy, pulling me from my thoughts. I turned to see Maya, her bright eyes sparkling like the twinkling lights overhead, her curly hair bouncing as she rushed toward me. "You've got to try the peach-infused beer! It's amazing!" She tugged my arm, her enthusiasm infectious.

"Sure," I replied, my voice a little flat despite her eagerness. But the flicker of warmth in her gaze drew me in, and I allowed her to lead me to the booth, the aroma of grilled peaches and barley wafting through the air. We squeezed through the throngs of people, their laughter and chatter buzzing like bees in a field of wildflowers. Maya didn't let go of my hand, a tether that kept me grounded amidst the swirling chaos.

As we reached the booth, I noticed the way the light caught the frothy beer, illuminating the rich amber hues. I raised the glass to my lips, and as the sweetness washed over my tongue, I felt a momentary reprieve from the emotional storm brewing inside me. "Okay, that's actually incredible," I admitted, a genuine smile breaking through my façade.

"I told you!" she exclaimed, her eyes shining with mischief. "You're going to win the competition at the festival. Just remember, you need to showcase what you love. The people want authenticity."

Her words struck a chord, echoing Jackson's advice. Maybe I needed to embrace the joy in brewing again, to return to the roots of why I fell in love with it in the first place. But in the back of my mind, the unresolved tension with Ethan hung like a stubborn cloud, threatening to rain on my parade. Could I really dive into my passion while our relationship felt so frayed?

"Right. Authenticity," I murmured, my thoughts drifting back to Ethan. "It's just... complicated."

Maya's brow furrowed, her enthusiasm dimming slightly. "What do you mean?"

I hesitated, debating whether to pull her into the whirlwind of my feelings or keep my struggles locked away. But before I could answer, the music shifted to a slower tune, a melodic thread weaving through the air, and suddenly, my heart raced with a sense of urgency. I wanted to heal, to reclaim the laughter that once filled my life. Perhaps, like the vibrant festival around me, I needed to find my way back to the color and connection I had lost.

Maya raised her glass in a mock toast. "Here's to authenticity then! And to whatever it takes to fix your rift with Ethan!"

I clinked my glass against hers, a quiet determination settling within me. I would find a way, even if it meant facing the storm head-on. The festival buzzed with life around us, and I felt a flicker of hope in the darkness. Somewhere amid the swirling lights and joyous laughter, I knew I could mend what was broken. It was time to bridge the gap, to find the courage to step beyond the shadows and reignite the flame we had almost extinguished.

The warmth of the sun dipped low in the sky, casting long shadows that danced playfully along the cobblestone streets of Alderwood. I stood at the edge of the festival, the echoes of laughter mingling with the sweet melodies drifting from the stage, creating a symphony of sound that enveloped me. Maya's exuberance faded into the background as I let my gaze wander, landing on the familiar booths lined up like colorful sentinels, each brimming with life and possibility. The festival felt like a carnival of dreams, yet my heart was anchored by the weight of my unfinished business with Ethan.

As I turned to walk away from the booth, Maya tapped me lightly on the shoulder. "Ava! You can't run away from this. It's your moment." Her eyes sparkled with an intensity that made me feel simultaneously supported and cornered. "Go talk to him."

"Right, because approaching the guy I just had a colossal fight with sounds like the best plan ever," I said, trying to keep my tone light, but the edge of my voice betrayed the anxiety swirling within me.

Maya rolled her eyes, a gesture of playful exasperation. "Come on, it's not like you're asking him to marry you. Just be honest. You've always been better at talking to him than you are at talking to yourself."

I let out a laugh, the tension in my chest easing slightly. "You know me too well." The truth was, the thought of confronting Ethan filled me with equal parts dread and determination. The very essence of our relationship was tied up in the brewing business we had built together, a bond forged over late-night concoctions and shared dreams, now teetering on the brink of collapse.

"Just think about the summer festival," she urged, her voice dropping to a conspiratorial whisper. "You'll be showcasing your creations. Ethan's going to be there. You need him on your team. Just go find him."

With her words swirling in my mind, I made my way through the crowd, my heart racing as I scanned faces, searching for the familiar one that made my pulse quicken and my worries fade. But each stranger felt like a ghost, reminding me of the laughter we used to share, the plans we had for the future. I kept my feet moving, propelled by a mix of anxiety and hope, until I spotted him near the center of the festival, his silhouette cutting a striking figure against the backdrop of bright lights and joyous chatter.

Ethan was engaged in conversation with a group of fellow brewers, his smile wide and easy, the kind that made it seem like he hadn't a care in the world. Yet I knew better. The undercurrent of tension that had seeped into our lives was palpable even from a distance. I hesitated, suddenly feeling small and fragile, the weight of our disagreement pressing down on me like a heavy cloak.

Just as I took a step back, second-guessing myself, he caught my eye. For a fleeting moment, the world around us faded, the laughter and music dimming to a dull hum. He looked surprised, maybe even a bit uncertain. I could feel the anticipation crackling between us like static electricity, and I took a deep breath, forcing my feet to carry me forward.

"Ava!" he called, a hint of warmth in his voice that stirred something deep within me. "Hey, you came! I wasn't sure if I'd see you here."

"Of course, I'm here," I said, attempting to sound casual despite the whirlwind of emotions swirling inside me. "I wouldn't miss it. Not when I have so much to show off." I gestured vaguely at the bustling festival, where the scent of cinnamon and fried dough wafted through the air.

His gaze softened, and for a moment, it felt like the old days—before the fight, before the doubts crept in. "You're going to blow everyone away with your brews. I just know it."

"Thanks, but I might need a little help," I replied, biting my lip, the words tumbling out before I could censor them. "I mean, we did this together before, right? The festival, the brewing—it was always a team effort."

Ethan studied me, his expression shifting, a mix of vulnerability and guardedness. "You know I'm in your corner, Ava. Always. Just... I'm not sure if I'm the right fit for your vision anymore."

That simple statement pierced me, the words landing with the weight of a thousand unspoken fears. "What do you mean by that?" I asked, my voice firmer than I felt. "I thought we were building something together."

"We are. But I feel like I'm holding you back. Maybe it's time for you to spread your wings without me." The finality in his tone chilled me, and I could see the flicker of pain behind his bravado.

"Ethan, no. You're not holding me back. I want you there. I need you there. I've always needed you there." My heart raced as I tried to catch his eye, willing him to see how intertwined our fates had become. "This festival is about more than just brewing; it's about us. About everything we've built together."

He shifted his weight, looking down at his hands as if the answers were written on his palms. "I don't want to be the reason you fail, Ava. What if I can't keep up with you? What if you shine brighter without me?"

"That's not how it works," I insisted, stepping closer, my voice low and earnest. "We shine together, like we always have. We balance each other out."

Silence hung between us, thick and heavy. I could feel the festival buzzing around us, vibrant and chaotic, yet all I could focus on was the rising tide of emotions threatening to spill over. The fear of losing him felt insurmountable, an avalanche of "what ifs" cascading through my mind.

"I don't want to hold you back," he finally replied, the conviction in his voice wavering. "But I also can't pretend that things are the same as they were. I think we need to be honest with ourselves."

Honesty. The word echoed in my mind, a reminder of the raw truth that lay at the heart of our conflict. "What if being honest means we have to confront our fears together? We can't keep pretending everything is fine if it isn't."

Ethan looked up, his eyes searching mine, and I could see the flicker of hope mingling with uncertainty. "Okay, let's be honest then. Let's find a way to navigate this together."

I felt a surge of determination, as if the festival's energy had woven itself into my spirit, urging me forward. "Yes. Together. I don't want to lose you, Ethan. Not now, not ever."

In that moment, the festival around us transformed, the colors brighter, the laughter more vibrant, as if the world was conspiring to align our paths once again. With a shared glance that held the promise of reconciliation, I knew we were on the precipice of something new—an understanding that would either forge our bond stronger or reveal the cracks that had begun to form. I chose to believe in us, in the power of honesty, and in the fiery spirit of Alderwood that would guide us through the chaos, hand in hand.

The air crackled with an unspoken tension as we stood in the midst of the festival, our hopes and fears intertwined like the threads of a tapestry. I searched Ethan's gaze, looking for the familiar spark that had ignited our journey in the first place. It was there, hidden beneath layers of doubt and uncertainty, but it flickered with promise. "Let's figure this out," I urged, my voice steady despite the turmoil raging within me. "We owe it to ourselves—and to what we've built together."

He hesitated, his brows knitting together as if he were solving a puzzle whose pieces refused to fit. "You really mean that?" His voice was low, almost vulnerable, and I could sense the walls he had built around his heart beginning to crack.

"Of course I do," I replied, determination swelling in my chest. "This festival is a celebration of everything we are, everything we've worked for. I don't want to face it without you." The words poured from me, honest and raw, and I saw the flicker of hope grow brighter in his eyes.

"You know I want to be part of that celebration," he said, running a hand through his hair, a familiar gesture that tugged at my heartstrings. "But I need to know we can navigate whatever comes next without losing each other in the process."

"Then let's commit to that," I said, my heart pounding in my chest. "Let's be honest, not just with each other, but with ourselves. We can't let fear dictate our future."

With that declaration hanging in the air, a wave of relief washed over us. I felt lighter, as if I had shed the heavy cloak of uncertainty that had clung to me since our fight. "So, what do we do now?" he asked, a hint of a smile creeping onto his lips.

"We take this festival by storm," I said, my voice gaining momentum. "We showcase our best brews, the ones that represent us—together. I've been experimenting with a new recipe, a blend of summer fruits and spices. It's vibrant, just like this place."

Ethan's eyes lit up at the mention of the fruit-infused concoction, a glimmer of excitement dancing in their depths. "You mean that peach-lavender ale? The one you were raving about last week?"

"Exactly!" I said, my enthusiasm contagious. "We can serve it at the festival. I want to create a memory, something that screams summer and partnership. People need to see us working together again."

"Then let's do it." He grinned, the warmth of his smile sending a thrill through me. "We'll knock their socks off. But, let's make it a little more interesting."

"What do you mean?" I asked, a playful suspicion creeping into my voice.

"How about a little competition?" His eyes twinkled with mischief. "We each come up with our own brew. The best one wins—whatever that means. We'll have the festival-goers vote. If I lose, I'll help you with your project, no questions asked. But if I win..."

"What's your stake?" I interjected, intrigued yet wary.

"If I win, you agree to try to work with me on something completely new. Something we haven't tackled before. A collaboration."

The challenge hung between us, a thread of tension woven with the potential for growth. I felt a rush of exhilaration at the idea of pushing our boundaries while also fearing the risk it posed. But I wouldn't back down. "Deal. But don't underestimate me, Ethan. You may be in for a surprise."

"Good. I wouldn't have it any other way." The playful banter returned, and for the first time in what felt like an eternity, I felt the familiar rhythm of our connection pulsing back to life.

As we began brainstorming ideas for our brews, the festival faded into the background, the colors and sounds morphing into a vibrant canvas for our creative energies. Ideas flowed like the beers we'd serve, and with each suggestion, the anticipation built between us, each laughter igniting the embers of our relationship.

"I could add some hibiscus to yours," he proposed, his voice a mix of seriousness and jest. "It would totally make your peach-lavender ale look like a neon sign."

"Not if I add more lavender than you can handle," I shot back, a playful smirk dancing on my lips. "I'll have you dreaming of lavender fields and buzzing bees in no time."

He chuckled, the sound deep and rich, and I realized how much I had missed the easy camaraderie we shared. The weight of our previous argument slipped further away, replaced by the thrill of what lay ahead.

As we jotted down ideas, a sense of unity enveloped us. The festival continued to whirl around us, but we were in our own little world, where laughter reigned and creativity flowed. I could see Ethan's passion igniting as we discussed ingredients, our conversations seamlessly blending into laughter and teasing jabs.

But just as I felt we were moving forward, a flicker of doubt crept into my mind, like a shadow passing through a sunlit room. What if this was just a momentary reprieve? What if we were simply masking the real issues that lay beneath the surface?

My thoughts were interrupted when Maya, with her infectious energy, bounded over to us. "You two look like you're about to conquer the world! Or at least the festival."

Ethan shot me a sideways glance, his brow raised in amusement. "Well, if we can survive this competition, we'll certainly feel invincible."

"Oh, a competition? This I need to see!" Maya grinned, clearly intrigued. "What are the stakes?"

"Just a little friendly wager," I said, keeping my tone light even as my stomach twisted in a mix of excitement and anxiety. "The winner gets to choose a new project for us to tackle."

Maya's eyes sparkled with mischief. "Count me in as your cheerleader! I can already see the festival banners: 'The Battle of the Brews!'"

Before I could respond, the atmosphere shifted, a chill creeping through the warm evening air. Suddenly, a loud crash echoed from one of the nearby booths, snapping everyone's attention away from us. The vibrant colors of the festival dimmed for a heartbeat as people gasped, some rushing toward the commotion while others stood frozen in place.

"What was that?" I asked, my heart racing.

Ethan's eyes widened, and we exchanged a worried glance. "Let's check it out."

As we hurried toward the source of the noise, a knot of dread twisted in my stomach. What could have happened? My mind raced with possibilities, each more troubling than the last.

When we reached the scene, my breath caught in my throat. The booth where the local cider maker had set up was in disarray, glass bottles shattered across the ground, the sweet scent of cider mingling with panic. But it wasn't just the mess that froze me in place; it was the figure standing at the center, their face a mask of shock and despair.

"Ethan!" A voice broke through the crowd, sharp and urgent. It was the cider maker's assistant, his eyes darting around as if searching for someone to blame. "You need to help us! The shipment for the festival is ruined!"

The implications of that simple statement crashed over me like a tidal wave. This was bigger than a spilled drink; it was a blow to the entire festival. As the chaos unfolded, I felt the air shift, the weight of uncertainty and dread settling back into my heart.

"Ethan, what are we going to do?" I whispered, my voice trembling as the reality of the situation set in.

His brow furrowed in concentration as he surveyed the scene, determination flooding his features. "We need to step up. If we can help them salvage this, it might just turn the tide for us—and for the festival."

But before I could respond, the crowd shifted again, a ripple of voices rising as they pointed toward the horizon. My heart raced at the sight: dark clouds rolling in from the distance, the festival's celebration suddenly overshadowed by an impending storm.

I felt a chill creep down my spine as the realization dawned on me. "Ethan, what if—"

The winds began to howl, whipping around us with an urgency that mirrored my own rising panic. "We have to act fast!" Ethan shouted over the growing din, his eyes blazing with resolve. "We can't let this festival go down without a fight!"

And just like that, as the storm loomed and chaos erupted around us, we were thrust back into the heart of uncertainty, the very thing we had vowed to confront. The stakes had never been higher, and I could feel the ground shifting beneath our feet. The question now wasn't just about our brews or our relationship—it was about survival and the fight to reclaim everything we held dear.

With the storm approaching and the festival in disarray, the path ahead was murky. My heart raced, and I couldn't shake the feeling that this was only the beginning of something much larger than either of us could have anticipated.

# Chapter 28: Brewing Unity

The scent of hops mingled with the sweet aroma of roasted barley as I stepped into the brewery, a place that felt like home yet carried the weight of unspoken words. The sun hung low in the sky, casting a golden hue across the wooden barrels stacked haphazardly, each one a vessel of possibility. Today was more than just a gathering; it was a chance to stitch together the frayed threads of my family, a tapestry that had become tangled and torn over the last few months. My heart raced with anticipation and dread as I prepared for what I hoped would be a turning point.

With the sun setting, I busied myself with the final touches—hanging string lights that danced gently in the breeze, their soft glow promising warmth. A subtle playlist wafted through the air, a mix of upbeat tunes that would, ideally, pull us away from the shadows that had lingered too long. My fingers grazed the edge of a freshly labeled beer bottle, the bold script a reminder of the craft that united us, a craft I was desperate to share, to celebrate. Each label was a promise, a testament to the love and effort that went into every batch. Yet, amidst the excitement, my mind danced with questions—would this work? Would Ethan and I find common ground, or were we merely two ships passing in the night?

Ethan arrived just as I was lighting the last candle, his silhouette framed against the twilight sky. He looked hesitant, his hands stuffed deep in the pockets of his worn-out jeans, a contrast to my brightly colored dress that felt far too vibrant for the weight of our history. "You look... ready," he said, his voice a hesitant compliment, his eyes scanning the room like he was searching for a sign, perhaps a sign that this wasn't a colossal mistake.

"Ready? Maybe more like frantic. I was just hoping the beer wouldn't spontaneously combust before we can serve it," I quipped, injecting humor to break the ice, though the underlying tension crackled like static between us. I moved to the cooler, retrieving our latest brew, a citrus-infused pale ale that had taken weeks of trial and error to perfect. "What do you think? Will it make people forget the awkwardness?"

Ethan cracked a smile, a rare moment of levity I cherished. "If this fails, I'll take the blame. We can drown our sorrows together in whatever's left." He extended a bottle, and we clinked our caps together, a silent toast to what could be, and I felt a flicker of hope.

As guests began to trickle in, the atmosphere shifted. Familiar faces from the community, patrons who had supported us through thick and thin, filled the space with laughter and stories. It was a tapestry of warmth—each person weaving their thread into our story. The brewery transformed into a lively celebration, echoes of laughter bouncing off the walls like a heartbeat, resonating with the pulse of something greater than just us. Yet, even amidst the joyous reunion, I sensed an undercurrent of uncertainty, a subtle tension that lingered like a ghost at the fringes of the evening.

As the night deepened, I watched families reunite, friends share memories over foaming glasses, the camaraderie palpable. I smiled, but the back of my mind kept drumming the same unsettling beat: the unresolved between Ethan and me loomed larger with each passing moment. He flitted between groups, his natural charisma lighting up the room, but I could see the way he stiffened when our eyes briefly met, an electric jolt that ignited the air around us, lingering long after our gazes slipped away.

"Do you remember the first batch we brewed together?" I asked him as we stood on the periphery, watching the joy unfold like a well-brewed lager, bubbling with life. "It tasted like socks, but we still had the audacity to serve it."

"Right? I think I nearly cried that day," he replied, a laugh escaping his lips, echoing the carefree essence of our past. "But it wasn't just about the beer. It was... everything else."

Everything else. Those words hung in the air, laden with implications. I turned to him, hoping to crack open the safe we'd both been guarding so fiercely. "Ethan, I know things haven't been easy between us lately. We've both been... avoiding the elephant in the room. What if tonight is our chance to address it? To face what's been brewing beneath the surface?"

His expression shifted, the humor fading like the last light of day. "It's complicated, isn't it?" he said, his voice dropping to a whisper, as if afraid the night itself would overhear our confessions. "I don't know if tonight is the right time."

I stepped closer, feeling the warmth radiating from his body, a stark contrast to the cool evening air. "But what if it's the only time? What if we keep waiting, and all we're left with are regrets?" My words spilled out, raw and unfiltered, igniting a fire in my chest that I couldn't ignore.

He ran a hand through his hair, a gesture I recognized as one of his most vulnerable. "You have no idea how much I want to talk about it, but every time I try, I freeze. I'm scared, Ava. I don't want to ruin this night for you. For us."

"Then let's make it work, Ethan. Together." The sincerity in my voice felt like a pledge, a shared promise to navigate the choppy waters ahead.

The buzz of the crowd enveloped us, a warm blanket of familiarity that both soothed and frayed my nerves. Laughter floated through the air, punctuated by the clinking of glasses and the comforting low hum of conversation. It felt like an embrace, yet the weight of Ethan's gaze, heavy with unsaid words, lingered just outside the periphery of my thoughts. I turned back to him, determined to breach the chasm that had formed between us. "What if we started with the basics? Like what went wrong?"

Ethan rubbed the back of his neck, a telltale sign of his discomfort. "Right. Because diving headfirst into our emotional dumpster fire sounds like a great idea," he said, attempting a playful smirk that only half-reached his eyes. "But hey, you're the one who organized this event. Let's just throw caution to the wind, shall we?"

His sarcasm stung, and I shot him a pointed look, ready to defend my earnest intentions. "I'm not suggesting we sit down with a therapist. Just... maybe we could be honest with each other?"

He sighed, his expression softening. "Okay, okay. Honest. Let's start with why we stopped talking in the first place."

I took a deep breath, the warmth of the brewery grounding me. "I think it was the pressure. Between the brewing and the expectations, it felt like we were losing our connection, and I didn't know how to fix it. So I backed off."

Ethan's brow furrowed as he processed my words. "You think it was just you? I thought I was the problem. I kept thinking if I could just figure out how to balance the business and our friendship, maybe everything would be fine. I'm the one who distanced myself."

Our eyes locked, and for a heartbeat, the world around us faded. The clamor of our patrons became a distant murmur, and the flickering lights dimmed to a gentle glow. In that moment, the walls we had both built began to crack. "So we were both being idiots?" I said, trying to lighten the mood, a half-hearted laugh escaping my lips.

"Welcome to the club," he replied, a genuine smile breaking through. "Membership includes free therapy sessions with yours truly."

I chuckled, the tension in my shoulders easing just a bit. "Okay, therapist. What's the first step in our recovery plan?"

"Let's start with that first batch we brewed together—the one that tasted like a mix between a dirty sock and desperation. Remember how we tried to sell it anyway?"

"Oh, how could I forget? The look on everyone's faces when they took a sip was priceless," I said, shaking my head at the memory. "It was like we served them liquid regret."

As the laughter subsided, I realized we were stepping into uncharted territory, one where vulnerability could lead to healing. "It's funny how we thought we could solve everything with beer," I mused. "As if every problem could be washed down with a pint of our finest."

Ethan nodded, his expression turning contemplative. "But isn't that the beauty of brewing? It's all about experimentation, right? A little this, a little that. Sometimes you hit gold, sometimes you end up with a concoction no one wants to drink."

"That sounds suspiciously like life."

He tilted his head, amusement dancing in his eyes. "So what's our next experiment? Because I think I'm ready for something a bit more palatable this time."

With a newfound confidence, I leaned in closer. "How about we start by being honest about what we want? From each other, from the brewery, from everything?"

His gaze intensified, the playful banter fading as the weight of the moment settled between us. "Ava, I want us to work. Not just as business partners, but as friends, as... whatever this is."

"Whatever this is." The words hung in the air, filled with a thousand unspoken hopes.

Before I could respond, a shout erupted from the crowd, pulling our attention away. A group of regulars had started an impromptu toast, raising their glasses high as if challenging the very stars. "To Ava and Ethan! May your beers be as strong as your friendship!"

Laughter erupted again, and I couldn't help but roll my eyes, the sudden shift breaking the tension. "They have no idea what they're cheering for, do they?"

"Not a clue," Ethan agreed, his smile returning as he joined in the merriment.

As we poured drinks, the atmosphere shifted again, buoyed by the camaraderie that surrounded us. I caught snippets of conversations, the hum of shared memories and hopes threading through the gathering like a tapestry of connection. Each clink of glass, each hearty laugh, pulled us further away from the edges of our unresolved past, creating a cushion of warmth that felt both inviting and frightening.

"Hey, Ava," one of our friends called, his voice cutting through the laughter. "What's the secret ingredient in this new brew? It's like drinking sunshine!"

I grinned, feeling the pride swell within me. "It's a mix of optimism and a little bit of lemon zest, but mostly the love we put into it."

"Sounds like a recipe for happiness," Ethan added, catching my eye as he poured a fresh round for the group.

As the evening progressed, I found myself leaning into the laughter, letting the joy of the moment wash over me. Yet, the ache of unresolved feelings simmered beneath the surface, demanding attention. With each shared joke and toast, the thought nagged at me—how could we navigate what was brewing between us when the air was thick with laughter and shared dreams?

"Hey," Ethan's voice pulled me from my reverie, his eyes earnest. "Can we step outside for a minute?"

The request sent a jolt through my chest, a thrill of anticipation mingling with the flicker of anxiety. "Sure," I replied, our unspoken understanding drawing us away from the warmth of our friends and into the cool night air, where stars twinkled like distant possibilities.

Outside, the night wrapped around us like a cloak, the sounds of the celebration fading to a soft murmur. Ethan leaned against the wooden railing, his gaze fixed on the horizon, a hint of vulnerability softening his features. "I've been thinking about what comes next. About us."

"Us," I echoed, my heart racing.

"Yeah," he said, his voice barely above a whisper. "What if we don't have to choose between the brewery and our friendship? What if we can find a way to make both work?"

Hope sparked within me, yet I couldn't ignore the fear that trailed close behind. "What if it's too late?"

Ethan turned to face me, the intensity of his gaze stealing my breath. "I don't believe that. It's never too late to try."

With the night wrapping us in its embrace, I felt the walls between us begin to crumble, the weight of unspoken words finally lifting.

The night air hung thick with promise, a gentle breeze ruffling the leaves of nearby trees as Ethan's gaze anchored mine. I could feel the current of our emotions intertwining, heavy and electric, as if the very universe had paused, waiting for us to take the next step. "What if we don't have to choose between the brewery and our friendship? What if we can find a way to make both work?" His words danced in the cool night air, daring me to consider the possibility.

"I want that," I replied, my heart racing at the thought. "But it's not just about us, Ethan. It's about the business, the customers, everything we've built together." My voice was firm, but the tremor underneath betrayed the conflict stirring within me.

He nodded slowly, clearly processing my words. "And what if the business thrives because of us? Because we're good together? Not just in brewing, but... everything?"

The idea sent a thrill down my spine. The possibility of rekindling not just our friendship, but something deeper, something that lingered beneath the surface, felt exhilarating and terrifying all at once. "You really think we can do that?"

"Honestly? I think we've already started. Look at tonight. People are happy. They're celebrating us—what we've created. If we can focus on that, maybe we can figure out the rest." His eyes shone with determination, and in that moment, the weight of the past began to feel a little lighter, more manageable.

I let out a breath I didn't realize I was holding. "Okay, then let's make a pact. We'll figure it out together, no matter what it takes."

"Deal." His hand extended toward me, and I met it halfway, our fingers intertwining in a brief yet powerful gesture of commitment. The connection sparked like a firework, igniting a warmth that traveled through me.

Just then, a sudden commotion from inside the brewery broke our moment. I turned toward the door, curiosity piquing as laughter erupted once more. "What now?" I asked, a grin creeping onto my face.

Ethan chuckled. "Probably someone trying to outdrink their own bad decisions."

As we stepped inside, the atmosphere was electric, the room alive with people sharing stories and laughter that felt like a soothing balm. But my heart sank as I caught sight of a familiar figure, standing slightly apart from the revelry. Melissa, my cousin, her expression a mix of amusement and mischief, was chatting animatedly with a group of regulars.

"Uh-oh, trouble's brewing," Ethan whispered, a playful glint in his eye. "What's she doing here?"

I rolled my eyes, but a smile broke through. "Probably planning her next scheme to make me the butt of some joke."

As we approached, Melissa caught sight of us and waved exaggeratedly, her grin widening. "Look who finally decided to join the party! The dynamic duo of hops and awkwardness!"

"Hey, at least we're not making sock-flavored beer tonight," I shot back, laughter spilling from my lips.

"True, but you two should consider that for your next batch. It could be a hit with the right audience." Her tone was teasing, but there was an undertone of sincerity. "You know, I heard a rumor that you two might be... working things out?"

I felt my cheeks warm, glancing at Ethan, whose expression was a mix of surprise and amusement. "Just trying to keep our business afloat, that's all," he replied with a light chuckle, but I could see the playful glint in his eyes as he leaned closer, his shoulder brushing against mine.

Melissa arched an eyebrow. "Right. Business. Sure."

"Don't you have someone to annoy?" I asked, trying to redirect her.

"Oh, plenty! But where's the fun in that?" she replied, leaning in conspiratorially. "But really, I'm glad to see you both here. I've missed you two being... well, you."

"Thanks, Mel. It means a lot," I said, my heart warming at her sincerity.

Ethan caught my gaze again, his eyes glimmering with something unspoken. "Let's grab another round. This celebration can't end on just that toast."

As we made our way to the bar, the excitement of the night pulsed around us. I felt lighter, as if the burdens of our past were slowly lifting, replaced by the thrill of what lay ahead. The rhythm of our conversations flowed easily, peppered with laughter and shared stories. The warmth of the crowd felt like a protective cocoon, shielding us from our insecurities.

But just as I was beginning to believe that perhaps we could navigate this path together, a loud crash echoed through the brewery, cutting through the laughter like a knife. The sound drew every eye in the room, including mine, to the corner where a table had tipped over, glasses shattering across the floor like fragments of our earlier tension.

"What the hell?" I exclaimed, rushing over, Ethan hot on my heels. As we reached the scene, I was met with chaos—a couple of our regulars were on the floor, clearly more inebriated than was wise, and they were engaged in an animated debate that had turned physical.

"Not exactly how I envisioned the evening going," Ethan muttered under his breath, his eyes scanning the crowd for signs of escalation.

I stepped forward, trying to separate the two men, who seemed more intent on proving their strength than their point. "Guys! Come on, let's not ruin this night!" I urged, my voice rising above the chaos.

One of the men, a familiar face named Brad, glanced up, his cheeks flushed with embarrassment. "It was just a misunderstanding, Ava! I'm just trying to prove that I know beer better than he does!"

"By throwing punches? Really?"

Before I could intervene further, Ethan slipped past me, his voice steady yet authoritative. "Hey! This isn't how we do things here. Put your fists down and your beers up!"

His presence commanded attention, and slowly, the men began to back down, confusion marring their features. The energy in the room shifted as people began to murmur, intrigued by the spectacle. "Let's remember why we're here!" Ethan continued, raising his own glass high, calling attention to the real reason we had gathered. "We're here to celebrate our craft, our community, and the friendships we've built! Not to fight!"

With a collective breath, the tension seemed to dissipate, the crowd rallying behind Ethan's words. The men exchanged sheepish glances, their bravado evaporating in the face of Ethan's earnestness.

"Okay, okay! We'll settle this over drinks," Brad said, his tone sheepish as he picked up a glass from the floor, careful to avoid the shattered remnants.

"Good choice," I said, my heart racing as the crowd began to cheer, clinking their glasses in solidarity.

Ethan's eyes found mine amidst the chaos, a knowing smile breaking across his face. "See? Just like brewing, it's all about handling the heat when things get messy."

I nodded, feeling the weight of the moment sink in. "But let's keep the drama to a minimum. I've had enough excitement for one night."

Just then, a shadow fell across us, and I turned to see Melissa's face pale as she stared past us. "Um, Ava? You might want to look at the door."

I followed her gaze and froze. Standing there, framed by the doorway, was a figure from my past, one I hadn't expected to see tonight. My heart sank as a wave of dread washed over me. "What is he doing here?"

Ethan's eyes narrowed, his expression shifting to one of concern as he registered my reaction. "Ava?"

"Just... just give me a second," I murmured, my heart racing as I faced the unexpected specter of my past, knowing that the fragile unity we had begun to build was now teetering on the brink of collapse.

# Chapter 29: Revelations in the Foam

The air in the brewery was a heady mix of hops and nostalgia, a place where the echoes of laughter mingled with the gentle clink of glasses. It felt like stepping into a warm hug, with the soft golden glow of twinkling fairy lights draping the room like a constellation caught in amber. I stood at the front, feeling the weight of my family's history pressing down on my shoulders, a silent reminder of the sacrifices and dreams that had woven us together. Ethan was beside me, a solid presence in a sea of familiar faces, and his quiet strength was my anchor in this moment.

As I looked out at the crowd—friends, neighbors, the occasional curious stranger—I could feel the anticipation humming in the air, like the first spark of carbonation in a freshly poured pint. I cleared my throat, the microphone cold and foreign in my grip, but I squared my shoulders, drawing in a deep breath that tasted of stale beer and courage.

"Thank you all for coming tonight," I began, my voice wavering slightly, but firming as I continued. "I wanted to share a bit about our family's journey, one that's been anything but smooth." I paused, catching Ethan's eye, and saw the flicker of understanding there. We had both felt the tremors of our father's dreams and the weight of unfulfilled promises, but tonight felt different—tonight, we were not alone.

I delved into the stories of our childhood, painting a picture of sun-soaked days spent chasing after dreams that seemed just out of reach. "You see," I said, my voice steadying, "our father always believed in building something bigger than ourselves. He envisioned a legacy, one rooted in passion and perseverance, but the path was riddled with challenges." The crowd was rapt, leaning in as if I were drawing them into our family's tapestry, each thread woven with love and heartache.

As I recounted the moments that had shaped us—the late nights spent studying in a cramped living room, the tears shed over failure, the small victories that felt monumental in the shadow of our father's expectations—I felt a swell of emotion rising within me. It was a bittersweet symphony of nostalgia, but also a call to arms for the present. "Family isn't just about blood; it's about connection," I continued, letting the words wash over me like the warmth of a summer breeze. "It's about understanding, forgiveness, and love, even when it feels impossibly far away."

The atmosphere shifted as I spoke, a palpable wave of emotion rolling through the crowd, sparking murmurs of agreement and nods of empathy. I could see tears glistening in the eyes of some of the older patrons, their faces lined with the weight of their own stories. And in that moment, I knew I wasn't just sharing our struggles; I was offering a piece of hope, a reminder that even the most tangled family ties could be mended with a little love and understanding.

After the speech, I felt lighter, as if I had shared a burden that had been too heavy to carry alone. I stepped down from the small stage, the applause still ringing in my ears, and made my way to where Ethan stood, a corner of his mouth curled into a faint smile. His eyes shone with something like pride, and I felt a rush of warmth surge through me, a recognition of our shared journey.

"Wow," he said, shaking his head slightly. "You really laid it all out there."

"Yeah, well, it felt necessary," I replied, my heart racing. "We needed them to understand us, to see us beyond just the family name." The words spilled out before I could stop them, my vulnerability stripped bare in the glow of the brewery's lights.

Ethan glanced around, then leaned in closer, his voice dropping to a whisper. "You know, I've been thinking a lot about everything—how we've drifted apart. I miss you, sis." His admission was simple yet profound, and it settled over us like a soft blanket.

"I miss us too," I confessed, the truth hanging heavy between us. "It's just been so hard, navigating everything without Dad."

"Yeah, I feel like we've been holding onto our wounds instead of healing them," he replied, his brow furrowing. "Like we're trapped in this loop of hurt."

The realization settled in—a shared acknowledgment of the unspoken barriers we had both erected, walls built from years of misunderstanding and unaddressed grief. But in the dim glow of the brewery, with the laughter and camaraderie surrounding us, I felt the possibility of change stirring like yeast in a warm mixture, ready to rise.

As we embraced, I felt the promise of a renewed bond, one that might finally allow us to break free from the shackles of our past. The crowd around us faded into a gentle hum, the chaos of the world outside quieting as I breathed in the familiar scent of his cologne mixed with the rich aroma of malt. It was an intimate moment, one of those rare instances when time seemed to stretch, allowing us to linger in the warmth of newfound hope.

We pulled back, and I saw it in his eyes—a glimmer of the brother I had adored as a child, the one who had shared dreams and secrets beneath the stars. "Maybe we can figure this out together," I suggested, my voice barely a whisper.

He nodded, the corner of his mouth quirking up in that familiar way that used to make me laugh. "Together," he echoed, and it felt like a vow.

The night wrapped around us like a cozy quilt, the laughter and chatter of the brewery fading into the background as we stood there, two souls finally ready to heal.

The night wore on, the hum of conversations blending with the clinking of glasses, and I felt buoyed by the warmth of shared laughter. The air was thick with the comforting scent of fresh beer and the faint sweetness of pretzels, their saltiness a reminder of our childhood snack wars, where we'd steal from each other's plates with mischievous glee. I stood beside Ethan, feeling an electric energy between us, a spark igniting the possibility of a new beginning.

As the crowd began to thin, I spotted our old friend Clara at the bar, her hair a riot of curls framing a face full of mischief. She was nursing a pint, one eyebrow raised as she surveyed the room like a sly fox. I felt a rush of nostalgia—Clara had always been the one to pull us into trouble with her wild ideas and irresistible charm. I motioned to Ethan, and we made our way over, his hand brushing against mine, a subtle reminder of our newly rekindled bond.

"Look who it is!" Clara exclaimed, her smile infectious. "The prodigal siblings return! You two look like you just conquered a mountain." She leaned in, her voice conspiratorial. "What's the secret? Did you finally put the 'fun' in family dysfunction?"

I laughed, the sound bubbling up unrestrained. "More like we decided to tackle the 'dysfunction' head-on. Turns out, a little honesty goes a long way." I felt Ethan's presence beside me, steadying me, his subtle smile reflecting his own relief.

"Honestly?" Clara scoffed playfully, her finger wagging. "How boring. I was hoping for drama—like you threw a chair or something!" She laughed, and it was easy to fall back into our familiar banter, the comfort of old friendships wrapping around us like a warm blanket.

"Believe me, the drama is a bit too real without any furniture flying around," Ethan interjected, and I could hear the undertone of sarcasm that we both shared, a family trait I cherished. Clara rolled her eyes dramatically.

"Fine, but you two are clearly too well-adjusted for my taste. Next time, I'm bringing popcorn!" She grinned and took a long sip from her glass, her gaze shifting to me. "But seriously, I'm proud of you for speaking out tonight. It's not easy, sharing your heart like that."

"Thanks, Clara. It feels... freeing, I guess," I admitted, a flutter of vulnerability still hovering in the air. "We've been tiptoeing around things for too long, and it just got to a breaking point."

"Sounds like you could use a bit of mischief to shake things up, though," Clara suggested, her eyes glimmering with mischief. "How about we throw caution to the wind and do something reckless? Like karaoke!"

Ethan groaned good-naturedly, but I could see the challenge sparking in his eyes. "I don't think my vocal cords are ready for that level of punishment. Last time, I made a room full of people question their hearing."

Clara laughed, her eyes alight with the thrill of possibility. "Oh, come on! It'll be fun! I promise I'll bring earplugs."

As she continued to pitch her idea, I felt a wave of exhilaration wash over me. The prospect of karaoke was absurdly appealing, and the thought of shaking off the remnants of family tension felt like a much-needed release. "Alright, let's do it! But only if we can pick the songs. No power ballads that require actual singing skills."

"Deal!" Clara declared, her enthusiasm infectious. "You two go pick the first song. I'll save our spot." She bounded off toward the makeshift stage, leaving us laughing behind her.

Ethan turned to me, shaking his head with an amused smile. "What have we just signed ourselves up for?"

"The most embarrassing night of our lives?" I teased, poking his side lightly. "But I think we could use a little laughter—preferably at our own expense."

"True," he agreed, a hint of mischief glimmering in his eyes. "I'd rather face karaoke than a family therapy session, anyway."

We shared a laugh, the sound echoing between us like a breath of fresh air. I felt lighter, the weight of unspoken words and long-held grudges lifting, if only temporarily. Together, we made our way to the stage, where the neon lights flickered with a promise of outrageous fun.

As Clara introduced us, I took a moment to soak in the atmosphere—the excitement, the camaraderie, the rush of daring to step into the spotlight. We had each faced our shadows, and now, we were ready to embrace a little chaos.

"Alright, what's our first song?" Ethan asked, scanning the options flashing across the screen.

I spotted "I Want It That Way" by the Backstreet Boys, and my heart skipped. "How about this one? It's a classic!"

Ethan raised an eyebrow, feigning disdain. "Please tell me you're joking. Do you want to lose every ounce of dignity we have left?"

"Dignity is overrated! Besides, it's a crowd favorite," I argued, laughter bubbling within me.

With a mock sigh of resignation, he conceded, "Fine, but if we embarrass ourselves, I'm blaming you."

I stepped up to the mic, adrenaline coursing through my veins, the crowd's buzz invigorating. The music started, and as the familiar chords filled the air, I couldn't help but sing along, the words spilling out with an infectious glee. To my surprise, Ethan joined in, his voice blending with mine, a harmonious blend of nerves and exhilaration.

The crowd erupted into cheers, and for those few glorious minutes, we were not just siblings mending old wounds; we were performers basking in the spotlight, laughter spilling from our lips like confetti. As we sang, I caught glimpses of Clara dancing in the crowd, her wild curls bouncing in time with the music, and for the first time in a long while, I felt truly free.

In that moment, surrounded by the echo of laughter and the thrill of our shared experience, I knew this night would be one to remember—not just for the karaoke, but for the renewed bond forming between us, strong enough to withstand whatever storms lay ahead.

The laughter echoed off the brewery walls, mixing with the clinking of glasses as Clara seized the microphone, her enthusiasm radiating like the warm lights overhead. "Alright, next up! This duo of delightful siblings has just set the stage ablaze! Let's keep the energy rolling!" She gestured dramatically, her wild curls bouncing as she hopped off the stage to join the cheering crowd, effectively leaving us to bask in the spotlight.

Ethan chuckled, nudging my shoulder with a playful grin. "Great, now we're officially the main attraction. No pressure, right?"

I could hardly suppress my laughter. "Just think of it as a bonding experience, complete with potential humiliation!" The crowd roared, egging us on, and I felt a rush of exhilaration. It was the perfect distraction from our family's weighty past, a chance to revel in the absurdity of the moment.

As the next song came on—an upbeat pop anthem that I was quite sure we had belted out during our teenage years—I glanced at Ethan. His expression was a delightful mix of uncertainty and amusement. "Are you ready for round two?" I teased, enjoying this newfound lightness between us.

"Only if you promise not to post this on social media," he replied, mock-seriousness etched across his face. "I have a reputation to uphold, you know."

I raised an eyebrow, fighting back a grin. "Ethan, you're a software developer. What kind of reputation do you think you have?"

"An impeccable one!" he shot back, his laughter spilling out effortlessly. "But I can't risk the world knowing my karaoke prowess."

The music swelled, and we launched into our rendition, the lyrics flowing easily between us, buoyed by the crowd's energy. For those blissful moments, it felt as if nothing could touch us, as if all the frayed edges of our family ties had been woven together in laughter and song. But beneath the surface of the joviality, I could feel a tension building, an undercurrent that spoke of the unspoken truths we still needed to face.

As our performance came to an end, a cacophony of applause erupted. I turned to Ethan, exhilarated. "That was surprisingly fun!"

"Surprisingly? I expected nothing less than a Grammy," he teased, slapping my back. Just then, Clara returned, practically vibrating with excitement. "You two are a karaoke dream team! Next time, I'm definitely joining in, but for now, we need a celebratory drink!"

She waved over a waitress, her order a delightful blend of the most colorful cocktails on the menu. As the drinks arrived, Clara held up her glass, eyes sparkling. "To family, to laughter, and to the world's worst karaoke!"

We clinked our glasses together, the sound ringing with promise. "And to a night without regret!" I added, downing half my drink in a single gulp.

Ethan's brow furrowed, his eyes darting toward the entrance. "Hey, is that...?"

Before he could finish, I turned to see a figure stepping through the doorway, the silhouette unmistakable. It was Mom, her presence heavy with unspoken words. My stomach twisted as she glanced around the room, her gaze landing on us.

"Uh-oh," Clara whispered, her playful demeanor fading. "Do you think she came to crash the party?"

"Or to crash our newfound bond," Ethan muttered, his tone shifting from playful to serious. I could sense the tension prickling in the air, a sudden chill that contrasted sharply with the warmth of the brewery.

Mom made her way toward us, her expression unreadable, a mix of concern and determination etched into her features. "There you are," she said, her voice steady but tinged with an urgency that pulled at my heartstrings. "I've been looking for you two."

"Uh, we're kind of busy," I replied, my tone attempting to brush off the seriousness of the moment.

"Busy with karaoke and cocktails?" she replied, a hint of sarcasm creeping in. "Look, we need to talk. Now."

Ethan exchanged a worried glance with me. "Can't it wait until after our 'victory lap'?" he asked, a slight edge in his voice.

"No, it can't," Mom insisted, her gaze unwavering. "This is important."

A heavy silence hung in the air, the laughter and music fading into a dull roar. I set my drink down, the weight of her words sinking in. This wasn't just about the karaoke or the fun we'd shared. It was about the walls we had built, the words we hadn't said, and the wounds that still festered beneath the surface.

"Fine," I relented, the word feeling like a weighty admission. "What's going on?"

She took a deep breath, her hands clasped tightly in front of her, as if she were trying to hold herself together. "I received a call earlier today. It's about your father."

My heart raced. The words hit me like a cold wave crashing against the shore, leaving me gasping for air. "What about Dad?"

Her expression faltered, and I could see the struggle within her as she searched for the right words. "There's something you both need to know—something he's been keeping from us all."

Ethan stepped closer, his protective instinct flaring. "What are you talking about?"

Her eyes flicked between us, revealing the storm brewing just beneath her composed surface. "It's about his past—things he never told us. Things that could change everything."

A thick tension filled the space between us, and my pulse quickened. "Change what? What are you saying?"

Before she could respond, the ground seemed to shift beneath my feet, a sudden realization dawning on me that threatened to unravel everything I thought I knew. My heart pounded as I grasped the enormity of her words. Just then, Clara, who had been watching with wide eyes, leaned in. "Is this about his past? Like... secrets? Family drama? Please tell me it's as juicy as it sounds!"

Mom opened her mouth, but before she could answer, a loud crash resonated from the back of the brewery. The crowd turned, and a collective gasp echoed through the room. A group of rowdy patrons had knocked over a table, sending glasses shattering to the floor. The momentary distraction was enough to break the tension, but not before I caught a glimpse of my mother's haunted expression, the weight of her revelations still heavy in the air.

"Mom, wait—" I started, but she stepped back, her face paler than before, her lips pressing into a tight line.

"I'll explain everything, but we need to go—now."

As we all stood there, the laughter and celebration fading into the background, I felt the grip of uncertainty tighten around me. The night had begun with hope and laughter, but as I watched my mother retreat into the shadows, I knew our family was on the verge of unraveling in ways I couldn't begin to comprehend.

Milton Keynes UK
Ingram Content Group UK Ltd.
UKHW040257181024
449757UK00001B/102